Callie possessed a keen intuition about others' feelings. Except for one terrible exception, Callie had found it to be true. She'd learned to observe people. And saw what they needed, what she could do to bring a smile or ease a worry.

As they strolled along the tree-lined walk toward town, she decided to give that strategy a try. "You're an excellent carpenter, Mr. Smith."

He took her arm and a jolt of electricity shot through her. "Watch your step," he said in a calm voice, but the gaze he shot her said he'd felt that same wild reaction. "Carpentry comes easy to me," he said, "like building a nest comes easy to you."

Once past the hump in the walk, he released his hold on her, leaving her feeling strangely bereft. "Building a nest?"

"Yes, making a home, a welcoming place for friends like Elise, even a stranger like myself. That's a gift." His eyes warmed. "I've seen my share of places and the people who live there. Hospitality like yours isn't something you see every day."

Everything inside her turned to jelly. Why did this man have such an effect on her?

Janet Dean
and
Janet Lee Barton

Wanted: A Family
&
A Place of Refuge

HARLEQUIN® LOVE INSPIRED®CLASSICS

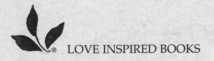

LOVE INSPIRED BOOKS

Recycling programs for this product may not exist in your area.

ISBN-13: 978-1-335-45469-0

Wanted: A Family & A Place of Refuge

Copyright © 2020 by Harlequin Books S.A.

Wanted: A Family
First published in 2011. This edition published in 2020.
Copyright © 2011 by Janet Dean

A Place of Refuge
First published in 2013. This edition published in 2020.
Copyright © 2013 by Janet Lee Barton

www.Harlequin.com

Printed in U.S.A.

CONTENTS

Janet Dean grew up in a family with a strong creative streak. Her father and grandfather recounted fascinating stories, instilling in Janet an appreciation of history and the desire to write. Today she enjoys traveling into our nation's past as she spins stories for Love Inspired Historical. Janet and her husband are proud parents and grandparents who love to spend time with their family.

Books by Janet Dean

Love Inspired Historical

Courting Miss Adelaide
Courting the Doctor's Daughter
The Substitute Bride
Wanted: A Family
An Inconvenient Match
The Bride Wore Spurs
The Bounty Hunter's Redemption

Visit the Author Profile page at Harlequin.com for more titles.

WANTED: A FAMILY

Janet Dean

And be ye kind one to another, tenderhearted, forgiving one another, even as God for Christ's sake hath forgiven you.
—*Ephesians* 4:32

To Karen Solem, my savvy agent.
Thank you for overseeing the business end of my career. To Tina James, my gifted editor, and Shirley Jump, dear friend and talented critique partner these past thirteen years. Thank you both for your insights that make me a far better writer. To my readers. A huge thank you for your encouraging words, a blessing I never take for granted.

Chapter One

Peaceful, Indiana, April 1900

How long before someone got hurt? How long before she couldn't pay the bills? How long—

Lord, help me find a way to keep my house and make it safe. For Elise. For my baby.

Automatically, Callie Mitchell's hand cradled the swell of her unborn child. Martin had been gone a few weeks when she realized that she was pregnant. She wanted this baby with an intensity that stole her breath away. In less than four months she'd hold a tiny infant in her arms. Soon she'd be too clumsy to make repairs herself.

She swiped a strand of hair clinging to her damp skin and let her gaze roam the old Victorian, the house where she and Martin had lived the past two years. Once majestic, now the house's peeling paint demanded another coat, the rickety porch begged for solid boards and rails, the roof pleaded for shingles. The house looked like a princess down on her luck.

Her breath caught. Martin had called her his princess, usually when he sought her forgiveness for some infraction. Those infractions usually involved skipping work or spending money they didn't have. But how could she not forgive that happy-go-lucky charmer almost anything? Her throat tightened. Especially now?

Of their own volition her eyes traveled the steep gabled roofline, to the spot where Martin had lost his footing in November and tumbled to his death.

The words she'd said to him that morning echoed in her mind. *If you don't repair the leak, one night the ceiling's going to fall on us while we sleep.*

Her gaze darted away. She wouldn't think about that now.

She wouldn't remember how he looked lying there. She wouldn't.

Tightening her grip on the milk pail, she trudged toward the small barn at the back of the property, the prospect of tearing out and replacing each board on the porch slowing her steps. Lady needed oats. Bossy needed milking. The garden needed hoeing. That much she could do.

But the list of chores she couldn't handle grew longer every day. The roof leaked. The window casings on the north side of the house had rotted. The staircase railing wobbled.

Inside the barn, she fed and watered the mare, then moved to the open stall where Bossy waited. Callie pulled up the stool, giving the jersey a pat. Laying her forehead against the cow's wide side for balance, she closed her eyes, taking a minute to inhale the familiar scent of livestock, hay and manure. Across the way, the mare snuffled her ration of oats. As always the serenity of the place soothed her and eased the weight of her responsibilities.

The cow placidly chewed her cud, paying Callie no mind. As the first stream of milk hit the galvanized pail, she prayed for strength and wisdom to handle the needed repairs. To rally around Elise and regain harmony with her father-in-law, a strong-minded man she didn't usually buck.

Callie had grown weary of Commodore fussing about her dilapidated house, yet not lifting a finger to help. Instead he pressured her to move in with him and Dorothy. He blamed the house for his son's death. And though he'd never said as much, he blamed her, too.

Sometimes lying in bed at night, sometimes rising at the dawn of a new day, sometimes at the cemetery standing before Martin's headstone, she blamed herself more.

But nothing would stop her from giving Elise and other unwed and pregnant women refuge. Her home would be a place for them to live, free from judgment.

Not long after she and Martin moved into the house, she'd talked to him about that very thing. He'd rejected the idea, citing the cost as the reason. A valid concern, but Callie suspected his main objection centered on the work involved and the lack of privacy, something she'd understood.

Now she had only her baby to consider and a large, empty house. Once she completed the repairs, she'd seek funds and community support and make her dream of an unwed mothers' home a reality. God would work it out in His time. A blessed sense of peace stole over her, renewing her awareness of God's provision.

Stripes trotted over, tail high, and rubbed against

her skirts, purring like a well-oiled engine. "Where are your kittens?" No doubt on the back stoop waiting for breakfast.

Bossy's tail swished Callie's way. A signal the milking was done. "Thanks, girl."

Accompanied by her strutting cat, Callie hauled the pail to the house. In the kitchen, she skimmed cream off the top and poured the rest into two pitchers. She crumbled day-old bread into an iron skillet, soaked it with milk, and then stowed the pitchers in the icebox.

Outside, Stripes and her offspring crowded around the pan, lapping the meal with dainty pink tongues. The male of the litter shoved one of his sisters aside and stuck in his paw.

"Mind your manners. There's plenty for all of you," Callie said.

Finished with her morning chores, Callie gathered tools from the barn and walked around the house to the front porch. The fistful of nails she'd driven into the boards a few days back made no difference.

With one gloved hand clutching Martin's toolbox, the other gripping the crowbar and her dyed-black skirts, she climbed the wobbly steps, careful to avoid the rotten wood. Once she removed the deteriorating planks, she'd replace them with the lumber stacked in the barn.

She forced the tip of the crowbar under a board and pushed down with all her might. Instead of coming up, nails and all, the plank splintered, pitching her forward. Gasping, she staggered, dropped the tool, but remained on her feet.

Heart pounding from her near fall, she knelt and used a hammer to knock off the remaining pieces of wood until she'd removed one board. At this rate, the task would take weeks. Callie wiped a hand across her moist brow and let her gaze roam the neighborhood.

Up the street, a stranger strode up the walk to Mildred's house. He was not a salesman. He carried a sack, not a sample case, and looked strong enough to handle this job. But if he sought work, she couldn't spare a penny to hire him.

She repositioned the crowbar and shoved again. Nails squeaked in protest, then slowly the board lifted. A few more shoves and it pulled free. Smiling, she tossed the plank aside.

The screen door creaked. Elise Langley, just eighteen, her family home a few doors down, stood in the opening, resting an arm on the bulge beneath her apron. "That job's too hard for you. Why not hire someone?"

From a family with money to spare, Elise wouldn't realize that Callie didn't have funds to hire anyone. Nor would Callie tell her, lest her houseguest feel unwelcome.

"It's good exercise." Callie grinned.

"I'll help." Before Callie could stop her, Elise, heavy and awkward with child, stepped onto the porch. The boards sagged and she stumbled, lurching sideways. "Ouch!"

The crowbar clattered to the floor. "Are you hurt?"

Elise hobbled to the door, pushed open the screen and lowered herself to the threshold. "I twisted my ankle is all." She lifted her skirts and rubbed the injured spot.

Callie picked her way to Elise's side and took a look. "It's already swelling."

Wrapping an arm around her middle, Callie helped Elise shuffle inside, settling her on the parlor sofa, then removed Elise's shoe and elevated her foot on pillows.

She hurried to the kitchen, returning with chunks of ice wrapped in a dish towel and propped it on Elise's ankle with more pillows.

"I'm sorry, Callie. You warned me about the porch. Why do I always have to learn the hard way?"

"You were only trying to help." She patted Elise's hand. "If you're all right, I'll get back to work."

After Elise's mishap, Callie edged her way across the porch, determined to remove a few more planks before she had to change the ice on Elise's ankle. She reached for the crowbar. A movement out of the corner of her eye stopped her.

The man she'd seen earlier ambled toward her, a jacket and sack tossed over his shoulder, his sleeves rolled to the elbow, revealing tanned, muscled forearms. He moved with a loose-legged ease, suggesting he'd covered his share of ground on foot.

Strangers were rare in Peaceful.

What did he want?

At the bottom of the steps, he tipped his hat. "Ma'am." His gaze landed on her rounded abdomen then slid to her face. "I'm looking for work. Heard at the Corner Café you'd lost your husband and might need help."

"If I did, I've no money to pay you."

His eyes roamed the house. "Your roof's missing shingles, the wood siding needs scraping and a couple coats of paint."

Hadn't he understood what she'd said? "Lots needs doing, but—"

"Nothing I can't handle." His self-assured tone held no hint of arrogance. He reached into his jacket pocket and removed a paper tucked inside. "This backs my claim."

When had she encountered a pushier man?

When had she been as desperate for a man with push?

Callie picked her way down the steps, took the paper from his hand and read the reference praising Jacob Smith's skill and work ethic, even his character.

What did that prove? He could've written it himself.

Above-average height with a wiry, broad-shouldered build, the man's angular face looked hard, chiseled from stone. The power radiating off him reminded her of a caged tiger pacing its enclosure, ready to spring. A guarded look in his eyes, as if he'd lived under scrutiny and been deemed defective told her this man had been hurt by life as much as she had. But that didn't make him honorable. It could mean exactly the opposite.

"Does anyone know you in this town?"

"No, ma'am."

"I'm sorry. I don't hire strangers." Not after the incident with the last handyman. She gave an apologetic smile, then returned to the porch and began prying up the next board. As she shoved against the lever, a jolt of pain streaked up her arms. She bit back a moan.

Eyes flashing, he bounded up the steps and hauled the crowbar from her hands. "You can't raze this porch in your condition."

Angry tears flooded her eyes. She wanted to slap that disapproving scowl off his face.

As if reading her mind, he took a step back. "I don't mean to criticize, but that much exertion could harm your baby."

Ignoring her refusal to hire him, he bent to the task,

removing the board with ease, and then tossed it to the yard. "How do you plan to replace the missing shingles on your roof?"

The mere thought of that roof made Callie queasy. "If I trusted you—which I don't." Her tone should make that perfectly clear. "I can't pay you."

Again his gaze roamed the house. "I'll restore this beauty for a roof over my head and three meals a day, a price most folks appreciate."

She appreciated the price all right. But he was still a stranger. "I've got to wonder why a man with your experience would work without a wage. I'll still have to say no."

"I can't allow a woman to harm herself, even a head-strong woman like you."

Of all the nerve! She glared at him. "I'm perfectly capable of handling whatever task I set my mind to."

His eyes held a flicker of respect. "I'm sure that's true, if setting your mind to a task got it done. But this job requires more brawn than brains." He winked, bold as brass. "That makes me perfect for the job."

Aghast at the rush of attraction that shot through her, Callie folded her arms across her chest, more determined than ever to send this rogue packing.

"One day I want a business of my own. Why not give me a chance to test my mettle by bringing this Victorian back to life?"

Though he'd used that spiel to manipulate her, she couldn't argue with his logic. Fixing up her house would prove his ability and allow her to keep her home.

Besides, she didn't see anyone else lining up to help her.

If the house wasn't safe, Martin's parents would insist that she live with them, putting an end to Callie's dream. What would happen to Elise and her baby then?

As she grappled with the decision, the man returned to the task of ripping up boards. As if enjoying the effort, his sinewy muscles danced, her stomach dancing right along with them. She dropped her gaze to her feet, tamping down the ridiculous reaction. What had gotten into her? Those muscles of his merely proved he could handle the job.

Stranger or not, what choice did she have? Jacob Smith had a reference and the skill. Had offered a price she could afford.

Lord, I've prayed for an answer. Is this drifter Your solution?

The knot between her shoulder blades eased. The final assurance she needed. "I'll risk hiring you."

The corners of his mouth turned up. "Reckon we're both taking a risk."

"How so?"

"I'm taking a chance you're a passable cook."

She couldn't contain a grin. "I'll cook as ably as you work."

"Good enough for me," he said, the rumble of his voice ending on a chuckle.

"Have you had breakfast?"

"No, ma'am."

"I'll prepare a meal to fuel a working man."

He shoved his hat brim up his forehead. "Appreciate it."

The morning sun lit his face. A smile softened the hard edge of stubble on his unshaven jaw and spread to his eyes. Green. They were green as jade.

Callie's mind went blank. "Ah." What was she about

to say? "While you're, ah, waiting, you can put your things in the lean-to attached to the barn. The last hired hand had no complaints about the accommodations." At the mention of that scoundrel, her hands fisted. "Thanked me by running off with the money from my sugar bowl. You don't plan on doing the same thing, do you?"

His jaw jutted. "No."

"In that case, settle in. I'll serve your breakfast on the back stoop." She turned then pivoted back. "Oh, I'm Callie Mitchell."

"Folks call me Jake."

"Just so you know, Mr. Smith, there's no money in my sugar bowl or anywhere else in the house."

He met her gaze, his eyes as steely as his muscles. "Just so you know, Mrs. Mitchell, I'm no thief."

Her hand flew to her throat. Giving a brisk nod, she hurried toward the chicken coop, glad to put distance between her and the stony-eyed drifter.

Smith was a common enough name. Her heart tripped in her chest. Too common.

Suspicious name or not, he'd come along when she needed his help. Badly. Still, she'd trust him only as far as her stoop.

Jake removed his hat to get a better look at the spitfire who'd hired him. The snippety woman had all but accused him of being a thief with that prickly tongue of hers. And those probing eyes, suspicious, reproachful, as if he had *burglar* stamped in capital letters across his forehead.

He sucked in a breath of free air and watched her march across the lawn, a woman on a mission. Even dressed in black, with those brown tendrils escaping her pompadour and feathering her neck, she looked beguiling. Taller than most women, she carried her delicate frame with a dignity almost disguising her condition. Surely she was heartier than she looked. Still, no matter how strong-minded, a pregnant widow wouldn't have an easy road. But then who did? No point in getting sappy about it.

What sort of a woman would risk unhitching that baby she was carrying?

A woman with no one to help her.

The haste of his recrimination pricked his conscience. He of all people should know better than to leap to conclusions. Mrs. Mitchell wouldn't have agreed to hire him if she knew he'd spent time behind bars. Framed by Lloyd, his so-called friend, vying for the affections of the woman Jake had thought loved him. He'd experienced firsthand that women were disloyal, even deceitful.

What a fool he'd been. Well, not even a fool made the same mistake twice. Jake might be a lot of things, but stupid wasn't one of them. He had no intention of trusting another woman.

Still, he'd handle Mrs. Mitchell's work for now. See that she didn't get hurt. Or harm her baby.

Perhaps in this town, several counties away from the penitentiary, he could stay a spell. One thing he'd learned—innocent or not, a man who'd done time wasn't free. He'd merely traded jail bars for barriers he couldn't see, but those invisible barriers were equally as solid. Prejudice. Suspicion. Judgment.

Not that he blamed folks, at least those who didn't know him. But those who did—

Well, after his release, except to get a reference from his boss, he didn't linger in Bloomington, the town where he'd been tried and found guilty, railroaded by flimsy evidence and an overeager sheriff. He couldn't face the skepticism, couldn't face being treated like a criminal.

But what he hadn't expected…

No matter where a man traveled, his past dogged his every step. One day, Mrs. Mitchell would look at him with the same doubt he'd seen often enough in the eyes of others. Not that he'd get close to anyone, not even to a woman with a stubborn tilt to her chin and dazzling sea-blue eyes.

He strode to the lean-to and opened the door into a room the size of a cell. A cot sat against the wall, bedding stacked at the foot, even a pillow for his head. Next to the bed a washstand held a kerosene lamp. Beside it, a chair where a man could fold his clothes at night and pull on his boots in the morning. A small window let in fresh air and a slice of the sky. Even under this roof, the moon and stars would keep him company.

He needed lodging. And whether Mrs. Mitchell wanted to admit it or not, she needed his help. He could mend a run-down house even if he couldn't repair the mess of his life.

A mess built by another.

No point harping on the past. The truth had come out. Lloyd was in jail. His treachery had cost Jake a year of his life, but he'd done Jake a favor by saving him from a life sentence with a fickle woman. Still, that year had deprived him of his good name and destroyed the last flimsy thread of his optimism.

Before his record caught up with him, he'd try to set this neglected, regal old house to rights.

More importantly, if she lived in Peaceful, he'd find the woman he sought.

Once he did, he'd leave. Moving from town to town, exposed to the elements. Not the greatest life, but he was free. Not only from the bars of prison, but unencumbered by relationships that had given him nothing but grief. When a man got burned, it didn't take him long to learn that the stove was hot.

A lesson he wouldn't forget.

On the chair, he laid the sack, holding a change of clothes and the Bible the warden gave him upon his release. Jake couldn't fathom why he bothered hauling that tome around. Tossing his jacket on the bed, he tried out the mattress. Not bad. Everything was clean and serviceable. Mrs. Mitchell treated hired hands well—that said plenty about her. He'd give her a full day's work and then some. All he had.

Maybe in a town with the unlikely name of Peaceful, he'd find his roots. Not that the insight would give him a moment of peace, no matter what the town's name was.

He shoved the thought away. Soon he'd sit down to a home-cooked meal. The prospect brought a rumble from his stomach.

Things were looking up.

Chapter Two

In Callie's large kitchen, cabinets ascended from wide baseboards on the plank floor to crown molding bordering the pressed-tin ceiling. At the enormous cookstove, Callie prepared breakfast. Hot grease popped out of the skillet and landed on her hand, bringing a hiss from her lips. That's what she got for frying side meat as if her life depended on it.

Her hands trembled. Maybe it did. She wanted Jacob Smith, if that was his real name, making repairs. Repairs Martin never got around to. Yet, within minutes of meeting her, the rugged stranger had taken charge as if he owned the place. An urge to slap his bossy face battled with an undeniable longing to savor his concern. He'd made her feel protected, cared for, as if he wanted to ease her load. When had Martin ever done that? Still, she didn't fancy relying on an outsider.

Through the window, she watched Mr. Smith haul an extension ladder from the barn. By the time she'd taken the pan of biscuits out of the oven, he'd made another trip, this time carrying an armload of shingles and a small keg of nails. The man didn't waste a minute, which she admired.

He stopped at the pump, splashed his face and neck with water, then scrubbed his hands. For a drifter, the man took responsibility and valued cleanliness. Virtues she respected.

Elise, leaning on an old cane Callie had found in the attic, hobbled to Callie's side. Her auburn hair was pulled into a low knot that failed to corral her mass of curls. "Can I help?"

"You're supposed to keep your weight off that ankle."

"It's stronger today." As she took a seat at the table, Elise glanced out the window. "Who's that?"

Callie set a plate of food in front of her. "His name's Jacob Smith. He's going to fix the roof and the porch." She smiled down at her. "So you won't twist your other ankle."

"I was more concerned about you hurting yourself than my ankle. That man's a blessing."

"I'm reserving judgment, but I hope you're right."

While Elise ate her breakfast, Callie poured a mug of coffee, then scooped onto a plate scrambled eggs, fried potatoes, two slabs of pork and three biscuits hot from the oven.

"Come meet him," Callie said. "Oh, and bring the flatware, please."

Under a smattering of freckles, Elise paled as if she wanted to refuse, but took the napkin-wrapped utensils and followed Callie to the door.

On the stoop, Jacob Smith doffed his hat then opened the screen. His hair, black as a moonless night, met his collar. Callie had an urge to grab her scissors, but introduced Elise instead.

"Nice to meet you, Mrs. Langley," he said, taking the utensils she offered.

Color dotted Elise's cheeks. "It's Miss Langley."

Mr. Smith's gaze landed on Elise's stomach then darted away, matching Elise's speed as she left the stoop and ducked into the kitchen.

Callie fixed a disapproving gaze on the newcomer. "Elise may be unwed, but she's a sweet girl. I expect you to treat her accordingly."

The hard set of his jaw gave Jacob Smith the look of a man ready to do battle. "I'm not one to judge."

"Good. Lord knows plenty of folks are." She motioned to the bench. "Have a seat, but watch the cats. They think the stoop's a feline café."

He plopped his hat beside him on the bench. "Breakfast looks mighty fine." He took the plate and mug from her hands then waited, as if expecting her to leave, so she did.

Glancing back, she watched him dive in. The man was hungry. Too hungry to pray? Or the action of a man without faith? Time would tell. Either way, she'd keep her doors locked at night.

As she entered the back door, a wave of light-headedness swept over her. She'd been up since dawn. The bowl of cold cereal she'd eaten was long gone.

In the kitchen, her food untouched, Elise drooped at the table, as limp as a rag doll, tears running down her cheeks.

Callie splayed her fingers over the girl's nape and massaged her muscles. "Are you all right?"

"You saw how he looked at me."

"Don't take it to heart. You know we expectant moms

can't trust our perceptions. Why, we're laughing one minute, crying the next."

"I know I'm right, Callie. I've seen that look of censure before."

"Well, if that's the case, he'd better keep his opinions to himself or I'll send him packing faster than a camel can spit."

"Camels spit?"

"I've heard they do. And I can, too, if I'm riled."

Elise's snuffles ended on a giggle, a rainbow in the stormy ups and downs of expectant motherhood.

Callie headed to the stove, slipped an egg and a slice of pork onto her plate. "I'll see what Jacob Smith has to say for himself."

While Elise finished eating, Callie left the house.

Across from Mr. Smith, she sat on a weathered chair with splayed legs. Her full skirts all but touched the scruffy toe of his boot.

As if uncomfortable with the contact, he yanked his foot back, then lifted the last forkful of food to his mouth. His hand was large, long-fingered. The nails were clean and he had a sprinkling of dark hair between his knuckles.

"Looks like I'm too late to ask if the food needed salt."

"Breakfast was perfect, as is. Every bite."

She'd missed cooking for a man, especially an appreciative man. She smiled. He smiled back. The dimple winked in his left cheek, giving his angular face a boyish look.

Bowing her head, she offered a silent prayer then cut into the pork.

Stripes wove between them, rubbing against Mr.

Smith's boot. He gave her ears a gentle scratch and was rewarded with a grateful purr. The way people treated animals said a lot about them. "Where's home?" she asked.

"Nowhere in particular."

Eyeing him, she scooped egg onto her fork. "We're all born somewhere, Mr. Smith."

"Yes, ma'am, but… I don't know exactly where."

Her hand stilled. "Care to explain?"

"I grew up in an orphanage." He'd said the words in a matter-of-fact voice, with no trace of emotion, yet his eyes didn't meet hers.

The bite of egg lodged in Callie's throat. If not for Aunt Hilda, Callie would've met the same fate. Swallowing hard, her gaze darted his way.

He looked tranquil enough, but a twitch in his jaw suggested otherwise. "Not a happy experience?"

He shrugged, but the raw bleakness in his eyes confirmed her opinion.

"You got kin around these parts?" he said, deftly changing the subject and avoiding his past.

"My late husband's parents live a few blocks west."

"I'm sorry about your husband." Green eyes locked with hers. "Must be comforting, having his family nearby."

She nodded. Those searching eyes noticed her lack of enthusiasm. The man missed nothing.

"So what brings you to Peaceful?"

He gave a lopsided grin. "Reckon I'm here to help you."

"Are you saying you came to Peaceful by chance?"

"The town's name drew me." He laid his plate on the bench. Except for a few biscuit crumbs, he'd wiped it clean. "Thank you for the meal." His gaze settled on the lean-to. "And for the lodging." He plopped his hat in place. "I'd say I got the better end of our deal."

"You may think otherwise once you wrangle with the roof."

"I'm part mountain goat." He rose. "If it's all the same to you, I'll repair the roof this morning. Tackle the porch during the heat of the day."

"Do as you think best."

A flicker of surprise skidded across his face. That boss at the construction company must've been a stickler.

"I'll bring your dinner out at noon. Wait a minute." She walked inside, grabbed a fruit jar with a galvanized lid from the kitchen. "It's going to be a scorcher. Fill this or you'll wear yourself out making trips to the pump."

He took the jar and tipped his hat. "Much obliged."

"Take care on that roof. It's steep."

"Yes, ma'am." His eyes sobered. "I will."

He strapped on a pouch of nails and stuck the hammer under his belt, then leaned the ladder against the back of the house, making adjustments until he had it centered to suit him. Before she could steady it, he'd grabbed an armload of shingles and scrambled to the top and out onto the roof. As he clomped up the incline, she held her breath and then slowly released it, noticing his confidence and agility.

And the way his back muscles rippled through his shirt.

At the unwelcome response to the man, her cheeks burned. With her hands full to overflowing and no idea where she'd get the money to take her and Elise through the winter, how could she keep noticing a man's muscles, a *drifter* at that?

Her father-in-law would say only a no-account man chose to work for room and board, instead of settling down with a good-paying job.

Callie shivered. Jacob Smith had been closed-mouthed. Was he running from something? Or to something?

Whatever his motive for coming to Peaceful, she didn't need another complication in her life. How long before he could get the work done and leave?

Couldn't be soon enough to suit her.

Sweat stinging his eyes and blurring his vision, Jake pulled a nail from the pouch and fastened a shingle in place. He yanked a handkerchief from his hip pocket, threaded it under the crown of his wide-brimmed hat, then plunked it on his head.

Laying shingles in this unseasonable heat was hard, dirty work, but he welcomed the exertion, liked being in control. Control he'd lost in jail, but needed badly. A man felt alive when he pushed the limits of his endurance. Afterward, his muscles might ache, but nothing equaled the satisfaction of repairing something broken. If it sometimes ate at him that remodeling houses came as close as he'd get to a home of his own, he forced the thought away. No reason to expect anything more. He had no interest in forming a family.

Every half hour like clockwork, Mrs. Mitchell came out to check on him. No doubt scared he'd break his neck. Not that he blamed her, considering what happened to her husband. If she knew how at ease he felt perched on this roof, she'd worry less.

He liked the expanse, the sense of freedom, the clear view of nearby gardens with slender rows of leaf lettuce and green onions. A few patches overgrown with dead pumpkin vines and cornstalks bordered red barns, whitewashed sheds and outhouses, all tucked behind clapboard houses.

Did one of these homes hide the woman who'd given him birth?

Not his mother. A mother took care of her child. Fed him. Tucked him into bed at night.

Or so he understood.

But one thing he knew—a mother didn't toss her baby away like an unwanted trinket. Clenching his jaw, he slammed the hammer into the head of the nail, driving it in place. He wanted that woman to know the price he'd paid for her negligence. The orphanage had provided the basics to sustain life, but no affection, no encouragement, no joy, merely existence.

She sent a yearly birthday greeting to the orphanage addressed to Jacob, not even using his last name, as if Smith was a lie. Those cards didn't diminish her desertion. Merely proved she knew his location yet never bothered to see him. Never bothered to reveal his roots. Never bothered to make sure he survived.

As he pounded shingles into place, his mind drifted back to the winter he was seven. He'd fallen from a tree on the orphanage grounds. With pain searing his broken arm and emptiness branding his heart, he'd lain on the frozen earth staring at the bare branches, silhouetted against a cloudless sky. A boy surrounded by people, yet starving for love, he'd cried out for his mother. No one came.

From that moment, Jake dropped the pretense he'd

clung to and faced the truth. He had only those post-cards. Postcards couldn't hold him. Postcards couldn't wipe away his tears. Postcards couldn't atone for her abandonment.

At last he'd quieted, then struggled to his feet. Cradling his broken arm against his chest, he'd shuffled toward the orphanage, a vow on his lips.

Never again would he care about that woman. Never again would he deceive himself into believing that one day she'd come for him. Never again would he hold on to hope for a family.

His arm had mended. But in the sixteen years since that day, nothing had proved him wrong.

Even as an adult, when he knew circumstances might've made her coming for him difficult, even impossible, he couldn't find it in his heart to excuse her.

The postcards had been postmarked Indianapolis. Once, just once, a card had come from Peaceful. He'd kept all those postcards. Just to remember the town names. Not that they meant anything to him.

As he hammered another nail home, his stomach clenched. In truth, he'd studied each stroke of the pen, compared the handwriting to his own, searching those pitifully few words for some connection. Never finding one.

After his exoneration and release from prison, he'd spent a month in Indianapolis, searching birth records, locating every Smith he could find, but he hadn't turned up a clue. For some reason, he had the strong feeling she'd sent the postcards from there to throw him off her trail and he'd find her in Peaceful.

Well, if she'd found peace in this town, perhaps he would, too. Once he'd given her a huge hunk of his opinion. Not charitable of him, but the best he could do with all the bitterness burning inside him.

He didn't wish her harm. He didn't even want to disgrace her. He merely needed her to know the penalty he'd paid when she'd swept him under the rug of her life.

The beat of his heart pounded in his temples with the rhythm of his hammer. If there was a God and He was the Author of Life, as some claimed, He hadn't gone out of His way to lend a hand to Jake's life story.

Not in the circumstances of his birth.

Not in those years in the orphanage.

Not in the injustice exacted in that courtroom.

He sighed. Why not admit it? He wanted to see his mother with a desperation he couldn't fathom, yet couldn't deny. He wanted to meet her. See if they shared a resemblance. Learn the identity of his father. Maybe then he could move on with his life. If only he had a way to make his search easier, a sign with an arrow pointing in the direction to turn. He huffed at such absurdity. What would the sign say? This way leads to Jake Smith's mother?

"How's it going?"

Whirling around, Jake scrambled for footing, scraping his knuckles against the hot shingles.

Mrs. Mitchell looked up at him, eyes wide with alarm. "I'm sorry. I didn't mean to startle you, but dinner's ready."

"My fault, I didn't hear you coming." He forced his lips into a grin that pinched like ill-fitting shoes. "Your timing's perfect. I just replaced the last shingle."

Her eyes lit. "Oh, now I won't have to cringe at the first peal of thunder."

Forcing his gaze away from that sparkle in her eyes,

that sweet smile on her lips, he tucked the hammer into his belt. She drew him like a mindless moth to a candle's flame, a lure that would prove as lethal.

"Any damage inside?" he said, barely able to concentrate with her peering up at him.

"My bedroom ceiling's cracked. I moved the bed to ensure that I won't awaken one morning blanketed in plaster."

Knowing the danger of entanglement, yet unable to stop himself, he said, "Can't have a chunk of ceiling marring that pretty face of yours."

The apple of her cheeks colored, but her eyes turned wary. "You men know the words a woman likes to hear."

Why didn't an attractive woman like Callie Mitchell appreciate a compliment? "I'll take a look at the ceiling when I've finished the porch." Jake pivoted out onto the ladder, descending the rungs two at a time, the ladder vibrating with each footfall.

By the time he'd reached the bottom, she'd dashed over and gripped the sides. He all but bumped into her coming off the last step. Wide-eyed and obviously shaken, she quickly moved aside. When had anyone worried about his safety?

"I'm accustomed to ladders and this one's sturdy."

"Even a careful man can meet disaster, Mr. Smith."

No doubt she referred to her husband's fall, but her remark summed up his life. "Your words don't give a man much hope."

Her eyes narrowed, as if trying to see inside of him. "Hope doesn't come from words of mine. Hope comes from God's Word."

A man couldn't manufacture something he didn't believe. "I don't see a point in opening a Bible."

"Without God's Word to point me in the right direction, I'd lose my way." Mrs. Mitchell looked at him with eagerness. "You might give the Bible and church a try."

"From what I've seen, churchgoers aren't likely to offer clemency." The words shot out of his mouth before he could stop them. What about this woman made him bleed his innermost thoughts?

Her gaze bored deeper. "Do you need clemency?"

Jake removed his hat and slipped the handkerchief stuffed inside into his hip pocket then swiped the sweat off his brow in the crook of his elbow. It didn't take a genius to recognize prying. "Reckon we all do."

A flash of remorse traveled her face. Her eyes lifted to the roof, filling with anguish and self-reproach that pushed against his core. If he didn't know better, he'd believe Mrs. Mitchell shoved her husband off the roof. Well, he had no interest in getting involved with her or her problems. Yet she looked so fragile standing there fighting back tears.

An overpowering urge to tug her to him, to tell her everything would be fine, mounted inside him, yet his hands remained at his sides.

Everything had never been fine.

He couldn't promise such a thing.

To her.

To anyone.

"I'll get your dinner." She headed to the house, shoulders bent, as if carrying a heavy burden.

No doubt she did. A burden he could ease by repairing this house. But the rest—unwed mothers, babies, grief over her husband's death—he'd stay clear of all that.

At the pump, Jake stuck his head under the spout.

Cold water sluiced down his throat and into his sweat-soaked shirt. Perhaps the dousing would cool his empathy for the young widow.

The woman tried to shove God and church down his throat, a prescription Jake couldn't swallow. She'd indicated that the Bible would point a man in the right direction, as if the road ahead lay with God. He'd more likely find that arrow he wished for earlier than answers in an ancient gilded book.

And as for prayer—

If God existed, He didn't give a fig about Jake. No matter what Callie Mitchell said, God wouldn't be helping him. Jake would need a sensible way to find his mother.

Wielding a crowbar, Jake pried a rotted board from the porch floor, easy to do with the missing or inadequately set nails. He'd make repairs and ignore Mrs. Mitchell's attempt to get him to church. Yet, he could feel himself getting drawn into her life. Worse, drawn to her. That scared him silly.

The faint scent of roses drifted through the air. Mrs. Mitchell stepped onto the porch, a straw boater perched at a jaunty angle on her head, wearing a high-neck white shirtwaist and gored skirt that rustled at the hem as she moved.

Jake sat back on his heels and drank in the sight of her, the gentle arch of her brows, her almond-shaped aquamarine eyes, her thick tresses the shade of rich coffee.

"Hello." He'd sounded like a smitten schoolboy instead of a man who'd been burned.

"Hello." She smiled at him. "Lovely afternoon."

"It is." Especially since she'd appeared, but he wouldn't say that. If he had one speck of control over his addled brain, he wouldn't think it, either.

"I'll try not to get in your way." She edged across the porch to check the flower boxes of pansies.

"You aren't bothering me."

When had he told a bigger lie? He could barely keep his eyes off her as she nipped off some dying blooms.

He clenched his jaw and pried up another board. What had gotten into him? The woman might be pretty, might even have a good heart, at least if her desire to take in an unwed expectant mother meant anything, but she was a woman after all.

If he could read her thoughts, he suspected her motive for helping wasn't as pure as it appeared. Most people had an underlying scheme for everything they did. He'd figure hers out eventually.

"Does Miss Langley have family?" Jake asked.

"Her parents live up the block."

"Then…why is she living with you?"

Mrs. Mitchell hesitated, as if deciding what to say. "Her father insists that she give the baby up."

Jake's stomach tensed. "What would he have her do? Dump it in an orphanage?"

She sighed. "Either that or put the baby up for adoption far from Peaceful."

An urge to tell Elise's father what kind of a life his grandchild would have in such a place gripped Jake, holding him firmly in its clutches, then tightening like a vise. "Nice and tidy for everyone," he said in a voice as rough as sandpaper.

Why was Callie Mitchell getting involved with such ugliness? "If Miss Langley had thought of the consequences, she wouldn't have gotten involved with a no-account man."

Her eyes flashed. "Your censure doesn't solve anything. What's done is done."

"I'm sorry." He swallowed against a sudden lump in his throat. "I'm just...angry."

"I'm sorry you spent your youth in an orphanage." Compassion filling her gaze, she reached a hand toward him.

He'd revealed too much. He took a step back, avoiding her touch. "As you say, what's done is done."

That morning she'd tried to pry into his past, tried to see inside of him. He knew better than to let anyone get close.

Mrs. Mitchell sighed. "If only Mr. Langley could see that an orphanage isn't the solution."

How many kids had Jake seen tossed into that orphanage from every situation or circumstance imaginable? Few thrived. If he tried to tell Elise's father anything, he might resent Jake's interference enough to dig around in his past. Perhaps discover his stint in prison. If word got out, he'd be forced out of town before he had a chance to find the woman who'd given birth to him.

Avoiding her penetrating gaze, he turned to his task. He'd repair this house, look for his mother and avoid more than conversations about the weather.

"Oh!" Mrs. Mitchell's hand darted to her stomach.

Jake leaped to his feet. "Is something wrong?"

Like a rosebud opening, her smile unfurled. "Something's very right," she said, her tone laden with wonder. "I think my baby just moved for the first time."

Of its own volition, Jake's hand moved toward her

middle, hovering inches away. Had his mother reacted like this when he'd moved inside her? No, if she had experienced Callie Mitchell's joy, she couldn't have tossed him out like yesterday's garbage.

"In four more months, I'll have a child." Her voice trembled with emotion. "A family of my own."

Behind the emotion, Jake heard Mrs. Mitchell's determination to create a family with her and her baby.

Family.

The word conjured up birthday cakes and bedtime stories, kisses on small hurts and hugs after a nightmare. All the things he'd never had. "Not every woman would want to raise a child alone."

"I have God and my baby. I'm never alone."

Her eyes reflected a faith so bright, so pure, Jake felt filthy in comparison. The idea that he could have such a woman in his life ricocheted through him. He tamped down the ridiculous notion. Callie Mitchell grieved for her husband. He grieved for his past. Not a foundation for second chances.

Chapter Three

Callie cringed, heat blooming in her cheeks. How could she have shared with Jacob Smith, a man, a *stranger,* the first movement of her baby? An intimate detail too personal to share with anyone but her doctor, her friends and the baby's father, but Martin was gone and she hadn't been able to contain her joy.

Worse, Mr. Smith appeared as overcome and delighted by the news as a prospective father. This would never do. Her breath caught. Jacob Smith was turning her world upside down.

Across from her, he took a long drink of water from the fruit jar, his Adam's apple bobbing with each swallow. His sweat-soaked shirt clung to his torso, a surprisingly broad chest on that sinewy frame.

Martin had been soft, pudgy. The unkind comparison of her deceased husband to a drifter knotted in Callie's stomach. "I'm going to town for my mail," she said, eager to be on her way.

"Mind if I join you? I could use a break."

At the thought of walking side by side with this man, a shiver snaked down Callie's spine. Why couldn't he have stuck to the task at hand? She ought to make an excuse and hurry inside, but she heard herself say, "I'd enjoy the company."

He smiled, flashing that fascinating hollow in his cheek. "Give me five minutes."

Looking pleased, as if accompanying her mattered, he vaulted over the railing to the ground with the grace and the quickness of a deer. Callie's belly flopped like one of Martin's landed fish. She tamped down such silliness. Mr. Smith merely needed a breather, exactly as he'd said.

Slow-moving clouds threw shadows on the house, pulling Callie's eyes to the turret rising in the sky. Her family home had resembled this old Victorian, except the upper-story windows had worn stained-glass crowns, throwing splashes of color on the walls, delighting her little-girl heart. From those windows, donned in the cloak her mother had sewed and a beaded cardboard crown, the princess of her domain, she'd surveyed her kingdom—the fertile valley nestled in the foothills of Tennessee.

But the dam had been compromised and rushing water had whipped through the valley, sweeping the house and her family along in the flood.

She'd survived their loss. She'd survived Martin's death. She'd survive whatever life threw her way. Her faith would keep her strong. But the deep ache of loneliness stirring within left her vulnerable. Vulnerable even to a man she knew nothing about.

Hadn't she learned anything from her marriage to Martin?

Alone and adrift after Aunt Hilda died, Callie had soaked up Martin's cheerful disposition and affectionate nature like parched ground and missed his lack of responsibility.

The minute he proposed, Callie had said yes. They set the wedding date for less than a month away. When the old Victorian came up for auction, Martin coerced his father into buying it as a wedding gift, insisting that the large family he wanted wouldn't fit into Aunt Hilda's tiny house. Once Callie sold the house, they used the proceeds to purchase furniture and had enough left over to put some money in the bank.

On her wedding day, Callie had never been happier. Martin had a secure job at his father's store. They had some savings. His parents had accepted her with open arms.

It didn't take long for the glow of marital bliss to fade. With Martin's penchant for guns and fishing gear and the cost of supplies needed to rebuild the house, they tore through their savings. The more that Commodore did to keep them solvent, the more he expected to run their lives.

Not that anyone could control Martin.

Perhaps with a baby on the way, he would have stepped up to his new role. She'd never know.

But she'd learned a hard lesson. A man wasn't always what he appeared.

Mr. Smith strode toward her, his hair damp under his hat, wearing a clean shirt and a contented smile that set her pulse racing. She folded her arms across her chest, vowing that she wouldn't let him have this effect on her. No matter how much she admired his responsible nature and impressive accomplishments, she wouldn't care about another man, especially a drifter.

When he reached her, their gazes locked. The yearning in his eyes lodged in her heart. They were two peo-ple cramming their days with meeting the needs of others, yet hungering for closeness. Every single bit of logic and misgiving vanished like dew on a summer day. Replaced by a pull towing her to him with a power she couldn't explain.

A pull she wouldn't heed.

Yet, her feet took her toward him. His eyes flared. Something meaningful and disturbing passed between them. Callie quickly looked away, breaking the hold this man had over her.

As she strolled beside him along the tree-lined walk toward town, she was all too aware of his height, the firmness of his stride, the power and energy he barely contained.

That first day she'd suspected he wasn't a believer. How could she be drawn to such a man?

Martin had possessed faith, well, faith of sorts. Not much for combing Scripture, he'd left his edifying to the preacher at those times he didn't snooze in the pew. In the two years they'd been married, they'd never shared a spiritual discussion.

Yet within hours of meeting, she and Mr. Smith had touched on their faith. From what he'd said, the man needed God. She would not get emotionally involved with a faithless man, but with God's help, she could try to fill more than his stomach. She could nourish his soul. Help him find the answer to the pain she sensed lurking beneath the surface.

Callie gulped. As long as that answer wasn't her.

Aunt Hilda had said Callie possessed a keen intuition about others' feelings. Except for that one terrible ex-ception with Nell, Callie had found her assessment true.

She'd learned to observe people. Saw what they needed, how she could bring a smile or ease a worry. Perhaps she could give that strategy a try with Jacob Smith.

As they approached a hump in the walk, he took her arm. "Watch your step."

A jolt shot through her. The startled look in Mr. Smith's eyes said he'd felt that same wild reaction. She quickly released her hold on his arm, yet felt strangely bereft. She groped for a safe topic. "You're an excellent carpenter."

"Carpentry comes easy to me," he said in a husky voice, "like building a nest comes easy to you."

"Building a nest?"

"Yes, making a home, a welcoming place for friends like Elise, even an outsider like me." His eyes warmed. "That's a gift. I've seen my share of places and the people who live there. Your hospitality isn't something I encounter often."

Everything inside her turned to jelly. Why did he have such an effect on her? The answer came. He understood what she valued, the importance of home and family.

"My house is a gift from God and way bigger than I need. I want to share it with others."

As if he doubted that God gave gifts, he didn't respond. She'd do what she could to share her faith. And leave the outcome to the One who controlled the universe. In the meantime, she'd focus on the arrival of her baby, on giving refuge to unwed mothers and ignore this transient man at her side.

As they passed Elise's family home, Callie's steps slowed. In the shadows of her porch Sarah Langley sat on the swing. She was a good Christian woman and

Callie always thought the same way about Mr. Langley, but Elise's decision to keep her baby called for strong support from her father, not opposition.

Sarah waved. "Callie, can you spare a minute?"

Callie glanced at Jacob Smith. "Elise's mother may have something important to say."

"I'll walk on ahead." He strode off, his lanky, easy gait eating up the distance to town, leaving a baffling void. A void she would ignore.

Sarah left her porch, motioning Callie toward the shelter of her lilac bushes. Did she think neighbors would report the conversation to her husband? "I hoped I might catch you on your walk to the post office." She fingered the collar of her dress. "When the baby decides to come, get word to me. If I can sneak away…" Her voice trailed off.

New lines of worry etched Sarah's plump face. Shots of gray Callie didn't remember seeing before streaked her auburn hair. "I understand."

"I talked to Doc Wellman. He'll let me make payments on his fee. Get him to help Elise when it's her time." She dug into the pocket of her apron, then thrust a stack of bills at Callie. "This is for diapers, a dress."

Callie put the money in her purse. "This will mean the world to Elise. After our doctor's appointments tomorrow afternoon, we'll go shopping for the baby."

"I know that girl can eat." Sarah gave a shaky smile. "Wish I could help more, but…"

Obviously, Elise's father wouldn't let go of a dime to help his daughter. "I have shelves of canned food in the cellar and soon we'll have produce from the garden. We'll manage fine."

Eyes filling with misery, Sarah stared off into the

distance. "We had such plans for Elise. You know, for schooling, a good marriage." Her voice faltered. "Now that's gone."

Callie laid a hand on Sarah's sleeve. "Elise can still have those things, Sarah. Maybe not right away, but her life isn't over. God will bring something good from this."

A spark of hope lit Sarah's eyes. "You're right. God will work it out. I know it. I do."

"You and Mr. Langley are in my prayers."

"God bless you, Callie. I don't understand why you're doing this for my girl, but I thank you."

But Callie knew. And if Sarah weren't wrapped up in her own worries, she'd know, too.

With a hug goodbye, Callie walked up Serenity Avenue, her eyes on the uneven brick, her mind filling with the image of Nell. Callie swallowed around a lump in her throat. Redheaded Nell—upturned nose with a dusting of freckles, blue eyes sparkling with innocence. They were only sixteen, sheltered from the facts of life. Nell had trusted a man, fallen hard. A lesson Callie ought to remember.

At the corner, she turned left on Liberty. Jacob Smith lounged against a tree. At his thoughtfulness something inside her twisted. "You waited." But then she remembered how fooled Nell had been by a man.

"I'm in no rush," he said as they continued up Liberty. "Life must be more complicated with Miss Langley in your house."

"Elise is a help and I enjoy her company."

"I know you don't like me saying so but no man should leave a woman in her circumstances."

"Perhaps he did Elise a favor."

"How do you figure that?"

"Marriage to some men would be intolerable."

"Why would a woman involve herself with such a man?"

No one could be that naive. "What's hidden can't be seen, Mr. Smith."

He studied her, his eyes filling with compassion, as if he suspected that she referred to her late husband. Well, he could keep his ill-placed sympathy to himself. She'd never met anyone more secretive.

Up ahead, the street bustled with activity by Peaceful standards. Carriages and wagons clattered over the brick. Shoppers stopped to chat on the walk. The one family in town with a newfangled automobile rounded the corner, honking its horn, frightening horses and young children.

"What do you know? Someone in Peaceful owns a Waverley Runabout."

"That's Mr. Burch, president of the bank."

"I visited the Waverley factory in Indianapolis," Jake said. "Can't think battery-powered carriages will come to anything. Now those gasoline motor automobiles Haynes-Apperson is turning out in Kokomo interest me."

"Really? You'd want one? My mare is a lot more reli-able."

"If they can get the kinks ironed out and a way to lower the cost, it wouldn't surprise me if one day the streets were teeming with automobiles."

"Sounds dangerous."

"Danger is a sign of progress, I reckon."

An odd thought. One she'd examine later.

Callie greeted passersby as they strolled by the variety of shops dotting the main street: Langley's Barber Shop, Lily's Millinery and Gloves, Harrington's Grocery, Cunningham's Pharmacy. Up ahead the Mitchell Mercantile. A dog sniffed his way along the walk beside her, and then trotted across the street, successfully dodging horses' hooves and buggy wheels.

Outside the post office, Jacob turned toward her. "I think I'll look into getting a haircut."

"Your hair *is* a bit shaggy," she said with a smile.

He doffed his hat and plowed his fingers through his ebony hair. "We mutts aren't groomed as often as those fancy lapdogs."

"Nothing about you suggests mutt, Mr. Smith."

His lips tilted up into a soft smile that climbed into his eyes and settled on her with such intensity that her mouth went dry as dust. She glanced away. "The barber is Elise's father."

"Thanks for the warning." He plopped his hat on his head, flashed his dimple, then strode off, turning more than one woman's head in his direction.

Jacob Smith was all male, more cowboy than any man she'd met. Unable to take her eyes off his lanky figure, she watched until he entered the barbershop. Chiding herself for such foolishness, she pivoted toward the post office and stepped inside, letting her eyes adjust to the dim interior.

Marlene Thompson, the postmistress, looked up from sorting the mail and punched her wire-rimmed glasses up her nose with her index finger. "Afternoon, Callie. How are you feeling?"

"The fatigue and nausea are long gone." She smiled. "I just felt the baby move." So much for telling only her friends such personal news, but she couldn't seem to keep it to herself.

"What do you want? Boy? Or girl?"

"I want whatever I'm having."

"With that attitude, you won't be disappointed. Mr. Thompson was determined to have a girl. Five boys later, he decided I was girl enough for him." She chuckled. "I could've told him that a whole lot sooner."

Callie giggled. "Do I have any mail?"

"Nothing today. Nothing that is, except a question." She motioned her closer. "I heard Elise Langley's staying with you."

"She is."

"Good." Mrs. Thompson's brown eyes warmed with interest. "My nephew Albert and his wife, Sally, would love to have that baby if Elise is looking for a good home for it."

"I believe Elise plans to keep her baby."

Marlene's shoulders sagged. "Well, if she changes her mind, ask her to talk to Sally."

"I will."

Callie knew the Thompsons and their desperate desire for a child. They would make wonderful parents. Callie doubted that Elise would consider such an arrangement. Yet her heart ached for the Thompsons. Why did some women long to have a child, yet remained barren, while others conceived babies with no interest in or means of caring for them?

What circumstances had led Jacob Smith's mother to put her son in an orphanage? Or perhaps she had been forced to give up her child, as Elise's father was trying to do.

If Callie had questions, she could only imagine Mr.

Smith's desire for answers. Could that be the reason he'd come to Peaceful? She sighed. Why was she getting involved with this man's life? He'd only bring her grief.

A block down, Callie entered Mitchell's Mercantile. The cavernous room held every utensil, tool, canned good, fresh-baked good and ready-made article of clothing imaginable. She dreaded running into her father-in-law. Yet, if she shopped elsewhere, the news would get back to him. She glanced around. No Commodore. No customers. Callie breathed a sigh of relief.

Since Martin's death, her father-in-law had badgered her to move in with him and Dorothy, and Callie suspected he wanted her and her baby to fill the void in their lives after losing Martin. She understood that, but the vehemence of his insistence unnerved her. Did something beside grief motivate him?

At a table piled with an assortment of tiny garments and fabric for making blankets and diapers, Callie plucked a white gown from the stack. Silky ribbons closed the neckline, cuffs and hemline, every detail precious. She couldn't imagine caring for an infant small enough to wear this. But in four months, she would. Would she even know how to be a good mother? What if the baby got sick? Or—

No, she refused to worry. Just because her parents and Martin had died tragically didn't mean disaster lurked around every corner. Countless women had children and managed fine.

But alone?

She knew very few who'd handled that responsibility without a husband. She laid a hand on her abdomen. *Please, God, keep my baby safe. Help me be a good mother.*

If only she could talk to her mother, to ask advice, to share the specifics of motherhood. Her throat clogged. She didn't have her mother, but she did have a mother-in-law and the ladies at church to advise her. She'd have support.

As she fingered the soft blanket, visualizing cuddling her baby swathed in its folds, filling her arms and her heart with a family of her own, tension drained out of her.

"Small, aren't they?" Commodore's gentle, almost reverent voice startled her. "Takes me back to Martin's arrival."

Surprised by this sentimental side of Commodore, Callie met his moist gaze and smiled. "From the pictures I've seen, Martin was a beautiful baby."

"Sure was. And strong. Why, he held up his head that first week." His voice sounded gruff, thick with emotion. "If you want material to make our grandbaby anything, I'll, ah, wrap it up." He shifted. "No charge. Get some dresses, too."

"Thank you. That's most generous." Callie had no idea how she'd manage it, but somehow she'd find a way. "I'll work here on Saturdays to repay you."

"Nonsense. We want to help. We still have Martin's crib, high chair, baby carriage. Dorothy saved everything he touched."

Commodore's effort to build a bridge between them softened Callie's wariness. "I could put the crib in the small bedroom."

His gaze hardened. "If you'd move in with us, we'd see to your and the baby's every need."

At the familiar argument, a constant sting between them, Callie sighed. Could she make Commodore understand? She had to try. She took a fortifying breath. "I need a place of my own to raise my child and make a life. Not to shut you and Dorothy out, but to have my own traditions, my own routines."

"You can do all that at our place. Why are you being stubborn? You used to be reasonable, someone we could talk to." He exhaled impatiently. "Why not be honest? All you can think about is housing that Langley girl."

"That's part of it, but not all. I wish you could understand."

"I understand, all right." He folded his arms across his barrel chest. "You'd rather remain in a house that caused Martin's death than move in with us. My son would want you and his baby with us."

As if Commodore had known Martin's mind. They'd been at odds for years. Fighting to control her emotions, Callie inspected several baby things.

"Commodore, I appreciate your concern about the house, but I want to assure you I'll be fine." She forced a smile. "I know the house's every flaw and will be careful."

"I can't stomach the sight of it." Commodore's tone was harsh, condemning. "If not for that eyesore, my son would be alive today, not laid out in Walnut Grove Cemetery. But no, *you* had to have this house. Nothing but that monstrosity would do."

Callie wrapped her arms around herself. Did he blame the house for Martin's death? Or was he dancing around the fact that he blamed her? "I'm heartsick about Martin's fall, his death." A sob tore from her throat. "But leaving my house won't bring him back. Nothing we do will bring him back."

Her nagging had cost Martin his life. If only Callie had asked someone with experience to replace the shingles, instead of fussing about the cost, about yet another bill they couldn't pay.

Perhaps living with Martin's parents would be her penance. But she couldn't cope under Commodore's accusing eyes. Decrepit or not, she had to keep the house, the one place where she felt at home. The one place she could re-create the family she'd lost.

And fulfill the promise she'd made to Nell. The promise she'd made to God to provide for unwed mothers.

"Commodore, please. Martin saw our home as a perfect place to raise our children."

"It hardly makes sense for Dorothy and me to rattle around in that big house of ours, while your place drains you dry. From where I stand, you're going to lose it anyway."

His words tore through Callie and ricocheted in her chest. How would she provide for Elise and two babies, once they arrived? "I've got to go." She whirled toward the door.

If God wanted her to give Elise a home and others like her, He'd show her a way to handle the expense, just as He'd brought her a carpenter to make the repairs.

It would all work out.

She was sure of it.

Chapter Four

Sporting a new haircut and a surly attitude toward the barber who'd shorn him like a spring lamb, Jake returned to demolishing the porch. Elise's father had bombarded him with questions. No doubt suspicious of a newcomer. Or, if Jake chose to think the best of people, perhaps Langley merely was making conversation.

In any case, Jake admitted that he was renovating the Mitchell place and had met the barber's daughter. Neither spoke of Elise's condition, though obviously her father had her on his mind. He'd had the gall to suggest that Callie Mitchell had persuaded his daughter to move in with her. Jake had leaped to her defense, raising Langley's ire. The man used his scissors to emphasize his points. Jake was fortunate to still be in possession of his ears.

Mrs. Mitchell opened the screen door. "Do you need the fruit jar refilled?"

Did this woman never stop thinking of others? "I'd appreciate it." He carried the jar to her, promptly getting lost in the depths of her dazzling blue-green eyes.

"Did Mr. Langley say anything about Elise?"

"He's not happy she's living here."

Her eyes dimmed. "I know."

An urge to teach Langley a thing or two for upsetting Mrs. Mitchell this way gripped Jake. But what did he know about being a father? About dealing with an unwed daughter in a family way?

"Yoo-hoo! Callie!" A twig of a woman, white hair frizzing around her face like a windblown cloud, lurched up the walk pulling a loaded wagon, impressive for someone surely approaching eighty.

"Mildred, whatever are you toting in that wagon?"

"Memories, dear. Births, deaths and everything in between." The lady's hand swept the stacks of newspapers and scrapbooks crammed to overflowing. "Some of this memorabilia dates back to the town's beginnings."

"That's nice but... I don't understand why you're bringing all that here."

"You will as soon as I explain." She tilted her head toward Jake. "You're that fellow who stopped at my place looking for work. I'd have hired you, but I'm not sure of my plans for the house."

Jake nodded.

"It's about time you got help, Callie, before this house falls down around your ears. Not an easy way to get them pierced." She gave an unladylike snort.

"Mr. Smith's already replaced the roof shingles."

"Ah, a hard worker *and* easy on the eyes." The woman winked. "I may be old as dirt, but I can still appreciate a good-looking man. Not why I wed my dear husband, but I enjoyed that handsome face of his more than dessert after a meal."

At Mrs. Uland's perusal, Jake's neck heated. The

feisty older woman merely grinned, as if enjoying his discomfort.

"This old Victorian sat empty too long. All it needs is someone who cares like Callie here and someone with the know-how to give it life." Her approving gaze rested on Jake. "Appears that's you, Mr. Smith."

"Sitting empty isn't good for a house," he said.

"Sitting in an empty house isn't good for a person, either." Mrs. Uland laughed. "I'm not in mine, more than I have to be."

He motioned to the wagon. "Let me help with that."

"Oh, a knight in shining armor." She wagged a knobby finger. "Just keep your nose out of them. Took me hours to get those issues in order of publication."

"They're safe with me." His mind raced like a hound dog after a fox. The information in this wagon could possibly unlock his birth mother's identity. If he examined these newspapers, he might find his birth announcement.

"I'm not following you," Mrs. Mitchell said, looking slightly dazed.

"Of course, you're not, dear. If you have time for tea, I'll explain."

"I do."

Jake scooped up an armload of newspapers. "Where do you want these?"

From the flicker of dismay in Callie Mitchell's eyes, she didn't want them anywhere, but she didn't let on. "Follow me," she said, gathering the scrapbooks, then taking the older woman's arm. "Watch your step, Mildred."

They picked their way across the dilapidated porch. "A strong man around the place comes in mighty handy." She lowered her voice, but not so low that Jake couldn't hear. "Maybe you can find a way to keep him around permanently."

For a moment, Mrs. Mitchell hesitated, and then hurried her elderly neighbor along, as if fearing what would come out of her mouth next.

The women entered the house and led him down a wide hallway, the wooden floor gleaming, past a magnificent staircase nestled into the curve of the outside wall. The house was an extraordinary example of Victorian architecture.

At the back of the house, they stopped at a door opening into a small library, the book-laden shelves rising from floor to ceiling. He stacked the newspapers on the large desk, a desire to look at them building inside him. As soon as he finished the porch, he'd ask permission. He suspected both ladies would question his interest. But he wouldn't open that Pandora's box.

With the contents of the wagon stowed in the library and the wagon back in Mrs. Uland's yard, Jake returned to the porch.

Inside, Callie Mitchell sat across the table from her neighbor, a pot of tea and some kind of secret between them.

Callie poured Mildred's cup of tea. "What's this about?"

"I've spent days rummaging through every nook and cranny in my house searching for that memorabilia, then getting it in order."

Callie's usually dapper neighbor looked like she'd gotten into a brawl and lost. Her hair appeared uncombed. The lapels on her dress tipped like a bird in flight. Her stockings were drooping around her ankles. Finding and putting those newspapers in order had taken its toil.

"I'll tell you it wore me out. I'm not what I used to be. Why, last week I had to rest while weeding the garden." She smiled. "Isn't the early lettuce yummy? I love wilting it, though it's tender enough to eat straight out of the garden."

Though she had a sharp mind, upon occasion Mildred went off on some tangent and forgot the point of the conversation.

Her eyes met Callie's. "Oh, sorry, dear. You asked about the newspapers."

"Why did you bring them here?"

"Those newspapers and scrapbooks are records you'll need." Her voice had a slightly impatient tone, as if unable to understand Callie's dim-wittedness.

"Why would I need them?" Callie asked gently.

"So you can write our town's history."

"Why me?"

"Your wonderful essays and poems used to make me cry. You love history. Told me that yourself. I wouldn't trust anyone else with the job."

"That's nice of you to say, but why do you want a history written?"

"I've lived in Peaceful all my life. One look at the obituary column makes it clear we oldsters are dying off. Soon no one will be left to answer questions about the town. Down the road, young people will want to know." She rolled her eyes. "They don't realize that now, of course, but it's true. Most of us never think to ask our elders anything until it's too late. I know my ancestors came over from England. But I have no idea what part and..."

As Mildred went on about her heritage, Callie thought about the countless times she'd wished she could've asked her parents some detail about their lives. Like when and where her father and mother first met. Either Aunt Hilda couldn't remember or never knew. Her pulse tripped. These articles might reveal something new about her mother or her mother's parents. The prospect of learning even one fact to fill the blanks on her family tree was reason enough to take the job.

"You've got the talent. And I've got the facts." Mildred sat back, looking pleased.

Callie hated to refuse her friend, especially since she'd enjoy delving into the town's past, but could she squeeze in another task? "It'll require a lot of time to organize the information and write it up."

"I know. That's the reason I will pay you and pay you well."

Was this God's answer? Not only for her longing for information about her family, but also for her financial predicament? As certainty filled her heart, a smile curved her lips. This put the lie to Commodore's prediction that she'd lose the house. God had provided a way to handle expenses, not with a miracle but through Callie's hard work.

She'd need other sources of revenue to increase the number of women she could help. As soon as the house was safe, she'd seek community support. If her plan were God's will, He'd provide. Her eyes misted. She'd been unsure, even discouraged about how she'd manage. God cared about every detail of her life. She'd lean on Him, the one constant in her ever-changing circumstances.

"I have the money," Mildred was saying, "and I'm running out of time to spend it." She grinned. Every line in her face stood at attention like a squad of eager recruits. "Mr. Uland, God rest his soul, always said I could squeeze a penny until Mr. Lincoln hollered."

Knowing the truth of that statement, Callie bit back a grin.

"All my life, I fought letting go of a dollar. Last I looked, those dollars were breeding. Why, I've got more than enough money to last me and then some. And you…" She paused. "With Commodore's attitude toward this house, I doubt he's helping with your bills. You need income, especially with Elise living here."

Who would've thought Mildred Uland, a tight-fisted friend, and Jacob Smith, a closed-mouth drifter, would be the keys to launching her dream? "Thank you, Mildred, for the opportunity. I'll work on the town's story in the evenings."

"I'll help all I can. It'll be good to have a new purpose, since that husband of mine up and died on me. Why, I'm as adrift as a rudderless sailboat."

Though her husband had been gone for more than twenty years, Mildred often groused about his passing, as if the poor man had died just to annoy her. Perhaps her way of handling grief was better than holding everything inside, as Callie often did. "I'm sure Elise would help, too."

"If she does, tell her to keep quiet about the book. It'll be my gift to the town at Peaceful's seventy-fifth anniversary two years from now. I don't want it blabbed about until it's in print." Mildred reached a blue-veined hand. "I'm paying for your talent and your reticence. Agreed?"

"Agreed." Callie gave her neighbor's hand a squeeze. "You're an answer to a prayer."

"Not surprised. God's been nudging me to get moving on this." She sighed. "Lately it's been more of a shove. I don't hanker to wrestle with God and end up with an out-of-kilter hip. Got me enough aches and pains as it is." She smiled. "I'm late learning the lesson, but when God says, 'Do it,' I do it."

Callie rose and came around the table, wrapping her arms around Mildred's shoulders. "Remember the spring after I came to live with Aunt Hilda? I picked your tulips." She kissed her cheek. "I still can't believe you forgave me for ruining your front flowerbed."

"You were only seven and meant well, wanted to give them to Hilda on her birthday. You weren't the brightest vandal I've come across." Mildred grinned up at her. "You left a trail of petals clear to her house."

"You followed that trail. Carrying a bouquet of tulips you'd picked from your flowerbed out back, claiming I'd missed a few. Then you helped me put together a bouquet, though you surely wanted to paddle my behind."

Tears flooded Mildred's eyes. "No, dear girl. You'd lost your brother and your parents. I lost only petals."

A sudden spasm seized Callie's throat. Her baby brother, Ronnie, just starting to walk. Mama and Papa going about their routine with no warning that the dam was about to give way. All gone.

When she could finally speak, Callie said, "Where would I be if not for Aunt Hilda and people like you, who took a frightened little girl into your hearts?"

"You'd be fine. You were born with all the strength

you needed, just like your mother. She's up in Heaven chatting with that inconsiderate husband of mine." She patted Callie's cheek. "That faith of yours will see you through. I'm proud of you, Callie Marie Mitchell."

Callie's smile trembled. "You've been my rock. I'm happy I can do something for you now. Writing this history will be fun. Imagine, Peaceful's past at my fingertips."

Mildred removed some bills from her pocket. "This'll get you started."

At the generous sum, Callie shook her head. "I can't accept this."

"You'll soon have four mouths to feed." Mildred said, then left through the back door and disappeared between the shrubs separating their houses.

In Callie's hands was enough money to meet their needs for months, maybe more. As she tucked the bills into her purse, the weight of obligations she'd had no idea how she'd pay fell from her shoulders. And she knew—

A naughty little girl's petal trail had brought Mildred Uland into her life, a very special friend. God had seen Callie through her troubles every step of the way. He'd given her this home. He'd sent Jacob Smith to make repairs. And Mildred with an offer of much-needed funds. Ensuring that she'd be able to take care of her baby and keep the promise she'd made to Nell, a desperate young girl who'd believed she had nowhere to turn.

With her heart filled to overflowing for the good fortune God had brought into her life, Callie could barely contain the unfettered joy pounding through her. A walk would help expend some of that energy.

She opened the screen door and jerked her foot back.

Most of the porch floor was missing. The boards had been stripped away, revealing support timbers underneath. Thankfully, they appeared solid and wouldn't need to be replaced.

Jacob Smith turned from tossing another plank to the lawn.

Callie smiled. "I'm amazed at the progress you've made while Mildred and I have been visiting."

"I don't believe in wasting time."

Truer words had never been spoken. Jacob might not be an open book but he could be trusted to do a good job in a timely manner.

"If all those newspapers your neighbor brought get in your way, I could haul them to the barn."

"They're fine where they are."

"I'm curious why Mrs. Uland dumped them on you."

"Mildred's—" She wouldn't spoil her neighbor's surprise. "Asked me to handle a project for her. I have plenty of room."

"Might make interesting reading. I like looking into the history of old houses. When you're finished, I'd like to take a look, see what I can find."

"I won't be done anytime soon." She cocked her head at him. "Are you planning on staying in town that long?"

"Only long enough to…repair your house. Then I'll move on."

Exactly as she'd thought. She wouldn't get involved with Jacob Smith or the problems she felt lurking beneath his polite, standoffish exterior. Why, he could walk out of her life as quickly as he'd walked in and never finish the job. She straightened her spine. Another reason to steel herself against this strange attraction she had for him.

"You might want to lock the screen so you and Elise don't use that door and fall through the floor joists."

Nodding, Callie closed the screen, hooked it, closed and locked the wooden door, and then found a red ribbon and tied it around the knob. Satisfied that Elise wouldn't miss the warning to avoid the porch, she left for her walk by the back door.

A warning she'd take to heart. The truth was Jacob Smith could hurt her. Not physically. She'd never think that. But hurt her nevertheless. She'd lock her heart against this drifter. And focus on making a family with her baby, with Elise and her child and focus on her dream. She'd have a full life.

The excitement bubbling within her like an effervescent underground spring sputtered and died. In truth, she'd been lonely for years—most of her life. Marriage to Martin hadn't filled that aching void.

Hadn't she learned anything? Attraction meant nothing.

Jacob Smith was the last man on earth she wanted in her life.

In a matter of hours, Jake had torn the planks off the porch. He'd found ample lumber in the barn to replace them, the boards covered with a layer of dust and mice droppings, evidence that the intent to make repairs exceeded Martin Mitchell's follow-through.

As Jake pounded in another nail, he cringed at his rush to judgment. If he'd been married when he'd ended up in jail, he'd have no doubt left some things undone.

Not everyone was suited for restoration. The poor guy lost his life trying.

Still, Martin's widow lived in a house all but unfit for human habitation. Jake couldn't let a woman endure such conditions. Not that he blamed the house. Time and effort would bring this place back to its former grandeur. Though enough work was here to tether a man indefinitely, a sentence without parole.

Yet to walk away, when he'd witnessed Mrs. Mitchell's relief and joy at the house's revival would be cruel. In the time he remained, if possible, he'd see the task to completion.

His heart lurched. Was the pull more the woman than the work? Either way, he doubted he'd get the job done. Someone was sure to discover his jailbird past.

The aroma of something sugary drifted on the air. Jake pulled the tantalizing scent of home into his lungs then released it in a gust.

Who was he fooling? This wasn't home—at least not his.

He grabbed the length of lumber he'd cut. Grasping another large nail between thumb and forefinger, he pounded it into the pungent pine, the perfume of Jake's life. Far better than the stench of prison, but nothing like the aromas floating out of Mrs. Mitchell's kitchen.

A shadow fell across the porch floor.

He turned to face a man and woman standing on the flagstone walkway. Offering a tentative smile, a round-faced, sturdy woman wore a feather-adorned hat atop her salt-and-pepper hair.

The burly man's brow furrowed beneath the brim of his hat. "Who are you?"

Jake laid the hammer down and rose. "Jake Smith," he said offering a hand.

The visitor didn't take it. "The name means nothing to me."

"Doubt it would. I'm new in town."

"What are you doing to our daughter-in-law's porch?"

So these people were Callie Mitchell's in-laws.

The screen door opened and Mrs. Mitchell stepped out on the solid boards he'd laid, looking fresh as a summer morning after a rain. She glanced at Jake, then at her in-laws. Her bright smile slipped. "I see you've met Mr. Smith, the carpenter who's fixing up the place. I'm sure you're pleased to see I'm taking action to ensure our safety."

Square jaw set in a stubborn line, Mitchell folded beefy arms across his chest. "The best thing you could do is torch this place."

Callie sighed, obviously not the first time she'd heard such nonsense. Father-in-law or not, Mitchell had no right to badger his dead son's wife, a gentle woman with a heavy load.

He turned his gaze on her, ready to toss the idiot off the property if she showed the slightest inclination, but she continued to wear that calm expression of hers. How did she keep her patience, when Jake would like nothing better than to punch the guy?

"We aren't here to argue, Commodore." Dorothy Mitchell laid a hand on her husband's sleeve. "Tell Callie why we've come."

Mitchell shifted on his feet. "I, ah, we brought the fabric and some of those baby things you were looking at before we, ah, got off on the wrong foot."

"Thank you." Smiling, Callie Mitchell motioned to the house. "Would you care for tea? I just took an angel food cake out of the oven."

Ignoring his daughter-in-law's peace offering, Mitchell swept a hand toward Jake. "Can't see how you can afford a handyman."

"Mr. Smith agreed to do the work for a roof over his head and meals."

He turned narrowed eyes on Jake. "Why? When you could get a good-paying job at the grain elevator or lumberyard?"

"I don't plan on staying long."

"That so? Then why did you come?"

Jake kept his expression blank, a skill that had held him in good stead in prison. "Peaceful sounded like a nice town."

"Peaceful is the way we aim to keep it. Most folks around here distrust drifters."

"I appreciate your concern, Commodore, but I've already arranged for Mr. Smith to do the work." Callie Mitchell tapped the toe of her serviceable shoe on the newly laid porch floor. "His work speaks for him."

"Let's have that tea," Callie's mother-in-law said. "Please."

Ignoring his wife, Mitchell frowned. "You're hardly a good judge of character, Callie. The last man you hired ransacked the place and took every cent in the house."

Jake took a step forward. "Where I come from, a man speaks kindly to a lady."

Mitchell turned suspicious eyes on Jake. "And where is that, Smith?"

"Does it matter? I believe good manners are the same everywhere."

"I'll tell you what I believe. A drifter has something to hide." He smirked. "As soon as someone gets close to his secret, that's when he leaves." He turned to Callie. "Reckon I'll stop at the sheriff's office. See what he knows about 'Smith' here."

He thrust the bundle at his daughter-in-law, then took his wife's arm and stomped down the walk.

The threat tore through Jake, heating his veins. Even if the sheriff didn't find out anything about him, that didn't mean he wouldn't come around asking questions. It wouldn't be long until his past caught up with him and forced him out of town.

Jake didn't know where to pin his gaze, but he couldn't look at Callie Mitchell. He couldn't risk the suspicion he'd see in her guileless eyes. He couldn't risk her seeing the alarm surely hovering in his.

"I'm sorry about that. About him," she whispered, then stepped inside.

Something frozen inside him knotted tighter. Callie Mitchell had lost her husband. She managed this run-down house and her daily chores while giving refuge to a young unwed mother—all that responsibility rested on her slender shoulders.

Yet without a moment's hesitation, a member of her family had piled on more burdens. No doubt Commodore Mitchell would call himself a Christian. The man was a hypocrite. The world was full of them, further evidence that if God existed, he had little impact on anyone's conduct.

Anyone that is, except Callie Mitchell. From what he'd seen, people in this town either harassed or leaned on her. The woman needed someone to look after her. Someone who'd help carry her burdens. Someone like…

Not him.

Anyone but him.

Jake knelt on the porch, then grabbed a nail and swung the hammer. This time, he found his thumb, not the nail's head. Through gritted teeth, he bit back the cry of pain and cradled his throbbing thumb in his palm.

No point in getting all riled up about Mrs. Mitchell's load. He wouldn't—couldn't—get involved with her. He'd never known a woman he could trust.

He was in Peaceful for one reason and one reason only. He had a woman to find. Soon as he finished for the day, he'd visit the Corner Café.

If the waitress proved as informative as she'd been on his way into town, she might lead him to the woman who'd discarded him like a broken tool. Then he could finish what he came for—and get out of town. Before he got tied to things he couldn't have.

Chapter Five

Callie found Elise in the parlor, her feet propped on a footstool, a ball of yellow yarn spinning with each knit-purl. "How's your ankle?"

"Good as new." Elise raised her needles, her face glowing. "I'm making a blanket for my baby."

The joy Callie read in Elise's face matched her own. Sometimes Callie thought she'd burst with the wonder of her impending motherhood. Still, considering Elise's circumstances, she might have had a far different attitude.

She sat beside her and ran a palm over the softness. "It's going to be beautiful and warm."

Elise's lips curved in a smile. "As soon as I'm finished, I'll make one for your baby. What color would you like?"

Precious babies—each one pure as the first dusting of snow. "White. I'd like white."

"That's not as practical as I'd expect from you, but white it shall be."

"I'll use it for church and special occasions. I'll get the yarn on my next trip to town."

"I have enough money to pay for it. It'll be my gift." Her eyes flashed. "No arguing."

"You win," Callie said with a grin then sobered. "I've been asked to tell you something."

Elise laid her needles down, met Callie's gaze then looked away. "From your expression, I'm not sure I want to hear it."

"Hearing what I have to say doesn't mean you have to agree to anything, but I thought you should know." She took Elise's hands. "Sally and Albert Thompson are interested in adopting your baby."

Elise sucked in a gulp of air. "They've wanted a baby forever."

"They have. But what they want isn't important. You need to make the decision that's right for you and your baby."

"Sally would be a wonderful mother, but— Oh, Callie, I know I'm young and don't have a way to earn a living, but I want this baby." She sighed. "Is that selfish?"

"If it is, then I'm selfish, too. We're both facing some of the same issues. I'm not sure how I'll handle all the expenses of raising a child, but with God's help, I'll find a way."

"Mama said a child means fevers, defiance and turmoil. But hugs and jelly kisses compensate for every worry and sacrifice." Her eyes glistened. "Taking the bad with the good—that's love. I love my baby. I can't let it go."

"Then that's settled."

Tears brimmed in Elise's eyes. "I don't know what I would've done if you hadn't taken me in, but I won't live on your charity forever."

"I'm sorry for the trouble between you and your father, but I enjoy your company."

"I've been thinking. Do you think my knitted baby things, shawls, caps and mittens would sell? I want to help with expenses."

"What a great idea! You're a wonderful person, Elise."

Elise's face fell, as if she saw nothing good in herself. A husband would simplify her life. "We've never talked about this and I haven't wanted to pry, but would you consider marrying the baby's father? Or isn't that an option?"

"He's not from around here." She withdrew her hands from Callie's and knotted them in her lap. "Remember the trip I took to North Carolina to see my cousin Carol Ann?"

"Yes, you were excited about taking the train and getting away from the cold for a couple months."

"I met Gaston at a square dance. I fell hard." She sighed. "I sneaked out of the house to meet him several times. I got caught up in his kisses...one thing led to another." Her cheeks flushed. "I was devastated when I had to leave him. We corresponded. I lived for those letters..." A sob tore from Elise's lips and she hung her head. "I was such a fool."

Callie laid a hand on Elise's arm.

"Once I told Gaston about the baby, he...stopped writing. Aunt Audra said he must've left town the day he got the news." Elise swiped at her tears. "My aunt blames herself. No one's to blame but him. And me." She met Callie's eyes. "He said I was pretty and he loved me."

"You *are* pretty." Callie pulled a handkerchief from her sleeve and handed it to Elise.

She blew her nose. "I'm not using his sweet talk as an excuse for breaking God's commandment. Papa wasn't much for praise. Gaston's words…were so different from what I was used to hearing from Papa. I believed every thing he said."

The baby's father wasn't an answer, but would Elise's dad relent and allow Elise to return home? "Can the rift between you and your father be mended?"

Fresh tears filled Elise's eyes. "Papa doesn't love me. How could he love me and say the things he's said to me? Mama says he's hurt and he'll get over it." Her lower lip trembled. "When?"

God gives His forgiveness quickly, at the speed of lightning. But mankind often took longer. "Have you asked your parents to forgive you?"

"More times than I can count. Mama's forgiven me, but I've disappointed her." She gave a strangled laugh. "I've disappointed myself. But Papa…"

"Give him time. Once the baby is here, he'll come around."

Elise fingered the yellow blanket in her lap. "I've asked God to pardon me, but I don't feel forgiven."

A lump formed in Callie's throat. She understood. Too well. Hadn't she asked for forgiveness for her part in bringing about Martin's death? Yet as much as she knew Scripture, as easily as she could quote the Psalm—"As far as the east is from the west, so far hath He removed our transgressions from us"—sometimes she didn't feel absolved. "The Bible makes it clear we're free from sin when we repent. But sometimes it's hard to feel pardoned. Perhaps clemency seems too easy, like we got off scot-free."

Elise snorted. "Memories are longer than Methuselah's beard. From what I've seen, folks expect forgiveness for their mistakes but aren't quick to offer it. I don't mind so much for myself, but I won't be able to bear it if anyone looked down on my baby," she said, her hand hovered over the movement of a little foot or hand.

How could anyone begrudge a kind word to an innocent child? Callie tilted up Elise's chin. "When things look dark and you and I can't see what lies ahead, we'll have to rely on God to light the way. Will you try that with me? One step at a time?"

Elise offered a wobbly smile and nodded. "This unmarried forgiven expectant mother is on the march."

Grinning, Callie glanced at the clock. "We'd better get on the march. We're due to see Doc Wellman in less than an hour. After our appointment, we'll stop at the Mercantile." She pulled the money Sarah gave her from her pocket. "Your mother wants you to use this to buy things for your baby. She cares about you and your child."

"I know she does, but she won't go against her wedding vows and defy Papa."

"Those vows are important."

Vows. Callie had taken them and from that first week wondered—

She refused to finish the thought. Even if Martin had never matured, even if she'd had to carry the load for both of them her entire life, even if sometimes that load wearied her, she'd always be grateful for the baby she carried.

She forced her thoughts back to Elise. "Even if your

father never changes his mind, you'll have a home here with me."

Elise burrowed into Callie's open arms. "What would I do without you?"

"We're in this together. We'll be fine," Callie spoke softly against Elise's copper curls, "if we seek God's guidance at the start of each new day."

Elise straightened and met Callie's eyes, the misery in their depths banged against Callie's heart. "If I'd done that last summer, I... I wouldn't be in this mess. I'm a fool for falling for a footloose man."

Through the lace curtains in the parlor window, Callie watched Mr. Smith climb the porch steps. A strong, handsome...drifter. Her breath caught. *Footloose* described Jacob Smith. She'd remember that. Both she and Elise had learned they could be fooled by a man.

Elise rose and tugged Callie to her feet, hugging her or trying to, but her round belly got in the way. They both laughed, easing the tension.

A half hour later, they headed out the door with Elise showing no sign of a limp. Elise looked pretty with her auburn hair swept into a French twist, her shawl pinned in place with a lovely old broach, a keepsake from Callie's Aunt Hilda. Nothing would disguise the girl's advanced pregnancy, but the shawl softened her silhouette.

Jacob Smith rounded the back of the house, tools dangling from his belt and slapping against his denims. He might be a drifter, but she appreciated his help. Goodness, the man never stopped. How long could he keep up the hectic pace?

He tipped his hat. "Afternoon, ladies."

His eyes locked with Callie's, his eyes pools of jade she felt she'd drown in. When had green become her favorite color? Even though she didn't trust him, her feet had a life all their own and brought her closer.

At the sound of Elise's giggle, Callie gathered her wits about her. "Tomorrow's the Lord's Day. You've earned your rest, Jacob," she said unable to look away from the intensity of his gaze. "If you're looking for a place to worship, church service begins at ten o'clock."

His full lips thinned, turned mulish. "Thanks, but I plan on sleeping late tomorrow."

"If God changes your mind about that, we're having a potluck after service. It's your chance to eat food prepared by the best cooks in town."

"Can't see how anyone could improve on your cooking."

The warmth of Jacob's regard spilled into the empty places inside her. "If you're aiming for larger portions, you're succeeding."

Chuckling, he bounded onto the porch and got back to work. He'd accomplished a great deal. Only a few boards needed replacing. Strange how quickly she'd gotten used to having him around the place. His long strides, the noise of saw and hammer, the scent of soap on his skin after washing up at the pump. An image of damp hair curling at Jacob's nape filled her traitorous mind. She shivered and quickly said goodbye.

As Callie and Elise strolled along at a snail's pace, Mildred Uland's cocker spaniel trotted over for a pat until a squirrel captured his attention. He sped after it, chasing it up a tree. "Sandy's feeling feisty this afternoon. Maybe we could use him to round up Mr. Smith for services."

Her attempt at humor fell on deaf ears. Apparently,

Elise had her mind elsewhere, probably missing her parents. For all her bravado, Elise loved her father.

Lord, Elise and her father are hurting. Please heal their wounds.

God controlled the outcome. He loved them all and in time would bring them peace. With that assurance, Callie filled her lungs with the soft afternoon air, listening to the chirping birds.

"Only three weeks until the baby comes," Elise said in a wobbly voice. "Oh, Callie, I'm scared."

"I am, too, a little." Callie smiled with as much assurance as she could muster. "Just think, by the time my baby arrives you'll be giving me advice."

"I can't imagine that." Elise laid a hand on her abdomen. "The way this baby's doing somersaults, it has to be a boy."

"So what do girls do while waiting to be born? Read?"

"Silly." Elise giggled. "They knit."

Laughing, they turned onto Liberty toward Doctor Wellman's office, a couple blocks down.

Up ahead, Lowell and Naomi Burch stepped outside the door of the First National Bank. As the bank's president, Mr. Burch had power and influence in town. His wife always wore the latest fashions. Naomi adjusted the skirts of her gown, the jet beads catching the light, then raised her lace-trimmed parasol and took her husband's arm. As the couple ambled toward them, Callie knew the moment they spied Elise by the hitch in their stride.

Elise's steps slowed. "Turn around."

"We'll do no such thing. You're neither a criminal nor contagious." As the couple approached, Callie smiled. "Good afternoon, Mrs. Burch, Mr. Burch."

"Hello, Mrs. Mitchell," Mr. Burch said. "Fine day."

Mrs. Burch gave a nod. "Hello, Callie."

The couple passed by, not uttering a word to Elise. Behind her, Callie could hear Mrs. Burch whispering. The word *disgrace* and *shameful* reached her ears. No doubt Elise's, too.

Did these people believe they'd never done anything wrong? Mrs. Burch was known to gossip. Mr. Burch had an affair with his secretary a few years back. The woman left town and the marriage survived. Still, what right did they have to treat Elise like an outcast?

Elise clenched a shaking hand over her shawl. "If I keep my baby, it'll never be accepted in this town." She turned sorrowful eyes on Callie. "I want to talk to Sally and Albert Thompson."

As much as seeing Elise snubbed hurt, Callie knew sin had consequences. But those consequences shouldn't spill over onto an innocent baby.

A lump rose in her throat. For all intents and purposes, Callie was an unwed mother herself. Not with the social stigma Elise faced, but with the same realities. "Talk to Doc Wellman. Talk to Pastor Steele. If you still want to give up your baby after that, I'll arrange a meeting with the Thompsons."

But inside Callie wanted to scream—don't let anyone force you into that decision. She remembered the loving arms of her mother. Arms she still missed. If Elise wanted her child in her arms, then that's where her baby should be, but Callie had no right to interfere.

She hoped Elise understood that once she gave up her baby to the Thompsons, she couldn't change her mind, no matter how much that decision broke her heart.

Lord, give Elise wisdom to make the right choice.

Here she'd been advising Elise and praying for the girl's wisdom, but what about her own decisions? Could she be both mother and father to her baby? Could she provide for her baby's needs? How long could she take care of her child and still provide support for the unwed mothers' shelter? The money she made writing the town history wouldn't last forever. Callie swallowed against the lump in her throat.

What would she do then?

What she would not do is worry. The tightness in her chest eased. If God gave an assignment, he enabled its success. She'd find a way to care for these girls and her precious child.

Unbidden, the image of Jacob Smith popped into her mind. She forced it away. Nothing good would come from her attraction to that man.

After securing the last board on the porch, Jake stowed the tools, his work done for the day. The idea of examining those newspapers and scrapbooks for information about his birth crept into his thoughts. If he asked to see them, Mrs. Mitchell would want an explanation. An explanation he couldn't give.

The temptation to enter her house uninvited lurched in his stomach. Unlocked or not, such an action would be deceitful. Time in jail didn't mean he'd lost his standards. Perhaps she'd give him an opportunity. But for now he'd visit the café, talk to that chatty waitress and see what he could learn. Nothing to stop him now that he'd finished the porch.

Not so long ago he'd lived behind bars, confined to a space the size of the lean-to. Now he could move about the Mitchell property, the town of Peaceful, why, the

State of Indiana, even the whole country if he got the itch to roam. Grinning, he gave a whoop, then headed out.

On Liberty, he entered the Corner Café, a nondescript colorless place, but spotless as a shiny penny. All eyes turned to him, the stranger in town. Some filled with curiosity. Most appeared welcoming. Not the reaction he'd come to expect. He removed his hat and gave a friendly nod.

Small-town scrutiny was a far cry from what he'd experienced in prison. The warden, guards, convicts serving time appraised each new inmate. All formed judgments, putting a man into one of two slots—troublemaker or target. Troublemakers got respect. Targets got contempt. That first day, Jake learned he'd have to wear a tough-guy persona to survive.

Better remember that welcoming smiles didn't mean these folks wouldn't probe into his past. A past he wanted to forget. But couldn't. No, shouldn't. That past taught him a valuable lesson. Never trust anyone. Even those he felt close to.

Especially those he felt close to.

"Hiya, handsome." The waitress, a crisp apron tied around her waist, approached the counter.

"Hi, Jessie."

A dazzling smile lit her pixie face. "A gal likes to be remembered. What can I get ya?"

He laid his hat on the stool beside him. "Coffee, black."

She grabbed a cup with one hand, the pot with the other and poured mid air, never spilling a drop. "Heard you're working at Callie's."

"Word travels fast." Jake took a sip, strong and hot.

Not as pungent as Mrs. Mitchell's, but good. "Thanks for the suggestion."

"Plenty wrong with that old mansion to keep a man busy for months." She poured a cup for herself then sidled closer. "I hope this means you're staying."

"My plans are indefinite."

She chortled. "Isn't that always the way with you good-looking types?"

Jessie's interest was obvious, even to him, a man who avoided connections. She was cute, but lacked the gentle refinement of Mrs. Mitchell.

Why was he thinking about either of them? He had no intention of getting entangled with anyone. No right to consider it, especially with the attractive young widow. He had no idea about what made a family. No idea how to create one. Even if he trusted a woman enough to consider settling down.

Conversation resumed in the café, permitting Jake to pursue his objective. "You get lots of people passing through?"

"No such luck. Life would be more exciting if we did." She leaned a hip against the counter. "You're the first stranger to come into town in ages."

"Have you lived here long?"

"All my life." She leaned toward him. "So tell me, is it true that Elise Langley's staying with Callie?"

Here was the opening he needed. Surely Jessie had heard the local gossip, even back twenty-four years. "Yes. I reckon a young lady in her fix is a rare occurrence in Peaceful."

"Not as rare as you'd think. Most get married before word gets out, but folks can count." She smirked. "And usually do, if you get my drift."

"Yes, ma'am, I do." He took a sip of coffee. "You keep up with the news."

"I hear things. Most folks have a skeleton or two in their cupboard."

Jake would choose his words with care. Anything he said to this woman wouldn't stop there. "A distant relative of mine may have lived here once, years ago. I don't know exactly where."

She stirred sugar into her coffee. "What's the name?"

"That's the catch. I don't recall. Just remember someone saying the woman lived here. The town name stuck."

She chuckled. "Reckon it would. Well, if you remember her name, ask that neighbor of Callie's, Mildred Uland. She's the town's oldest resident and never forgets a thing." She fiddled with her hair. "Or even better, come in and talk to me."

Ignoring the not-so-subtle message, Jake took another sip of coffee. Jessie sighed and took a step back.

The waitress made a good point. Mrs. Mitchell's neighbor would know all the secrets in this town. "I've met Mrs. Uland. She appears to be a good friend of Mrs. Mitchell."

"Callie attracts friends like pollen does bees. And she needs every one. Can't imagine your husband dying then discovering you're expecting." Jessie picked up the pot. "Reckon what don't kill you makes you strong." She patted his arm, then made the rounds, pouring coffee.

Jake drained his cup. On top of the heavy load she carried, Mrs. Mitchell would cope with motherhood alone. Why did that trouble him? Wasn't that what he thought his mother should've done? And hadn't?

He paid his bill, adding a generous tip. He'd come, hoping Jessie would rattle off a list of other unwed mothers in town, but he'd gotten nowhere. From what she'd said, unwed mothers weren't as rare as he'd thought. One thing for sure, the waitress had a soft spot in her heart for Callie Mitchell.

Much like the feelings he had for the woman.

Jake's stomach plunged as it had when he'd heard the jury pronounce the guilty verdict. He wouldn't care about Callie Mitchell. Caring carried a stiff penalty. He wasn't here to get involved with anyone. Not even with a woman whose heart appeared to be the size of Texas.

Jake knew better than to pin his happiness on how someone appeared. Both Lloyd and Susan had taught him that even a loving demeanor could hide a devious heart.

Chapter Six

As she sat on one of the two chairs in the examining room, the scent of antiseptic tingled in Callie's nostrils. Across the way, Doctor Wellman, a thatch of blond hair falling across his forehead, moved his stethoscope along Elise's stomach. Doc looked like he could use a wife, to see he got a haircut and his suit pressed, but the life of a small-town doctor probably didn't give a man much time to court.

Doc straightened and removed the earpieces of the stethoscope. "Everything's fine. From the baby's heart rate, I'm guessing you're having a girl."

Elise beamed. "If it is, I'm naming her Kathryn Marie. Marie is Callie's middle name."

Callie grinned. "I'd be honored."

If she had a girl, Callie would give the baby her mother's name. If a boy… She probably should name him after Martin, but she thought of her father and brother and knew she wouldn't.

"If you're wrong, Doc," Elise said, "and this baby's a boy, I'm naming him David."

"Thank you."

"David's your name?"

"Joseph David Wellman. My folks call me Joe David."

"King David was God's man, a perfect name for my baby if it's a boy." Elise's smile drooped. "Oh, David sinned with Bathsheba. Maybe I should select another name—"

"Nonsense." Doc tapped her on the hand. "God used David in a mighty way, sin and all. None of us are perfect."

"Obviously, I'm not." Laying a hand on her abdomen, she flushed. "My sin is out there for everyone to see."

"That baby was knit in your womb by God Himself. That makes her special." He waggled his brows. "No more of that harsh talk, you hear?"

Callie wanted to hug Doc for reassuring Elise.

"Some people make sure I don't forget what I've done." She sighed. "Not that I should."

Doc helped Elise to a sitting position. "If I thought it would do any good, I'd crack a few hard heads together." He lifted Elise's chin. "But it's folks' hearts that need softening. Only the good Lord's got a cure for that."

Something close to adoration filled Elise's eyes. Did Doctor Wellman realize how much he meant to Elise? Perhaps she saw him as a father figure, a substitute of sorts.

"Your baby's healthy and hardy, Miss Langley. Most likely, she'll make an appearance around May Day."

"I like the name David."

"You can use David for the next baby," Doc said with a laugh. "This one's a girl."

Elise smiled up at Doc as he leaned over her, a teasing look on his lean face. Why hadn't she noticed the magnetism between them at other appointments? Doc always joked with Elise, tried to ease the guilt she wore like her personal scarlet A.

Up until now, Callie had thought Doc's kindness toward Elise stemmed from a physician's concern for his patient, but now she wondered if it could mean more.

Just as she'd decided that Elise and Doc had forgotten her presence in the room, Doc motioned to Callie. "You're next."

Callie traded places with Elise and stretched out on the narrow table. Doc Wellman leaned over her. "Have you felt movement, Mrs. Mitchell?"

"I've felt fluttering sensations of late."

"Good, exactly what you should be feeling at five months. That's your baby waving hello. Enjoy it." He grinned. "It won't be long before he'll wallop you awake at night."

Elise giggled. "And send you racing to the chamber pot."

Doc chuckled. "Ah, the inconveniences of motherhood."

After he'd finished his examination, Doc helped Callie upright. "Your lives are about to change, ladies. Don't get me wrong. I grew up in a big family, oldest of seven. I've seen babies bring great joy…and a heap of responsibility." He ran a hand through his hair. "Not easy for either of you, since you'll most likely raise your children alone, at least, in the beginning. That first week or two, enlist the help of others."

"Doc, I'd like to enlist your help, if I may," Callie said then went on to explain her plans for housing unwed mothers and concerns for their care.

"You can count on me, Mrs. Mitchell."

"You've relieved my mind. I'm not sure I could deliver babies alone."

"I'll be glad to take care of delivering their babies. If they can pay, fine. If not, I won't allow them to go without medical care." He sighed. "Too many women die in childb—" He closed his eyes then opened them. "I'm sorry. I'm not much of a doctor to voice that in front of two expectant mothers."

"A walk through Walnut Grove Cemetery makes it clear." Callie glanced at Elise. Hoping the talk didn't scare her.

"Most women do fine. These days, doctors know the importance of hygiene. Not that many years ago, doctors performed surgeries wearing street clothes and without washing their hands. We've come a long way." He smiled. "I like the idea of your unwed mothers' home. I can see that Elise has flourished since she's moved in with you." Doc looked at Elise. "Miss Langley, your mother told me she'd pay for your care."

Elise smiled. "She did?"

"Others may be able to do the same," Callie said, "but it's a huge blessing to know a young woman without money will have the care she needs."

"That's why I'm a doctor." He looked at Elise. "See you next week—same time, Miss Langley. Mrs. Mitchell, schedule for next month. Enjoy this pretty afternoon, ladies."

After making their appointments, Callie and Elise left the office, heading to the Mitchell Mercantile, a smile suffusing Elise's face. Perhaps the prospect of shopping for her baby had put it there, but more likely Doctor Wellman was responsible.

Perhaps it would lead to something. That was fine

for Elise, but not what Callie wanted. She'd live her life taking care of her child, giving unwed mothers a home. If a smidgeon of loneliness chaffed on occasion as it did now, she'd follow the advice she'd given Elise and take it one day at a time.

Up the street, Jacob Smith emerged from the Corner Café and strode toward them, his long legs eating up the distance. Mere steps away, his gaze connected with hers. He gave her a brilliant smile, putting a sudden hitch in her breathing and a wobble in her knees and confirming her worst fear.

No matter how much she told herself she shouldn't, she was attracted to this stranger. His smile might make her feel special, but meant nothing more than a passing interest. These unwanted feelings came from her gratitude to the carpenter for shouldering some of the weight of responsibility on her shoulders.

How could she let a drifter throw her off balance this way? Clearly, the uncertainty of her circumstances and a handsome face had overruled her common sense. When it came to Jacob Smith, Callie questioned if she could trust her judgment.

One look at Callie Mitchell, her face glowing in the afternoon sun, and Jake's heart galloped like a racehorse nearing the finish line. The strangest longing twisted inside him, pressing against his lungs. Callie's eyes reflected goodness, warmth, a gentle spirit, everything he admired. What would it be like to have someone like Callie sitting across the breakfast table from him? What would it be like to have someone like Callie to come home to after a hard day's work? What would it be like to have someone like Callie to inquire about the details of his day?

He had no idea. But, oh, how he wanted to find out.

"I, ah, finished the porch." Like a tongue-tied toddler, he could barely get the words out of his mouth. "Got a hankering for coffee and walked to the café."

"I'd have made you an entire pot for finishing that porch. But I can't blame you. The café's coffee's the best in town."

He knew better. "Your brew has the Corner Café beat."

At his words, her cheeks took on the hue of a summer peach. "Jessie should've made a fresh pot for you. I would have. I'm sorry I wasn't home."

As the colorless cloak of dusk settled around them, streetlamps flared to life. The clamor of the afternoon had softened to a sigh, leaving a sense of serenity that whispered the town's name. Peaceful. If only it could be for him. But he knew how quickly life could change. He had to be on guard and resist believing in what looked like an idyllic life.

He'd had a reason for coming here, though with that sweet smile on Callie's lips and the lemony scent of her hair, his motive fled his mind.

"Hi, Mr. Smith."

Jake jerked toward Elise. "I'm sorry, I didn't see you there, Miss Langley."

Elise giggled, heating Jake's neck like a branding iron.

"Few people miss me these days. I think I know the reason for your poor eyesight," she said, then glanced at Mrs. Mitchell.

What did a man say to that?

Jake heard footfalls behind him. A man, tall, burly, appearing forged of steel, tipped his hat to the ladies. "Callie, Elise, good to see you."

"Hello, Hal." Mrs. Mitchell smiled. "How's Loretta?"

"Strong-minded as usual. If my wife says jump, I jump."

Mrs. Mitchell's eyes lit with humor. "Better keep that to yourself in an election year. No man's going to cast his vote for a coward."

"Loretta's the best shot in these parts. That makes me a mighty brave fellow. Not a man in Peaceful would dare disagree."

Elise giggled.

He chucked Elise under the chin, and then swung his gaze to Jake, appraising him with one long look. He stuck out a hand. "I'm Hal Frederick, town sheriff."

The news thudded in Jake's stomach, squelching every thought of Callie from his mind and filling him with foreboding, the familiar tightening in every muscle. "Jake Smith, Sheriff."

"I've heard the name. Appears you've got some folks fired up, Smith."

That could only mean one thing. Commodore Mitchell hadn't wasted a minute getting to the law.

Mrs. Mitchell let out a gust. "If you mean my father-in-law—"

"Commodore paid me a visit. As I told him, a town by the name of Peaceful treats our visitors accordingly. That's assuming visitors are the peaceful sort." The smile never left his face. "How long you planning on staying?"

"Long enough to repair Mrs. Mitchell's house."

The sheriff nodded. "Glad you're giving Callie a hand."

Mrs. Mitchell tapped the sheriff on the arm. "Don't forget that you and Loretta are coming to dinner at my house Tuesday evening at six o'clock."

"Not likely to forget, especially if you're serving pie for dessert. Now that Loretta's bagging rabbit and quail, she's got no interest in rolling dough."

Callie laughed. "How's apple sound?"

"Like music to my ears."

"The boys are invited, if they'd like to come."

"A delicious meal would tempt them but they practice baseball on Tuesdays."

With the conversation off him, Jake felt his muscles ease and made a mental note to be scarce Tuesday evening.

"Jacob and Elise will join us, I hope." Callie turned to Jake, her azure eyes full of entreaty, as if his attendance mattered.

He bit back a refusal. Trying to get out of the dinner invitation would look suspicious. He wanted to have as much time with Callie as he could. Not smart but how could he say no to a woman with eyes that blue? "Thanks, I'll be there."

Mrs. Mitchell's eyes fairly danced with pleasure at the prospect. "It'll be fun."

The woman loved cooking and helping others. She'd made him feel at home, had cared about his safety. When had anyone ever done that much for him?

The sheriff turned to Jake. "That'll give us a chance to get acquainted."

How long before the sheriff learned about his past?

Sharing a meal with the law was the last thing Jake wanted to do. But he supposed moving from the stoop to the table proved that Callie Mitchell had begun to trust him. One thing he knew—any pie of hers would be worth the hassle of spending the evening with the sheriff.

"I'll look forward to it, Mrs. Mitchell," Jake said.

Frederick gave Jake and Callie a speculative glance then strolled on, stopping to chat with the few folks lingering on the street.

"Mrs. Mitchell's too formal for a dinner guest. Please, call me Callie." She smiled. "Would you mind if I called you Jacob? I love biblical names."

No one had ever called him Jacob before, but the gentle, dignified sound of it coming off Callie's lips coiled within him. "That's fine, ma'am."

"My, you make me feel old. Callie, remember?"

"Callie."

The prospect of spending time with her rippled through him. They'd share a meal around the dining-room table he'd glimpsed from the hall. All the meal-times in his entire life had been eaten at a row of long tables. Or alone. What would it be like to stick his feet under Callie's table? And pretend for a while that he was part of a family?

Jake glanced up the street. The sheriff stood watching him, dousing his mood faster than a rainstorm quenching a campfire.

Hal Frederick tried to throw a man off with humor, but Jake never doubted the sheriff's competence.

A lawman would have questions.

They always did.

Callie awakened at dawn with a knot in her stomach and a prayer on her lips. *Please, God, help people to treat Elise kindly today in church.*

Lying in bed expecting trouble wouldn't solve anything. God was in control. She grabbed her robe and headed for the kitchen to prepare food for the basket dinner following service.

By the time Elise plodded into the kitchen, Callie had chicken frying, green beans with ham bubbling on the stove, slaw made and a pie cooling on the counter alongside the stove.

Elise yawned. "Smells good in here. You should've awakened me so I could help."

"You needed your rest. I made oatmeal." Callie pointed at the sink. "I'd appreciate your cleaning up the dishes after breakfast."

"It's the least I can do." Elise took a bowl and filled it, then sat at the table and added sugar and milk. "I've been thinking," she said between bites, "I could stay home today and do the morning chores."

"I've milked. The rest can wait until we're back." She smiled. "You're not fooling me, Elise Langley. You're scared."

"Papa locked me in. And you're shoving me out." She jutted her lower lip. "Not sure I like either one."

Callie moved to Elise's side and laid a hand on her shoulder. "You won't be alone."

"Speaking of alone—what's going on between you and Jake?"

"What do you mean?"

"In town yesterday Jake behaved as if you two were the only people on earth."

"He did not."

"He didn't even know I was there—me, as big as a barn door." She giggled. "You had this goofy grin on your face. You're falling for him."

"Why wouldn't I grin? Do you know how long it would've taken me to replace those rotten boards?"

Elise snorted. "You were grinning about the porch? I don't believe that for a second."

"You're imagining things." Callie plopped her hands on her hips. "Probably because Doc couldn't take his eyes off you."

Color climbed Elise's cheeks. She ducked her head and concentrated on her oatmeal.

"You don't have much to say now."

"Mama taught me never to talk with my mouth full." Eyes twinkling, Elise popped the spoon in her mouth.

Callie laughed, relieved that Elise wasn't fussing about going to church.

A knock at the back door summoned Callie.

Jacob stood on the stoop holding a basket of eggs. At the sight of him, Callie's traitorous heart stuttered in her chest.

"I thought you might need these."

"Thank you." She reached for the basket. "I thought you were sleeping in."

He rubbed a hand along the back of his neck, avoiding her gaze. "Woke before the sun was up."

"I told you God might change your mind."

He harrumphed. "I figured you ladies could use help with chores this morning."

"That's thoughtful of you."

Obviously, Jacob refused to credit God for anything. Perhaps she could still get him to attend church.

She thumbed toward the kitchen. "I've made oatmeal for breakfast, but I could fry a couple of these eggs."

"Oatmeal's fine." Though his tone wasn't convincing.

"You sure?"

"Positive." He took off his hat and dropped to the stoop.

Jacob worked like a dog around the place, but that didn't mean he should be treated like one and continue taking his meals on the stoop. Callie still knew next to nothing about him, but one thing she did know—he wouldn't do them harm.

"Don't be silly. Come in and eat at the table." Callie stepped aside to let him enter. "I won't apologize for being leery at first. But you've proven that you're trustworthy."

His eyes leapt to hers then looked away.

As Jacob stepped inside the back hall, Callie realized that, with the exception of her father-in-law, Jacob Smith was the first man she'd had in her home since Martin died. The first man she'd had in her life. In any way.

Could Elise be right? Could he have an interest in her?

No, he was a drifter. Drifters didn't stay.

Roused by the puzzled expression in Callie's eyes, Jake kept his mouth shut and crossed the threshold before he blurted out that he didn't belong there, even though that was the barefaced truth.

At the arched doorway leading from the hall into the kitchen, he removed his hat and held it in both hands, spinning it between his fingers. Tantalizing aromas drifted toward him. The serenity of the room, reflecting Callie's gentle spirit, wrapped around Jake, tugging him in.

He felt jumpier than a freshly broke bronco. When had he ever been invited inside a home, a real home, where folks shared their meals, their lives, their hopes and dreams? Never. Well, except for hauling in those newspapers for Callie.

He'd slept in the back room at the construction company where he worked, took his meals at a nearby café or carried food in from the neighborhood grocer. Not so different from others he knew. Someday he'd buy a home of his own and put down roots, so why didn't that prospect hold the appeal of this kitchen?

"Hi, Jake." Elise's eyes twinkled as if she found something funny, but he had no idea what.

Callie moved to the stove. "Come to church with us this morning and stay for the potluck. I've made plenty of food."

"Smells great." He was certain he'd do no such thing.

His gaze roamed the kitchen, took in the cupboards, their patina mellow with age, then the checked green-and-white curtains framing the windows, the soft green walls, the vase of bleeding hearts in the center of the table. Everywhere he looked he saw Callie's penchant for making a nest. "This is cozy."

"My aunt always said the kitchen's the heart of a home." She motioned to the sink. "Feel free to wash up while I pour your coffee."

Jake eased past her, keeping his distance. At the washbasin, he scrubbed his hands and dried them on a towel. Not the rough, threadbare towels he'd used in the orphanage and in prison. When had he felt anything softer?

Turning from the sink, unsure where to sit, he glanced at the three empty chairs. Callie handed him a mug. As he took it, his hand brushed hers, sending a jolt to his spine and his feet toward the table. "Thanks for the coffee. Uh, which seat is yours?"

"I sit here." She pointed to the head of the rectangular table. "Now."

Had that been Martin's place at the table? Did she fill it to avoid seeing the seat empty? If so, that proved Callie Mitchell grieved for her husband. As if those widow's weeds she wore weren't enough of a reminder.

"I've already eaten. Sit wherever you like," she said.

He dropped to the middle seat. Callie put a bowl of oatmeal in front of him. Nothing about this cooked cereal resembled the winter fare he ate every day in the orphanage, either runny as gruel or solid as cement.

Jake added sugar and cream then scooped a spoonful of oatmeal and took his first bite. "Delicious."

Callie gifted him with a smile. "I'm glad you like it. From your expression earlier, I thought you didn't."

"I've never had oatmeal that tasted like this."

Elise rose and took her bowl to the sink. "Please come to church with us, Jake. You'll be doing me a favor."

Did she believe his presence would take the focus off her?

"Nothing like a visitor to get folks excited." Callie met his gaze. "This will be Elise's first time to attend…in months."

Jake would prefer taking a thrashing than to darken a church door, but one glance at Elise's drawn face and he understood. Walking into this home had made him uncomfortable, as if he didn't belong and had no right to be here. But it was nothing compared to the stares, the whispers, the muttered comments at his trial and upon his release from jail.

No doubt Elise would experience the same thing at church with her pregnancy in full bloom. He'd go if for no other reason than to shield her from that nightmare. And to please Callie. "I suppose you could use reinforcements."

"We're all going," Callie said in a contented tone, then turned to Elise. "If anyone is impolite to you, they'll answer to me."

Elise grinned and winked at Jake.

Callie folded her arms across her chest. "Do you doubt I'm a formidable opponent?" She attempted a glower and failed.

"No." Elise was laughing now.

Jake chuckled. "I wouldn't want to go up against you, Callie." Then he thought better of it. Going up against the young widow might just be fun.

Callie grinned. "I'm glad you both see I'm a force to be reckoned with." The grin faded as she tucked the dishes she'd prepared into a large woven basket. "Some people believe they're pure as driven snow, but pew sitters are sinners, too. Saved, but not by their goodness."

From what Jake had seen, people who ranked sin were quick to judge. Innocent or not, he'd been in prison. To most, prison spelled guilty. Callie would probably feel the same way if she knew he'd served time.

"If your father-in-law's reaction means anything, Callie, my presence at church might make things worse."

A flash of disquiet crossed Callie's face. She quickly controlled her expression. "As long as the house is unsafe, Commodore assumes I'll have to move in with him and Dorothy. He's upset that you're thwarting his plan."

Elise's brow furrowed. "Can he take your house away?"

"No, it's mine. I'm staying and you are, too, for as long as you want." She glanced at Jake. "Once Commodore sees you in church, he'll have to admit that you're not the scoundrel he makes you out to be."

Jake suspected that Mitchell didn't change his opinions that easily. Still, he'd go. What choice did he have with Elise looking at him with those soulful eyes of hers? With Callie's gaze issuing a challenge?

This cozy kitchen and its occupants enveloped him in the warmth of home and family—all the things he'd missed and yearned to have. He wouldn't let Commodore run him off.

But Jake suspected that his and Elise's presence in church today would stir up trouble. For years he'd avoided trouble. Now it appeared he'd go looking for it.

Chapter Seven

Callie jabbed a hatpin in the crown of her Sunday best,
facing the mirror in the elaborately carved hall tree with
more appendages than an octopus—hooks for coats,
slots for umbrellas and canes, a shelf for men's hats or
ladies' gloves and a bench to ease off one's boots. She'd
get far more accomplished if she could handle that many
tasks at once. Though, at times like this morning, she
felt more octopus than human.

With all she had going on, she'd had little time to
consider Jacob's baffling demeanor in her kitchen earlier. She'd entertained a host of friends and family, but
had never witnessed the kind of discomfort he'd ex-
hibited.

In his realm, making repairs to the house, he appeared totally at ease. So why would a take-charge man
who handled one chore after another with confidence
become hesitant, look as if he didn't know whether to
sit or stand or run?

Tucking a wisp of hair in place, her hand stilled, as
an idea took hold in her mind. That first day, Jacob told
her he'd grown up in an orphanage. Was it possible he'd

always lived in an institution or rented a room somewhere, taken his meals in cafés and never stepped foot inside a private residence?

That didn't make sense. Perhaps the reason for his uneasiness had more to do with attending church. No doubt the reason his lack of faith. Yet, he'd agreed for Elise's sake, almost as if he felt a kinship with her, and then gulped his breakfast and left, supposedly to change for services.

Would he reconsider? No, he'd said he would attend. One thing Callie believed—Jacob kept his word.

The grandfather clock chimed the half hour. While the clock ticked away, she'd been dillydallying, trying to decipher Jacob Smith, a puzzle she couldn't solve. "Elise, are you ready?" she called up the stairs, tugging on her gloves.

Her young charge appeared on the landing, her hair corralled in a tight bun, her cheeks pale, her gaze tethered to Callie's like a lifeline. "Ready as I'll ever be," she said, but her voice wobbled.

Smiling to impart courage to Elise, even as a lump rose in Callie's throat, she motioned her down. "We don't want to be late."

As Callie stepped onto the porch, the odor of pine wafted from the newly laid boards. Her mind flew to long ago Christmases. Freshly cut tabletop trees, the branches adorned with strings of popcorn and her paper ornaments. Ornaments, pictures, keepsakes, all swept away in the churning water. Along with her parents, baby brother and three others who drowned that tragic day. With trembling hands, she took Elise's elbow and they descended the sturdy steps.

"Is Jake planning to paint the porch boards?"

The odor of pine couldn't be obscured fast enough to suit Callie. "Yes, once he gets the railings fixed." Callie's gaze roamed the yard, but she saw no sign of the carpenter. "I hope Jacob didn't change his mind about going."

The words had no more left her mouth than he appeared, his raven hair damp and glistening, his jaw clean-shaven, his rangy frame sporting creased pants and a starched white shirt.

Callie's breath caught and held as she drank him in. Not his usual denims, but no matter what he wore, clothes draped on his lean muscular build with an elegance that made him stand out in a crowd. Something told Callie he'd prefer to blend in.

He greeted Elise, then turned to her. "I bought these clothes in town yesterday for that dinner you invited me to. Didn't expect to need them this soon."

"You look very handsome," she said, pleased that he'd wanted to make a good appearance for her.

His gaze traveled her purple dress, the snowy-white high neck and wide lapels covering her shoulders, then slid down her length to the hem. "You look beautiful. Like violets in bloom."

Their eyes locked and something significant passed between them, deepening the connection Callie didn't want but couldn't resist. "Thank you," she managed, trying not to let him know his compliment had melted her insides into a puddle.

"You look pretty, Elise."

With downcast eyes, Elise gathered her shawl more tightly around her bulging middle. "Your mother raised a polite son."

The light in Jacob's eyes dimmed. Elise had forgotten he'd never had the comforting presence of a mother. Callie had a crazy notion to pull him into a hug, to try to make amends for the years he'd spent in an orphanage. But, of course, she wouldn't.

"Where's your basket?" he asked.

Callie motioned to the porch, trying to turn her wayward thoughts to the task at hand. Jacob bounded up the steps, lifting the heavy load with ease. He was considerate. Considerate and reliable, a combination Callie respected. Yet without a family, life had left him wounded. Something Callie understood all too well. Her heart went out to this loner, yet his lack of openness warned her to keep their relationship impersonal. Or was it already too late for that?

Returning to their sides, he swept a hand up the walk. "After you, ladies."

With Elise all but dragging her feet, the four-block walk to Peaceful Christian Church took far longer than it should have. At the entrance, Elise froze.

"Be brave," Callie whispered. "We're marching, remember?"

Biting her lip, Elise straightened her spine. Jacob held the door and they walked into the vestibule, Elise with her head held high. Callie had never felt prouder of anyone. Once her eyes adjusted to the dim light, Callie got her bearings. Most folks sat in the pews or were moving in that direction.

"Jacob, would you please put the basket over there with the others?" She pointed to a bounty-filled bench.

He did as she asked, jaw rigid, eyes straight ahead. The look of a man prepared for trouble. When he returned to her side, Callie, her heels clacking on the wooden floor, led the troop toward the last pew on the right. Every head turned in their direction, eyes focusing on Elise. From some of the startled, then stern expressions, not everyone rejoiced that Elise had returned to services.

Behind the altar the stained-glass window sparkled, radiating the joy and peace of the Lord. Or so Callie saw it. How she loved this beautiful church with its dark woodwork and whitewashed walls. She hoped nothing would happen to bring ugliness to this house of worship.

"Please stand. Open your hymnals to page 37, 'What a Friend We Have in Jesus.'"

Sandwiched between Jacob and Elise, Callie flipped to the hymn and held the book for her companions as the song leader signaled the organist, then led the singing.

Callie glanced to the right, to Elise's trembling lips and wondered what thoughts filled her mind—guilt, humiliation or elation to worship once again in God's house? She put an arm around her and squeezed. Elise's lips turned up in weak smile.

To her left, Jacob's tight-lipped profile looked rigid, as if chiseled from marble. Was he angry at their reception or merely loath to be in church? Perhaps years in an orphanage had erected stumbling blocks between him and God. Stumbling blocks he needed to demolish, as he had the rotten boards of her porch, before he could find peace.

As she turned the pages to the next song, Callie prayed that after the service, congregation members would welcome Elise and Jacob. Whether they intended it or not, their behavior would send a message—censure refuted a loving God. Mercy revealed God's love.

Jacob had said the church wanted their pew sitters clean. She'd argued the point then, but now...

Now she wondered if he'd been right.

Callie took a shaky breath. She'd come this morning to worship and worship she would. And perhaps, just perhaps, God would soften hearts and transform what looked like trouble into harmony.

Please, Lord, help everything that's done and said this morning be in accordance with Your will.

Having laid it before the throne, Callie released the weight of her concerns and sang with abandon, filled with expectation that God would bless Elise and Jacob for setting aside their qualms and attending church.

Just as He'd blessed her when she'd come to Peaceful, a frightened little girl. This church family had opened their arms to her, giving her guidance, love and support.

Surely two hurting people would be welcomed with the same love as a grieving child.

Wouldn't they?

Jake half listened to the sermon on harvesting the sheaves, guessing that most folks sitting in the pews didn't care to save every soul, and considered some not worth saving.

After the sermon, a ruddy-faced gentleman read a list of the sick and announced the potluck to follow. The preacher gave the benediction and the congregation spilled into the aisles, hauled by their noses toward the tantalizing aroma of food.

Jake rose from the pew and stepped aside, letting Callie and Elise lead the way. As in jail and the towns he'd stopped in since his release, he felt eyes on his back. A stranger would naturally arouse curiosity. How long before those stares turned hostile? And curiosity became judgment?

Why he'd agreed to stay for the meal baffled him. With an instinct that rarely failed him, Jake sensed that few would welcome Elise or him into the fold. Fine. He'd never seen anyone until Callie do more than mouth their faith anyway.

When Gerald Swartz had picked him out from the lineup of orphans, right after Jake's sixteenth birthday and taken him home, Jake had believed he'd attained his childhood dream. As long as he could remember, his fantasies had centered on having a family, a home, perhaps sharing a room with a brother or two. At last, someone wanted him.

They'd wanted him all right.

To work from sunup to sunset, handling every imaginable chore they threw at him. Eager to please, he'd slept in the barn, bathed in the creek, worn hand-me-down clothes, done exactly as he was told without complaint, certain he'd earn their trust and prove he wouldn't be a burden.

Soon they'd include him in the tight circle of family.

Soon never came.

Not that the Swartzes were cruel. They'd filled his belly. Had taken him to church and sent him to school, exactly as the rules required. But he'd never been welcomed in. He'd never spent a single night under their roof. He'd never received an affectionate hug or a kind word.

Each Sunday, they'd sat in their church pew, nodding at the message of love, but never showed him a speck of it by word or deed. The night of his seventeenth birthday, he'd run away. Better to expect nothing than to live with unfulfilled hope. Better to learn a trade and earn a wage than depend on scraps of a family that shut him out. Better to go through life a loner than count on anyone.

Hadn't Susan given him further proof of that?

One church visit brought it all back. If these folks resembled the people he'd spent that year with, they were welcome to their songs. Welcome to their sermons. Welcome to their God.

Hypocrisy. All of it.

He couldn't wait to leave, to reject the stifling pretense of piety, but he couldn't desert Elise and Callie in case they needed him.

In the vestibule, parishioners flowed around the three of them, as if steering clear of an uncharted island, an obstacle on the way to their baskets.

"Good morning, Callie," a woman said, then she turned to Elise. "How are you feeling, dear?"

"Fine, Mrs. Thompson."

"You've got that glow about you. It won't be long now."

"Marlene, I'd like you to meet Jacob Smith, who's doing some work around my place. Mrs. Thompson is Peaceful's postmistress."

The woman shook his hand like a long-lost friend. "I hope you're staying for the meal, Mr. Smith." She glanced toward the door. "Speaking of which, I'd better get going. I'm in charge of setting up the tables." She darted off.

Mrs. Thompson appeared nice enough, but that didn't ease the tension knotting inside Jake. Like a greenhorn on a cattle drive, Jake trailed the women toward Callie's basket, meeting a few friendly parishioners along the way. For a man who'd been misjudged, he'd been quick to do the same. Perhaps he'd been wrong about these folks.

Carrying Callie's basket in one hand, Jake ushered the ladies toward the door where the pastor stood shaking hands. Callie introduced Jake.

Pastor Steele greeted him and Elise with warmth, then took Elise's hand. "Good to have you back."

"Thank you," she said softly then hurried to Callie's side.

"I'm looking forward to a slice of your pie, Callie," Pastor Steele said. "What did you make this time?"

"Cherry with a lattice-top crust."

The pastor all but smacked his lips. He turned to Jake. "Lots of benefits to this calling. Eating the ladies' fine cooking is one of the best. Now don't go tattling to my wife." He winked, then shook Jake's hand. "Good to have a new face in the pew, Jacob. I hope you'll come back."

Jake merely nodded. No point in telling the preacher he wouldn't. They descended the steps, turning toward the tables set up in the side yard already loaded with food, and into the path of a couple blocking their way.

Jake recognized Elise's father and was immediately struck by their resemblance. Except Mark Langley's eyes reminded Jake of thunderclouds before a storm.

Callie laid a hand on Jake's arm. "Would you mind putting the basket on one of the tables?"

Obviously, she wanted to protect Elise from the embarrassment of facing her father in front of him. Jake didn't like leaving them alone with this angry man. He shot Langley a scathing look, then did Callie's bidding. Wishing he could punch the good barber in the nose. The man was another example of a Christian's lack of clemency.

* * *

As Mr. Langley glowered at Jacob's retreating back, Sarah put a protective arm around her daughter.

"That guy was in my shop yesterday. Is he the father?"

"No! He just arrived in town. You know who the father…"

"Who's to say that scum didn't come here?" He leaned toward Elise. "How could you shame us by flaunting your condition at church?"

Elise's eyes glistened. "I'm shaming myself. Not you."

"Elise came for the same reason we all do, Mr. Langley. To hear God's Word, worship and have the support of the church family."

"God's Word is clear. Honor your father and mother. By insisting on keeping your child, Elise, you're defying my authority." He pointed a finger at Callie. "You've made that possible, Mrs. Mitchell, by inviting her in. I don't know how you live with yourself."

Callie reached a hand, then pulled it back. "What's happened can't be changed, but that baby you're disgraced by is your grandchild."

Color drained from Mr. Langley's face, as if she'd struck him. "We're not staying," he said. "I'll fetch your basket, Sarah."

Eyes brimming with tears, Sarah wrapped Elise in a hug. "I've missed you, sweetheart. How are you? What does the doctor say?"

Elise's father pivoted back. "Are you coming?"

Mrs. Langley didn't answer, didn't move. Her silence lengthened—a mutiny of sorts. Then she heaved a sigh and followed her husband.

"It's almost time to eat." Callie ushered Elise toward the tables. "You can help set out our food."

Elise went through the motions of helping, but Callie could see that her heart was breaking. Callie longed to smack some sense into Mr. Langley's mulish head. He was hurting, but he needed to think of his daughter. She needed his forgiveness.

Why couldn't her father count his blessings? He had a family, a grandchild on the way, an innocent baby needing his love and protection. Callie would give anything if her parents could see her baby.

Signaling the group to silence, Pastor Steele bowed his head. "Lord, thank You for this food and time of fellowship. Open our hearts to visitors and members alike that our actions might be a pleasing offering to You. Surround us with awareness of Your love and the gift of Your grace. Amen."

The unseasonable high temperatures of the past few days had eased, bringing a gentle breeze—a perfect day for a picnic. Even with the run-in with her father earlier, Elise relaxed and managed to eat. Parishioners came by to say hello and wish her well. The pastor's pointed prayer a possible reason.

Several men stopped to talk to Jacob about the work at Callie's, a few asked his opinion on projects of their own. Jacob joined them in a game of horseshoes, tossing ringers almost every time. From the serene, even happy expression on his face, Jacob was having fun.

With her heart overflowing with peace, Callie walked to the dessert table. A piece of Mrs. Uland's chocolate cake would be a delicious finish to a lovely day.

Mrs. Sunderland, the corners of her mouth drooping like the bedraggled flowers on her hat, cornered Callie under an elm. "How could you bring a fallen girl to church? What kind of an example does that give our young people, to rub elbows with a sinner?"

"We're all sinners, Mrs. Sunderland."

The woman sniffed. "Next thing you'll have a party for her and ask for baby gifts. Invite the whole church or some such nonsense."

"Elise made a mistake. She's remorseful—"

"I didn't see her come forward at the altar call. No decent girl would grace this sacred building carrying a baby out of wedlock without begging forgiveness. She should've done that in front of the entire church."

Callie couldn't believe her ears. "You and I are allowed to repent in private. Shouldn't we offer that same grace to Elise?"

"Her sin isn't some little white lie or a bad word voiced in anger. Her sin is fornication. *And* out there for all to see."

Callie's hands balled into fists. "Would an altar call have made a difference to you? You're ranking sin, as if some deserve forgiveness and others don't. Elise needs our love, not condemnation."

The woman smirked. "I'd say she's had all the love she can handle."

"That's just cruel." Unable to bear the presence of this judgmental woman a moment longer, Callie pivoted, tears flooding her eyes until she could barely see and hurried around the church where she'd have privacy.

"Callie?"

She turned, colliding with Jacob. He grabbed her by the shoulders to steady her. With a callused thumb, he brushed away the tears sliding down her cheeks. "Don't pay attention to that battle-axe."

At his caring touch, Callie's breath caught. She longed to step into his arms and accept the comfort of being held.

"I overheard," he said. "I'd regret making a spectacle for your and Elise's sakes, but give the word and I'll deposit that woman's judgmental carcass on the lawn."

At the image popping into her mind, Callie gave a shaky smile. "She probably deserves it, but she's just one person. Everyone else, well, except for Elise's father, has been kind."

"I've noticed. Several men welcomed me to the community. All and all, this is a nice little town."

The exact words Callie hoped to hear. Perhaps that welcome he'd felt would bring Jacob to church. And in time, he'd find his way to God.

"Now that you've seen that most Christians are compassionate and loving, maybe you'll like Peaceful enough to settle here."

The smile on Jacob's face ebbed. A guarded, unreadable expression clouded his eyes. She took a step back.

What made a man look ready to run?

What secret was Jacob Smith hiding?

Chapter Eight

The fishing poles were a ruse. Not that Jake would admit it to Callie. Standing on her stoop, holding the two rods he'd borrowed from the large stash in the barn, he waited for her to answer his knock with the impatience of a kid waiting his turn in a candy store.

The door opened. In Callie's eyes, he saw weariness he hadn't seen before. As if something with the weight of an anvil were perched on her shoulders, sapping her of the energy to take a step. He'd been right. Callie needed to unwind, to dangle a line. Take time for her. And him.

He smiled. "Nice afternoon for fishing."

A spark of interest lit up her eyes. "Yes, it is. You'll find plenty of earthworms in the garden if you're looking for live bait."

"Got them right here." He pointed to the bait box.

"Good, hope they're biting." She turned to step back inside. Away from him.

"Why not find out for yourself?"

She cocked her head, looking as puzzled as if he'd spoken in a foreign tongue.

"I'm asking you to go with me."

"Fishing? With you?"

"Yep, why else would I have two poles?"

"Martin always propped a number of poles along the bank."

"Keeping all those lines straight must've made casting complicated for you."

She fiddled with her collar, averting her gaze. "He never... Well, he never asked me to go along."

"Why's that?"

"I asked him once. He said...he just said he needed time away."

Her words banged against his heart, penetrating his defenses as if they were made of putty, instead of bricks and mortar. "With that patience of yours, I'm guessing you're an excellent fisherman," he said, struggling to keep his tone even.

A sudden smile came to her lips. "I used to be. When I was little, my dad took me fishing. And a friend and I went as kids, every chance we got."

Callie's deceased husband knew she liked to fish and never once took her. The man hadn't appreciated what he had. All the more reason Jake wouldn't take no for an answer. He intended to erase that exhaustion from her face and give her some fun, especially after that biddy's attack at the church picnic.

He could do that much for her.

"I'd like to spend time with you, Callie, doing something besides work. Fishing will be fun."

A sparkle lit her eyes. She glanced inside. "I should probably stay with Elise."

Jake bit back a sigh. "Elise is welcome to come along."

A lie.

He wanted Callie to himself. He wanted to hear her soft laughter again. He wanted to see the delight in her face when a nibble jerked her line. Most of all, he wanted to be an ordinary man out with an ordinary woman.

"I'll ask her." Callie whirled away. "Be right back."

Kneeling, Jake opened the tackle box at his feet to an impressive array of floats, hooks and manmade bait and flies. Mitchell hadn't spared any expense with his fishing gear. Jake had always done fine with a worm dangling from a hook.

A moment later, wearing a straw bonnet and a dazzling smile, Callie appeared with a basket. "Elise dislikes worms and fish, alive or dead, and wants no part of our adventure. She's curled up in the parlor reading a book."

The news that he'd have Callie to himself exploded in his chest and pumped through his veins. "Guess we'll have to manage without her." He'd tried to sound disappointed but from the way Callie's cheeks turned rosy, he'd failed.

"Would you like me to make sandwiches? I always did for Martin. He said fishing made a man hungry."

The only hunger Jake had was for time with Callie. This woman captivated him like no other, made him want to please her, to protect her, to—

He told himself to pull back. This was a fishing trip, not a lifetime commitment. No one's getting hooked here, except a bluegill.

"I'm still stuffed from the church picnic."

"Me, too." She indicated the basket. "Just in case, I've brought cookies."

"What kind?"

"Snickerdoodles."

"Mmm, sugar and spice."

"And all that's nice."

He tapped her chin. "That's what little girls are made of."

"I hope I have a girl." Her mouth formed a circle of surprise. "Oh, what if it's a boy and he heard that?"

"If he did, he'll no doubt make you regret saying it by living up to his reputation." He grinned. "Let's see, frogs and snails and puppy-dog tails, that's what little boys are made of." Unable to take his eyes off her, he offered the crook of his elbow. "Girls are wonderful, especially the grown-up variety."

"Thank you, kind sir." She took his arm as they started down the walk. "Boys are special, too."

"Not according to the girls at the orphanage. They never let us forget our less than impressive makings."

She giggled, looking young, carefree and beautiful.

As they strolled along, the distance between the Victorians lengthened until they reached the edge of town. Across the way, between the trees, Jake spotted a strip of flowing water glinting in the afternoon sun. The scent of loamy soil mingled with the hum of gurgling water. Birds chirped, leaves whispered in the breeze. A sense of peace settled over Jake, as pleasant as the scent of Callie's fragrance.

He helped Callie descend the bank, guiding her toward a large rock at the water's edge. At their approach, a frog, nose barely above water, leaped out of reach. Down the way, the deep drone of a bullfrog geared up for his nightly serenade. Everywhere Jake looked, creatures took part in the mating dance of spring, building homes, re-creating their kind. A deep ache of loneliness throbbed anew inside him.

He dusted the rock off with his hand. "Have a seat, fair lady."

Then he joined her, sitting on the edge, barely on the rock at all, and baited the hooks.

Callie watched, smiling. "You've done this before."

"The orphanage wasn't too far from a pond. We'd sneak off to fish whenever we could. If we cleaned what we caught, the cook would fry them. Nothing's better than a mess of fresh-caught bluegills."

"Bluegill is my favorite. Catfish was Martin's."

How often had Martin considered Callie's likes and dislikes? If at all? If Jake were married to Callie, he'd bring home a bucket of bluegills every week. But he wasn't. He needed to remember that.

Jake handed Callie a pole. "You know how this is done."

"Well, it's been a while."

"Watch the float. If it goes under, yank the pole up to set the hook. Then reel it in. Simple unless the fish aren't biting and all you catch is a twig or an old shoe."

Callie laughed, the melodious sound mingling with the serenity of their secluded surroundings, charming Jake down to his toes.

"To cast, just whip the tip of the pole back, then forward toward the river. As you do, put your finger on the spring to release the line."

Fingers posed hesitantly over the mechanism, she gave him a quizzical look.

"Would you like me to cast for you?"

"Let me try." She rose, swung the rod back, the line shot out…and snared on the undergrowth behind them.

Jake untangled the line and asked her to reel it in. Absorption in the task easy to read on her face, she tried again. Again, the line caught in the bushes.

As he worked to free the line, she shook with laughter. "Maybe you'd better show me."

He came around behind her and laid his hands over hers, wrapping her in the circle of his arms. Aware of the proximity of her body, the warmth of her skin, Jake longed to pull her against him, to nuzzle her soft nape, kiss her.

Callie glanced over her shoulder at him, bringing her face mere inches from his and dropped her gaze to his mouth. Just one step and he'd feel those soft lips beneath his. His grip tightened and he lowered his head.

She spun away, facing the river. "How, uh, how do you do this again?"

With yearning mounting within him, he guided her hands through the motions. The line sailed through the air. As soon as it hit the water, Callie moved out of his arms.

He watched the float drift in the current, aching to pull Callie back in his arms. But she held herself apart, her grip tight on her pole, as if her life depended on it, avoiding the attraction sizzling between them.

How could he blame her? He had nothing to offer her and her baby except a past that would surface one day and suck them into a maelstrom of trouble.

"This is fun," she said, keeping her gaze glued on the float and off him.

The float dipped under the water, Callie yelped with surprise, then whipped up the tip of the rod, cranking with all her might, the line growing tauter with every spin of the reel.

A fish emerged, skimming through the water toward her. "I got one!"

Jake grabbed the net, skidded along the bank and scooped up her catch, a bluegill. "It's a beauty," he said, smiling.

As he strode the bank to show her, she laughed again, her face alight with delight. She was having a good time, exactly what he wanted to give her.

After they'd estimated its length, he removed the hook from the bluegill's mouth, put it on the stringer he'd tied to a sapling and eased it into the water. With his stomach flopping like that bluegill had in the net, Jake fought the truth. He was falling for Callie. And he couldn't. But he'd enjoy this day. Wrap it in his memory to take out again and again.

As they fished, he and Callie munched cookies, swatting at an occasional mosquito, exchanging fishing stories and talking about their love of nature.

"Imagine how much fun God must've had making all this." She swept her hand. "And Adam, too, when he got to name all the creatures God created." She laughed. "I can't even decide what to name one little baby."

Looking at her face, aglow with enthusiasm for life, for her God, for her baby, Jake wanted what she had.

"Keep seeking God, Jacob. If you do, you'll find Him."

She must've seen that longing on his face. But she hadn't seen him reading Scripture every night. Nothing had changed. He switched the subject and they moved on to other topics. The time passed quickly, with each of them pulling in several bluegills. Jake even caught a good-sized bass.

"I'll fry them, if you'll filet them," Callie offered.

"It's a deal."

Callie gathered the basket as Jake corralled their catch and fishing gear. "Thanks for bringing me, Jake. I couldn't have a better friend than you."

The smile on his face faltered. She didn't want a romantic relationship. Wasn't that what he wanted, too? So why did her words hook his heart with a painful sting?

On the walk home, the sounds of approaching night enveloped them. Birds called to one another in the trees. Insects hummed, joining the bullfrog chorus, a cheerless chatter that to Jake spoke of endings, not beginnings.

No matter how much he pretended otherwise, he'd been fooling himself about wanting to give Callie only a fun afternoon. Or that he cared one whit about fishing. He cared about this woman. She charmed him, like no other. Yet he had no hope of reeling her in.

She needed a husband, a father for her child. A jailbird wouldn't do.

He'd seek information about his birth mother and forget this foolishness. He was meant to walk through life alone.

As he always had.

Callie stood as far back from the stove as she could and still keep an eye on the fish sizzling in the large iron skillet. Another skillet of fried potatoes and onions was set to the side. Once Jacob finished stowing the gear and washed up at the pump, he'd be in. He'd sit at her table and eat with the gusto of a man who loved home cooking. And fill the emptiness in her heart.

Across the way, Elise set the table for three. "You actually had fun?"

Her incredulous tone made Callie chuckle. "I did. Catching fish is fun. The river was peaceful. Jake ate a slew of cookies. The man has a hollow leg."

"Did you bait your own hook?" Elise wrinkled her nose with displeasure.

"He insisted on doing it for me, though I could've."

"I feel sorry for the worms. Fish, too." She gave a wry grin. "Guess that makes no sense, since I'm looking forward to supper."

"Me, too."

"So what was it like to spend time alone with Jake?"

Fishing might have been the goal. And they'd caught quite a few, but nothing had prepared Callie for her reaction to the man. Perhaps it had been the solitude, the two of them alone surrounded by the beauty of God's creation and an ever-deepening awareness of each other.

God created man and woman, planting within them a yearning for intimacy, a desire to walk through life two by two. Surely that was the reason, the only reason, she'd had that response to him.

"He's attentive, thoughtful."

Elise grinned. "And a hard worker. He's perfect for you."

But Callie knew Jacob Smith wasn't the right man. God knew that, too. Jacob didn't have faith. He was a mystery. She wouldn't allow herself to get entangled with a man who kept his past and his future hidden.

She sighed. His future wasn't hidden. From the moment he'd arrived, he'd spoken of leaving. For her baby's sake, she would not get wrapped up in this man. She'd keep it impersonal. Avoid being alone with him. Surely with Elise in the house, that would be easy enough to do.

The back door banged shut and Jacob stood in the

kitchen, his hair wet from a dousing at the pump. Her treacherous heart leaped at the sight of him. He shot her a smile, his gaze meeting hers with an absorption that suggested he had eyes only for her. Some compulsion lured her closer.

What was wrong with her? Where would this attraction lead?

To yet another loss.

Loss had permeated her life, each one leaving her battered, clinging to God.

She whirled to the stove and checked the fish, crispy on the outside, flaky within. "I'm sorry. I need to lie down. Would you serve, Elise?"

"Don't you want to eat first?" Elise's brow furrowed. "I thought you were hungry for fish."

"Are you sick?" Jacob took a step toward her, his tone laced with concern.

"No, just tired. Too tired to eat." Unable to meet his gaze for fear he'd see the panic in her eyes, she hurried out of the kitchen.

In her bedroom, she wilted onto the bed and hugged a pillow to her chest, aching to hold Jacob in her arms.

Jacob. A man without faith.

A man without a past.

A man without permanence.

Even with all his shortcomings, Martin had given her that much.

She'd protect her child from a broken heart by holding Jacob at arm's length. She released the pillow and laid her palms over her unborn child. A flutter of movement, as if her baby leaped within her, wrapped around her heart. All she needed was this precious little one, God's gift and her future.

* * *

Jake knelt on the staircase, tightening the screws in the banister, eliminating the wobble. Steadying the railing with both hands, Callie stood looking up at him with those startling blue eyes. He could've managed without her help, but it gave him an opportunity to ask questions that might lead to information about the woman who'd given birth to him.

"Once I'm finished, this railing should be solid enough to support my weight with two mules on my back."

As he'd intended, she grinned, looking happy.

Unlike the expression she'd worn last night, when she'd raced out of the kitchen with the excuse that she was too tired to eat fresh-caught fish. But she hadn't been able to look him in the eyes when she said it. No, she'd been unsettled by the intimacy sizzling between them at the river.

Well, she wasn't alone.

What he hadn't counted on was his overwhelming reaction to having her near this morning, aware of her scent, her sea-blue eyes and slender, toil-toughened hands. A woman like Callie shouldn't have to work that hard. She ought to find a reliable man, a God-fearing man, and remarry. Yet the notion of Callie attached to another man tightened his jaw until his teeth hurt.

He sat back on his heels and absorbed the tendrils of her hair curling around her neck, the delicate arch of her brows, her full, kissable lips. What would it be like to have that sweet mouth against his? To feel her soft curves pressed against him?

With every ounce of his strength, he concentrated on his objective. "How long have you lived in Peaceful?"

She hesitated, a troubled look filling her eyes. "I moved here when I was seven to live with my aunt after…" she took a deep breath "…after my parents and baby brother drowned."

That Callie had been orphaned twisted in Jake's stomach.

She cleared her throat. "Our farm sat in a valley, the school on high ground." She laid trembling fingers over her lips as if trying to hold back the words. "I wasn't the only child to lose my family that day."

"You were a little kid." He touched her jaw, wanting to take her into his arms, but didn't. "That had to be terrifying."

"You understand better than most," she said softly. "It happened because a disgruntled husband sought to punish his wife's lover and blew a hole in the dam. The whole thing gave way. He claimed he was innocent but the evidence was overwhelming and he finally confessed."

The news crashed into Jake with the force of an avalanche. He couldn't imagine the horror of losing her family, especially that way. A lawbreaker had destroyed Callie's world and now sat in jail, as he should. If she learned of Jake's sentence, how could she not question his innocence?

"I'm so sorry." Knowing the words weren't enough, not nearly enough, for all Callie had missed.

"I was luckier than you. My mother's sister took me in and helped me adjust."

Jake ached to somehow erase all she'd suffered. "Not luckier. You knew what you had. What you lost. I could only guess what it meant to have a family."

Avoiding her eyes, he rotated the handle of the screwdriver, twisting the screw tighter and tighter into the wood. Something despicable must live inside him that prevented others from stomaching his presence. "Even when I lived with one for a little while, I was never part of their circle."

She laid a gentle hand on his arm. "It's better to have had a family and lost it than never to have had a family at all."

That delicate hand burned through his sleeve. He wanted to cover it with his own, to show her he cared, but even a fine woman like Callie, with all she'd experienced would be suspicious of his stint in jail.

"Losing my parents and Ronnie was…" She shivered. "Terrible. But I have memories, happy memories to remember them by. Aunt Hilda had a few pictures of us, pictures I cherish. Pictures I can pore over, hold, touch. They don't replace my family, but they keep them alive in my heart." Her eyes glistened. "I wish you had that."

Jake wanted that, too. Some sense of where he came from and who his parents were. That lack of connection twisted inside him. A constant ache he'd learned to live with, so much a part of him he barely noticed. If only he could share his search for his mother. But if he found her and she rejected him… He couldn't bear for Callie to witness his humiliation.

He forced his thoughts to Callie's aunt. She'd know all the scandals in town, might know the identity of his mother. "The day I arrived, when I asked about your family, you didn't mention an aunt."

"Aunt Hilda had a stroke and died."

The news thudded in Jake's stomach. "You've endured the loss of your family, your aunt and your husband. I've never heard you utter one word of complaint or resentment. You're strong, Callie Mitchell."

"I'm weak, Jacob. God is strong. I lean on Him."

Callie didn't realize what a rare creature she was, an uncommon woman, but Jake knew. And his admiration for her grew. Her baby was fortunate to have such a mother.

A desire to know the woman who'd given him birth gripped him. Perhaps she was a woman of strength with an inner beauty like Callie. He'd judged her, condemned her. But he didn't know her circumstances.

"Even with everything you've been through, you've made friends, gotten involved, put down roots. Probably not much happens in town that escapes you."

"Are you implying that I'm a gossip?"

"I'd never believe that of you. I thought people in small towns generally knew everyone's business."

She sighed. "That can be a problem, like with Elise on Sunday. Some folks poke their noses in more than they should."

Here was an opening. "Elise can't be the first young woman to find herself in those circumstances. Your aunt probably saw young women in the same fix in her day."

"If she did, she kept it from me."

Callie had lived with a woman who'd protected her from the harsher side of life. "Losing your aunt must've hurt."

"Aunt Hilda was a wonderful, giving woman. I miss her. I married Martin soon after she died. Now he's gone, too," she said softly.

Suddenly her mouth contorted as if she might cry.

Jake brushed her cheek, then stood helplessly, unable to break away. In Callie, he recognized the signs of bone-deep loneliness. Loneliness he lived with every day. Or he had until he came to Peaceful.

He lifted her chin, bringing her face within inches of his. Almost losing his composure at their closeness, he wanted to comfort her, to hold her, to make her pain vanish. But the widow's weeds she wore served as a vivid reminder that she mourned her husband.

"What can I do? Should I call Elise?"

"I'm fine," she said, though her voice trembled. "Once in a while it hits me anew that all the family I had in the world is gone."

"You have Martin's parents."

She nodded but remained mute. No wonder. Commodore Mitchell could've made things easier for Callie. Been the supportive father figure she needed badly. But he badgered her and criticized her. Losing an opportunity Jake would give anything to have. Callie appeared to cope with loneliness by re-creating that family with Elise.

Callie looked away, letting her gaze meander toward the railing. "Martin meant to get around to fixing up the place. But something always interfered." A hint of a smile appeared on her lips. "The fish were biting or his buddies would invite him hunting."

Jake couldn't imagine a go-getter like Callie married to a slacker, even a slacker with good intentions. What had been wrong with the guy? Martin Mitchell had possessed everything of importance. A beautiful wife, a great old house, parents. Why hadn't he put them first, before his amusement?

"Don't judge my husband and find him wanting," Callie said, as if reading his thoughts. "You might see Martin as lazy, but he had many good qualities." She raised her eyes to his.

Jake met her moist, forlorn gaze, all but tearing a hole in his self-control, his eyes stinging and swallowed hard. "I know he did, Callie. You wouldn't have loved him otherwise."

"He liked to have fun, to tease. I never had a dull moment with Martin around." She smiled. "He appreciated nature. He'd call me to watch a pretty sunset or see a rainbow." Her voice faltered. "He died so young. I'm glad he got to enjoy those things as much as he did."

Her forceful tone and the intensity of her gaze dared him to disagree. He craved that loyalty. Loyalty he'd never had. But if Callie discovered his past, she'd never talk about him the way she talked about Martin, with that sweet acceptance, with that tolerance.

Still, what would it be like to have a woman like Callie stick up for him? What would it be like to have a woman like Callie to watch a sunset with? What would it be like to have a woman like Callie to call his?

No point in speculating. He might be a hard worker, his one edge over Martin Mitchell, but Callie could never care about a taciturn jailbird the way she'd cared about her happy-go-lucky husband.

Today had proved that Callie knew nothing about unwed mothers in the town all those years ago. He'd have to find a way to look at the newspapers cluttering her library. Surely somewhere in that pile was the information he sought.

Once he found the woman who'd given birth to him, he'd be on his way, though the prospect of leaving sank inside him with the weight of an anchor. But what was the point of staying? He had no hope of forging a family with Callie.

Chapter Nine

Callie put the finishing touches on the tulip center-piece. As she rearranged the height of one flower, her hands trembled. Silly to be this shaken by her first dinner party since Martin died. Some would see entertaining this soon as unseemly, but too many deaths, too many funerals had taught Callie to live in the moment. She believed God's Word supported that lesson. As much as she could, she wouldn't let past losses or future uncertainties cast a shadow on her today.

The dinner party gave her a chance to offer Jacob a taste of hospitality, of the pleasure of gathering around a table, sharing a meal and conversation with friends. His edgy demeanor in her kitchen implied that this wouldn't come easily for him. But once he got acquainted with her friends, he'd relax.

She heard a rap on the door. Jacob stood on the other side, clean-shaven, wearing his church clothes and a wary look in his green eyes. She wanted to assure him that which fork he used didn't matter one whit, but a man raised in an institution wouldn't have confidence in social situations.

"Thought I'd fill screw holes then polish the banister. I wouldn't want your guests to think I'd left a project incomplete."

"How thoughtful." Smiling, Callie stepped aside to let him enter.

"I'll try not to get in your way."

Just his presence in the house chased every task from her head. "You won't bother me." When had she spoken a bigger lie?

As he set to work, Callie returned to the dining room, reliving their conversation yesterday. She'd opened up about her past. He'd cared about her losses, understood her loneliness. What would it be like to lean into those strong arms of his?

The prospect of counting on another man skittered along her spine. Caring brought heartache. And she'd had all the heartache she could handle. She'd focus on her baby and refuse to get involved with Jacob, except to help him repair the house.

Through the archway, she had a view of the foyer. Jacob bent over the banister, his black hair catching the light. His haircut gave him a refined appearance, but she missed the rugged masculinity of his collar-length hair.

A loner, Jacob shunned the limelight. She appreciated the care he took with the house, not only to make it safe and functional, but also attractive. He had a patient touch.

Aunt Hilda had possessed that same unhurried way about her. She'd devoted her life to teaching Peaceful's children, first in a one-room schoolhouse, then in the new larger building in town. She hadn't earned much money but with the little left over, her aunt had bought everything on this table.

Callie smoothed a slight wrinkle in the white linen tablecloth, letting her gaze sweep over her aunt's candlesticks, flatware, lovely china. The mahogany table and chairs had come from her aunt, handed down from Callie's grandmother, a link to her mother's childhood home, something she cherished.

When Callie arrived with nothing but the clothes on her back, Aunt Hilda's income went toward providing for a growing child, but she never complained about the sacrifice. Her example taught Callie the importance of giving, of helping others. She couldn't repay her aunt, but she'd taken in Elise, as her aunt had taken her in. She hoped to make a difference for Elise, for any woman in her situation, by opening her home and her heart.

Even to her lonely neighbor. Mildred had accepted the invitation to dinner before Callie had gotten the words out of her mouth. Knowing the effort it took to prepare food, only to eat alone, she should ask Mildred to join her more often.

To ensure that she hadn't forgotten anything, Callie let her eyes meander over the six place settings. Satisfied that nothing was amiss, she stepped back, took in the room's high ceilings, deep moldings, crystal chandelier and gleaming wooden floor. Mere days after she and Martin had moved in, she'd painted the wainscoting white and hung above it the striped navy, pink and white wallpaper. She'd delighted in bringing even this small part of the house back to life.

Strides in the hall announced Jacob's approach. He stood under the archway, his stance wide, as if maintaining his balance on the deck of a wind-tossed boat. His gaze swept the table, then lifted to her, the expression in his eyes as skittish as a seasick landlubber heading to open water.

"We can't all fit around the kitchen table," she said by way of explanation, though he hadn't asked.

"You have the right to eat where you want." His tone mild, unconcerned, yet he glanced toward the front door as if he were ready to make a run for it.

She chuckled. "Eating in a dining room isn't a jail sentence."

His gaze swiveled to hers. A flash of alarm traveled his face then vanished so quickly she wondered if she'd imagined it.

"It'll be fun. You know Mildred. You've met Hal Frederick."

"I remember."

"I've known Hal's wife, Loretta, for years. She's more big sister than friend. We're exact opposites. She loves to hunt, while I have to work up my courage to kill a chicken for the pot."

The warm depth of his gaze enfolded her. "I'll be glad to handle that chore for you."

Jacob's kindness rippled through her. Martin had known about her squeamishness, yet rarely was around to handle unpleasant tasks. Jacob made her feel cared for. Protected. Cherished.

Inside her chest her heart rat-a-tat to a wayward beat. All because Jacob Smith looked at her with those burnished jade eyes, suggesting that he cared, suggesting they had a future, suggesting—

She wouldn't finish the thought.

"I'm sure Loretta's a fine person," he said. "That all your guests are. Otherwise, you wouldn't care about them."

"Then why look like you've been given a life sentence?"

His smile faltered. "You're imagining that."

"Am I?" Not waiting for his answer, she moved toward the kitchen and tossed over her shoulder, "Want to help put the finishing touches on the meal?"

He followed her in, the staccato of his footfalls discordant with hers. Nothing about the two of them fit.

She enjoyed people. He avoided them.

She loved God. He denied God.

She cherished family. He cherished solitude.

Even so, Jacob's tough beginnings and his commitment to her house connected them, along with a huge dose of attraction she didn't trust. Whenever he was near, that attraction pulled her into a swirling eddy of conflicting emotions. Jacob Smith had a past he avoided and he wasn't staying. She wouldn't let feelings rule her head.

Not this time.

In the kitchen, she handed Jacob a knife. "Please slice the pie. I promised Hal apple, but decided on cherry."

"He'd be a dunce not to appreciate any pie made by your hands."

"Thank you." Callie checked the roast, releasing an aroma bringing a growl from her belly. Across the way, Jacob divided the pie into wedges with the precision of someone accustomed to measuring every cut he made.

She bit back a smile. "The vegetables are almost tender. Everything's ready…except me. I'd better change."

"That'll give me time to polish the banister."

Side by side, they walked to the foyer, Callie aware of the man, towing her to him with a strength that left her shaken.

He looked around him. "Where's Elise?"

"Upstairs taking a nap. I'll awaken her so she can get ready."

When they reached the staircase, Jacob took a jar and a rag out of the sack she hadn't noticed him carry in. "Beeswax and linseed oil should give it a nice finish." He set to work.

"If you don't need anything else, I'll go upstairs."

"I'm all set," he said. "Take your time."

As Callie climbed the steps, she planned what she'd wear. Perhaps the gray silk dress she'd altered to give more ease in the midriff and Aunt Hilda's lavaliere. Normally, she saved the pendant for special occasions, but the ruby would sparkle in the candlelight. Her breath caught. Here she was a widow, trying to look pretty for a Godless drifter.

Forgive me, Lord, for such foolishness. Protect my heart from a man who can destroy it.

Jake watched Callie climb the stairs. Gripped by a desire for her to turn back, he waited. Waited for a brief glimpse of her face.

Another step.

A third.

He kept watching, hoping she'd look at him as she ascended the broad staircase, her hand gliding along the banister, totally unaware of his presence below. No doubt she had her mind on last-minute details.

With the rag poised to wipe down the banister, the mixture in the jar at his feet, the tools of his trade—tangible things he could count on, unlike relationships with others, he took one last look.

She pivoted and smiled down at him.

Joy exploded in his chest and spread through every muscle and tendon, holding him transfixed, captured by her beauty—inside and out. He drank in her warmth and goodness the way sun-bleached boards absorbed the first coat of varnish.

Then, in a blink of an eye, she moved out of view.

Every feature and contour of her lovely face was fixed in his memory. The prospect of an entire evening with Callie burned within him. To watch her slim, expressive brows rise and fall. To watch her full lips turn up in a smile. To watch every nuance of her expression transform her face. What a privilege.

But then he remembered that the sheriff would share that table. How long before Frederick discovered the truth? Truth had not set Jacob free. Truth had imprisoned him.

With the sheriff at the table, Jake would have to watch every word he said. But the invitation gave him an excuse for finishing the railing, the little job a convenient ploy to get into the house early.

On silent feet, Jake moved down the hall toward the library. The knowledge that Callie trusted him alone in her house tweaked his conscience, but seeking the woman who gave birth to him wouldn't bring Callie harm.

At the last door on the right, he turned the knob. Inside the library, he strode to the desk. He'd leave the door open, listen for Callie's return.

The first stack of newspapers looked recent, but over to the side a pile, brittle and yellowed with age, looked promising. He'd start there. Rummaging through the stack, he discovered the newspapers dated decades before his birth.

His hand moved to another stack, yellowed but in better condition. His throat clogged. This stack might hold the information he sought. Flipping through the dates, he located the year 1877. With shaking hands, he looked for May 21, 1877. His birthday.

Or so he'd been told.

A squeak of the floorboards overhead. Jake jerked to his feet. One of the women would soon arrive downstairs. He straightened the newspapers and eased the door closed after him.

He made it to the foyer, grabbed the cloth and polished the banister, revealing the soft glow of the wood's patina just as Callie made it to the landing.

"Oh, that looks much nicer," Callie said, descending the final flight of stairs. "Lovely."

The description fit her perfectly.

As she reached the foyer, Jake got a whiff of roses, the delicate scent she wore. Her dress accentuated her soft curves and the swell of her baby, and then swirled to the hem. The lower neckline revealed the jewelry she wore, the pale skin of her throat, the pulse hammering in its hollows in rhythm with his.

"You look…stunning."

A smile curving her lips, she laid a palm on his cheek and he covered it with his, looking into her eyes. He yearned to cup her jaw, to lift her face to his. To kiss her.

Elise appeared at the head of the stairs. Their hands fell away.

Callie took a step back. "Doesn't Elise look pretty?"

"Very pretty."

Elise blushed, appeared ready to deny it, but Callie took her arm. "Help me pour water in the glasses."

Once the ladies had entered the kitchen, Jake returned to his work. If the woman who'd given birth to him lived in this town, she'd had twenty-three years to claim him as her son and hadn't. Jake saw no reason why she'd welcome him now. Still, he needed more time to search those newspapers.

His jaw clenched. He couldn't bear the idea of Callie learning of the woman's existence, only to see him rejected and humiliated. Nor could he allow his birth mother to be disgraced.

After spending time with Elise, he cared about his mother's reputation. Getting others involved would stir up a hornet's nest. Someone would get stung.

Chapter Ten

The candles were lit, the food served, the prayer given. At Callie's side, Jacob sat stiff in his chair. Even inexperience in social situations didn't explain his obvious uneasiness.

Talk ceased while everyone tasted the first bites, then resumed as they declared the food delicious. Callie released the breath she'd been holding and thanked her guests.

"I'm glad you've stopped wearing black, Callie. It's never been your color." Loretta gestured across the table to Jacob. "I'm also glad to have the opportunity to meet you."

"The pleasure is mine, Mrs. Frederick."

"Please, call me Loretta. And whatever Hal has said about me, take it with a grain of pepper."

Hal chuckled. "Salt is too bland for my wife."

Winking at her husband, Loretta took a bite of potatoes. "I'm impressed with your skill, Jake. That new porch floor is as solid as Marlene Thompson's fruit-cake."

Callie snickered. "You're terrible."

"You know I'm speaking the truth. Marlene carries that fruitcake of hers to church suppers and carries it home untouched. Wouldn't you think after all these years, she'd get the message?" She smiled. "Course if she did, folks would probably miss it. Grumbling about Marlene's fruitcake is as much a Christmas tradition in Peaceful as caroling on Christmas Eve."

At Loretta's assertion, Elise choked on her sip of water. "That's like Papa fussing about Mama's dime novels. If he stopped, he'd take away half the fun of Mama's reading them."

Eyes on Jacob, Hal cut a slice of beef. "Smith, tell us about yourself. Where did you learn carpentry?"

"I apprenticed at a construction company. The owner took me under his wing and saw that I learned more than the basics."

Though Jacob sounded at ease, the tight look around his mouth verified that he didn't relish being the center of attention. His discomfort touched a spot deep inside her.

She glanced at Mildred, wearing a beribboned gown, the round neck edged in lace and trimmed with seed pearls. "You look lovely this evening, Mildred."

"You're sweet, dear, but truth is I look as overdone as a dried out turkey at Thanksgiving." She smiled. "But I'm here. At my age, every day I wake up is a good day."

Elise giggled and the others joined in. Callie could see the tension ease in Jacob's shoulders. "From what I've been reading in the papers," she said, keeping the conversation off him, "President McKinley should win reelection in the fall."

"McKinley and Roosevelt make a good ticket," Jacob said.

"Papa reads the newspapers from front to back," Elise groaned. "At supper he dishes up the news like stew, chunks of politics, dash of the gold standard, pinch of Spain, on and on until Mama and I have indigestion."

Callie chuckled. "I take it you'd appreciate a change of topics."

"I could use some work done on our house, Smith." Hal buttered his roll, apparently determined to return the conversation to Jacob. "Once you're finished here, I'd appreciate it if you'd take a look. Maybe you could teach me and those sons of mine to handle some carpentry."

Jacob shifted in his seat. "Not sure how long that'll be. Most likely I'll move on after I'm finished here."

Not news, but still Jacob's words banged against her heart. As soon as Jacob repaired her house, he would leave.

"Too bad you're moving on. Lots of buildings in town could use repairs, new roofs. There's enough work here to keep an honest man busy for years."

Mildred patted Jacob's hand. "Maybe Jake will change his mind. The Granger place over on Harmony could use some attention. The roof leaks like a slotted spoon. After Elmer died, Louise took in boarders for a while, but didn't earn enough to keep the place up."

"I arrested one of her boarders for forgery, a man from out of town." Hal leaned back in his chair and gave a smug grin. "Found his face on a wanted poster."

Jacob's mouth flattened. He quickly wiped it with his napkin, averting his gaze.

"A squirrel got in there once. The poor thing tore the parlor curtains and upholstery to shreds," Elise said. "That squirrel was the talk of the town."

Loretta grinned. "Louise asked me to trap the varmint. I suggested she just open the door, but she was afraid that the squirrel's pals might see it as an invitation."

"Houses in Peaceful have more stories than floors." Mildred grinned. "Just imagine what we could learn if lumber and plaster could talk."

The sheriff nodded. "The McGuire place at the edge of town has this big old tree, once used to hang a man."

Loretta wagged a finger at her husband. "That's hardly dinner-table conversation, Hal. There's a difference between trapping squirrels and stringing up a man."

"I apologize, ladies. Such talk is routine in my line of work. I forget the sensibilities of the womenfolk."

"No need to apologize on my account," Mildred reassured him. "It's only natural you'd remember houses involved in crime."

Loretta glanced at Jacob. "Any houses with tales to tell where you grew up, Jake?"

"I wasn't interested in houses until I got into construction."

Hal glanced at Jacob. "Where's the construction company where you worked located?"

Lifting a forkful of potatoes toward his mouth, Jacob's hand stilled. "Bloomington."

Elise gasped. "Indiana? Callie, isn't that the hometown of the unwed pregnant girl you said would be arriving soon?"

"Yes, someone in Bloomington knows someone, who knows someone who knows me." She grinned. "I'm expecting a letter any day now with the date of her arrival."

Under his tan, Jacob paled. Callie frowned. If the arrival of someone from where he'd lived upset him, he must have something to hide. His skittish behavior suggested that he'd felt more on trial than carefree, as if he had something to fear from the law.

As Callie walked to the kitchen for dessert, she knew her attempt to give Jacob a nice evening had failed. And worse, all the evening had accomplished was to put a large knot of mistrust of Jacob Smith twisting inside her.

Dinner churning in his stomach, Jake all but applauded when he saw the pie heading his way. Dessert meant the meal would soon end and he could leave. During dinner, Frederick had quizzed him several times, real friendlylike, as if his answers didn't matter. Jake knew better.

Worse, an unwed mother would soon arrive in Peaceful from the town where he'd been arrested and found guilty. She might recognize his name, even his face, since the story had hit the papers. He had to get out of town before she arrived.

A knock sent Callie to answer the door. "Commodore, come in," she said, her voice carrying to the dining room.

"You've got company. I don't want to interrupt. Dorothy asked me to drop off this sack of Martin's baby things. Said to tell you that she aired and washed them."

"Thank Dorothy for me. I'm glad my baby will get to wear his father's things. Join us for a piece of cherry pie." Callie tugged Commodore into view. "You know everyone."

Mildred smiled a welcome. "Commodore, settle a

quarrel for us. Who owned the Adams place when you were a boy?"

Frederick pulled a chair up to the table and gestured to Commodore. "Have a seat."

As Callie hurried to get his pie, her father-in-law looked like he'd rather be anywhere else, but he sat. Everyone greeted him, followed by an awkward pause.

"Reckon that would be the Prendergast family," Commodore said. "John Prendergast was one of the town's first settlers."

"That's what I thought," Mildred said. "What a relief to get something right for a change."

Callie sighed. "You don't forget as much as I do."

"That happens to expectant mothers," Loretta said. "I remember my brain turning to mush with our two." Loretta leaned toward Jake. "All evening, I've had the feeling I know you from somewhere."

The bite of pie Jake had swallowed caught in his throat. He gulped it down. "Can't imagine where."

"Your face looks so familiar."

"I've never been to Peaceful before. I probably remind you of someone."

"You do, but I can't think who." A puzzled frown furrowed Loretta's brow.

"Good to know I'm not the only one with a lagging memory, though I rarely forget a face, especially a handsome face." Mildred patted Jake's hand. "If I'd seen Jake before, I would've remembered. Now names… don't always stick."

"This house sat empty all my life," Elise said. "Who owned it before you, Callie?"

"I'm not sure."

Mildred smiled. "Wesley Squier, an Indiana state

senator built this house, one of the finest in these parts, even in the state. Strangest thing—the family moved out in the middle of the night."

"Why would someone do that?" Elise asked.

Frederick scooped a bite of pie onto his fork. "No *good* reason I can think of. Did they leave a pile of debts?"

"No, nothing like that. They were upstanding citizens." Mildred frowned. "A fancy Realtor over in Indianapolis tried to sell the house for years, but big-city folks didn't hanker living in what they saw as a Podunk town. And the price was bigger than Peaceful's purses. So it sat empty."

"Until it got into such terrible shape that the house was sold at auction for next to nothing." Callie smiled. "I'm grateful. Otherwise Commodore and Dorothy couldn't have bought it for our wedding present."

"I heard gossip about why the Squier family left but that's all it was—gossip," Mildred said.

Commodore snorted. "People like to talk. What they don't know, they make up."

Elise's gaze dropped to her lap. "Gossip's a terrible thing."

"Yes, it is," Mildred said. "I make a point not to repeat it. I'm glad Callie's giving this beautiful old house new life. And Jake here is handling the renovation."

Why had the Squier family moved out of the house? Did they have a daughter? Perhaps Jake should talk to Mildred, see if she'd open up about the gossip she'd heard. No matter what she said, most people couldn't resist wagging their tongues. He'd offer to do some chore. See what she knew.

Commodore rose. "This house should've been left

to rot. You all enjoy your pie." Though he hadn't taken a bite of his, he left the dining room.

The front door slammed. No one said a word.

Jake supposed he could understand Commodore Mitchell's resenting the house he blamed for his son's death. But each time he condemned it, he stomped on his daughter-in-law's heart.

As the tension of Commodore's remark ebbed, conversation resumed. Yet, for some reason Jake couldn't decipher, a whisper of questions hung in the air.

Callie and Elise hugged Loretta and Mildred goodbye. Jacob shook hands with Hal, then headed to the kitchen to start the dishes, a generous offer, but one Callie wished she'd refused. She wanted Jacob gone. Too much about him raised questions.

Callie closed the door after her departing guests and glanced at Elise. In her last weeks of pregnancy, the poor thing looked limp as a wrung-out dishrag. Callie gave her a gentle push toward the stairs, sending her up to bed, then walked to the dining room.

As she loaded glasses onto a tray, she reconsidered Jacob's behavior. Perhaps she was unfairly suspicious, a fault of hers, when he might just be a private man who didn't open up easily. Most people had painful circumstances in their pasts they'd rather not dwell on. Like Martin's fall. Like Nell's tragedy. Like her family's destruction.

Still, she didn't trust a man who kept to himself. If she had any sense, she'd ask him to leave and handle the dishes alone. Yet, the prospect of spending time with him sent her pulse skittering and her aching feet to the kitchen.

Jacob stood at the sink, the sleeves of his shirt rolled up to the elbow, his hands submerged wrist-high in suds. The shadow of a beard defined his rugged jaw.

As he scrubbed a plate, muscles in his back rippled beneath the shirt tucked into his trim waist. Her gaze moved lower to slim hips and long legs. Gulping, she quickly looked away, determined not to give in to these wild feelings of attraction to a man she didn't trust. Hands shaking, she planted the tray of glasses on the counter with a clunk.

"Nice party," he said, glancing over at her with a smile.

"You didn't look like you were having a good time."

"Formal meals aren't normal in my world. But I enjoyed the evening. I've never had better food."

Pleased that he'd at least enjoyed her cooking, she wouldn't argue the point. "You appear to know your way around a kitchen."

"Washing dishes was one of my chores at the orphanage."

"I'm sorry there are so many." She gave a nervous laugh. "Aunt Hilda complained that I could dirty every pan in the kitchen just making toast."

Grinning, he lifted a hand dripping suds, indicating the waiting stack. "This little batch will be a cinch."

Martin would never have helped with what he'd called woman's work. He never put himself in another's shoes—especially a woman's shoes. To have Jacob's assistance in the kitchen left her rattled, as if her world had tilted and she couldn't get her bearings.

Taking a deep breath, she focused on what needed doing, then proceeded to cover bowls of leftovers with plates and put them in the icebox. Then she grabbed a towel to dry the plates draining on the counter.

He turned toward her, letting his gaze roam her face. "You look tired. But pretty," he added as if afraid he'd hurt her feelings.

"I hadn't thought about it, but I suppose I am." Inside her shoes she wiggled her toes and winced. "My feet hurt."

"We can't have that."

He dried his palms, then took the towel from her hands, ushered her to the table and pulled out a chair, gently guiding her into it. Then he knelt and cupped her foot. Before she could protest, he removed one of her shoes, then the other.

Callie's heart galloped like a runaway horse. "I, uh, my shoes aren't as comfortable now that my feet have started to swell."

Why had she said such a personal thing?

"I can see that."

The concern she heard in his voice and the gentle, caring expression on his face heated hers. What was this man doing to her with just a look?

Moonlight filtered through the window, highlighting his features. His woodsy scent drifted closer.

"Though from what I've seen, ladies worry about fashion more than comfort."

"I, uh, won't make that mistake again. Well, at least until after my baby's born," she finished, not sure if she made sense.

With still-damp hands, he encircled her right foot and massaged her toes through her stockings, something far too intimate for a man who wasn't her husband to do. She tried to retract her foot from his grasp, but his nimble fingers continued kneading her toes, sending waves of pleasure crashing through her until she almost groaned.

She should stop him. She would. "Jacob."

"Hmm?"

"You shouldn't."

But her eyelids drifted closed under his gentle, yet firm touch. His hands slid down her foot to her arch. He rubbed the curve, his fingers easing her aching bones. It was all she could do not to purr like Stripes. His hands moved to the heel, then back to her toes.

When he set her foot on his knee, her eyelids flew open. The intimacy heated her cheeks and she yanked her foot out of his grasp. "I... My feet are fine. Let's finish the dishes."

"Let me do something for you for a change."

He lifted her other foot, ministering to that one as he had the first. Each stroke of his fingers eased the throbbing in her feet and fulfilled her need to be cared for. A need she hadn't known she possessed. Since adulthood, she'd been the one to take care of others. Until now.

She reminded herself that Jacob Smith couldn't be trusted. He might be kind, considerate and hardworking, but he kept his past secret. Why? Had he been harmed by others? Had he done something evil? No, she couldn't believe him capable of harm. Was he simply a lonely man?

Whatever his past, something had brought him to town.

Jacob lowered her foot to the floor. At the loss of his touch, disappointment slid through her. A silly reaction.

He tugged her to her feet then handed her shoes to her. "Go on up to bed. I'll finish here and lock up."

His no-nonsense tone kept her from expressing her gratitude that for once, someone had eased her burden. That someone took care of Callie Mitchell, instead of the other way around.

"Are you sure, Jacob?"

"Very." His tender gaze collided with hers, and then he cupped her jaw. His touch made her wobbly on her feet. "You work too hard. It's the least I can do."

He stepped closer and closer still, until he stood mere inches away. Tiny gold flecks bordered the dark mesmerizing pupils of his eyes glittering in the lamplight, and then settling on her lips. And stayed.

"I see you every day. Every day your beauty socks me in the gut. Not just outside, but inside too, the heart of who you are. And I wonder what it would be like to hold you in my arms." His Adam's apple rose and fell. "Do you wonder that, too?"

She couldn't look away. Couldn't speak. Could only nod.

"May I kiss you?"

Every rational thought fled her mind as she looked into those clear pools of jade. And saw nothing to harm her. What if… What if Jacob Smith was the caring man he appeared to be? What if she could trust and lean on him? What if God had brought Jacob here to mend more than her house? To mend her aching heart? Knowing Jacob would turn to Him in God's time?

With all those questions burning in her mind, Callie looked at his lips—soft, full, slightly parted—waiting for her answer. The slight pressure of his hand under her jaw felt right, as no touch ever had.

She wanted his kiss. Wanted it badly. Refusing to heed the warnings churning inside her, she rose on tiptoe, the only answer she could give. As she slid her arms around his neck, her shoes clattered to the floor.

His lips captured hers. Gentle, teasing, sending shivers up her spine and curling her toes inside her stockings. He pulled her closer and she clung to him, then she raised her palms to caress the sandpaper of his jaw. The pressure of his lips grew stronger, bolder. She returned the pressure, her response to the man left her weak-kneed and wobbly.

Jacob's breathing grew rapid, matching hers. Oh, when had she ever felt like this? His fingers splayed in her hair, sending pins to the floor, unleashing her hair—and triggering her faltering common sense.

Chest heaving, gasping for breath, she pulled away from his arms. Like a starving man, his eyes devoured her. Something passed between them, something unspoken yet powerful. So powerful it frightened her.

She took a hurried step back. "Good night," she said, then fled the kitchen, leaving her shoes and the last remnant of her composure behind.

Struggling to control his breathing, his need for Callie, Jake planted his palms on the counter, hunched forward, the memory of Callie's sweet lips beneath his searing his mind. Sheer torture. Nothing had prepared him for his strong reaction to their kiss.

With shaky hands, he washed and rinsed the tumblers, almost dropping the last one as he set it on the counter, then loaded the dishpan with the pots and pans. While they soaked, he dried the tumblers, peering though the kitchen window at the patch of night sky and the stars twinkling overhead, and relived that kiss. Beneath his tense fingers, the glass squeaked.

One kiss wasn't enough. He wanted more. He wanted Callie.

He released a shuddering breath and laid the towel aside, tackling the roasting pan. Nothing in his relationship with Susan prepared him for his powerful feelings for Callie.

After sharing that kiss, a kiss that bonded him to Callie in a way he couldn't understand, he knew he would do anything for her. He'd go to the ends of the earth to protect her. To comfort her. To take care of her.

Yet, he'd read the panic in her eyes, the resolve to keep him at arm's length immediately before she stepped away and fled from him. The truth slammed against his lungs. She knew what he just now recognized. Callie was a strong, independent woman who didn't need his protection or comfort. What she needed from him, he couldn't give. Or fix. Or build.

She needed his heart.

His heart wasn't worth having.

Shriveled from years of neglect. Frozen at the hands of Susan and Lloyd's betrayal. Etched with the filth of prison.

Callie deserved more. So much more.

Why had he, even for a moment, believed they had a future together?

He hadn't robbed that store. He hadn't deserved that year in jail. What did it matter? Those who learned about his time behind bars didn't believe in his innocence. Didn't trust him.

If only he could tell Callie, be honest with her, but he didn't dare take the risk. If she reacted as others had, he would be destroyed.

But hadn't he also seen her response, that undeniable pull between them? A pull that would disappear the moment Callie knew about his past. He'd witnessed the lowest depths of man's depravity. Freed months ago, he still felt dirty. Unclean. No matter how often he scrubbed his skin.

As he finished drying the last pot, he glanced around the tidy kitchen. Nothing more to do here.

He locked Callie's house, about to return to the lean-to out back, then hesitated on the stoop. He should leave. Tonight.

That's what a smart man would do. Get out of town before the ugliness of his past touched Callie. But he couldn't leave her in the lurch. Not with all the work that still needed to be done.

Not only did the past stand between them. The future did, too. The baby Callie carried would need a strong, wise father. A Godly man. He didn't know how to create a family. He had never experienced such a thing. Didn't have that faith in God she prized. His past had taught him to run, to keep moving on before staying brought pain.

Better to remember why he came.

He entered the lean-to and dropped onto the cot, staring at the drawer that held those postcards. If he hoped to find his mother, he didn't have much time. Any day now, the unwed mother from Bloomington could arrive and expose his past.

Tomorrow, he'd look at the newspapers. See what he could find. And move on.

He released a gust of air, together with the pent-up desire to get close to Callie Mitchell.

He didn't dare. Some things were better left alone.

Chapter Eleven

Callie handed the tray loaded with plaster up to Jacob as he stood on the ladder, repairing the ceiling.

In her *bedroom*.

After the kiss they'd shared last night, she couldn't look at Jacob without her stomach fluttering like it held a bevy of butterflies. Every word, every glance and movement, multiplied her awareness of the man and their location.

The bed seemed to have doubled in size, her personal items scattered around the room—her hairbrush, robe and slippers—left her feeling edgier than chickens facing a dog in the henhouse.

As Jacob packed the crack with plaster, smoothing the edges as he worked, each stroke bunched the muscles in his arm and back. Callie's mouth went dry, yet she couldn't look away.

After last night, nothing would be the same between her and Jacob. She wanted to shrug off the significance of that kiss. Wanted to pretend that there would be no consequences from that kiss. Wanted to forget that the blood in her veins had surged with that kiss.

The truth was undeniable. She was attracted to Jacob Smith. The man was a drifter.

Without faith.

A mystery.

And worming his way into her life.

Her heart lurched. That scared her silly. She would not care about this man. Especially since he behaved as if that kiss they'd shared had never happened. Yet that kiss shouted in the silence, tightened in her shoulders and shook in her hands.

She had to do something to cut the tension stretching between them like a taut rubber band about to snap. What could she talk about? "Commodore certainly put a damper on things last night."

"The man's scowl could topple a hot-air balloon."

"He's never been an easy man. But losing his only child... That wound won't heal."

"Maybe it would, if he quit picking at the scab."

"What do you mean?"

He glanced down at her. "Instead of harping at you about giving up this house, if he'd pitch in to help, he'd fill that chink in his heart."

Good deeds, exactly as Jacob did now repairing the crack in her ceiling, fixing the porch and rails, making the house livable, doing every conceivable chore to make her life easier and in the process becoming indispensable.

Well, she wouldn't allow herself to need him that way. Hardworking didn't equal trustworthy. Trustworthy meant everything to her. So why did his presence make her feel more alive, more energized and eager to greet each new day?

"Commodore blames the house for Martin's death,"

she said, determined to keep the focus on her father-in-law and off all these thoughts about Jacob.

"Until Commodore lets that go, he'll never find peace."

Would Commodore ever find peace as long as she lived in this house? Her gaze traveled the crown molding, slid to the imposing chandelier, then dropped to the wooden floor she'd waxed until the boards gleamed. Most of the rooms in the house resembled this one—elegant, yet not fussy—and spacious, the height of the windows matching the lofty scale. The house wrapped her in a cozy cocoon of childhood memories.

She ran her hand along the windowframe in need of a fresh coat of paint. The house needed restoring, much as the unwed mothers who would fill its rooms—each with her own story, her own struggles, each with a heart—in need of mending. Here they'd find peace, acceptance and God's love. She'd see to that.

"I'm surprised that Martin's accident hasn't destroyed my love for this house, but, if anything, I cling to it more than before," she said softly.

"I've never had a place to call home, but I can see how this house reminds you of happy times with your family."

They both avoided the subject of that kiss and all it implied, pretending it meant nothing, when each small touch or glance sizzled. Still, more than attraction, more than that kiss connected them. She and Jacob knew the heartache of not having or losing family.

"You understand," she said, knowing he did, yet wishing he didn't. For that link was powerful.

As Jacob descended the ladder, her gaze locked with his. "I do." He smiled—a gentle, encouraging gift. "In some ways the house is your security and your father-in-law's adversary, or so he believes."

"With Commodore dead set against my living here, if I didn't love the house, I'd let it go rather than deal with his attitude. But the house means more to me than feeling at ease here. It provides plenty of room for Elise and her baby, and room for several unwed mothers who may need a harbor in the storm."

"Tell me why you want to open your home to these girls."

"They're wounded and desperate. I know how desperate." She swallowed against a sudden lump in her throat. "You see, my dearest friend, just sixteen years old, got with child. She and I were naive, barely knew the facts of life." She gave a wistful smile. "Nell was beautiful. Red hair, blue eyes, full of life…"

Life was fragile.

"She fell hard for a college boy home for the summer. When he returned to school, he wrote that he was engaged to someone else. Nell was devastated. She never told me about the baby. She never told anyone." Tears stung the back of her eyes. "Rather than face the shame of having a baby out of wedlock…"

The words stuck, but determined to make Jacob understand why she had to give these girls a home, she forced them out, each word scraping against her throat. "One night she slit her wrists and bled to death. Her baby died with her."

The sorrow on his face threatened to undo her. Unable to hold his gaze, she studied her hands. "The day before Nell took her life, she'd been examined by a doctor." She blinked rapidly, holding her tears at bay. "Otherwise, we'd have never known why she took her life.

"At her funeral, I made a promise. A promise that I'd never let another girl I knew go through that alone." She folded her arms across her chest. "I intend to keep that promise. These girls need someone to care about them. Someone to listen to them. Someone to help them without judging them."

Jacob cupped her face in his hands then drew her into his arms. "I'm sorry about your friend. What a tragedy. I understand why you want to help."

That Jacob's arms felt like home made Callie step away.

"But, Callie, others may not see it the same way. Housing unwed mothers will bring trouble. You've got a lot to handle as it is, without dealing with opposition from the community."

"I can't let public opinion sway me. Not when I believe this mission is from God."

The skeptical look on his face only proved what she already knew. Jacob Smith didn't have faith. Didn't understand that God could speak through His Word, through listening to His quiet voice or by providing opportunities. Proving once again that Jacob Smith was exactly the wrong man for her.

"Why do you think you need to advise me?" She thrust the plaster mixture at him and stalked toward the door. "You can handle this job alone."

Jake didn't understand Callie at all. One minute, she'd been sharing memories, even a personal tragedy. The next, she'd stomped off like she couldn't stand the sight of him. Well, he'd have no problem handling repairs to Callie's ceiling alone. Though the job would take more time, as he ran up and down the ladder to mix and carry plaster.

Though he'd only been trying to help, his warnings upset her. Even if this was a mission from God, as she'd said, did that mean she couldn't look at the facts? He'd seen enough of life and enough of this town to know that Peaceful wouldn't allow her to give unwed mothers sanctuary without resistance. Trouble was brewing, starting with that biddy at church.

Yet he admired Callie's dedication. Yes, and that very pretty mouth of hers. He sighed. How could a man think clearly when Callie Mitchell had stood mere inches away?

His heart tripped in his chest. If his mother had had someone like Callie in her life, someone to provide help instead of hindrances, perhaps she'd have kept him. Instead of leaving him in an orphanage, as if he wasn't worth the turmoil he'd caused. Why had she made that decision? He couldn't rest until he found the answer. Until he'd unlocked his past.

He just had to find the key.

Callie opened the newspaper to the Society page and a headline leaped off the page.

Callie Mitchell Opens Home to Fallen Girls

Mrs. Callie Mitchell hosted a dinner party in her home Tuesday evening, May 8. Guests in attendance were Sheriff and Mrs. Hal Frederick, Mrs. Mildred Uland, Miss Elise Langley, and newcomer Mr. Jacob Smith. Mrs. Mitchell's menu included beef roast, mashed potatoes with gravy, carrots and peas, dinner rolls and cherry pie.

Sources told this reporter that Mrs. Mitchell revealed that an unwed mother from out of town would soon take up residence in her home at 7133 Serenity Avenue. Mrs. Mitchell served a delicious meal, but her plans give this columnist indigestion.

News must be scant this week. Which of her guests had been the source? Certainly not Jacob. Elise was unlikely. That left the Fredericks or Mildred. Whoever was responsible, this item could be a blessing in disguise.

Callie had planned to wait until work on the house was completed before raising funds for the unwed mothers' home, but this publicity would give her an opening she needed. Or breed more opposition. If so, what choice did she have? The time had come to seek community support. She'd go to the town fathers, to the newspaper with a plea for backing.

But first she'd talk to Pastor Steele. If trouble brewed, perhaps he'd help stem the tide of negative opinion.

Lord, again I ask, if this endeavor is in Your will, please provide as only You can.

No time like the present. She grabbed her purse, slapped her hat on her head, drove a hatpin through the crown, and then tugged on her gloves.

As she left the house, Jacob strode up the walk, his long strides swallowing the distance between them, a smile lighting up his face. He took her breath away.

"Looks like you're heading out. Mind if I walk along? I need to stop at the Mercantile and get supplies to fix that chimney."

"I'll pay for them." Callie dug through her purse. "Any idea how much?"

He laid a hand on hers. "I'll take care of it."

"I can afford to handle the expense of materials." She frowned. "What I can't afford is to pay you a wage."

"Who'd want money and lose the great deal I have? I like eating at your table..." His gaze locked with hers. "...and having you near."

The intensity of his regard rippled through her. "I... I like that, too."

And she did. Too much. She forced a light tone. "I may not be back until time to fix supper. Don't worry. You'll get your next meal."

"I look forward to it."

Callie fought the desire to be that woman Jacob looked forward to. She wouldn't get wrapped up in a man who didn't love God.

They parted ways at the corner of Liberty and Serenity. He gave her one last lingering look, then turned west toward the Mitchell Mercantile. With her heart thudding in her chest, evidence that Jacob meant more to her than she wanted to admit, she turned east toward the church.

She found Pastor Steele in his office, preparing his sermon for Sunday. She took the chair across from him.

He gave her a warm smile, the kind of smile that welcomed confidences. "What do you have on your mind, Callie?"

"Perhaps you read in the Society page that another unwed mother will soon arrive at my home."

"I did." He chuckled. "Which I suspect has something to do with why you're here."

Callie leaned forward in her chair. "I'm here to ask

you to support my plan to house unwed mothers, to provide for their needs and give them shelter from reproach."

"I applaud your plan. Too often these girls are thrown to the lions." He sighed. "And the babies' fathers go their merry way." He fiddled with the fountain pen on his desk. "Has it occurred to you that Peaceful might not welcome this home?"

The concern in his eyes dampened Callie's enthusiasm, but only for a moment. "I suspect a few will criticize, one in particular."

"We both know who that would be."

"But isn't that always the case with something new?"

"You make a good point. Far be it from me to try to talk you out of what I believe is an important calling. But I need to warn you that it's possible more than a few will oppose this." He sighed. "Plenty of believers feel sinners deserve reproach. That they've broken God's commandments and should be ostracized. They forget the command, 'Judge not, that ye be not judged.'"

How could she ask? "Could you preach a sermon that would take a stand welcoming these girls to our community?"

"I'll preach on judging others, on forgiving others. Sermons based on God's Word. I can't endorse the unwed mothers' home from the pulpit, but I'll give my time and a donation and hope others will do the same." He peered at her over his glasses, then shoved them up his nose. "Human nature being what it is, I'll be praying this doesn't divide our congregation."

With the pastor's prayers and her own, surely God wouldn't allow that to happen. "I'll do the same. I'd hoped everyone could see the value of helping these girls."

"Everyone rarely agrees on anything, even the meaning of Scripture." He grabbed a sheet of paper. "There's much to consider here. If one of these girls leaves her baby after it's born, just slips away in the dead of night, you'll need the services of a lawyer."

Pastor Steele's words put a knot in Callie's stomach. She hadn't even considered such a possibility.

He wrote a name and address on the page. "I recommend a fine man in Indianapolis who can advise you. Write and explain what you're planning. He'll know the legalities involved."

"Oh, thank you." Callie took the sheet. "I'm going to have to keep you stocked in pie."

"If any of these young women are struggling with tough issues like incest and rape, I'll be available to counsel them. With God's help, I'll try to help them find peace."

If only Nell had talked to her pastor.

Pastor Steele rubbed a hand over his eyes. "I suppose you could find yourself housing a prostitute."

Callie gasped.

"You'll need to make the rules crystal clear. Nothing illegal or immoral can go on while those young women are under your roof."

She'd need a list of house rules. Something she hadn't considered.

Pastor Steele took a look at Callie's face, then came around the desk and perched on the corner. "God has called you to this, but that doesn't mean you can ignore the important details of such an undertaking."

"You've given me a lot to think about. And act on." She released a breath. "I feel overwhelmed."

He smiled. "I feel the same way much of the time."

"All I know to do is take it one girl, one day at a time."

"When we're doing God's work, we can expect opposition. But these women will be blessed to have you on their side." He pulled a chair next to hers. "Shall we pray about this unwed mothers' home? Ask God to provide everything you need to make it a reality, including wisdom and support."

After the prayer, Callie left the church filled with peace. They'd asked God for His help. With His power, she'd strive to anticipate and deal with every obstacle, every problem. But, ultimately, the outcome rested with Him.

Pastor Steele would prepare hearts and counsel those who needed him. Mildred would donate funds to support it—Callie was sure of it. Perhaps even Commodore would contribute items to clothe fatherless babies.

Callie headed home, eager to share Pastor Steele's reaction with Elise. Perhaps even with Jacob. He'd lived in an orphanage. Surely he'd be pleased to hear that the pastor had given her counsel and supported her plan.

Jake finished his errand in town and arrived back at Callie's house, toting a bag of cement. A load of bricks would be delivered tomorrow. He saw no activity around the place, then remembered that Elise was visiting her mother. Callie hadn't returned from town. And shouldn't for a while, giving him the perfect opportunity to examine the newspapers.

He entered the house by the back door and strode to

the main hall, then on toward the library. The door was closed. Not unusual with Callie's dislike of clutter. Inside he discovered that the piles had been separated by decades. Much easier to find what he wanted. Within minutes he found the year and month of his birth. To make sure he didn't miss a birth announcement, he'd check June as well.

He carried a stack to a chair and went over each one with painstaking care, searching for anything that would give him a clue to his identity.

And came up with nothing.

No one by the name of Smith appeared to have lived in the town. Had his mother given him an alias when she left him at the orphanage? If that were true, what was the likelihood that she'd stay in town to give birth? The only baby born on May 21, 1877 was a girl. If that was even the year he was born.

He rose and returned the stack to the desk. What to do next? With the newspapers a dead end, he'd talk to Mildred Uland, the woman most likely to know town gossip, especially from twenty-three years ago.

"What are you doing?"

Jake jerked toward the open door. Callie. He hadn't heard her enter the room. He stepped away from the desk. "I uh, thought I'd kill some time looking at these newspapers. Hope you don't mind."

Her accusing gaze locked with his. "Why didn't you ask permission?"

"I didn't think it mattered." He took in her tight mouth and the pucker between her slim brows. "Obviously, I was wrong."

She shoved back her shoulders. "Why go behind my back? I would have gladly shown you the papers."

"I'm sorry, I didn't realize you'd be upset."

"After that kiss… After what we've shared, I thought I could trust you. Obviously, I was wrong."

Jake wanted to deny her claim, to tell her she could trust him. To tell her the reason he needed to look at the newspapers. But if he did, she'd want to know more. He couldn't risk telling her everything.

By the look in her eyes, he'd not only made her mad, he'd hurt her. He hadn't meant to, but saying that wouldn't impress Callie. If anything, his denial would make her angrier.

A man's actions proved his trustworthiness.

From the frown puckering her brow and the icy chill in her eyes, she wanted him gone. He had money enough to stay somewhere else, but he wanted to be here, to make this house habitable for her and for Elise. With that crumbling, faulty chimney that risked their safety, he had to say something to ease her disquiet.

"I'm sorry. I should've asked first." He motioned to the newspapers. "I was looking for information on the Odd Fellows' building downtown. The edifice is unique, made me think of the work of an architect my boss talked about."

The guardedness in her eyes didn't ease.

He'd just lied to Callie. And she knew it.

"I want you to leave."

Her words cut into him like a knife. "I can't. Not yet. The chimney isn't safe. If it isn't fixed, you risk being overcome by carbon monoxide."

A flash of consternation swept across her face. "Nothing would make me happier than seeing you go. But I need to ensure the house's safety." She folded her arms across her chest. "We'll forget this happened." She turned to go, then pivoted back. "This time."

He heard the warning. She'd given him another chance.

If only he'd been able to tell Callie the real reason he'd needed to look at the newspapers. But if he did, she'd want to help. She'd want to get involved. She'd want to get close.

And that meant she'd learn the truth. The truth of who Jacob Smith really was. That he'd spent almost a year in prison. That *Smith* might not even be his real name. That a jury of his peers had judged him a loser.

But when Callie had looked at him, he'd seen a different reflection in her eyes. A faith in him that made him feel seven feet tall, instead of like a lowly worm. She'd made him believe in himself, something he'd lost.

If she discovered that he was a former convict, that look of respect he'd seen in her eyes would disappear forever. Better to endure her ire, and hope she'd forgive him, than lose her regard.

Callie watched Jacob leave the house and walk to the barn. His shoulders hunched like he carried the weight of the world on his back. She felt the same way. Until he repaired the chimney, she would try to put the incident with Jacob behind her.

What choice did she have? Unless the flue was repaired, fumes could kill them all this winter. She couldn't take such a risk. A list of jobs he'd planned to do paraded through her mind. The windows on the north side of the house needed replacing. The house needed to be scraped and it needed a coat of paint. Nothing hazardous there, but the possibility that the house wouldn't be returned to its former glory sank inside her.

Jacob had entered her home without permission. He'd only needed to ask to see the newspapers. That he hadn't asked left no doubt in her mind. His excuse for examining the newspapers had nothing to do with architecture and everything to do with concealment.

Concealment had been Martin's forte. Her throat tightened as memories raced through her mind. Martin had hidden his selfish nature behind a jolly exterior. He'd hidden overspending, keeping bills from her until a storekeeper in town would ask her for payment. He'd hidden his frequent absences from work to go fishing and hunting by telling Commodore he was sick or handling a chore for her. A chore he never intended to do. Time after time, he'd lied to her. Each time had chipped away at her respect for her husband. Caught red-handed, he'd always been sorry.

Just like Jacob.

She'd thought Jacob Smith was the exact opposite of Martin—hardworking, dependable, a man who meant what he said. How wrong she'd been.

Loretta had said Jacob looked familiar. A chill snaked down Callie's spine. Could she have seen Jacob's face on a wanted poster?

No, Jacob might be devious, might not be the man she thought, but he wasn't a criminal.

Then what was he up to?

She'd thought they might have a future together. What a fool she'd been to even consider a relationship with a man without faith. With a man who kept things hidden. With another man who concealed his true nature.

She'd thought Jacob's past had left him wounded. That he didn't want to open that pain to others. Now she questioned the motive for his secrecy. Did he have a more sinister reason for not opening up and sharing his past?

The attraction between them was undeniable. Well, she wouldn't act on it. How could she have started to care for the wrong man?

Again?

Once he made the repairs on her house, he would leave, exactly as she wanted it. Her breath caught. Who was being dishonest now? For when he did, Jacob would take a piece of her heart with him.

That was all he'd get. She'd protect the rest with every particle of her will. And never let Jacob Smith get close again.

Chapter Twelve

Callie greeted Loretta, stepping aside to let her in.

Across the way, Jacob hauled bricks in a wheelbarrow toward the barn—no doubt, preparing to repair the faulty flue in her chimney. At the sight of him, her heart skipped a beat. She quickly looked away, tamping down the silly reaction to a man who was all wrong for her. A man who deceived. A man without faith.

Loretta handed Callie a basket of muffins, still warm from the oven, then wrapped Callie in a hug, eyeing her. "You're upset about something."

"Actually, I've had a good day." Until her run-in with Jacob, her statement was true. For some reason, Callie couldn't share Jacob's uninvited entrance into her house and obvious lie with her friend.

"Any special reason?"

"The water's hot. Join me for a cup of tea and one of these muffins." She inhaled. "They smell wonderful."

While Callie prepared a pot of tea, Loretta leaned against the counter, fiddling with the button on her dress. "How are you feeling?"

"Fine." Callie smiled. "Great, in fact. I'm not so tired these days."

With Callie carrying the pot and Loretta following with cups and napkins, Callie led the way to the table in her sun-drenched, sprawling kitchen.

As they took their seats, Loretta turned to her with a grin. "That handsome handyman of yours is getting more done in a few weeks than Hal accomplishes all year. Does he help with the chores?"

"He does." She wanted to deny that Jacob made her life easier, but she couldn't. Helpful or not, if Loretta knew the reservations Callie had about Jacob, she'd insist that Callie send him packing.

Callie would, as soon as he repaired the defective chimney. Others in town could do the repair, but the money to pay them would deplete funds needed for the unwed mothers' home.

Loretta lost her smile. "I saw the mention of your dinner party on the Society page and the columnist's reaction to your unwed mothers' home. That's why I'm here."

"I knew you'd want to help. Could you handle the funds while I took care of the details of housing the girls? We—"

Loretta raised a hand, cutting Callie off. "Before you get too far, let me explain. I didn't want to say anything in front of Elise, but I can't support your plan."

"You've been kind to Elise. I assumed..."

"Callie, its one thing to take in Elise, a neighbor girl we all love, but to bring total strangers with who knows what kind of pasts into your home is risky. Perhaps Hal's job makes me wary, but I'm afraid of what this unwed mothers' home will bring to our town."

"I thought you'd be my biggest supporter. Might help with fundraising." She sighed. "Everyone in town listens to you."

"I'm sorry. But, to speak frankly, I think your idea is crazy."

Loretta's words landed in her stomach like a stone. "Why?"

"A home for unwed mothers will cause trouble. Trouble this town doesn't need. Right now we have a close-knit community. People will take sides. One thing will lead to another until Peaceful is anything but."

"Once people get used to the idea, they'll see the importance of providing a refuge for these girls."

Loretta's eyes narrowed. "Those girls could be lawbreakers, have arrests or jail sentences in their pasts. We can't risk opening our children or this community to riffraff."

"Riffraff?" Callie's cup hit the saucer with a clink, splashing tea onto the table.

"Right now Hal doesn't do much to ensure the peace. Other than an occasional fracas in the saloon, the cells in the jail sit empty. That's the way we want to keep it."

"I want the same thing." She laid a hand on Loretta's sleeve. "You're overreacting. I'm taking in young women, not hardened criminals."

"Your heart is in the right place, but I can't go along with this idiocy."

"Have you prayed about it?"

"No, I guess I haven't." She moved her arm away. "But don't think making me feel guilty will change my stance. I have personal reasons for objecting to this unwed mothers' home."

"Like what?"

"Our boys are seventeen and eighteen, at that age when… Well, when young ladies are fascinating creatures. They're inexperienced and fool enough to fall for some girl's helpless charms. One or both could offer marriage to solve a need for a daddy for her baby and a husband to take care of her bills."

"Then tell your sons not to get involved with them."

Loretta harrumphed. "You have a lot to learn about parenting. Our boys are at an age when telling them what to do will only make them sneak around to do just the opposite."

"These girls will have been burned. I doubt they'll be hunting for a man, but—"

"You're naive. Who knows why these girls end up pregnant? Their babies could be the result of rape, even incest. Or maybe they'd slept with several men and have no idea who fathered their babies."

"You're expecting the worst, but—"

"Okay, let's give them the benefit of the doubt." Loretta rose and paced the floor, then stopped in front of Callie. "They've made a mistake like Elise. They're good girls who want to start over. And give their babies a happy life. But you can't know which kind of girl will be coming to your home. If you expect them to be honest about their pasts, you're mistaken."

Callie had to convince Loretta of the worth of her endeavor. "Sit down, please. Let's talk calmly about this."

Loretta did as Callie asked, but with a frown on her face.

"The Bible tells us to love our neighbor. Sometimes giving that neighbor what he needs is a risk, as it was for the Good Samaritan. While he ministered to the injured man, he could've been beaten and robbed. But he didn't consider the cost. Instead, he gave his time and his money to see that the man received good care and recovered fully."

Loretta threw up her hands. "The Good Samaritan stumbled across the victim. He didn't go looking for someone in trouble."

"Loretta, surely you remember what happened to Nell." Unable to continue, she bit her lip.

"I do. And I'm sorry, Callie, but surely you care about my sons more than girls you've never met. Give up this plan for George and Henry's sakes."

"Your boys know right from wrong. And who's to say—maybe these girls will be God's answer for their wives."

Loretta gasped.

Callie took Loretta's hand. "You don't really believe these girls deserve forgiveness, do you?"

"You're wrong. I'm not judging them. I'm afraid of where this will lead."

"All I know is that you're putting up roadblocks to these girls' chance to start over. To be loved while they carry and deliver their babies. Whether you see them as a mistake or not, these babies are created by God."

"Are you being honest with yourself? Is concern for these girls the real reason you want to do this? Or are they replacing the family you've lost?"

Callie winced. Loretta's words stung like a slap in the face. Yet she'd heard the truth in them. Her motive for the unwed mothers' home might not be as Godly as she'd thought, but that didn't make her decision wrong.

"It's true that I love having Elise with me. The house was like a tomb before she moved in. But the promise I made Nell at her funeral is my reason for this step.

I'd even talked to Martin about it. Not that his reaction was any better than yours."

"You can't know that these girls won't come to a horrible end, like Nell. If so, you'll be left to pick up the pieces."

"I can't run my life expecting the worst." She shivered, suddenly unsure if she could handle the job.

"I'm sorry, but my sons and the other young people in town are more important to me than these girls. Their loose behavior could spread like a rotten apple through a bushel. Our children might think intimacy before marriage is acceptable." Loretta rose. "Too much is at stake. I will fight you on this."

"What will you teach your children by your stand? That you don't trust them to do what's right? That you won't heed God's leading if doing so involves risk?"

Loretta's jaw jutted. "I'll do anything to protect my boys. You'll understand that better when your baby arrives."

Tears sprang to Callie's eyes. "You believe I'd make decisions that would harm children? I'm trying to help children."

"I'm sure your intentions are good, Callie. We both know where they lead."

With that her friend left by the back door. Without sharing their usual hug. The unwed mothers' home had put a rift between them. A rift that might never heal.

Oh, Lord, am I doing the right thing? Am I following Your will? Is my unwed mothers' home contrary to Scripture?

In the parlor, she pulled her Bible from the table and onto her lap. Grateful for privacy, she looked up Scriptures about orphans, about Jesus's treatment of prostitutes and sinners of every variety. Nothing she found convinced her that caring for these girls displeased God.

Quite the opposite.

In the back of her mind, a nagging worry took hold. Would this unwed mothers' home split the community? Peaceful had been good to her, had rallied around her. The possibility of her friends and neighbors turning against her twisted in her stomach.

What if Loretta was right that her motivation for establishing this home was to fill the hole in her heart rather than to fulfill a need for these girls?

Right motivation or not, she felt called by God to house unwed mothers. How could she refuse? She would obey. No matter what the cost.

Lord, help me be strong. Strong enough to handle the job.

Except for God, she might be handling it alone.

Callie sat across the table from Elise. Rain poured down the kitchen windows, all but hiding the outbuildings from view. Jacob had mentioned that the roof of the lean-to leaked during the last rain. He'd been too busy repairing her chimney and cracked ceilings to see to his own comfort. Here she sat in a snug, leak-free house, thanks to him. Even if she was still upset by the excuse he'd made for sneaking into her house, she couldn't allow Jacob to stay out there getting drenched.

"You should invite him in."

Callie turned toward Elise, her stomach fluttering at the prospect of having Jacob in the house again. In this kitchen. The place where he'd massaged her feet. But she wouldn't admit that to Elise. "You read my thoughts. Will you make some popcorn while I go out to the lean-to and invite him?"

"I'll get out the dominoes, too."

Callie wrapped her fringed shawl around her shoulders, grabbed the umbrella and slipped out the door, raising the umbrella over her head. Picking her way between puddles, she arrived at the lean-to door and knocked. "Jacob, it's Callie."

The door opened to the ping of water hitting metal buckets. One pail sat in the middle of the floor. The other stood between her and Jacob like a sentry. Her heart squeezed at the dismal cramped space where he spent his nights.

Jacob planted a hand against the frame and leaned toward her, his muscles bulging through the sleeve of his shirt. "Hi," he said flashing a lazy grin. The hollow in his cheek put a hitch in her breathing and rooted her to the spot. "Why are you braving this downpour?"

"You can't stay out here with the roof leaking. Come up to the house. Elise is making popcorn."

"Are you sure you trust me inside?"

She heaved a sigh. "I trust you inside the house, or I wouldn't have invited you. But that doesn't mean I believe your excuse for looking at the newspapers."

"I'm sorry, Callie. I shouldn't have lied."

She waited. No explanation came. What was he hiding? "You're not going to tell me why, are you?"

"Can you just trust that I have my reasons? Good reasons that I'm not able to share with you. Not yet."

Her eyes traveled his face, searching for furtiveness but seeing only candor. Yet, his admission didn't provide the answers she needed. She couldn't force him to confide in her, but she wouldn't open her heart to a secretive man.

"I guess I'll have to. Let's go before we both get soaked."

He shrugged into his jacket, then took the umbrella and wrapped an arm around her, shielding her with his body. As they navigated the puddles to the house, the heat from his skin drew her to him like a moth to a flame. She knew where that led.

Inside, Elise greeted them along with the aroma of popcorn. Elise dished up the snack into a large bowl, Jacob poured apple juice while Callie gathered napkins.

Elise set the bowl on the table. "Did you feel like a drowned duck in that leaky lean-to?"

"A smidgeon," Jacob admitted with a grin. "But my feathers are well-oiled."

Elise giggled. "At least you're not waddling like me." She proceeded to do a good imitation of a duck, as she moseyed to her seat.

Laughing at her antics they all sat and turned the dominoes black side up.

With Jacob at her side, taking up more space than a mere man should, the intimacy of their last private moment in the kitchen rose between them like a living, breathing thing. Callie vowed she'd never make the mistake of being alone with him again.

Her hand brushed Jacob's as they both reached for popcorn and every rational thought fled. Why did the slightest touch of this secretive man affect her this way?

"Remember you score if the dots total anything divisible by five." Elise laid down double-fives, grinning from ear to ear. "That makes ten." She wrote the number under her name. "I have a feeling I'm going to win."

"We'll see about that," Jacob said, plunking down a piece with five on one end, ten on the other. "That makes twenty."

Elise harrumphed and wrote the number under Jacob's name. "Are you sure you haven't played dominoes before?"

"Not this way." He grinned. "But it doesn't seem hard."

Callie had no play. Moaning, she drew a domino. This one played. She added her piece to the string of dominoes but didn't make any points.

Eyes dancing with mischief, Jacob rearranged his dominoes and cocked his head to her, looking handsomer than a man should. "Looks like things aren't going well for you."

"As if you care," she said, rolling her eyes.

As Elise studied her options, Jacob's gaze locked with hers. "Oh, but I do. More than you know," he said.

At his words, Callie's heart skipped a beat. His jade eyes continued to burn into hers with an intensity that left her insides quivering like a field of grain on a blustery day. To avoid his eyes and cool the heat in her veins, she reached for her glass of apple juice and practically drained its contents in one long swallow.

"You must be thirsty," Jacob said. "Let me get you more."

"It's the popcorn," she choked out.

About to make her play, Elise furrowed her brow. "Did I add too much salt?"

"No, a hull got stuck in my throat. I'm fine now."

Jacob leaned toward her. "I'd hate to lose a player to a hull injury, especially a player who looks to be losing."

While Jacob continued to grin as if he knew exactly

what was bothering her, he proceeded to add a domino. "Give me twenty more points," he said, sending a satisfied smirk in Callie's direction.

"You sound mighty sure of yourself, Mr. Smith."

Cocking his head, he eyed the line of dominoes in front of her. "The evidence is hard to deny, Mrs. Mitchell."

She laid down a double-ten. "That'll be twenty-five." Folding her arms, she smiled at Jacob.

"Appears you're getting the hang of it."

"I'm not one to give up."

Jacob took her hand and gave it a squeeze. "One of the many things I admire about you," he said, then released it.

Leaving Callie feeling bereft, which made no sense at all. She would concentrate on the game. Not that the outcome would've mattered one whit normally. But tonight, she couldn't let him best her.

"Papa likes to play dominoes." Elise put out her piece then lifted her eyes to Callie's. "I miss him."

"Have you thought about going home for a visit, Elise? Maybe he's had a change of heart."

"He still insists I give up the baby, either to a married couple not from here or…an orphanage."

"If your father ever spent time in an orphanage, he'd change his mind about having his grandchild there."

Elise sighed. "He's so upset he doesn't act like my baby's even human, much less his grandchild."

Callie took Elise's hand. "I'm praying that your father will change his mind once the baby arrives. Who couldn't help but love a newborn?"

"Oh, thank you. I hope you're right." Elise turned to Jacob. "What was it like in the orphanage, Jake?"

"Life was regimented. We were lined up and marched to meals that we ate in silence." He gave a wry smile. "Nothing resembling your meals, Callie. We didn't starve, but we came close. There never seemed to be enough food."

Jacob had gone hungry? And hadn't known the joy of conversation at mealtimes?

Elise's eyes filled with sympathy. "I had everything I needed and more."

Callie patted her hand. "We were fortunate."

"Depravation comes in many forms. We worked. We slept. No hugs at bedtime. No praise. Not that all the kids deserved it. Bullies terrorized younger kids. Disobedience was a problem. Every day some kid, sometimes several, got a switching or hit with a razor strap for serious or even slight infractions."

Callie gasped. "I've never been whipped."

Jacob grinned. "I earned a few. The belt didn't hurt as much as the lack of reconciliation afterward, no making up and being forgiven. Some kids cried most nights." He met her gaze. "You learned to be tough."

From what Callie had seen, a lesson Jacob hadn't forgotten. Everything he'd said about the orphanage twisted inside her. "Talk to Elise's father. Tell him what you've told us." She laid a hand on his. "Please."

"Maybe I will," Jacob said, playing his last domino. "Next time I need a haircut. Though, like most folks, I suspect he won't appreciate the interference."

"Can't you talk to him sooner? Elise's baby will be here before the month is out."

Jacob avoided her gaze. "I'll see what I can do."

"Thank you for trying," Elise said, then added up the scores. "Looks like Jacob won."

"Nothing to this game." Jacob grinned.

Callie cocked her head at him. "Are you sure you're a novice?"

"It was the luck of the draw," he said, trying to look humble but failing, his eyes twinkling with humor. "Or I'm a fast learner."

Callie laughed, enjoying this fun side of Jacob. But even more importantly, pleased he'd agreed to talk to Mr. Langley. "Let me know when you're going to speak to Elise's father. Elise and I will pray." An idea seized her mind and wouldn't let go. "Even better, let's pray now."

At the suggestion, Elise smiled, but Jacob looked as if he'd swallowed a persimmon. Still, she reached out her hands. Elise took her left. Jacob hesitated then took her hand in his. The solid strength of his callused hand, evidence of his occupation, filled her with reassurance. She gave him a smile, then bowed her head.

"Father God, Jacob has agreed to talk to Elise's father about his experience of living in an orphanage. We pray that Mr. Langley will listen and their talk will go well. And Lord, please meet the needs of orphans and all Your children, no matter who or where they are. Amen."

Jacob dropped her hand, as if the experience scorched his conscience. She doubted that he valued prayer. But perhaps, along with Elise's father, God would teach Jacob Smith a thing or two. She sent up a silent prayer that the experience of talking to Elise's father would somehow bring Jacob closer to God.

They'd just finished their second game when Elise yawned. "I'm tired. You'll have to play without me. I'm going to bed."

Jacob rose. "I'd better leave."

Elise walked to the window and peered out. "It's still pouring."

"A little water won't hurt me."

"Don't be silly." Callie packed away the dominoes. "Wait until the rain stops."

Elise said goodnight, then left the kitchen. The memory of the last time she and Jacob were alone in the kitchen brought Callie to her feet. She refilled the bowl of popcorn, moved about the kitchen, wiping grease off the stove, cleaning out the pan, straightening the hand towel, keeping her distance.

"Don't worry, Callie." Jacob shot her a teasing grin. "You and those pretty feet of yours are safe with me."

Her cheeks heated. "I'm not afraid of being alone with you."

"That's not what I'm seeing. I promise to keep my distance. Come sit before you wear yourself out and the wooden planks on the floor."

"You're imagining that." She set the bowl of popcorn down on the table, then took a seat across from him, careful to tuck her feet beneath her skirt.

Though every nerve in her body zinged at being alone with Jacob, a man who made her feel things she'd never felt before and didn't want to feel now, she didn't want the evening to end.

Jacob took her hand, rubbing his thumb across the palm. "I've had a wonderful time, playing a game with you and Elise, sharing a bowl of popcorn. It was like being a kid again."

She pulled her hand away. "What, ah, kind of games did you play as a boy?"

"When our chores were done and weather permitted, we played outside—kick the can, dodgeball, racing games and, of course, baseball. In winter, we had snowball fights and built forts." He chuckled. "Most of us had runny noses all winter."

"I was afraid from what you said that you never had fun."

"Kids find ways to have fun. Sometimes at others' expense, like the time we hid a frog in the silverware drawer." He laughed. "We scared the cook so badly she refused to fix our supper."

"You were an imp."

He grinned. "That's a kind description. What was it like at your aunt's?"

"Aunt Hilda liked to play board games and dominoes on winter evenings. In the summer I spent every moment I could outside playing jump rope, hopscotch, roaming around town." She giggled. "Getting into trouble."

"You?"

"No more than most kids."

"You were never punished?"

Callie laughed. "Occasionally, Aunt Hilda gave me a scolding. Once I had to sit in my bedroom without supper."

"What did you do?"

"I lied to her. I learned my lesson and haven't told a lie since."

He raised a brow. "Never?"

Their eyes locked and everything within her stilled, as a surge of connection to this man swept through her. Evidence that she was lying right now, to herself. No matter how much she wanted to deny it, no matter how wrong he was for her, Jacob Smith had gotten under her skin.

She wouldn't let him get close. Not until she knew what brought him to Peaceful and why he wanted to look at those newspapers. He'd admitted that he'd lied about his reason, but hadn't confided in her, either. Never again would she fall for a man without seeing what lurked beneath the surface.

"What about you, Jacob? Perhaps you're not telling a lie, but..." She took a deep breath, afraid of his answer. "Are you living one?"

A flicker of something lit in his eyes. He dropped his gaze. What had she glimpsed in their depths before he turned away? Something wary, something secretive, something leery.

Her breath caught. How could she have fallen for another deceiving man?

Chapter Thirteen

Jake had hightailed it out of Callie's kitchen last night before the rain had stopped, dashing to the lean-to, each footfall drenching his pant legs and his spirits. Callie had pushed to ferret out his secret, destroying the camaraderie they'd shared. Before she learned the truth, he'd finish his search for his mother and get out of town.

With a grunt, he shoved the wooden handles of the hedge shears together, cutting off the branches of the overgrown evergreens blocking Mrs. Uland's windows. A chore he'd offered to do, hoping to question her about the gossip she'd heard about the Squier family. But the search for his mother didn't preoccupy his thoughts. All he could think about was Callie.

Better to sever the relationship, as he did these branches, than to let her become involved with him, a man who'd rubbed elbows with depravity and ugliness in jail and smelled the stench of it in his nostrils still. A man who had no idea how a proper husband behaved. Or, for that matter, what it took to be a good father. Callie deserved better than him.

Not that he could take the risk of getting close, even

if he hadn't spent time in jail. He'd been burned by an indifferent foster family, a woman he'd thought loved him and an unscrupulous best friend.

As much as he felt Callie incapable of such treachery, he couldn't seem to let go of his mistrust. To avoid Callie and her questions, he'd gulped down breakfast, mentioning his plans to trim Mrs. Uland's shrubs on his way out the door. Callie hadn't tried to stop him. She knew as well as he did that Jake wasn't the man for her.

Mrs. Uland would no doubt insist on paying him, but he'd refuse. He had money, which he didn't need to use as long as he stayed in Callie's lean-to and ate at her table. But his time here was running out. Soon the unwed mother from Bloomington would arrive. Before she did, he'd be gone.

The thought of leaving drenched his good spirits like an April downpour. He tried to tell himself that his reaction had more to do with not finishing the renovations on the old Victorian than an interest in Callie.

But, no matter what Callie claimed, he'd never been a good liar. Since the age of seven, he hadn't even been able to lie to himself.

He swiped sweat from his brow in the crook of his elbow. A man had no problem staying warm working at this speed. He dumped the last armload of branches onto the tarpaulin, grabbed two ends and hauled it to the back of Mrs. Uland's lot. On a windless day, he'd burn them. Not today. He glanced toward the fast-moving clouds. Today was better suited to flying kites.

The idea of holding on to the string with Callie beside him, watching a kite soar into the sky, the tail whipping in the wind, held him in its grasp. He could visualize her delight, the huge smile she'd wear as she looked upward, holding on to her hat. He'd wrap an arm around her—

In reality, the blustery day would be better spent mucking the barn. Odors didn't linger on a day like this one. He'd handle that chore when he finished here. And forget what he couldn't have.

Jake stowed the hacksaw, clippers and tarpaulin in the small shed near the rear of her property, then walked around to the front door.

Mrs. Uland answered his knock, wrapped in a bulky shawl. "Gracious, you're a whirlwind on two legs! I'm practically dizzy from watching you. Come in, dear boy. I have coffee made."

He flicked evergreen needles from his sleeve. "I'm a mess. Just wanted to let you know I'd finished trimming your bushes. I'll burn the branches when this wind dies down."

"I've been walking between the windows, enjoying the view. My neighbors probably thank you as much as I do. All those overgrown shrubs looked like a hermit lived here with something to hide." She laughed, obviously not the least concerned about what her neighbors thought. "If you're sure you won't come inside, let me get you a cup of coffee to ward off the chill."

"Coffee sounds good."

"Sugar? Cream?"

"I like it the way it comes."

"I prefer to dress it up with both." She laughed. "My hubby said I didn't like coffee, only what went into it. He might've lived long enough to greet old age, if he'd indulged." She shot him a look. "You might want to give that a try."

He bit back a smile. "Yes, ma'am."

Accompanied by her dog Sandy, Mrs. Uland returned carrying a tray holding two mugs and a plate of gingersnap cookies sprinkled with sugar. "The older I get the more I can't tolerate the cold."

"Your windows may need caulking."

"That or my bones." Her grin crinkled the corners of her eyes. "Maybe that would stop their creaking."

Jake grinned, taking a seat in one of the wicker rockers on the porch across from Mrs. Uland's. Sandy laid his nose on Jake's leg. He gave it a pat. The porch was comfortable in the morning sun and they were somewhat protected by the wind.

He could set Mrs. Uland's house to rights in no time, but he'd move on before someone discovered his past. Though maybe this quirky dowager, who didn't appear to care what anyone thought and wasn't easily rattled, wouldn't be thrown by the news that he'd spent a year in jail. Perhaps, just perhaps, Callie wouldn't be undone by the information, either. Not that he'd take a chance by telling her.

Mrs. Uland wrapped both hands around her mug and took a sip. "This is nice. Help yourself to the cookies." She motioned to the plate on the table between them. "Don't waste them on Sandy. He's not fond of them, silly dog. My ma baked gingersnaps every week. They gave me a sore tongue, I ate so many." She chuckled. "That's what I got for being greedy. But they're still my favorites." She inhaled, closing her eyes. "The aroma makes me think of my childhood."

He took two. "I didn't realize I was hungry till I got a whiff of these." He took a bite. "They're delicious. Cookies are my favorites. At Christmas, a nearby church would bring gingerbread boy cookies to the orphanage. One for each of us."

"Ma made those, too."

"I'd prolong eating mine for as long as I could." He grinned. "I'd start with the legs, then the arms and finally the body. Left the head for last."

"Now why was that? I always ate the heads off first."

Jake shrugged. "I guess I...liked their smiles."

"You must've been a sweet little boy to care about that. You make me feel like a monster," she said with a laugh. "So we both have good memories of cookies."

A list of memories from his childhood tromped through Jake's mind: his mildewed pillow, beans of every kind, scratchy towels, limp shirts, a pile of work, the sting of a razor strap. The giant old bush behind the shed, the place disobedient boys were sent to get their punishment. He'd never smell a lilac without thinking of that bush. Odd that, now, he didn't mind the scent.

Mrs. Uland dunked another cookie into her coffee. "When you go shopping for a wife, make sure she can make gingerbread cookies. Your house will always smell like home."

To Jake, cookies—any kind of cookies—each individually made, often with kids in mind, were a small serving of affection. He used to help the cook in the kitchen, cleaning up, peeling potatoes, shelling beans. On rare occasion when cookies made the menu, she'd sneak Jake a couple of extras. He'd carry those cookies in his pockets as he'd roamed the woods or fished the pond. Just knowing he could munch on them whenever the notion struck put a smile on his face.

"Are you looking?"

"Pardon?"

"For a wife?"

"No, ma'am."

"I'm thinking Callie might change your mind about that."

Jake choked on his coffee. Curled at his feet, Sandy raised his head then lowered it again.

"Not just yet, you understand, what with her only months since Martin's death. But a woman needs a man. I'm a rudderless ship since my husband passed." She sighed. "Keeping up this house is more than I can handle. Those bushes should've been trimmed years ago, but I didn't know who to ask. Not Martin." Mildred shook her head, tsk-tsking. "He was a congenial fellow, but not partial to work."

"I got that impression."

"Take my advice. Don't say as much to Callie. She doesn't cotton to criticism of that husband of hers. I admire her loyalty. We've both lost husbands. Mine was a saint." She smiled. "I never deserved that man. The only time he made me mad was when he up and died on me, leaving me to manage without him for twenty years." She rolled her eyes Heavenward. "Or for however long it'll be before the Good Lord takes me home."

Jake didn't know how to respond to this talk of Heaven. Shifting in his chair, he let his gaze roam the house's exterior. "I'm impressed with the construction of these Victorian houses. They're solid. If properly cared for, they're almost indestructible."

"Changing the subject doesn't fool me, Jacob Smith. Call me a busybody, but you and your Maker need to have a talk."

If only he could believe. "Reckon you're right about that."

"Don't be waiting too long. As for that house of Callie's, it was hard to watch it fall into disrepair. Couldn't understand why the senator built a lovely home then left it to rot."

Here was the opportunity Jake sought. "Wonder what makes someone move under the cover of dark and never return?"

She tapped a finger against her lower lip. "None of the rumors made any sense. Some said the house was haunted." She chuckled. "Such foolishness, but people talk. Make up something if they don't know the facts." She sobered. "Another story, which makes more sense was that votes were the reason he left."

"Votes? How so?"

"He never did one thing unless he thought it'd get him a vote. Near an election, he'd attend church, faithful as you please. Sat in the front row. Once elected, he didn't darken the door, that is, till the next ballot. He'd attend Peaceful's festival in September if there was an election in November. Shake his way from gathering to gathering. But otherwise never joined in, never took part."

"Seems like people would've caught on and not reelected him."

"Reckon they thought he'd done a good enough job, but they weren't fooled, if that's what you're thinking. Folks aren't fooled long by a user." She narrowed her gaze. "Make sure you don't do the same thing, Jake. I don't know what brings you to Peaceful. I suspect you've got your reasons. An agenda, some call it, for coming and not joining in. We got enough folks living on the sidelines. Don't be one of them."

Jake felt heat climb his neck. In a couple sentences,

Mildred Uland lumped him together with Senator Squier, discrediting them both. "I'd say I've joined in by repairing Callie's house."

She raised a palm. "That work you do isn't what I mean and you know it."

Jake hated to admit that Mildred was right, even to himself, but he'd managed to stay on the sidelines most of his life.

"Now Lillian and their daughter, Irene, were nothing like the senator. They took an active part in the community."

"They only had one child?"

Mildred nodded. "Irene was a pretty little thing, petite, not much over five feet tall. Never understood why they'd uproot her with only another year till graduation from high school."

"Maybe the commute to Indianapolis got old." He took a swig of coffee.

"He didn't run for another term." She frowned. "Bothers me that I have no idea if Lillian and Irene are alive or dead. Guess that makes me nosy."

"I don't think so. When someone disappears without a word to anyone, folks want answers." He met her gaze. "Perhaps something bad happened here that ruined the house for them."

"Can't imagine what." She nibbled on a cookie, thinking. "Reckon I'll have to accept I'll never know. A mystery—that's what it is." She shook a finger his way. "Kind of like you." She turned questioning eyes on him. "You're mighty interested in the Squier family. Why is that?"

He forced a grin. "Making conversation is all. The family means nothing to me," he said, though he heard the wobble of his reply. He rose. "I'd better get to mucking out Callie's barn. Thanks for the coffee and cookies."

"Jake." Mrs. Uland held out the plate of cookies. "Take these with you." She walked to the step, Sandy at her heels, and handed them to him. "You're giving Callie's house new life. From the bounce in her step, you're giving it to her, too. Make sure you don't hurt that girl. She's had enough heartache."

"Yes, ma'am." He doffed his hat. "Thanks for the cookies."

If what Mildred said was true and Callie cared about him, even a little, he'd better hurry his search and get out of town. He would only bring Callie trouble.

As he strode toward her house, he relived the conversation. He'd said the Squier family meant nothing to him. But if Senator Squier moved his family because Irene got in a family way, that could mean she was his mother. Though he didn't have evidence to support that conclusion, he couldn't dislodge the idea from his mind. If she had given birth to him, she no longer lived in Peaceful. Where was Irene Squier now?

Mildred was obviously puzzled about that, too. Thankfully, she'd given Jake a name to go on. He'd see if he could discover why the senator gave up politics. And what had happened to the family. He might have to make a trip to Indianapolis. Whatever it took, he intended to pursue the only lead he had.

One thing he knew. If a senator's daughter had given birth to him, her family had possessed the material resources to raise him in their home, and a motive to avoid scandal.

Hiding a baby in an orphanage would've been a

convenient solution to the problem of an illegitimate grandchild. At his sides his hands fisted. Convenient and corrupt.

If Irene gave her baby up to save her father's career, then the ploy had backfired. Senator Squier hadn't run for a second term. Why?

Perhaps Jake was making too much of the family's disappearance. Yet, the fact that they'd left in the middle of the night, and appeared to have dropped out of sight, certainly raised his suspicions. What did all this speculation mean? He might be no closer to the identity of the woman who gave him life than when he first arrived in town. But he wouldn't know the truth until he investigated this new lead.

Mucking out the barn could wait. He'd head to the depot and buy a ticket for the first train to Indianapolis.

Yanking a leggy weed and tossing it to the ground, Callie wished she could do the same to Jacob. He'd finished trimming Mildred's bushes hours ago, then said he had an errand to run and left. If that errand involved purchasing supplies, he should've been back by now.

Where had he gone?

She sighed. This was yet another example of Jacob's secrecy. When they'd parted last night, she'd asked Jacob if he was living a lie. He'd laughed off the question as if she'd been joking, but from the disquiet in his eyes, he knew better.

Well, she refused to let that man ruin the joy of today. Soon another unwed mother would arrive. She'd help the newcomer get settled in and see what she could do to make Refuge of Redeeming Love feel like home.

While she waited, Callie took the opportunity to

clear dried leaves and weeds from the front flowerbed. Thankfully, the wind had died down. The bonnet she wore protected her face from the late-afternoon sun, warm through the sleeves of her dress.

Across the way, Stripes rose on his haunches and batted at a moth. A dog barked. Most likely, Sandy had treed a squirrel. A robin flew off with strands of dead grass to incorporate in its nest. All around her, Callie saw and heard the signs of life, of renewal—all part of God's plan. She loved spring.

Though she still had three months before her baby arrived, this bending and stretching was getting difficult. She chuckled, hoping she could get to her feet once she finished. Elise was off visiting her mother while her father cut hair at his shop.

Callie hoped the newcomer—Grace—would fit in. She'd grown accustomed to Elise in the house and Jacob nearby. As time went on, more women would come. Each one would affect the tone.

A sound alerted her to someone's approach.

A woman, carrying a satchel, her dark hair pulled into a severe bun, wearing a plain skirt and shirtwaist and, from her expression a chip on her shoulder. Her no-nonsense look fit Callie's image of a spinster school-marm more than an unwed mother.

The woman glanced at the newly painted sign Callie had hung that morning alongside the front door. Grace wasn't as young as Callie first thought, probably older than Callie herself.

"This is the home for unwed mothers."

"It is." Callie smiled a welcome. "You must be Grace."

She gave a cursory nod.

"If you'll give me a hand up, I'd appreciate it."

Grace took Callie's hand and with one fluid motion pulled Callie to her feet.

"Whew, you don't mess around." Callie tugged at her skirts.

"Some would say that's exactly what I did." Grace's tone held the biting edge of a well-honed knife.

The smile on Callie's face faltered. "I'm Callie Mitchell." She offered her hand, which was ignored. "Welcome to Refuge of Redeeming Love."

"How much does it cost to stay?"

"I'd ask for help with groceries if you can afford to pay. If not, you're still welcome. We share the chores."

Grace nodded, but didn't look pleased. Callie had an urge to chastise her for that haughty attitude but her conscience walloped her in the stomach. If God blessed His children according to their gratitude, there'd be far fewer rays of sunshine, drops of rain and bites to eat.

"I didn't catch your last name."

"I didn't give it."

Callie waited.

"Grace. I'm not saying more."

"Are you on the run?"

"Not from the law, if that's what you mean."

"From your family?"

"What's it to you?"

"I own this house. I don't want trouble, not here or in town. If we fail to keep the reputation of Redeeming Love spotless, I could be forced to close."

"No one's looking for me."

Every trace of disdain in her eyes evaporated, replaced with a raw pain that shut off Callie's questions. This girl needed someone to care.

"I'll show you to your room."

They walked to the house, Grace trailing a few steps behind. Along the way, Callie pointed out the location of the privy and other outbuildings. Inside, they climbed the stairs without Grace making one comment about her surroundings. A disappointment to Callie, who enjoyed seeing the house appreciated.

Sensing that the girl needed privacy, she led Grace to the back bedroom, the furthest from hers and Elise's. The space to rest, to cry, to work out whatever had happened to put that baby in her belly and bring her here.

"I hope you'll find your room comfortable."

Grace glanced at the double bed topped with a blue and white quilt, the dresser, washstand and armoire. "It's better than I expected."

Not exactly praise, but it would do. "Unpack, take a nap if you'd like. Or you might take a walk around the grounds and the house."

"I could use a nap."

"How did you get here?"

"Hitched a ride on a wagon. Walked the rest of the way."

"You must not live far."

"I won't be answering questions about where I'm from or who the father of this baby is. If that ain't acceptable, then say the word. I'll leave before I muss the sheets."

At the hostility in her voice, Callie frowned. "Who should I contact if you get sick?"

"No one cares if I live or die."

Callie folded her arms across her chest. "There are things I'll need to know."

"Like what?"

"Like how far along are you in your pregnancy?"

"Six months."

"Have you seen a doctor?"

"No."

"I'll get you in to see Doctor Wellman."

"I don't need no doctor."

"If you're worried that you can't pay, he's agreed to tend to residents of Redeeming Love whether they can afford a doctor or not."

She shrugged, as if medical care didn't matter, one way or another.

"I'd appreciate help preparing dinner. Come to the kitchen around five o'clock. It's at the back of the house behind the dining room. There's food to make, the table to set, cleanup after."

Grace's eyes turned cold. "I've worked as a domestic. I know what needs doing."

A piece of information Callie would remember. "Well, I'll leave you to unpack." She stepped toward the door. "Unless you need something before I go."

"What I need you can't give."

"Are you sure about that?"

"I'm sure."

"Well, if not me, then God can provide for your needs."

"If you're into preaching, I'm leaving."

"I don't preach, Grace. But talking about my faith is who I am. I did before you came and I will after you leave. If that's not all right with you, maybe you should walk out that door."

The young woman glanced at her feet. "I need a place to stay," she said in a subdued voice, without a trace of belligerence.

No matter what the woman claimed, Callie could provide a need—the roof over Grace's head. "I'm glad to have you."

Grace turned her back, walked to the window, all but dismissing Callie.

"Well, I'll be in the parlor. I've done all the gardening I care to for one day."

No response, as if Callie hadn't spoken. She left the room with the warnings Loretta had raised dancing through her mind. Most likely, Grace wasn't a lawbreaker. But her cold demeanor left no doubt. She wasn't interested in building relationships.

What had happened to her?

Well, whatever Grace had experienced, God had brought her here. Time would help. Affection would help. Prayer would help.

Or so Callie hoped. Yet doubts nagged at her. How would Grace's presence affect the household?

With three pregnant women under one roof, and who knew how many more to come, Callie wondered if she was equal to the task of keeping everyone's spirits up and trouble down. She'd gotten used to harmony in the house. Harmony she had no idea how to maintain.

She'd never felt more inadequate.

And more like giving Jacob Smith a piece of her mind. Just when she needed him most, the man was nowhere to be found.

A knot twisted in her stomach. When had she started relying on a drifter?

As Callie made coffee, she glanced out the window. Rays of morning sun bounced off the barn's tin roof. A glance at the kitchen calendar reminded her of the

Peaceful Ladies Club's Spring Tea later this morning. She'd agreed to bring a buttermilk coffee cake. Mercy, with the confusion of Grace's arrival yesterday, she'd forgotten the event, much less her contribution.

Donning an apron, Callie's hands stilled on the sash. This tea would be a perfect opportunity to lift Grace's spirits. Normally, she'd have obtained permission to bring guests, but all women eighteen years and older were welcome. There would be plenty of refreshments. Two more wouldn't matter.

Humming to herself, Callie set about the task. She'd use her talent for preparing food to help Grace feel welcome in the community. Along with Elise, they'd have a lovely time. And for a while forget their troubles. And have fun—something their situations may have denied them.

Callie measured flour, baking soda, baking powder and salt into the sifter then squeezed the handle back and forth, back and forth, mixing and refining the ingredients that dusted to the bottom of the crock.

God sifted his people, too, pushing them together to improve the whole. He'd used Grace's sullen attitude to show Callie that she could handle Grace's hostility. Without turning to someone exactly wrong for her. Jacob.

The man hadn't appeared for supper last night. Nor breakfast this morning. What did she care? Hadn't she learned not to rely on a man?

When Elise and Grace came into the kitchen, Callie talked long and hard to persuade Grace to attend the tea. She'd finally agreed, more to appease Elise, who wanted to go badly.

Finally, they'd dressed and walked the few blocks to

the Ladies Club. Callie carried the coffee cake. Elise wore a smile of anticipation. Grace wore that chip on her shoulder.

Inside the front door, a knot of women chatted, ooh-ing and aahing over each other's goodies.

Mrs. Sunderland noticed them first and stepped forward. "This is a private club."

Callie leveled a steely glance. "We've never turned anyone away, Mrs. Sunderland."

Coming around beside her, Loretta shot Callie a look of understanding. "I'm sorry, Callie, but we're not prepared for guests today."

Not taken in by that nonsense, Callie wanted to say as much, but doing so would only embarrass Grace and Elise more. Though with that scowl on Grace's face, Callie was surprised anyone dared confront them. Poor Elise looked ready to faint.

Mrs. Sunderland shook her head. "I can't believe how far you'll go to pursue your agenda."

Callie's mind went blank. "My agenda?"

"Everyone knows you need money to repair and keep up your house. Soliciting funds for unwed mothers is a clever way to look out for *your* interests, not the community's." She swept a hand. "Or these girls. Elise should be home with her parents." She folded her arms across her chest. "Honor your father and mother is a commandment, yet you've aided her rebellion."

Callie wouldn't break Elise's mother's confidence. But even if she knew that Sarah supported her daughter's actions, Mrs. Sunderland wouldn't be moved. She didn't have a heart.

Tugging Elise along, they headed out the door. Grace shot her a glare. "You're using us for your own benefit." She scoffed. "I knew your motives were too good to be true."

"Grace," Elise said, taking her arm. "Mrs. Sunderland will say anything to destroy Redeeming Love."

As they retraced their steps toward home, Callie could barely put one foot in front of the other. What a fool she'd been to expose Grace and Elise to censure. She'd wanted to give hurting women some fun. Her intentions had been good. But everything she'd planned had gone awry. She'd failed. Yet again. Only this time, Elise and Grace had been affected by the consequences of her bad decisions.

After this, Grace would probably never trust her.

Where would all this lead?

Chapter Fourteen

Jake hadn't seen Callie since his return from Indianapolis. He hoped his absence hadn't built another wall between them, but he still wasn't ready to talk about his mother.

The hours he'd spent at the State Capitol hadn't produced any solid evidence about his birth mother. He'd talked to several senators. Only one had served in the Senate with Wesley Squier. He'd remembered conversations they'd had about his wife and daughter. Told Jake that Squier had lost his appetite for politics, moved back East to his wife's hometown, though he couldn't recall where. He assumed Irene had gone with her parents.

Jake checked records at the courthouse and back issues of newspapers in the city's library, but found no mention of Wesley Squier, except for his announcement not to run for a fourth term. The article didn't mention his wife or daughter.

Wherever the family had gone, they apparently hadn't lived in the area for years. Irene couldn't have mailed those postcards, which meant he'd been on a wild goose chase.

With his lack of success weighing him down, he slogged toward the barn to get the tools he'd need to repair the water-damaged parlor ceiling.

Across the way, Callie plopped the milking stool and pail down alongside the cow. Soaking up her presence, he brushed off the setback, wanting only to make Callie's load easier. "Hi," he said. "Let me do the milking for you."

At his greeting, Callie jerked up her head.

Her beauty socked him in the gut. He'd missed her, as if he'd been gone for days instead of less than twenty-four hours. His gaze swept over her, then settled on her eyes. Eyes as turbulent as stormy seas and weary, as if she could barely keep her seat.

His pulse ratcheted. "Are you feeling all right?"

"I'm fine."

She didn't look fine. Or sound fine for that matter. Was she upset about his absence? "Is something bothering you?"

She glanced away, as if she didn't want to confide in him. Disappointment at the remoteness between them sank to his belly. "Are you angry that I didn't tell you where I've been?"

"Why would you think I care?" she said in a tone as frigid as a mountain stream. "You have a right to come and go as you please."

"That look in your eyes suggests otherwise."

"If you must know, I didn't sleep well last night. I couldn't get Grace off my mind."

"Who's Grace?"

"If you'd been around, you'd know Grace is an unwed mother and a resident. And she and Elise were refused admittance to the Ladies Club this morning."

"Why?"

"Why do you suppose?"

"Mrs. Sunderland at work?"

She nodded. "I had every right to bring visitors, but no one spoke up, even Loretta."

"You care too much. You're going to get sick if you don't keep your distance emotionally."

She harrumphed. "That's occurred to me. And not merely regarding Grace."

It didn't take a genius to understand her meaning. Unable to meet that probing gaze, he looked away.

She sighed. "I believe God brings people into my life for a reason. I just need to understand what purpose He has for me." She rose and strode to Jake. "As for you, at first I thought God brought you here to repair my house. But now I believe His reason is far bigger, far more important."

Jake turned on a booted heel. "Well, if you're sure you don't need help, I'll be in the parlor plastering the chink in the ceiling. Purpose enough for me."

"Whatever reason you're in Peaceful, Jacob, *your* purpose may not be God's objective."

The comment stopped him, made him turn back. How could he respond to that?

With every particle of his being, he wanted her touch. Wanted her with a desperation that left him shaken. But what Callie needed, he couldn't give, didn't even possess. "I don't believe God works in a doubter's life."

She gave a gentle smile. "God works in anyone's life He chooses, even those who haven't accepted Him." Then she returned to Bossy, putting her back to him.

Callie's behavior left him baffled. One minute she appeared upset with him, the next she talked about his purpose as if she cared about his life. What man understood a woman's thoughts? All he'd wanted to do was give her a helping hand. Not dig into purpose and faith.

He gathered the ladder and tools, trying to put Callie out of his mind the only way he knew how—with hard work and steely determination to find his birth mother.

If she left Peaceful to give birth, she could've returned with no one the wiser. He'd talk to Mildred Uland again. See if a woman in town had disappeared for months then come back.

In the parlor, a woman he'd never seen before had holed up on the couch. She looked up from leafing through a magazine and shot him a scowl. Dark hair, dark eyes, dark disposition. This had to be Grace, the newcomer.

"Hello," he said, forcing a smile he didn't feel.

She gave him a cursory nod, not exactly friendly, but then he hadn't been, either.

"Excuse the interruption. I'm here to repair the ceiling."

"Fine with me."

"I'm Jake Smith. I'm remodeling the house for Callie."

She shrugged. Not giving her name.

While ignoring Callie's latest arrival and her attitude, he cleared out the furniture and rug, set the ladder beneath the water damage and went about the task of laying a thin coat of plaster.

He had no interest in getting to know Grace, but he would like to know why she had gotten involved with a shiftless man who lacked the decency to propose marriage. Who lacked one grain of commitment or responsibility, gave not one thought to the consequences of his actions.

The realization that he'd just described his father landed in Jake's belly with a thud. Why had he blamed only his birth mother all this time? Those postcards were the reason. How could a mother send an annual birthday greeting, yet make no effort to see her child?

His hand tightened on the handle of the trowel, digging into the wet plaster, marring the repair. With care, he added plaster then smoothed the edges until he could no longer see the gouge. He climbed down the ladder, leaving the repair to dry.

As he turned to go, something about Grace reading a magazine while everyone else worked struck him as wrong. "Callie's out milking. Elise is gathering eggs. You could be helping with chores instead of sitting here like a princess on her throne."

"I'm no princess. No mind reader, either. If she wants help, she should ask."

"Callie probably assumes that you're not up to working and is excusing you for not carrying your weight. Someone like Callie can't imagine that some people are takers, not givers."

Grace's eyes turned icy. "You're no doubt taking a wage. You hardly have room to talk."

"My wages are the same as yours. A roof over my head and three meals a day." He folded his arms across his chest. "I don't sit idle."

She shot him a glare. "Mind your own business. And I'll mind mine."

"Callie's having a baby, too. She shouldn't be waiting on you hand and foot."

At the reference to her pregnancy, the woman all but snarled. "Get lost."

Before she ruined her health, Jake would suggest that Callie set up a schedule to divide the work. Not that she'd appreciate his interference. But in a couple of weeks, Elise would give birth. A baby would make even more work for Callie.

If only he could stay until Callie's baby was born, and Callie was back on her feet. But the unwed mother from Bloomington could arrive at any time and identify him. Then all havoc would break loose.

Pretending to sip a lukewarm cup of tea, Callie sat on the fringed sofa in her mother-in-law's heavily draped parlor, surrounded by an abundance of knickknacks of every size and shape—a signed baseball, bronzed baby shoes, a tarnished silver rattle—all reminders of Martin. Martin's pictures filled the mantle and piano, lined the walls. With the stuffy room closing in on her, Callie couldn't wait to leave.

Dorothy sat at her side, her gaze traveling the room, the lone worshipper in a shrine to her son.

With a shaky hand, Callie set the teacup on the saucer with a clatter. She'd spent the last half hour choking down cup after cup, looking for an opening in the conversation to discuss the financial needs of the unwed mothers' home.

Once she broached the subject, Callie felt certain she could count on Dorothy's support. Unlike Jacob, who'd dared to disapprove of Grace's behavior. As if he had the right to object to anything. Why couldn't he see that Grace's fragile emotional state proved the newcomer needed their understanding and patience?

The sensation of a tiny moving arm or leg rippled across Callie's stomach. Awed at the miracle of the baby growing inside her, Callie laid a hand over the spot.

"Is the baby moving?" Dorothy leaned closer. "Can I feel it?"

Callie moved Dorothy's hand to her abdomen and held it there. At another kick, Dorothy closed her eyes, almost as if praying. "It's your grandma, sweet baby."

She lifted her gaze to Callie. "Bless you, dear. This child you're carrying will give us back a piece of our son. It breaks my heart that he'll never see his child." Tears sprang to her eyes. "Oh, we miss him. His absence aches in our bones, blankets our every moment with sadness."

Uncertain what she could say that would comfort Dorothy, Callie simply patted her hand. The promise of Heaven and assurance of seeing loved ones again eased but didn't eliminate the heartache for those who grieved.

Dorothy heaved a sigh laden with pain and weariness. "I know Martin wasn't a perfect husband. That's hard to admit about my only child." She gave a shaky smile. "He was gregarious, spontaneous, fun-loving and…irresponsible and self-centered." Dorothy's gaze clouded. "Commodore and I are at fault for that. We spoiled our son."

"I'm sure I'll do the same with my baby," Callie said, trying to soothe Dorothy's regrets, yet knowing Martin's mother spoke the truth.

Fighting for control, Dorothy looked around the gloomy space, more mausoleum than living room. Callie wanted to rip off the heavy curtains covering the windows, open the casements. Fresh air would do Dorothy good, more than anything Callie could say or do.

She wrapped her mother-in-law in her arms. "Martin had a kind heart. He never said a harsh word to anyone."

"You were patient with him. You gave our son happiness," Dorothy said, a tremor in her voice.

"His strengths were the reason I loved him."

"I understand." Dorothy fiddled with the narrow gold band on her finger. "More than you know."

How many women could acknowledge such a thing about their only child, especially after his death? Callie's breath caught. Perhaps a woman who lived with the pain of her own troubled marriage?

Fighting to regain her footing after Dorothy's emotional admission, Callie wondered if she should broach the subject of money. But with two unwed mothers in the house and their babies on the way, Callie needed funding now.

As she got to the reason for her visit, Dorothy straightened. "I agree with your unwed mothers' home. In principle. But I can't support it. I'm worried that you're being foolhardy and not putting your baby first." Dorothy plucked at something on her sleeve, lint or a thread perhaps, only visible to her. "I hate to tell you this, dear, but I thought you ought to know...before the letter arrives."

A python of foreboding wrapped around Callie's throat and squeezed, shutting off her air. "Letter?"

"The members of the Peaceful Ladies Club met yesterday and voted to revoke your membership."

"What?"

"Oh, Callie, I'm sorry." Her eyes flashed. "The women believe your unwed mothers' home is in conflict with Ladies Club bylaws and God's commandments."

Callie wanted to protest but the words lodged in her throat.

"They assert that providing refuge for these fallen girls is, in essence, coddling sinners and sending a message to the youth of this town that contradicts Scripture."

Callie's pulse pounded in her temples. These women thought she'd broken God's commandments. "I can't believe they'd do this. Aunt Hilda was one of the founders of the Ladies Club."

"I reminded them of that, but the leadership felt the home would bring nothing good to Peaceful. You'll get a detailed summary of their objections and action."

These women were her friends. They'd been there for her when Aunt Hilda died. When Martin died. They'd hugged her. Prayed for her. And she'd done the same for them. She'd served on Ladies Club committees, hosted meetings and social events, taken food into their homes in times of crisis. Last year, she'd cared for the president's children when Karen came down with influenza.

Now they were tossing her out.

"You know, Callie, you leaped into this without a plan in place. You don't have the money to finance the home, yet you have two unwed mothers living there. You're ruffling feathers of the people you need to help you. If you'd paved the way, perhaps they would've seen the unwed mothers' home from your perspective." She sighed. "I'm sorry, but I can't support what you're doing, especially when the consequences could hurt my grandchild."

"I'd never do anything that would harm my baby."

Dorothy's praise of Callie's treatment of Martin was mere words. She wanted to defend herself, to demand that the women of the Ladies Club show a Scriptural basis for kicking her out. The injustice of it all churned within her.

Vengeance is mine sayeth the Lord.

No, she didn't want vengeance. She wanted vindication.

Be patient.

She took a deep breath and counted to ten. These women would discover that the town wouldn't be turned upside down by these girls, as it feared.

Or would it? God had a way of doing that very thing. A flipped view of their world might be what the folks in this town needed.

"I have more bad news." Dorothy didn't meet Callie's eyes.

Every muscle in Callie's body tensed, sensing that losing her membership in the Ladies Club was only the beginning of the trouble ahead.

"I want you to understand that I don't believe a word of this gossip. I know you. Know your faith. But all this trouble with these girls is turning this town into something ugly."

"What are you saying?"

"Gossip has it that you and Jacob Smith are…" Dorothy sighed "…intimate."

"That's a lie!"

"Or course it is. Commodore doesn't believe a word of the gossip about you and Mr. Smith, either. Though, he is suspicious of the man."

Who wasn't?

Callie had met with disapproval. She'd endure removal. But slander? Where would this ugliness end?

How much would the unwed mothers' home cost her?

* * *

That evening at supper, Jake pulled out a chair for Elise, then another for Callie, who thanked him but didn't meet his eyes. Why? Grace had deigned to come to the table, undoubtedly reluctantly if her demeanor meant anything, scooting into her chair before Jake could assist her.

After blessing the food, Callie passed the serving bowls. Elise chatted away about her knitting, her baby, while Grace picked at her food, ignoring attempts to include her in the conversation. Elise shot furtive glances at the newcomer, obviously uncomfortable with Grace's stony silence.

Jake glanced at Callie. "The food is delicious."

Callie nodded her thanks, her gaze distant. Something had happened to upset her. Had her visit with Dorothy that afternoon gone badly? Or was she still angry with him for suggesting she divide the work? Hoping to dispel the gloomy atmosphere, Jake said, "How are you feeling, Elise?"

She sighed, resting her forearms on her belly. "Ready to have this baby."

"Won't be long now." Callie gave Elise a sweet smile, a smile Jake would've given anything to have directed at him.

"Have you made…uh, plans for your child?" he asked.

"If you're asking if I'm keeping my baby, the answer is yes. I thought you knew that's the reason I'm here."

"I wasn't sure if you'd changed your mind. Raising a child alone is a huge responsibility."

"My baby won't end up in an orphanage. After what you told me, I'd never allow that to happen."

Grace's head shot up. Her eyes darted to Jake then to

Elise. "Easy for you to say." She snorted. "You two have all the answers. Passing judgment, condemning women. You don't know anything." She plopped the glass she held on the kitchen table, sloshing water and glaring at him. "You bellyache about that orphanage, Jake. Why? You had food in your stomach and a roof over your head."

Had Grace lived on the streets? What had happened to put that sneer on her face?

Callie reached a hand to Grace. "You make a good point. Many children aren't given up by choice. Parents die." Jake heard the tremble in Callie's voice. Knew she still suffered from the loss of her family. "Or they can't provide." She sighed. "It's far easier to name the problem than to solve it."

Had an inability to provide motivated his parents to give Jake up? Maybe they didn't have two pennies to rub together. An orphanage would be better than living on the streets.

"I know of at least one couple in this town who'd love to raise a child," Callie said. "No baby born at Redeeming Love need end up without a family. God will provide."

"Another pat answer! I've lost my appetite." Grace shoved back her chair, tipping it over. As it crashed to the floor, Jake jumped to his feet. Grace stomped from the room.

"What's wrong with her?" Elise burst into tears.

As Callie pulled Elise into her arms, she met Jake's gaze, her eyes wide with alarm. "Grace is having a rough time adjusting. We'll need to be patient with her."

Jake righted the chair then stood by helplessly with no idea what to do or what to say that would restore harmony.

"I'm not hungry," Elise said, though she hadn't finished her meal. "I'm going to see my mother while Papa's at the shop."

The front door banged closed, the sound echoing in the silence. Grace might be troubled, but she'd brought strife into the house. Not good for anyone. Especially for Callie, who gave and gave, trying to make life better for those in her care. No doubt she'd see Grace's reaction as some failure on her part, rather than laying the blame at Grace's feet, where it belonged.

With the force of a tidal wave, awareness slammed into Jake. Grace reminded him of someone. Someone he knew all too well. Someone who'd railed at life. Someone embittered and spewing blame.

Himself.

Swallowing hard at the similarities between him and this troubled young woman, his gaze surveyed the kitchen. The stormy scene they'd witnessed was at odds with the beam of sunlight streaming in through the window, lighting the vase of peonies on the table, their scent mixing with the aroma of beans and ham.

This cozy nest Callie had created, along with that warm way of hers, had softened his edges. Perhaps in time, she'd do the same for Grace. But at what cost? Plenty, if the look of dismay on Callie's face meant anything.

Jake wanted to make amends for Grace's behavior. To protect Callie from this strife. Protect her from any ugliness.

He reached a hand. "Grace is upsetting you. Having her here isn't good for you or your baby."

"I didn't ask for your opinion." Eyes snapping, Callie slapped her napkin on the table. "You're leaving. So keep your advice to yourself."

Chapter Fifteen

As he hauled manure to Callie's garden, Jake bent into a gust of wind. Except for an occasional fast-moving cloud obstructing the warmth of the sun, the breezy day was pleasant, invigorating. Spring carried the promise of new beginnings. New beginnings he wanted but couldn't see, not with the shadow of prison eclipsing his every tomorrow.

He glanced toward the stoop where Callie washed clothes. Even from here, he could feel the tension between them, as thick and high as fortifications at the penitentiary. Her anger last night made it perfectly clear. Callie didn't want advice from him. She didn't want anything from him.

She heaved a heaping laundry basket to her middle, wrestling with it. He dropped the handles of the wheelbarrow and loped toward her. At his approach, she tilted her chin in that stubborn way of hers, as if she'd refuse his help.

Maybe if he started small, helping with the laundry, he could restore the harmony between them. "Let me carry that basket."

"If you insist." Callie looked away, as if she couldn't stand the sight of him.

"I do." He took the basket from her arms.

Callie pivoted and headed for the clothesline stretching between two poles, leaving him to follow along behind.

With hammer and nails, he'd taken care of the hazards threatening the women in the house. He could fix any object with the right tools, but he didn't know what it would take to fix things with Callie.

Jake watched the sway of her hips, wanting nothing more than to pull her into his arms. But after the way they'd parted last night, she wouldn't welcome his embrace. Callie understood the futility of building a relationship with a man like him.

At the clothesline, he lowered the basket to the ground. She reached for a lump of white just as he did. Their hands collided, zipping a flash of attraction from the tips of his fingers to the base of his spine.

"I'll do that," he said. Before she could protest, he pulled a sheet from the pile and unfurled it. The wind caught the cotton, whipping it in the air between them.

Callie grabbed clothespins from her apron pocket and pegged the first corner to the line, then the middle. When she jabbed the last pin in place, the sheet hung between them, a wall of sorts. They were in close proximity, but miles apart.

Sometimes Callie's determination to handle things alone had Jake clamping his jaw in exasperation. Perhaps, married to Martin, she'd had to do everything on her own and knew no other way. Was he any different? Empathy for this woman, a survivor like him, made him long to pull Callie into his arms.

Jake stomped past the sheet, determined to do that very thing, determined to tell her how much he cared. One glance at her belly stopped him. Her child would need a father. Jake had no idea how to handle that role. Getting out of her life was the kindest thing he could do. The fact that he cared about her kept his arms at his sides. His mouth closed.

He yanked a towel from the stack and draped it over the line. She pegged. He draped. Neither spoke, yet the air fairly crackled with friction as every touch and glance burned into Jake's awareness like a hot branding iron.

When he could stand the tension no longer, he threw up his hands. "Callie, why don't you just tell me what's on your mind?"

She whirled toward him. "What's the point? You'll do what you please, no matter what I say."

A cloud covered the sun, throwing them in shadow. He took a step closer. "You're putting barriers between us and not just with this laundry. You know I'd stay if I could."

"I know no such thing. You have no job to go to. No family waiting for your return. For once, drop the pretense and be honest. With me. With yourself."

Her words slashed at him. He hadn't been honest with her. He hid his past and his purpose the same way that cloud overhead hid the sun. Perhaps he could tell her why he'd come to town. Why he kept his past a secret. And she'd react differently than others had.

She turned back, as if she meant to talk to him, then her gaze fastened on something in the yard.

A few feet away, he spotted a baby robin hunched in the grass, its little beak opening and closing with soft chirps. The mother hovered nearby, fluttering her wings, panicked or maybe merely showing her offspring what to do. From the looks of it, the baby didn't get the message.

"Jake. Look." Callie pointed across the lawn.

Out of the corner of his eyes, he saw Stripes slink forward, eyes locked on its prey. The mother robin flapped her wings, hopped closer, alarmed by the stalking feline, but the baby bird remained huddled on the ground.

Callie crouched down, trying to shoo the cat away. Stripes kept coming.

Slowly, Jake moved toward the birds, then squatted in the grass. The baby bird looked weak, defenseless, its feathers stirring in the breeze. The mother robin flitted about, her dark, beady eyes on Jake. Wary. Scared.

"Do you think he's hurt?" Callie lowered herself in the space beside Jake.

"I don't think so." He kept his voice soft and low, but still the mother robin's gaze held trepidation. The baby let out a squawk. "Falling is part of learning to fly."

"What if he's not ready yet? Maybe he needs to go back to the nest."

"Maybe."

Jake studied the baby bird. Under its thin skin and feathers, he could see the delicate bones that would one day carry this small bird through the sky. At times like this, Jake marveled at the order and beauty of nature. Could a Master Planner have designed this world?

Callie laid a hand on his arm. Her gentle touch slid through him. "You need to put him back. I'd do it, but…" She waved at her belly. "Will you, Jake?"

That Callie needed him for more than repairs to her

house filled some ache inside him. Still, moving the bird might not be the right solution. "We need to give him a chance to fly. We'll chase off the cat—"

"Stripes will come back." Worry flooded her eyes. "I can't bear to think of him down here, helpless, with the cat out there, watching. Waiting."

"If I touch it, the mother may not accept the fledgling."

"The mother can't get it back in the nest. Someone has to." She turned pleading eyes on him. "Isn't it better to try than to let the cat get it?"

He glanced at the baby she carried inside her. He couldn't do anything for that baby, but he could do something for this baby bird.

He edged forward, one small step at a time. The mother bird flapped her wings, squawked a protest, but Jake kept closing in. The mother froze. Watched. Her heart beat so fast that Jake could see it through her breast. Stripes stepped closer and closer. With one last glance at her baby, the robin took flight and perched on a branch above his head.

Yanking his gloves from his back pocket, Jake shoved his hands inside, reached down, scooped up the trembling baby bird, and cradled it in his hand. It weighed almost nothing.

The warm smile Callie sent Jake slid through him, easing the impasse between them. "Any idea where the nest is?"

She pointed behind him. "Up in that tree."

As soon as the words left her mouth, the robin flew to a branch far above him. Jake grabbed a low limb and clamored up the trunk, heaving himself along with one hand and holding the bird in the other until he reached the spot where the robin waited. There he found her nest balanced between two branches, a miracle of twigs, dried grasses and loose threads. Occupied with two chirping siblings, beaks open wide, ready for a meal.

As he gently deposited the outcast alongside his family, Jake grasped in that moment that one of nature's creatures had placed its trust in him.

Him. Of all people.

He retraced his path, much easier with both hands free, then jumped to the ground. A foot away, Stripes sat on her haunches, eyeing Jake with reproach. "You're a mom. Shame on you."

Relief plain on her face, Callie chuckled. "Stripes is not happy."

Jake removed his gloves and stuffed them back into his hip pocket. "The wanderer is back in the nest."

"Thank you," Callie said then threw her arms around Jake, burrowing into him with a sob.

What was wrong? The bird was safe. Who would've thought a baby bird that had fallen out of its nest would bring this self-sufficient woman to tears? Yet that Callie needed him, even for a moment, slid through Jake. Filled with a sense of the rightness of having Callie in his arms, he rubbed her back, murmuring an endearment near her ear.

She jerked away, wiped her tears with both hands and shot up her chin. Back to her strong independent self. Unwilling to rely on him for anything. Anything except repairs.

"The baby bird would most likely have survived," he said. "Mother birds push fledglings out of the nest because they know the time has come to try their wings. It's what's best for them."

Callie's eyes locked with his, in their depths Jake saw tenderness. For him? "Do you think it's possible, Jake, that sometimes… Sometimes human mothers do the same thing?"

"I don't understand what you mean."

"I'm saying a mother may do what she sees as best for her baby, but the child may not see her actions that way."

Callie's words held a significance she wanted him to grasp. Why wouldn't a child understand his mother's actions? Unless…

As understanding dawned, he wrestled with the insight. "You think my mother believed that giving me up was the best choice for me?"

"It might have been. You don't know what she faced. What your life would have been like if she hadn't given you up."

The ground shifted under his feet, as if the earth had moved on its axis. Jake saw the truth with sudden clarity. "All these years, I've resented her decision. Until I know her circumstances, I can't say her decision was right or wrong."

Callie touched his face with a gentle palm, offering approval or maybe solace.

"That insight came through a baby bird. And you, Callie, the most merciful person I've ever met. You've taught me by your example how to live." He laid his hand over hers. "I need to give my mother the same clemency."

A smile bloomed on Callie's face. The beauty of it socked Jake in the gut. He wanted nothing to stand between him and this special woman. A woman he trusted enough to divulge his stint in prison, his search for his mother.

Grace called to Callie from the house.

Callie gave her a wave, then pivoted to Jake. "You're a good man, Jacob Smith. God is working on you." She gave him a smile, then walked to the stoop, tucked an arm around Grace's waist and walked her inside the house.

As Jake tramped toward the barn, filled with gratitude that the incident with the birds had led not only to an understanding about his mother, but to an easing of the rift between him and Callie.

One thing stood between them, a Grand Canyon of an impasse. He didn't believe in God. If only he had Callie's faith.

Perhaps the amazing order of nature wasn't an accident. Perhaps everything in this world had been designed by a Higher Power. If so, that lesson would outweigh all the others.

Jake had doubts. Still, he would examine them. Open that Bible of his. And see where it led.

Callie stared out the back kitchen window facing the tree Jacob had climbed that morning to return a lost baby robin to the nest. Sometimes she felt just as lost, unsure which way to turn. Had she been foolish to test her wings with this unwed mothers' home when her own baby's arrival was imminent?

The incident with the baby bird had made Callie realize that she wasn't taking care of her own baby as well as she'd thought. She'd put other things first, before her own child. That sense of failure had driven her sobbing into Jacob's arms. Her mind was a jumble of confusion. Her emotions were in shambles.

In such a state, how had she thought she could help Elise and Grace? Or any other unwed mother who appeared at her door?

Laying her hands on either side of her abdomen, Callie bowed her head. *Lord, give me wisdom. Help me put my baby's welfare first. Enable me to make plans that ensure his well-being, not put him at risk.*

Her baby had lost his father. Her breath caught. Had God brought Jacob into her life for that very reason? Not that she'd fall in love with an unbeliever, but she felt Jacob's softening toward God. Saw it in his attentive posture during Pastor Steele's sermons. Saw it in his growing forgiveness toward his birth mother. Saw it in his kindness toward Elise and, of late, Grace.

Callie glanced at the plate of food warming on the stove. Grace had skipped the noon meal, not something an expectant mother should do. If nothing else, perhaps God gave Callie this mission to ensure that Grace got proper nourishment.

Holding the plate, Callie walked upstairs and rapped on Grace's door. "It's Callie. May I come in?"

The door opened a crack. "What do you want?"

"I brought your food up. You need to eat."

The door widened. "I'm not hungry."

"Please, eat anyway, for my sake. If you don't, I won't get a wink of sleep tonight."

The door swung open. Callie breathed a sigh of relief. Grace looked pale, defenseless as if she didn't have the strength to keep on her feet. "No one has ever cared about me enough to lose sleep."

Callie set the plate of food on Grace's nightstand then put an arm around her. "I'm sorry you've never had someone in your life who cared."

Stepping away from Callie's arms, Grace turned to the bed, smoothed a wrinkle from the quilt with her palms. "Not many folks worry about a servant."

Underneath those quiet words, Callie heard Grace's resignation to her status in life, as if her job determined her worth. She had to make Grace understand that God loved her. And that made her a person of significance. But food for the body came first. "Eat while it's still warm."

Amazingly, Grace sat on the edge of the bed and took a bite of the chicken and noodles. "You're a good cook."

"I don't feel like much of a cook when you can't keep your feet under my table."

Suspicion rode in her eyes. "So why are you doing this? What's in this unwed mothers' home for you?"

Perhaps Grace had seen through her and suspected that her motives weren't entirely selfless. "I thought I wanted this home because of what happened to a friend of mine. But it's possible I want it so I can surround myself with people and forget the losses I've had, the loneliness."

Grace's gaze darted to her plate. As if Callie's admission was a hot potato she couldn't juggle.

This young woman needed to share her wounds with someone. If she chose to confide in her, Callie prayed her response wouldn't make matters worse.

While she ate, Grace looked at Callie's wedding ring. "What happened to your husband?"

"He passed away last November."

Toying with the band, Callie admitted that her marriage had been a disappointment. She'd been both wife and mother to Martin. Some days she'd felt more like a warden, trying to keep tabs on his whereabouts, his choices. He hadn't understood that she hated that role. Oddly, he'd never blamed her for taking it. She wondered why she still wore his ring. Maybe she saw it as a badge of legitimacy for her baby.

Grace took a sip of milk, then set down her glass.

"That's tough. I thought maybe you and Jake… I noticed a spark between you."

Callie gulped. Was the attraction between them that obvious? What did it matter? Nothing good would come from furtive glances, pounding hearts or stolen kisses. She wouldn't care about Jacob. She wouldn't care about another man who deceived. But even as that thought came to her, Callie knew it was already too late. She did care about Jacob Smith. But she'd never let him know.

"Jacob will be moving on." She forced a smile. "But thanks to him, this house is livable. I have much to be thankful for."

Grace took the last mouthful on her fork, wiped her lips then dropped the napkin on the plate. "I'm not interested in a list of your blessings."

Grace used that sharp tongue of hers to keep people at a distance. If Callie hadn't cared about Grace, hadn't taken the time to look into her weary eyes laden with pain, she'd never have seen past that wall she'd erected. Grace was wounded. What could Callie do to help?

The young woman rose and set the dishes outside the door, as if unable to tolerate one tiny thing out of place, then walked back to Callie, her expression closed. "Thanks for the meal."

Callie smiled. "You're very welcome."

"I'm sure you have things to do." She glanced at the door, an invitation to leave.

But Callie wasn't budging. Not yet. "What happened to your parents, Grace?"

As if her legs gave way, Grace sank to the mattress. "They died."

Callie sat beside her. "What did you do then?"

"I lived on the streets, like thousands of immigrant

kids." Her brown eyes, dark as storm clouds, met Callie's. "No matter what Jake says, an orphanage is better than sleeping in alleys, huddling together for warmth, eating garbage."

A huge lump formed in Callie's throat. Trying to clear it and the image Grace's words evoked in her mind, she swallowed convulsively. "That explains why you're upset with Jacob."

She sighed. "I'm not. Not anymore. I haven't walked in his shoes."

This young woman had endured a horrid life. Worse, Callie suspected that what Grace had told her revealed only the tip of the iceberg, that more was frozen below the surface.

"If we all did that, this world would be a better place." Callie faced Grace and took her cold hand. "I want you to know that you're a child of God. That makes you worthy. Servant and master, rich and poor, all are the same in the eyes of God."

Tears sprang to Grace's eyes. She squared her shoulders, obviously fighting powerful feelings inside her. Callie waited.

Grace swiped at her eyes. "So what happened to that friend you mentioned?"

Changing the subject, another tactic Grace used to put the focus on anyone, anything, but her. Well, Grace deserved to know. She explained Nell's pregnancy and suicide.

"Some boyfriend." Grace shook her head. "Women rave about the guys they love. But men get what they want then move on."

"You're not an admirer of men."

Grace motioned to her protruding belly. "Should I

be? Prince Charming exists only in fairy tales." She yawned. "I'm tired."

"Sleep well, Grace."

As Callie left the room, she thought about the make-believe castle of her childhood and the prince she'd envisioned riding up on a powerful steed to rescue her.

An image of Jacob popped into her mind. He was a far cry from her vision of Prince Charming. True, he was handsome, strong and capable. He'd made the house safe, helped with chores, did whatever he could to make her life easier. All things she appreciated. But when it came to giving his heart—

This prince hid his past. Had no interest in sharing a castle.

She'd go through life caring for her baby, handling this home and steering clear of men. Grace was right. Prince Charming existed only in childhood dreams.

Her baby thumped against her belly. She laid her hand on the spot. This precious baby growing within her deserved a father. A father to toss a ball. A father to demonstrate how to pound a nail. A father to give piggyback rides on his back. No matter how much Callie wanted to believe that she could be both father and mother to her child, the absence of a father would leave a void in her child's life.

She'd come to Grace's room to see that she ate and help however she could. And she'd left burdened with her troubles, problems she didn't know how to solve.

She'd never felt lonelier.

Chapter Sixteen

That morning, Callie had taken Grace to see Doc Wellman. After the visit, Doc had taken her aside. "Give Grace understanding, love, your time," he'd said. "Something is wrong. Very wrong, but she won't talk to me. I feel she's slipping away, as if she doesn't want to live."

Back at the house, Callie poured Grace a glass of milk and set out the wheel of cheddar she'd bought at the grocer and slices of homemade bread. "I always treat myself after a doctor's visit. The baby and I like cheese." Callie grinned, cutting off a slice.

Ignoring the food, Grace sipped the milk.

"You barely eat enough to keep a bird alive." Callie cut another slice and offered it to Grace.

Grace turned her head away, as if the sight made her sick to her stomach.

"Don't you like cheese? It's good for you."

Grace looked at her. In the depths of her eyes, Callie saw something that made her shiver. Something so horrible she said a quick prayer.

"I hate cheese."

"Oh." Surely that didn't explain the horror she'd seen in Grace's eyes. "Does the smell bother you?"

Grace swallowed convulsively. "It…makes me… remember."

Barely able to swallow the bite she'd taken, Callie rose and put the cheese in the icebox.

Grace lurched from the chair and staggered to the window, turning her back to Callie. Callie moved closer, put a hand on her shoulder. The seconds became a minute. A minute became two.

Just when she'd decided that Grace wouldn't explain, the young woman turned to her, perspiration beaded on her forehead, her face pale as paper.

"I've never told anyone." She lowered her eyes to the floor.

With a strong sense of foreboding tightening every muscle, a desire to run slid through Callie. But she held her ground. Whatever Grace had to say, Doc Wellman believed it needed to be said.

Callie's breathing grew shallow. *Lord, help me. Help Grace. Help us both.*

"My employer's husband…asked me to store some clothes in the attic. While I was putting the last of the things away, he…" She took a breath, as if the effort of saying that much had winded her. "He came in and locked the door behind him."

The air left Callie's lungs.

"He said—" She pivoted to the window. Callie heard a sob. "He said his wife was visiting her mother for a couple of days." She lowered her forehead, rested it on the glass. "He'd given the staff the time off." She gave a strangled laugh. "I wondered if it was with pay."

She began to sway back and forth, back and forth

in front of the window. The chill in Grace's voice and that rocking churned in Callie's stomach.

She put an arm around Grace, grasping her cold hand and turned her away from that window. "You're here with me. You're safe."

Grace fastened her gaze on the far wall. "I fought...but... couldn't stop him." She tore her hand from Callie's and clasped it over her mouth. A sob. "He dragged me to the floor." Another sob tore from her throat. "And...raped me."

Callie laid her cheek against Grace's face. Their tears mingled with the pain of her gut-wrenching admission.

"He came back time and time again. For three days, he...returned to the attic. At the end of each day, he'd bring water and—"

A moan escaped Callie's lips. "Cheese."

Legs giving out from under her, Grace slid down the wall to the floor, leaning back, eyes closed, as if trying to shut out the images. Images burned into her soul with the branding iron of brutality.

Callie sat beside her, held her trembling hand. "I'm sorry, so sorry." Yet nothing she could say or do would erase the horror of those days in the attic.

Birds chirping, Mildred's Sandy barking next door, the whistle of a distant train—ordinary sounds drifted in through the open window. As if this day were like any other. But Callie, a woman who'd never been mistreated, and Grace, a woman who'd been subjected to every cruelty, wounded to her core, clung to each other, and knew innocence was gone forever.

"On Monday, the day the staff and his wife were due back, he came in before dawn. He said he'd kill me if I told his wife or the police." She gave a harsh laugh. "Then he raped me one last time, unlocked the door and told me to clean myself up. Said not to worry, he wouldn't touch me again." Her chin quivered. "I was… used goods."

Inside Callie, anger raged. She wanted to hurt that man. To make him pay for what he did. *Oh, Lord. Oh, Lord, help us.*

"His wife and the staff returned within hours. He never bothered me after that. I needed that job. Entering that house each morning took everything I had. Fear kept me silent until the morning I knew I was pregnant. I saw him leave for work and followed him outside. When I told him, he said, 'Who's the father? Or do you even know?'" Grace beat a fist on the floor. "I hate him! I'll hate him till the day I die."

Callie tugged Grace into the circle of her arms. "He should be shot." And she meant it. That frightened her even more.

"I can't bear to see the face of this baby I'm carrying." Tears slid down her cheeks. "Yet as often as I thought about it, I couldn't end its life."

Callie shuddered. That baby, that poor baby, would always be a reminder of the violence of its conception.

Grace's trembling fingers found her lips. "What if… What if it resembles him? What if looking into that face the rest of my life is a reminder of everything he did to me? And I grow to hate the child, as much as the father?" She turned her face away. "Don't you see? Putting my baby in an orphanage would be a kindness."

Callie thought of Jacob. There were so many reasons a mother might abandon her child.

"I'd hoped I'd feel better once I told someone. But…" She sobbed. "I feel worse."

"I wish I could take away your pain."

"You won't despise me if I can't keep my baby?"

"Oh, Grace, I have no idea how I'd react if I had to endure that horror. I'm proud of you. Whether you keep your baby or not, you're giving him life, a chance. If you decide to let him go, I know a couple here in town who would love your baby and would give him a good home."

"What if… What if my baby is evil? Like him?"

Callie shook her head. "God is merciful. Your baby will be gentle, sweet."

A sob escaped Grace. "I can't keep it. I'm too filled with hate to be a mother."

Again thoughts paraded through Callie's head that she dare not examine, couldn't admit out loud. She wanted to track that evildoer down. She wanted him to pay for what he'd done. She understood in that moment the hate Grace carried.

Yet that hate festered, destroying Grace's future. Hate meant that brute would be victorious. "Don't let him win, Grace. Don't let hate destroy you."

"It already has."

"No! You're not destroyed. You're strong. That's why you didn't harm your baby. That's why you're here. That's why you will survive. You're battered and bloody, wounded, body and soul." She tucked a strand of hair behind Grace's ear. "We're going to clean, anoint and bind your wounds. With God's help and His power, you'll heal."

"I've been so ashamed."

"Of what? Not being able to stop a monster far stronger than you? God knows what happened. He knows your innocence. The suffering you endured. He hasn't left you. He loves you."

"I feel dirty." She sobbed. "I washed and washed, but I can't get rid of his hands on me. His mouth."

Callie laid both hands on Grace's shoulders. "You're not dirty! The love of God covers you. That man who raped you is dirty. He'll have to answer for his crime. One day he will. If not here on earth, then in eternity."

Grace twisted a hand in the folds of her dress. "Don't tell anyone. Promise me."

"I promise."

But someone should tell. What if he did that to another woman? Callie shivered. Perhaps he was doing it now?

"Thank you for trusting me enough to tell me what happened. But you need to tell someone else. Doctor Wellman. Or Pastor Steele. Someone who knows how to help."

Grace swallowed convulsively and let out a soft groan.

Laying her hands on either side of Grace's jaw, Callie peered into brown tormented eyes. "You've done nothing wrong. You've done nothing to be ashamed of."

A sob. Two.

In silent entreaty, Callie opened her arms. "Let it go, Grace. Let it go."

Burrowing into her arms, Grace wept. Callie wept with her.

God was faithful. Callie prayed that He would restore Grace, give her a new beginning as only He could do.

Callie hoped God would forgive her desire for vengeance. Perhaps Nell's suicide contributed to that. Nell had kept her pregnancy secret.

Grace had kept the crime against her secret, too. Letting it eat at her, nibbling away at hope, joy and love.

Secrets destroyed.

Her breath caught. Jacob Smith kept a secret. She saw it when his eyes grew wary. Felt it when he held others at arm's length. Heard it when his tone turned guarded.

Whatever Jacob hid, when that secret came out, there'd be consequences. Callie suspected that she'd also pay a price. Better to confront him now, with her defenses firmly in place, then wait for that secret to catch her unawares.

Bent over the hoe, sweat dripping off his nose, Jake hacked at the weeds in Callie's garden, exposing their roots to the sun. Freed from the soil that fed them, the weeds would wither and die. If only he could as easily cull the debris choking his heart. With every passing day, the tension between him and Callie intensified. How long could they go on like this?

"Looks like you could use a cold drink."

Jake pivoted. Callie leaned on the fence watching him, tendrils of her chestnut hair teasing her neck. A crisp white apron covered her skirt, the ribbons fluttering in the breeze.

She took his breath away.

With his forearm, he swiped the sweat off his face and smiled. "Nothing would taste better."

"I'll bring a glass of iced tea to the gazebo. We'll have a chat."

The afternoon sky encasing her silhouette brought out the startling aquamarine of her eyes, yet... The softness he usually saw in those eyes had grown watchful, conveyed a warning. A chill snaked through him.

"Sounds good. I'll meet you there."

As he watched her go, Jake wondered what Callie had on her mind. That somber demeanor of hers suggested that she intended to uproot him as he had these weeds. Only instead of a hoe, she'd remove him with a swift, sharp spoken word.

Across the way, Grace left the henhouse carrying

the egg basket. She waved at him and he returned the gesture. He couldn't help smiling at the new spring in her step. Callie hadn't told him what had transpired between them, except to say that Grace had shared her story. Everyone had a story. Perhaps sharing that story with a trusted friend was the first step to healing.

When he finished the last row, he strolled to the gazebo. Inside, Callie sat on the swing, a cold drink on the table at her side.

"Thanks," he said then swigged half the glass. "Hits the spot." He pulled up a chair and sat across from her. "You always know what I need."

Her eyes narrowed. "Are you willing to do the same thing, Jacob? For me?"

"What do you mean?

"I need something from you."

"I'd do anything for you, Callie."

"Anything?"

An alarm went off in his head. "If I can." His mind scrambled for footing. Where would this lead?

"You can— I'm sure of it. But the question is, will you?" She folded her arms across her middle, as if shielding her baby. "From that very first day you arrived looking for work, I sensed that you carried a secret. Hid something you didn't want anyone to know." She clenched and unclenched her hands in her lap. "I've tried to tell myself that you're just a private man, but…" Her eyes clouded. "Lately I've realized that keeping secrets isn't beneficial. Not for the one holding the secret. And not for the one taken by surprise." She met his gaze. "You see, secrets have a way of coming out."

From the very beginning, Callie had suspected that he hid something, yet hadn't pushed him for answers until now. The hard shell around his heart softened. That proved she cared about him, about their relationship. He could trust her with his past.

"Some things are hard to talk about, but you're right. I have kept something hidden." He took her hand. "I want to tell you."

As if his tension became hers, the spark in her eyes dimmed. "From your expression, what you're about to say is bad news."

His gaze dropped to her small hand, the feel of her calluses rough against his own. "I'm hoping you won't see it as bad news. But, even if you do, you deserve to know." He took a deep breath and met her eyes. "I thought once I'd found love. Love of a woman I met in Bloomington."

Callie lowered her eyes to their clasped hands. "What happened to her?" she asked, so softly that Jake could barely hear.

"Susan's actions proved that she didn't…love me. Never had." How could he find the words? Would she believe him? "I was accused of stealing from a jewelry store. Lloyd, a man I considered a friend robbed the store." His throat convulsed. "He left my wallet behind to…" his voice grew raspy, harsh "…make it appear I'd committed the crime."

She squeezed his hand. "Why would a friend do such a thing?"

"He wasn't a friend at all. He wanted someone else to take the blame. He picked me so he could have Susan."

"I don't understand."

"The woman I thought loved me didn't believe in my innocence." He gave a chilling laugh. "She turned to Lloyd for comfort, exactly as he'd planned, while I cooled my heels in jail."

Tears sprang to Callie's eyes. "Jail?"

He swallowed past the lump in his throat. "Because I didn't have an alibi and with that wallet as evidence, the jury found me guilty." He sucked in a gulp of air, trying to get enough oxygen to finish. "I spent almost a year behind bars for a crime I didn't commit."

"Oh, no!" Her hand covered her mouth her eyes wide with horror. "That must've been terrifying." She tightened her hold on his hand.

"I'd be there still, except Lloyd got careless. He gave a necklace to Susan. She recognized it from the description on the list of stolen items I'd supposedly taken and went to the police. They searched Lloyd's room and found more stolen property. I was released. Lloyd stood trial and now he's in jail."

Tears slid down her face.

"Life behind bars was…" He shook his head, refusing to return to that place, even in his mind. "It wasn't an easy time." He swiped the tears off her cheeks with his thumb. "I've allowed those months in jail, those years in an orphanage to make me bitter, to keep me in a prison of sorts."

"Those experiences would wound anyone."

Suddenly, unable to meet those sad, compassionate eyes, he jumped to his feet and turned away. Did she see him as pathetic? He wanted her respect. But could she respect a jailbird? Even one falsely accused? Or would the indignities he'd suffered in jail disgust her? Build a wedge between them?

She rose and put her arms around him. "I'm sorry, Jacob. So very sorry."

"Don't pity me."

"Pity you? Never! If I could, I'd erase that nightmare." She gazed up at him, her eyes glowing with what looked like admiration. "You survived a terrible ordeal. I'm proud of you. Of the man you are."

The snap of a broken twig.

Jake spun on his booted heel, searching beyond the screened enclosure. He didn't see anyone, but someone had been there.

"What's wrong?" Callie whispered.

"Someone may have overheard me. I'm sorry. That'll only complicate your life."

She shrugged. "I can't see how that'll make the attitude of this town any worse."

He wished he shared her opinion. "I've never known anyone like you. You're brave and kind and good and strong. Yet your life hasn't been easy. Your example has made a huge impression on me." He cupped her jaw in his palm. "I've learned to trust again, Callie, because of you."

"Don't put me on a pedestal. If you knew all the anger I've struggled with, the doubts about God's leading, you'd know how much I fail."

"Your actions say otherwise." He grinned. "You're even humble. See? You're perfect."

"Hang around long enough and you'll see the real me."

"I'd like that," he said, his heart in his throat.

"You would?"

"Yes, I would."

"I wish you could've trusted me with this sooner."

"I'm sorry. Nothing in my life made me believe I could trust anyone."

"I'm the one who's sorry. Sorry Susan and Lloyd betrayed you." She laid her head on his chest. Surely she could hear the wild beat of his heart. "But if all that hadn't happened, I would never have met you."

He'd never thought of it that way.

"Thank you for sharing your past, Jacob. Now no secrets lie between us."

As his throat constricted, Jake pulled her to him, wrapping her in his arms. He had one more secret. But if Callie knew why he chose Peaceful, she wouldn't rest from the search until she'd turned over every stone and examined it under a magnifying glass. With the controversy over the unwed mothers' home, Callie was coping with enough. Now with the strong likelihood that someone had overheard his confession, she'd face even more trouble.

She'd come to him determined to uncover his secret. He could only hope the price she paid for that discovery wasn't too steep.

At the entrance to Mitchell Mercantile, Callie tightened the hold on the bag she carried and released Jacob's arm. If only she hadn't pushed him into talking about his stint in prison. Whoever had overheard hadn't taken long to get the word out. The news had spread faster than wildfires on an arid prairie.

At the grocery yesterday, several people had come up to Callie, warning her to send that jailbird packing before he robbed her blind. She'd made it clear that she stood by him. Eventually, the gossip would die down. And Peaceful would once again live up to its name. Or so she hoped.

"I'll just be a minute," Jacob said, then headed toward the hardware section of the store. As he strode past aisles milling with customers, they put their heads together, no doubt whispering about his time in prison.

It didn't seem to matter to anyone that Jacob had been falsely accused and released with an apology. How could people add more pain to the injustice he'd endured by gossiping?

Sighing, Callie moved to the counter teeming with jars of every size and shape crammed to the top with gumdrops, peanut brittle, taffy, hard candy and pretzels. Fresh-baked goods were tucked under glass. Barrels of pickles and crackers lined the floor. One barrel with a spigot held vinegar.

On the other side of the counter, her father-in-law sat at his desk, examining a ledger. As if he felt her presence, he looked up. "Hello, Callie." Smiling as if he were glad to see her, he shoved back his chair and stepped toward her.

Seeing his good mood, hope leaped inside her. Perhaps he'd accept her proposition. "You look busy."

"Taking care of these books is a full-time job." He thrust the pencil he held behind his ear. "What brings you out today?"

She pulled the blanket Elise had made from the bag. "I'd like to barter Elise's hand-knit items like this lovely blanket and jars of my jams and maybe some pies, in exchange for store credit." She forced a smile. "Or, better yet, for cash."

"You're looking to raise money for the unwed mothers' home, aren't you?"

"That's true, but..." Her hands trembled on the blanket. "Frankly, I'm not sure I can put food on the table for me and my child, much less others, unless I get a steady income."

"I see." His brow furrowed as if her words pained him. "I don't agree with your plan, but I'd never let you or my grandchild go hungry." He sighed. "I haven't been as generous as I should've been, hoping you'd give up this foolishness." His jaw jutted then eased. "Reckon you're even more stubborn than I am." He chuckled. "I'll buy as many of your jams, pies and knitted items as you two can make. Pay a good price for them, too. They'll fly off the shelves."

"Thank you." She slid the bag toward her father-in-law. "In that case, I'll leave these with you."

Commodore opened the cash register and took out a wad of bills. "I'll let you know when we run out." He handed her the money. "You've always been able to stretch a dollar." His eyes filled with misery. "The ones my son didn't spend. This is a small way of saying thanks."

"You're a blessing, Commodore."

At that moment, Jacob laid his purchases on the counter and wrestled his wallet from his hip pocket. From Commodore's cold, penetrating stare, trouble brewed between the two men. Jacob suspected that Commodore had spread the news of his imprisonment and looked ready for a showdown.

Her father-in-law rang up the wood fill and plaster, bagged them and took the money, all without saying a word to Jacob.

As Jacob reached for the sack, Commodore covered it with his hand. "I can see you're trying to get close to Callie. No jailbird is raising my grandchild. Look at you, drifting from town to town. You really think you can stop here and become a father?"

"Commodore!"

"Let me handle this, Callie." Jacob turned to her father-in-law. "I'm innocent. My record's been erased. I'm no more a criminal than you are."

Leaning close, Commodore put his face mere inches from Jacob. "So you say, but this town is up in arms about that stint in jail. I won't have Callie's good name dragged through the mud. I want you gone."

"My name isn't being tarnished by befriending Jacob. He's done nothing wrong."

Jacob fisted a hand. "I've got an urge to plow a fist into your yakking jaw. But my principles won't allow me to harm Callie's baby's grandfather."

Commodore took a step back, no doubt suspicious of the strength of Jacob's principles. "Your reputation in this town is ruined. Gossip about you two is rampant. If you care about Callie, you'll leave."

"He can prove he's innocent," Callie said.

"Innocent or not, the damage is done." Commodore pointed a finger at Jacob. "Who'd hire you in this town? Who'd trust you in their home? Who'd want to share a pew with you in church? You've seen enough of Peaceful to know I'm speaking the truth. If you truly care about Callie," Commodore went on, "you'll get out of town. Her baby's future is what's important."

The uncertainty filling Jacob's eyes tore at Callie. "You might want to consider your stance, Commodore, if you care about seeing your grandchild."

"See what you're doing, Smith? Because of some misguided loyalty to you, she's threatening to cut me off from my son's child. Are you proud of yourself?"

"Don't blame Jacob for that. You're the one causing the problem."

"Only a few minutes ago, I was a blessing. Maybe you should remember, young lady, which side your bread is buttered on."

The threat squeezed against Callie's lungs. Before she said more than was prudent, she thrust the money in her pocket, took Jacob's arm and rushed from the store.

Outside, Jacob laid a hand on hers. "What Commodore said is true, whether it's fair or not. I won't be the reason this town hurts you and your baby."

"You could leave? That easily?"

In the end, didn't everyone leave?

Or deceive her at every turn?

Commodore had accepted her proposal, paid her well even praised her cooking and management skills, and then threatened to retract their deal unless she toed the line.

"I'm sorry, Callie, but sometimes a man has to make hard decisions to protect those he cares about."

No doubt Commodore believed he was doing the same thing. "If you could toss me aside at the first hint of trouble, that's evidence of how little you care." She yanked free of his hand then clipped along the walk, refusing to look back, every step thudding against her bruised heart.

Well, she needn't have worried. No steps sounded behind her. What did it matter? Without faith in God, Jacob was the wrong man for her. They had no chance of a future together.

This impasse was for the best. With Jacob out of the picture, Commodore would keep his end of the bargain, ensuring that the unwed mothers' home would survive. She needed nothing more than her baby and to help these women.

So why did a future without Jacob leave her feeling so lost and alone?

Chapter Seventeen

Nothing. Not a single clue.

Jake stretched his arms over his head. He'd been sitting here with Callie for hours, flipping through past issues of *The Peaceful Chronicles,* looking for some nugget of information that would reveal his mother's identity or help Callie write the town's history.

To restore the peace between them, Jake had come clean about his reason for landing in Peaceful. As he knew Callie would, she'd joined his search, eager to find any detail that might lead to his mother's identity. If Callie learned during that search that his mother had no interest in a relationship with him, Jake knew she'd never think less of him.

Grace had gone next door to clean Mildred Uland's house after Mrs. Uland's cleaning lady had quit. Elise had helped for a while, then said she wasn't feeling well and went upstairs to lie down, leaving just the two of them holed up in the library.

Across the way, Callie hunched over a newspaper, caught up in some article. He drank in the curve of her cheek, her upturned nose and tendrils of hair curling around her neck. Memorizing each small detail, storing them in his mind for the day she sent him packing. Though they'd forged a modicum of peace, thanks to some fast talking on his part, he didn't doubt that day would come.

Still, he'd been wrong to fall for Commodore's ploy to get him out of town. Not that Peaceful would ever accept him. On that much he and Commodore agreed. But he'd see the quest of finding his mother to the end and help Callie make her dream a reality. During one of his chats with Mildred, he'd given Callie's neighbor money for the home's support, asking her not to reveal the source. Mildred had added her own funds, then opened a bank account for Refuge of Redeeming Love.

That much Jake could do for Callie.

He returned to skimming titles, searching for names of the men and women who'd played a role in settling the town and helping it grow and flourish. He looked for significant dates, events and even human-interest stories that would bring Peaceful's history alive on the page. They'd clipped anything that looked promising and tucked each one into labeled boxes. From those clippings, Callie hoped to condense it into an interesting narrative. But to Jake, most of this information was as dull as unvarnished wood.

Callie took a sip of tea, then pointed to an article. "This lists the winners at the Marion County Fair. My grandmother's quilt won a blue ribbon." She swept a hand over the clippings. "Find anything of interest to you?"

Yes, nothing held his interest like Callie, but he wouldn't say that. "Not yet. But I'm grateful for the chance to look."

She picked up another issue of the newspaper. "I'm keeping an eye out for clues to your mother's identity. Have you been reading the Society page?"

"No, I'm sick of reading descriptions of ladies' hats and who attended the latest tea. I'm saving those tidbits for you." He pointed to the box labeled *Gossip*.

"Oh, I found something." Callie picked up the paper to read the words to him. "Listen to this: 'Occupants of a house on Serenity Avenue may wish to dub the street Stressed Avenue, since a young man from the wrong side of the tracks has been seen calling on their daughter.'" Callie laid down the paper. "Could that be a clue?"

"To what?"

Callie rolled her eyes. "If the columnist is referring to *this* house, then the daughter would be Senator Squier's."

"And?"

"That could mean some young man was courting Irene Squier."

"There're lots of houses on Serenity. But I suppose it's possible."

"And he could've… Well, might've gotten her pregnant."

Jake reached a hand. "What else does it say?"

"Nothing." She thumbed through the stack of issues. "Let's see if more is said about this in later columns." She turned to the next paper's Society page and read the gossip column. "Nothing in here, but I'll look through the next several issues."

Jake picked up the column and reread it. "Even if the gossip referred to the occupants of this house—and we have no evidence that it does—Irene moved away from here. Remember?"

"True. What's the date of that paper?"

"September 1876." Jake's breath caught as he did the math. "I was born in May of the next year."

Callie gasped. "Could Irene be your—?"

"Mother." Just hearing the word off his lips, a desire to know Irene Squier sprang to life inside him.

The date of the family's departure and this column were significant. He thought back on his conversation with the state senator in Indianapolis. The man had said Wesley and Lillian Squier had moved back East. He'd assumed Irene had gone with them. If she had, she couldn't have mailed those postcards.

But what if she hadn't left?

What if she resided in Peaceful? His heart pounded. What if he'd passed her on the street?

Callie gathered a stack of newspapers. "I've looked at the gossip columns for the remainder of the month. No mention of this relationship. But until we read them all, we can't be sure we're on the right track."

Jake grabbed the box labeled *Gossip* and leafed through the clippings they'd snipped earlier. A few minutes later, he found another mention of a romance on Serenity. "Here's another one! With a later date." He half rose from his chair. "'Young love on Serenity Avenue will find a way—better under the watchful eye of a chaperone than under cover of dark.'" Jake cleared his throat. "Sounds like they were sneaking off together."

"I wish we had more to go on."

He flipped through the rest of the gossip articles. "No sorrier than I am. I've looked at the columns in May, near my birthdate. There's no mention of a baby born to someone on Serenity."

"Wouldn't it be something if the young woman who

lived in this house was your mother?" She glanced around the room. "It's as if this house were meant to shelter unwed mothers."

"Perhaps we're making too much of this. Serenity's a long street. Several families could've had a daughter."

"Of courting age? It's the first lead we've had."

He reread the article. "Where was the wrong side of the tracks?"

Callie pointed south toward the downtown area. "The Monon railroad tracks cut Peaceful down the middle. Mildred might know more about the area south of those tracks."

"I'll see what she knows. She hadn't remembered Irene courting anyone, but this article might trigger her memory."

Again Jake thought about his visit to Indianapolis. He hadn't shared that trip with Callie, thinking that what he'd learned amounted to nothing. But now he was tempted to return. See if Senator Davis might have an address for the Squier family, something more to go on.

Callie jumped up and shot around the desk. "What an adventure this is turning out to be! Let's go see Mildred."

He gazed into her lovely, animated face. Callie appreciated the importance of family. Combing the newspapers had become important to them both. When had anyone cared that much about him?

"We'll go." He tugged her into his arms. "But before we do, I know another quest that interests me."

He lowered his head. The softness of her lips under his elicited a groan. She melted against him, encircling his neck with her arms. The gentleness of the kiss intensified with an urgency that set his heart knocking in his chest.

The door banged open. Jake and Callie jerked apart.

Elise stood on the threshold, her face twisted in pain, her hands supporting her bulging belly. "I think it's time," she ground out.

Springing into action, Callie rushed to Elise's side. "I'll help you upstairs." She motioned to Jake. "Get Doc Wellman. On the way, stop at the Langleys'. Tell Sarah that Elise has gone into labor."

"Consider it done."

Callie shot him a smile, then wrapped an arm around Elise and walked her out of the room.

On the way to the front door, Jake's stomach plummeted like a runaway wagon on a downhill slope. Not just about the arrival of Elise's baby, though his disquiet that her time had come surprised him. But after almost giving up on finding his mother, Callie had stumbled upon gossip columns that might be a clue to his roots. Who would've thought gossip would ever have merit?

Soon life would change forever. Certainly for Elise. And perhaps, if the clue meant anything, life would change forever for him. Where would those changes lead?

Jake paced the kitchen floor, tending the teakettles on the cookstove, as Callie had asked. With no idea what else he could do, he felt lost, like a man in the backwoods without a compass. He wanted to shut out the moans from upstairs, yet couldn't leave—as if his presence made an iota of difference. Poor Elise was suffering. The doctor had been here for ages. Her mother had arrived. Why wasn't that baby coming as well?

Maybe the baby was like his grandfather—too stubborn to come. How Mark Langley could refuse to be there for his daughter baffled Jake.

"Jacob."

He whipped around. Callie stood in the doorway. "What's wrong?"

"Nothing. Nothing at all." Callie's calm demeanor eased his stomach, righted his off-kilter world. "Doc Wellman says it won't be too much longer. I came down for hot water."

Wanting to protect her from that kind of pain, he touched her cheek, soft beneath his fingers, "Are you afraid? Knowing you'll go through that in a few months?"

"Bringing a baby into this world can be hard, but I'm not afraid." She laid her hand over Jake's. "Some things are worth any amount of pain."

"I've heard of women having ten-pound babies." He glanced at her petite frame. "It could be difficult to—"

She laid her fingers across his lips. "When did you become such a worrywart?"

He wasn't. Normally. When had Callie become his world?

He tugged her to him. She laid her head against his shoulder and snuggled close. Jake rested his chin on her forehead and soaked up the peace he felt at having her near. With Callie in his arms, life's concerns faded. All felt right with the world. This is where she belonged.

"Callie." She glanced up at him with those startling sea-blue eyes of hers. "I care about you—"

Abruptly, she broke away, clearly avoiding his declaration. "I'd better get that water," she said, not meeting his gaze.

Everything that had softened inside him, hardened. Callie didn't want him. He couldn't blame her. "I'll get it."

Jake followed her upstairs, carrying a hissing tea-kettle and a steaming pot by the handle. Outside Elise's bedroom door, he handed them over to Callie. "Let me know if there's anything else I can do."

"Pray all goes well and this baby arrives soon. Elise is tired." She sighed, no doubt remembering he wasn't a praying man. That sigh nearly did him in.

Jake knew one thing he could do. He raced down the stairs and strode out the front door, all feelings of abandonment inside him shoving to the surface. He'd do what he could to ensure Langley didn't abandon Elise.

At his knock, Mark Langley opened the door, looking as lost as Jake felt. "Is Elise all right?"

"The baby hasn't arrived yet. Callie says it's normal for babies to take their time coming."

Her father nodded, but didn't look comforted. Obviously, he cared for his daughter. But what about that child she would bring into the world?

"I'm here to tell you what it's like to spend your childhood in an orphanage." Then, not waiting for Mr. Langley's permission, he proceeded to do so. When he finished, he looked deep into Langley's eyes. "Be a father to your daughter. Be a grandfather to her child. The only thing you have to lose is your pride. If you don't, you'll lose everything that matters."

Without a word, Langley headed for the door. Jake had to hurry to catch up.

In Callie's parlor, Elise's father perched on the edge of a dainty chair. "Thanks for telling me about your childhood. It's got me thinking about a lot of things—"

A shriek from above brought him to his feet. "What's taking so long?" Pacing the rug like a caged coyote, he rubbed a hand over his eyes. "If anything happens to that girl, I'll never forgive myself."

"She'll be all right." Jake gulped. She had to be.

Langley stopped and looked at Jake. "Things aren't good between us. Haven't been in a long time. I wanted a boy," he said, choking out the words. "Never could relate to Elise and all that girly stuff. I loved her…but didn't show it much." He shuddered. "I wonder if I drove her into that scalawag's arms."

Langley feared his daughter had fallen for a smooth-talker to fill the void of a distant father. Jake had expected families to be warm, loving, supportive, never failing one another. He'd seen that few people had picture-perfect families. Yet they managed to go on and forge their way, hopefully as Elise and her father would do.

Langley went on pacing. "I couldn't deal with Elise having a baby." He sighed. "My baby having a baby. Just couldn't take that in. I wanted the problem to go away. That's how I saw the baby—as a problem."

"It's not too late to set things right between you and Elise. She's a generous, forgiving person."

"I said a lot of things I shouldn't have."

"What about the baby?"

The eyes he turned on Jake filled with misery. "That's my grandchild Elise is bringing into this world. A baby, not some shame I can shun." His voice broke. "Elise and I got to the point that I couldn't figure out how to mend things."

Jake would give anything if he had a relationship with his parents. Even with all that had happened. Even with the hurts he'd buried inside. If he ever found them, and they showed him one bit of interest, he'd forgive their abandonment. Family mattered. Families stuck by one another. Families worked it out.

"Just be there," Jake said. "Be there when Elise needs you most."

Another shriek, then another and another until the air all but vibrated with Elise's cries. Both men froze. Then they heard the high-pitched wail of a baby that sounded so hopping mad, Jake couldn't help but chuckle.

Mark Langley's face lit up. "It's here."

Jake shook his hand. "Maybe that boy you always wanted."

Elise's father shook his head. "I hope it's a girl. If it is, I'll show her girls are special. That is, after I show her mother."

Callie appeared in the parlor and stopped at the sight of Mr. Langley, her wide-eyed surprise changing to a huge smile. She motioned for the two of them to follow her upstairs.

The door to Elise's bedroom opened. Doc left the room, carrying his medical bag. "Elise and the baby are fine. You're a grandfather of a healthy baby girl."

"Thanks, Doc. Thanks for taking care of my girls," Langley said, in a shaky voice.

Callie ushered them inside. Elise sat propped up in bed, her face weary but wearing a stunning smile, her baby tucked in a yellow blanket and wrapped in her arms.

Mrs. Langley sat beside the bed. "Mark," was all she said, but Jake heard more in that word than an entire sermon on forgiveness.

Mr. Langley walked to his daughter. "I'm sorry, Elise, for everything I've said. Can you forgive me?"

"You're here, Papa. You came." Elise's voice strangled with tears. "You came when I needed you most." She pulled back the blanket to expose all of her baby's face, reposed in sleep during this momentous family reunion. "Meet your granddaughter, Kathryn Marie Langley."

Mr. Langley caressed the baby's face with one finger. "She's beautiful, Elise. Like her mother."

"Oh, Papa."

Elise laid the precious bundle beside her on the bed and lifted her hands to her father.

Mark Langley wept in her arms.

Callie led Jacob through the hedge to Mildred's, the only person they trusted who might remember the young man from the wrong side of the tracks who could've courted Irene Squier.

Mildred ushered them into her parlor. "Have a seat."

Every surface, shelf and chair was stacked with books and keepsakes. Not unusual these days while Mildred spent endless hours going through mementoes. All treasures Callie knew, but from the shocked expression on Jacob's face, he saw nothing but junk. Callie picked up a stack of books on one end of the sofa and set them on the floor.

With an apologetic smile, Mildred cleared books from the other end. "You'll have to excuse the mess. I'm going through things, trying to cull them out, but…" She picked up a McGuffey's reader and opened the cover. "This belonged to my husband. Has his name right here." She looked away. "It's hard to let go."

Callie understood the difficulty of letting go. Not with things, but with loved ones. Jacob had difficulty letting go of a past that affected him still.

"I'll get refreshments," Mildred said, then left the room.

Jake leaned toward Callie. "A house this size no doubt has a library. Isn't it large enough to hold her collection of books?"

"Like she said, she's been going through things. I think all these keepsakes make her feel closer to her husband." She sighed. "Now you can see why her cleaning lady quit. Grace will do the job as long as she can. Her way of helping with expenses."

Mildred returned, carrying a tray with three glasses of lemonade and a plate of those gingersnap cookies she loved. Callie shoved aside a box of postcards on the table to make room for the tray.

Mildred cleared the chair of today's newspaper and plopped down. "You're here for more than my cookies," she said. "Anyone with ears knows about your time in jail, Jake." She offered him the plate. "I'd like to hear your version."

After he explained, Mildred leaned toward him. "Life's not fair, plain and simple. But you hold your head up. In time, people will lose interest."

"Perhaps, but my past is tainting Callie's reputation and giving this town another reason to turn against her."

Mildred cocked her head at him. "Why not tell me why you're in Peaceful, Jake?" She raised a hand. "Better yet, let me guess. Considering how many times you've asked questions about the women in this town, about the Squier family, especially their daughter, Irene, I suspect you came here looking for your mother."

He met her gaze. "Yes."

"Why did you believe your mother was in Peaceful?"

Jacob told her about the postcards.

"Have you found her?"

"That's why we're here, Mildred. We found a few references in newspaper gossip columns that could be a clue. The columns suggest a young man from the wrong side of the tracks courted a young lady on Serenity. We're hoping that was Irene. Do you know who that young man might have been?"

Mildred munched a cookie, then leaned back, closing her eyes, hopefully deep in thought, not nodding off as she was prone to do. Her eyes popped open. "The wrong side of the tracks is easy enough. The folks with money lived on this side. Folks south of those tracks lived in small bungalows, a few in shanties." She furrowed her brow, staring at her shoes, as if the name of the young man was written on the toes. "What year was that?"

"Most likely the fall and winter of '76."

"That explains it. The reason I don't recall Irene having a suitor is my husband took sick about that time. He died a few months later, that next spring. I spent every moment at his bedside. I wouldn't have noticed if Irene had spooned with a young man on her front porch— or on mine for that matter. I'm sorry. I wish I could've been more help."

Disappointment sank to Callie's belly. "You were a wonderful wife, Mildred. Everyone said so."

"I hope you figure it out. Maybe talk to the folks south of town." She nailed Jacob with her gaze. "I've got a question for you. Are you planning to run? Or stick with Callie here?"

The shocked look on Jacob's face said it all.

Mildred harrumphed. "Don't let a little gossip direct your steps. Let me tell you, Jake, God expects better of you."

"God doesn't know me."

"Ha! You've got lots to learn, my young friend. Stay put. Open your heart to God. You're in for the ride of a lifetime."

Callie had come hoping to learn more about Irene Squier. Instead, Mildred had tried badgering Jacob into faith and into caring for Callie. Callie knew what Mildred had forgotten. Before a man could ride, he had to be willing to get in the saddle.

Jake sat in Callie's parlor holding Elise's baby against his chest. Inside the blanket, the poor little thing drew her knees up, screeching like an alley cat in a midnight skirmish. And Jake didn't know the first thing about comforting her. He'd never even held a baby before.

Not that he planned to hold this one for long. He'd come in from feeding the stock and surely didn't smell good enough to hold a newborn baby. But, with Callie off to a prayer meeting and Grace holed up in her room, Elise had come to him, close to tears from walking the floor with Katie.

He couldn't turn her down. Not after she gazed up at him with exhausted eyes and asked for his help, as if he knew the first thing about babies. He'd taken the tyke into his arms as gingerly as an explosive device with a short fuse and sent Elise off to bed.

Elise surprised Jake by staying at Callie's after she and her father had made peace, hoping Katie Marie would soften Grace's heart toward her baby. But Grace avoided the newborn. Even took food to her room if the baby showed up at meals.

How could she not open her heart to this baby? Katie Marie was perfect. Helpless. Tiny. And madder than a hen with a broken beak.

Patting her back, Jake walked the floor, swaying with her. Not enough to hurt her. He hoped. He kept patting. Kept walking. Every muscle tense.

What if he hurt her?

What if something was wrong?

Should he get Doc?

Where was Callie? How long could one person pray?

"Looks like you could use some help."

Callie stood in the parlor smiling at him. The relief of having her there washed through him clear to his toes.

An explosion erupted from Katie's mouth. A belch of gigantic proportions, one a teenage boy would be proud of, was followed by a stream of curdled milk that dampened his shirt, and an odor that left him gagging. Surely that couldn't have come from this dainty creature.

But the baby kept on crying, as if her little heart would break and Jake felt like joining her.

With an amused smile, Callie took Katie Marie from his arms, easing the baby into the crook of her arm and cooed softly to her, then tucked the baby up against her middle, swaying to the rhythm of some unsung lullaby. Immediately Katie quieted. Her eyelids drifted closed. She slept.

Callie sat on the sofa. Jake sank beside her as wrung out as an old dishrag. "I'm thankful you got home when you did." He grabbed the cloth Elise had left with him and dabbed the milk from Katie's rosebud lips, then mopped his clothes. "You're a natural mother."

"You were managing just fine."

Jake knew better. Commodore had said Jake wasn't cut out for fatherhood. He hadn't doubted Commodore's assessment. His failure to soothe Katie had added further evidence.

Callie lifted her gaze to him. "Isn't she beautiful?"

"She is."

Jake touched the soft folds of the baby's neck, ran a finger over the silky strands of her hair and along a tiny fuzzy ear. Katie emitted a soft sigh and snuggled deeper into the yellow blanket, a picture of contentment, tugging at his heart with a strength that left him dazed.

This precious infant would grow up without a father. Something hot flared inside him. Better to have no father than a bad one. At least she'd have one good parent.

"I can't wait to hold my baby," Callie murmured, ending on a soft sigh.

"Your baby is blessed to have you as a mother."

She smiled at him, beamed really. "Thank you, Jacob. I want what's best for my child."

"What's best for your child isn't me."

"Oh, you worry too much. Few feel up to the task of parenthood." She chuckled. "What's best for this little one is her bed. I'll put her down."

As Jake watched them go, tears stung the back of his eyes. Callie hadn't understood what he'd tried to tell her. Even as the admission stabbed like a knife to his heart, the truth was undeniable. Callie's baby needed a good father. How could Jake be such a thing when he'd had no role model? He'd heard enough from Pastor Steele's sermons to know a husband should lead his family. Yet Jake lacked the faith that would help guide a child and head a home.

The harsh truth of his incompetence sank inside him. He had to walk away. Leave this house. Leave the ministry to unwed mothers. Leave Callie. Leave everything and everyone who had become important to him. He'd vowed to toughen himself against caring, against opening his heart—

He'd failed. Callie Mitchell had his heart. He'd found what he'd been looking for all his life. Nothing in his past had prepared him for his feelings for this woman. Her presence made the bleakest day beautiful, the toughest task easy, and the most monotonous day exciting. She was merciful. Kind. Generous. Everything good.

He loved Callie. Completely, totally.

Only a few days old and Katie Marie had already taught Jake Smith a thing or two. He hadn't had a family. Never knew the privilege of sharing a home or of having the support of loved ones, but this baby had given him a peek at the responsibilities of fatherhood.

He wasn't fit to raise a child. To love this woman. Especially in a town that would never accept him.

He'd never tell Callie he loved her. If he did, it would be asking her to choose him over what was best for her child.

Even a faithless jailbird wouldn't stoop that low.

Chapter Eighteen

Wind howled in the trees, whipping the limbs into a frenzied dance. Rain pelted the windows, striking the glass with the clatter of hail. Callie prayed a tornado wasn't brewing and heading their way. Jacob had raced to Mildred's to cover a leak in her roof with a tarpaulin. Yet, even with nature blowing up a tempest, her house was sturdy and would weather the storm.

Katie Marie's cry drifted down the staircase. Within minutes, she quieted. Her needs met by Elise. Remembering the way Jacob had handled the newborn last night, holding her like a piece of crystal, as if she'd break, Callie smiled. His tender, awed expression proved he was smitten with the baby. He would be a good husband, a wonderful father.

For someone. Not for her.

What's best for your baby isn't me.

Jacob's statement didn't sink in—at first—but it hadn't taken Callie long to realize he meant every word.

She'd prayed and prayed for Jacob to come to God. Though she'd seen a change in his attitude in church and he'd acknowledged reading the Bible, he hadn't taken that step. And from his own mouth he'd dispelled the prospect of that changing.

He shared her concern for unwed mothers, understood her troubled background. She'd had hope that he might be part of God's plan for her life. But she and her baby needed a God-fearing man to lead their home. God would not send her a man without faith.

A knock at her door jarred her out of her thoughts. Who would be out on such a night? Whoever braved this weather was getting drenched. She hurried to answer it.

On the other side of the door stood a stranger wearing a long navy macintosh over his suit, lowering a silk umbrella. She shivered in the damp, chilly wind.

The man tipped his bowler, revealing his pate, bald and pale as a peeled onion. She noted the case in his hand. Surely even the most ambitious salesman wouldn't be out in this weather. "I'm sorry, but whatever you're selling—"

"Ma'am, I'm Robert Lovell, attorney with the Indianapolis law firm of Lovell, McGahan and Lovell." He replaced his hat. "I'm looking for Martin and Callie Mitchell."

At the mention of her deceased husband, Callie's grip on the door tightened. "I'm Callie Mitchell. Martin's widow."

"I'm sorry for your loss, Mrs. Mitchell."

"What's this about, Mr. Lovell?"

"May I come in? I'd rather explain my business in the comfort of your parlor than out here in this storm."

"Please excuse my bad manners. Come in." As Callie led the way, her stomach roiled like a vessel on a storm-tossed sea. What business would a big-city lawyer have with her?

She felt an urge to ask him to wait for Jacob, but that was silly. Whatever this was about, it had nothing to do with Jacob. The time had come to stop relying on that man.

They took seats at the parlor table. After an apology for dripping water on her carpet, the attorney reached inside his case and pulled out a ream of papers. He glanced through them, then met her eyes. "Just to verify, I'm at 7133 Serenity Avenue in Peaceful, Indiana."

"That's correct."

"This house was previously owned by Senator and Mrs. Wesley Squier."

"My father-in-law, Commodore Mitchell, purchased the Squier house at auction two years ago this month."

"The senator and his wife died in a trolley accident that same year. Their daughter, Irene, preceded them in death."

Something tightened in Callie's chest, pressing against her lungs until she could barely breathe. If Irene was Jacob's mother, she was dead. How could Callie break the news to him? "I had no idea. What a tragedy."

He cleared his throat. "Indeed. Senator Squier and his wife had moved back East. At the time of their death, as their attorney, I had a copy of their Last Will and Testament. Or so I believed." He mopped his brow. "As it turns out, not all their legal papers were in my possession. Recently, a safe was uncovered containing a later will, written in Wesley's own hand with the seal of a notary, negating the earlier one. A judge in Maryland has ruled that the later will is binding."

Through the window, lightning flashed, casting eerie shadows in the room. "What does this have to do with me?"

"Mrs. Mitchell, the house Commodore Mitchell bought shouldn't have been up for auction. The Squiers left this house to someone else."

Callie's pulse throbbed in her temples with the rhythm of rumbling thunder overhead. "I don't understand. Commodore paid for the house."

"I can appreciate your confusion. But, as I said, the house should not have been sold. It was left to Irene's son, Jacob Squier Smith."

All these years Jacob thought he had no family, but he did. He had a family that had looked out for him, left him in their will… That meant—

The room tilted then righted. Callie knew, in that moment, nothing would ever be the same again. She was losing her home, her baby's home and the refuge for unwed mothers. *Lord, help me handle this trial.*

"Could this be a mistake?"

"No mistake. I'm sorry."

Her body went cold. She shivered.

"A letter attached to the updated will explained that after Irene died in childbirth, Senator Squier placed the infant in an orphanage, giving Jacob an alias, the surname *Smith* to protect his daughter's good name. These documents were found weeks ago, but we haven't been able to locate Jacob Smith. The orphanage had no address for him. As you can imagine, we wanted to make sure Jacob Smith survived before we broached this rather sticky situation with you."

Should she get Jacob from Mildred's? He needed to hear the news, had a right to know. But to hear something this devastating from a stranger seemed cruel. "Mr. Smith is here in town, but not available at the moment."

The attorney smiled. "That's good to hear. I'm staying at the Liberty Inn tonight. Please give him my business card and ask him to meet me there tomorrow."

She nodded, taking the card.

"I suspected that he was in the area. A few days ago, Mr. Smith spoke to a friend of mine in Indianapolis."

Callie's head snapped up. "What?"

"Mr. Smith came to inquire about the Squier family. The state senator he talked to, David Davis, is a friend of mine. David knew I represented the Squier family and was looking for their heir. I'd never given David the name of the man I sought, but he thought Jacob Smith's inquiry might be important." He smiled. "It was."

"Jacob came to Indianapolis, asking about my house?"

"I'm not privy to every topic of their conversation." He handed a copy of the will to Callie. "You can rest assured that these documents are legal and binding."

The name Jacob Squier Smith leaped off the page. Callie's hands trembled so badly that she laid the document on her lap.

"Do you have the deed in your possession, Mrs. Mitchell?"

"Yes."

"Would you get it, please? I will make the necessary change of ownership in the recorder's office in the Marion County courthouse."

Callie's head pounded, fire filled her veins. Jacob Smith had lied to her again. Even his name had been a lie.

No wonder he'd been willing to make repairs without a wage. No wonder he'd worked from dawn to dusk to restore her house. No wonder he'd been reluctant to tell her about his past. Jacob Smith had manipulated her.

For two years, she'd lived in the shelter of these rooms, more shabby than stately, but home. Wasn't possession nine points of the law? "I will fight this, Mr. Lovell. I have no intention of turning over the deed to this house." She shook the papers. "This document could be a fake. I don't know you or your law firm." She rose. "Good day, sir."

Mr. Lovell's jaw jutted, but he got to his feet. "I assure you, these documents are legally binding. There is no mistake," he said, his tone steely.

"I assure you I won't be fooled again. I will look into this with an attorney of my own."

Not that she had an attorney or the money to hire one. She'd find a way. Perhaps Mildred would lend her the money. With the bond between Mildred and Jacob, the prospect of telling her neighbor about his deceit sank inside her like a stone.

She showed Mr. Lovell to the door, bracing against the wind then closed it after him.

Now she understood why Jacob told her he wasn't best for her baby. His reason wasn't some concern for her baby's welfare or a lack of faith. No. He knew he'd set up this betrayal.

What a fool she'd been.

Jacob Smith—no, Jacob Squier, a man she'd trusted, a man with a horrific past dominated by loneliness and injustice. She'd made his burdens her own. For this? Once again she'd missed what lurked beneath the surface of a man.

Yet that didn't eradicate Jacob's image from her

mind, didn't block those intense green eyes, the dimple in his cheek, that chiseled jaw—

Something Commodore once said stuck in her mind and came back to her now: *A drifter has something to hide. As soon as someone gets close to his secret, that's when he leaves.*

Jacob Smith hid secrets. But Commodore had been wrong about one thing. Jacob wouldn't be leaving. Not when he expected to move into the main house.

Jake had managed to get the tarpaulin in place before the brunt of the storm hit. The wind practically blew him from Mildred's to Callie's. Thankfully, the rain had let up enough to make the distance without getting drenched.

Callie opened the door to his knock. He brushed the rain off his hat, smiling. "I've battened down the hatches at Mildred's." He took another look at her. "Everything all right here?"

She moved aside to let him in. "How nice of you to take an interest in your house."

"What do you mean?"

She glared at him. "How could you do this to me?"

Her icy tone stopped him cold. "I don't know what you're talking about."

"I've had a visitor."

"In this weather? Who?"

"A Mr. Robert Lovell, an attorney who claims this house doesn't belong to me." She took a step toward him. "That it was wrongly sold."

"What?"

"A more recent copy of the Squier Last Will and Testament was found. How convenient to find that will after you've increased the house's value." She gave a choked laugh, verging on hysteria. "But then you know all about that."

Lightning struck nearby. Thunder shook the house. Callie never flinched. She didn't appear to notice the storm, but Jake could see by the glint in her eyes, the rigid set of her jaw, she had one raging inside of her.

He reached for her, but she batted his hand away. "I don't understand what you're saying. Callie, talk to me."

"You lied. How could you? I trusted you. I cared about you. Even thought, I lov— What a fool I've been!"

Another bolt of lightning, a clap of thunder. He pleaded with her, his composure crumbling. "Lied? I told you about my time in jail, the reason I came to Peaceful. I've told you everything."

"You're quite the actor." She poked a finger into his sternum with surprising force, as if wanting to give him pain.

What was going on?

"Don't pretend! I had all the deception I could stomach with Martin. Always pretending, always telling me what I wanted to hear and hiding what I didn't." She poked again, harder. "I trusted you! You and Martin are cut from the same cloth." She thrust the papers at him. "This proves you're lying!"

With an unsteady hand, Jake took the paperwork, never taking his eyes off Callie.

Her chest heaved. "Read it!"

Jake glanced at the page. Phrases jumped out at him. *The house at 7133 Serenity left to Jacob Smith.* Why?

"This doesn't make sense." The sneer suffusing Callie's face forced the air out of his lungs.

He read on—*Jacob Squier, also known as Jacob Smith, son of Irene Squier, born to her on May 21, 1877.*

His pulse ratcheted. The date of his birth. "Irene Squier's my mother." His gaze leaped to Callie and he looked into eyes as turbulent as storm-tossed seas. Unable to bear the coldness there, he dropped his gaze to the papers in his hand. *Irene Squier died in childbirth.*

Dead? She was dead? Died giving birth to him?

Again and again he read the same words. With each reading the horror of them shuddered through him. As he read them one last time, the pieces came together in his mind. Comprehension slammed into him, doubling him over. He sucked in air. All the time he'd resented his mother for not coming to him, she'd been dead.

Tears filled his eyes. He'd never get to know her. Never get to see her face. Never get to tell her he was sorry for years of blaming her for deserting him.

"I thought *you* were an answer to my prayers. How wrong I've been."

Jake straightened, tried to focus on Callie's words. But she didn't make sense—nothing made sense. He tried to tug her to him. Maybe in his arms, she'd listen. "I didn't know about this."

She laughed. The eerie sound slithered along Jake's spine.

"Do you expect me to believe that your coming here to Peaceful, to this house looking for work was a coincidence?"

"The waitress at the café suggested you—"

"Lies. All of it. Lies!" Her voice broke. "You were living in my lean-to, waiting like a vulture for the pickings."

"I'm not lying!"

"Do you deny that you went to Indianapolis?"

He frowned. How did she know about that? "No, but—"

"You set all this in motion!" Battling tears, she flung a card at him. "You're supposed to meet the attorney at the Liberty Inn tomorrow."

The anguish on her face tore at him, clawed at his heart, ripped it to shreds. Instead of thinking of Callie and what this meant to her, he'd been focused on his mother, on his loss. Callie was losing her home. To him. He wouldn't let that happen. He picked up the card: Robert Lovell, Attorney at Law. Tomorrow he'd contact the lawyer and get this straightened out.

Callie pointed a hand toward the door. "Get out of my house. I won't be moving, not until I'm forced. Stay in the lean-to tonight." She snorted. "I couldn't send even a dog out in this storm."

With that she turned on her heel and stomped off.

Callie was tossing him out. The closest thing he'd had to a family had been destroyed while he'd stood there holding that card in his hand, powerless to stop it.

The family he wanted and thought he'd found was exactly like that foster family so many years ago.

A figment of his imagination.

Jake slapped his Bible shut and stretched out on the cot, his back propped against the pillow. The storm had passed, but that hadn't eased the storm raging between him and Callie.

At first, her accusations had baffled him, then filled him with shock. Shock turned to anger.

That Callie believed him capable of treachery when all he'd ever wanted was to help, not harm, churned inside him. But he'd moved past his own pain and had seen hers. Everything between him and Callie lay in ruins.

Yet, even knowing that, he still listened for her footsteps outside, hoping she'd come to him. That she would admit she knew he'd never wrest the house she loved from her. She hadn't come.

No matter. He'd go to her. Surely, she must be calmer now. Together they'd work this out. If the will was legitimate and the Victorian did belong to him, he'd sign the house over to Callie. He'd ensure that she and her baby had a roof over their heads, as well as all the unwed mothers and their babies, both now and in the years ahead.

He leaped to his feet, striding to the door and opened it. Dusk had fallen but he could see Callie, standing at the back door, talking to a woman heavy with child. Then she ushered her inside. Callie had gone on with her life while he could barely function. She'd settle the newcomer in, as only she could do, and give the woman a sense of belonging.

As she once had him.

He closed the door and dropped to the mattress, tucking his hands under his head. Something about that woman nagged at him, hung on with the tenacity of a gorging tick. He'd seen her before. Where?

He jerked to his feet. With the turmoil of the afternoon, he'd put the incident out of his mind. Until now.

That morning he'd gone into Mitchell Mercantile to buy work clothes. He'd seen that same tattered cloak, that same disheveled woman, a furtive expression on her face, shoving something in her pocket as she slipped out of the store. No one appeared to notice anything amiss.

Most likely she was a downtrodden woman, down on her luck. He'd give it a few minutes then knock on Callie's door. Make sure the newcomer wasn't a problem. Then he'd tell her his plan to set things right.

First thing tomorrow, he'd talk to that attorney. They'd work this out. Everything would be fine. Picturing Callie's reaction, he grinned. If he handled it right, she might even let him give her a hug.

By now, Callie would've settled the woman in. He shoved on his boots, crossed the lean-to floor in a few strides and opened the door.

He found himself staring into the remote eyes of Sheriff Frederick, his hand raised as if to knock. Or break down a door.

"Money's missing from Commodore's cash register. He's thirty dollars short. He saw you in the store. Know anything about that?"

Jake shook his head. "I didn't take any money. Not from the Mercantile. Not from anyone."

"Mind if I check your room?" Not waiting for an answer, Frederick rummaged through Jake's bedding, his clothes folded on the chair, rifled through his Bible, as if a man would hide evidence of his sin in that book. Then jerked open the drawer and pawed through his personal items, his boss's reference, the fragile postcards, ragged from scrutiny and age.

The only connection he had left of his mother. A powerful urge to knock the sheriff into the next county seized him. But that satisfaction wouldn't accomplish anything except to give Frederick another reason to haul his hide to jail.

He slammed the drawer shut. "Where's the money?"

"I told you—I didn't take that money."

"Maybe cooling your heels in jail will improve your memory."

Jail. Reflected in the sheriff's eyes, Jake saw his guilt. Reflected in the tone of Frederick's voice, Jake heard his guilt. Once again, he was facing jail for something he didn't do.

Frederick wrapped a beefy hand around Jake's arm.

"Let go of me," Jake said, his tone rigid, "I'll come of my own accord."

Anyone seeing the two of them on the walk to the jail would've thought they were taking an evening stroll. But for Jake, each step relived another walk. A walk he'd taken from the courtroom to a cell, his fate sealed by a jury. He'd been no guiltier then than now, but innocence didn't keep a man free.

The prospect of being caged like an animal shoved against every nerve, every tendon, every muscle. A compulsion seized him—to run, to fight—to stop the inevitable clank of that barred door. But he kept moving, kept putting one foot in front of the other, holding tight to his control. The only thing he had.

Inside the jail, Frederick threw open the door of a cell. Jake flinched. Then with sheer strength of will, he took the last steps inside.

The door closed with a bang that ricocheted through the block of cells and echoed with a familiar finality that made his stomach heave.

Mere months before, he'd been in another prison where an innocent bump could send a man into a rage. And someone could end up dead. He'd learned to watch his back, always prepared for trouble. Trouble was a daily visitor in jail. Conditions made that inevitable. The bullpen, that dim, airless exercise room with inmates herded together like doomed cattle in the stockyards. The stench of unwashed bodies and urine invaded his nostrils. The slime of spit, slippery beneath his feet had him gulping for air. He couldn't survive that again.

Shoving the memory aside, he dropped onto the cot in the dim cell, elbows on knees, hands dangling, focusing on the fibers on his frayed cuffs. Those frayed cuffs had been the reason he'd gone into the Mercantile. Odd that something so trifling as wanting a new shirt determined a man's fate. He plucked at the fibers, unraveling from the times he'd scraped against shingles, plaster, lumber—typical in his line of work.

Yet, far more than his cuffs was unraveling. His life was unraveling, too.

That woman he'd seen in the Mercantile could've taken the money before she slipped away. Yet he had no way to prove it. Considering Callie's anger at the will, she wouldn't come to his defense.

Jake's throat knotted. He'd lost everything that mattered. His mother. His woman. His freedom.

Once again, he was confined to a cell, no one to hear, no one to care. Swallowing against the bile pushing up his throat, Jake understood with clarity. He didn't know how to handle his life. He didn't know how to handle even one night in this cell.

Tears stung his eyes. All he'd ever wanted was a family. Was that too much to ask for?

That yearning had brought him to Peaceful in search of his mother. In a way, he'd found her. His mother had lived in Callie's house during its grander days. Both he and his mother had walked those floors, spent time under that roof, been sheltered by those walls. Not much of a connection but something. Something he'd cherish. All he had.

A sob tore from his lips. All those years he'd resented his mother for not coming she'd been *dead.* Irene Squier, still in her teens died giving him life.

Someone should care that she no longer lived. Someone should mourn her. He did. He cared, yet too late to tell her.

Too late to thank her.

Too late.

He had nowhere to turn. No one in this town would help him. He hauled himself to his feet and walked to the window, staring at the star-studded night through the bars. Across the way, he spotted the silhouette of Callie's church steeple, pointing toward the sky. The Heavens, people said, God's home.

Did God exist? Were all those words in the Bible true?

He dropped to his knees in the striped moonbeam on the floor, gazing up at that scrap of sky, the only visible link to God, if He even existed.

Jake had read the Bible stories. There'd be no burning bush for him. No parted waters. No water into wine.

All he knew for sure was that he couldn't go on alone. He couldn't make it through another day under his own power. He'd prided himself on his skill with hammer and nails, on hard work, on his physical stamina. But he had nothing left. He was a hollow shell of a man.

A sob shoved up his throat. *If You're real, God, if You're up there and You...care about...me, help me. Please. Help me accept the loss of a mother I never knew. Help me find my way. Please, be that arrow Callie talked about. Show me the way.*

The arrows he'd been following had taken him to a dead end.

I've tried to live by my own strength, but I don't have any strength left. I don't have enough strength to spend the night in this cell. I don't have enough strength to fight Commodore's charge. I don't have enough strength to convince Callie to love me.

I love you.

Jake swiveled on his knees, searching the small space, the corridor. No one was there, but he'd heard a voice. A voice that was crystal clear, real. The tone gentle, with the warmth a loving parent would use with a frightened child.

Some child. *Him.* A twenty-three-year-old jailbird unable to handle his life.

He staggered to the window, peering into the night, searching for some change, some concrete evidence that the voice in his head, dare he think, was the voice of… God.

No falling stars, no flashes of lightning, no howling wind. A regular night. But in that moment, a night like no other. A blessed sense of peace filled him.

God was real. God cared. God loved him.

Jake felt that love. Felt that forgiveness. Nothing about his new conviction made sense. Yet with bone-deep certainty Jake knew God was there in that cell with him.

Him.

A man who'd walked this life alone. Or so he'd thought. Now he knew that choice had been his, not God's. God had been there all along, waiting for him.

At Jake's first step of trust, at his first plea for help, God had answered.

He'd read about Jesus in the Garden of Gethsemane. How he'd cried out to God the night before he hung on that cross. If Jesus could handle *that,* Jake could easily handle this night.

Tomorrow he'd share his faith with the only woman whose opinion mattered. He had the promise of a fresh beginning. It seemed so simple. Yet, so complex. To a man like him, who'd never been loved, the love of God was a mystery.

He had a father now. A Heavenly Father.

Thank You for loving me. Thank You for saving me. Thank You for never leaving me when I rejected You countless times. Help me be and do what You want.

Certain of what he must do, Jake closed his eyes and gave his burdens to the One who controlled the universe, even this small chunk of it. Let go of the anguish of those lonely years in the orphanage, the heartache of waiting for a mother who never came, of being framed by a friend for a crime he didn't commit, the months of degradation and fear in that other cell, of losing Callie's regard. All that weight lifted from his shoulders.

He still remembered every moment of his past. How could he forget? But his past no longer dominated who he was. His todays. Or his tomorrows. He felt reborn.

Hope spilled into every crevice. With God's help, he and Callie could be a family. He could be a good husband, a good father. He stretched out on the cot and slept.

Chapter Nineteen

The morning brought bright sunshine and chirping birds, but nothing was light about the load of uncertainties Callie carried. Yesterday's storm had moved on, as storms always do. But the storm within, the pain of losing her home, of losing Jacob raged. How could she have allowed herself to depend on him?

As she'd made her way to the barn, she hadn't seen Jacob. Not that she expected to after the way they'd parted last night. He'd no doubt already gone to meet that lawyer about his inheritance and would succeed in ripping the house out from under her and her baby. In effect, destroying her dream and leaving some desperate women homeless.

Leaning into Bossy's side, Callie bit back a sob. Now, she'd be forced to move in with Commodore, but at least she had a place to go. But what would happen to Grace and Joanna?

She had to tell them, though they might react as Mildred had when Callie had seen her neighbor earlier—with total faith in Jacob's integrity—insisting that he hadn't known about his mother's death or the Squier will. Once Mildred took Jacob under her wing, she had a blind spot when it came to him.

Callie rose, picked up the milk bucket and left the barn with Stripes at her heels.

"Callie!"

Hand on her hat, Loretta hurried toward her, skirts flying. What was going on?

When she reached her, Loretta took the pail and they continued walking toward the house. "Hal arrested Jake last night for stealing from Commodore's store."

"What?" Callie gripped Loretta's arm, slopping milk out of the pail.

"After closing yesterday, Commodore discovered thirty dollars was missing from his register. Jake had been in the store that morning."

Callie whirled on Loretta. "That's the only reason Commodore had for accusing him?"

"Hal said Jake looked more dead than alive when he walked into that cell. I think he felt sorry for him, but once a jailbird—"

"How can you condemn a man with no real evidence?"

Loretta's gaze sought the ground. "I'm sorry." She raised her eyes to Callie's. "But Commodore swears he knew everyone who stepped inside the store the entire day, had known them for years. Who else could've done it?"

Callie reached for the bucket, Loretta's question slowing her hand. Jacob had betrayed her but this act of thievery didn't ring true. "I have no idea."

"I can see you're upset. I thought you'd want to know."

"I'm glad you told me. I'm just sorry you always jump to conclusions about people."

Loretta worried her lower lip with her teeth. "I don't know why I do that. Maybe because I don't want anyone I care about to get hurt." Tears brimmed in her eyes. "I know things haven't been good between us, but I care about you, Callie."

With that declaration Loretta hurried off before Callie could respond. As she walked on to the house, Callie acknowledged that she cared about Loretta, too, though her friend didn't always make caring easy. She'd have to make amends for that hurt in Loretta's eyes. Her entire life seemed to be falling apart.

Inside the kitchen, one by one the others came in, dished up oatmeal, poured tea and coffee, and took seats at the table. Callie went through the motions, greeted Joanna, Grace and Elise, kissed Katie Marie's soft cheek, but the food in her stomach churned. She didn't have the heart to tell them about the Squier will and all that would mean.

Had she been wrong? Maybe Jacob hadn't known about the will. But he hadn't said one word or taken one step that indicated he'd refuse his inheritance. Her breath caught. Had she given Jacob a chance to explain before they parted last night? He couldn't very well come to her when he was locked in a cell.

Still, she couldn't expect a man who'd never had a home to relinquish ownership of a house he admired.

Brought out of her reverie when Grace and Joanna rose and cleared the table, Callie realized they'd finished their breakfast. "Jacob's been arrested for stealing cash from the Mercantile," she blurted out. She wouldn't mention the will until she knew for certain that she'd lose the house.

"What?" Elise, eyes spitting fire, laid the baby on her shoulder and patted her back. "I don't believe it!"

Joanna studied her fingernails, indifferent to the predicament of someone she'd never met.

Grace's eyes filled with disquiet. "Do you think he's guilty?"

That first day when Callie had asked Jacob if he'd steal from her, his jutting jaw attested that he'd found her question offensive. No wonder with the horror of being unjustly jailed for theft. She sighed. He'd never appeared to care much about money. He might not be candid, might've kept his purposes to himself, but he had principles.

"He'd never steal," she said and knew she spoke the truth. The man was innocent.

Elise's eyes snapped. "If you don't think he's guilty, how can you let him rot in jail?"

Dear sweet Elise, dramatic and loyal. "I won't let an innocent man be railroaded to prison," Callie said firmly. Even if Jacob had stolen her house. And her heart. She rose. "I'm going to the jail. Make sure Hal gets off his duff and looks for the real culprit. After that, I'll try to convince Commodore to drop this ridiculous charge."

Katie Marie gave a resounding belch, as if offering her displeasure at Jacob's treatment. "That's my girl," Elise said, grinning at her baby as she tucked Katie into Martin's wicker baby carriage. "I'm coming with you."

"Me, too," Grace shoved back her chair and lumbered to her feet.

Joanna lifted downcast eyes. "I'll go, too."

The women in this house knew the pain of being judged and convicted by a merciless town, yet had the courage to unite in Jacob's defense. Callie had never been prouder of anyone.

"On the way, we'll stop for Mildred. Hal had better be prepared. The women of Peaceful are on the march."

Leaving the dishes and the oatmeal sticking to the pan—not Callie's way—she strode out the back door, the others bringing up the rear.

Up ahead, Commodore and Albert Thompson, the sheriff's deputy, headed into the lean-to. With her entourage behind her, Callie hurried toward them.

"We're here to search the lean-to, Callie," Albert said. "Another set of eyes is—"

"A waste of time. Once you come up empty-handed, perhaps, Commodore, you'll drop this absurd charge against Jacob."

"I never thought my son's widow would fall for a jailbird."

Heat climbed Callie's neck. How dare Commodore use that hateful label for Jacob? "I haven't fallen for anyone." Callie planted her palms on her hips. "Admit it. You're accusing Jacob of theft because he fixed up this house and thwarted your plan to force me to move in with you."

Commodore harrumphed. "Think what you will. I knew every single person who came into my store yesterday."

Joanna tugged her sleeve. "Shouldn't we get to the jail?"

Callie nodded, then turned back to Commodore. "You often work on accounts at your desk. You can't see everyone who enters your store."

"I haven't run a successful business for years without keeping an eye on the clientele."

Which said plenty about her father-in-law. "Don't you trust anyone?"

Commodore stared into space. "Not much in my life has given me reason to. Maybe I don't even trust myself."

The air of despondency in his eyes pinged against Callie's heart. She took a step toward him but he turned away, avoiding her touch. "The deputy and I will be examining Smith's quarters with a fine-tooth comb."

For a moment there, Callie had felt sorry for Commodore. But she wouldn't waste time arguing with a man whose compassion died with his son.

Sheriff Frederick didn't use a cattle prod or whip. His method of getting Jake to confess was far less painful, yet monotonous enough to threaten his sanity. But in an attempt to conduct himself in a way that honored God, Jake bit his tongue. A tongue that was getting sore.

"Were you in the Mitchell Mercantile yesterday?" Frederick began again.

"Yes."

"What time was that?"

"Around eleven o'clock."

"What were you doing there?"

"I told you, Sheriff. I went in to buy a work shirt."

"Did you get that shirt?"

Jake exhaled. "You know I didn't."

"Does it strike you as odd, Smith, that a man would go into a store for a purchase, find what he needed, yet leave without it? I've got to wonder if that man went in for something all right, but it wasn't a work shirt. And he didn't leave empty-handed."

"For the fifteenth time—I didn't take the money."

The door banged open. Callie led the way, a warrior leading the charge, her expression resolute, eyes blazing.

Jake had never seen her look more beautiful and been gladder to see anyone.

The sheriff rose to his feet. "Callie, you can't come in here during an interrogation."

"You can't arrest a man based on his past."

Callie had come to his defense, even if it hurt his pride that she hadn't declared him innocent. Her action gave Jake a smidgeon of optimism.

Frederick rubbed his neck. "Jake's under suspicion, that's all. No point getting riled up."

"Why did you send Albert and Commodore out to search my lean-to?"

"Looking for evidence."

Cradling Katie Marie in her arms, Elise came up behind Callie. Grace on one side of her, the new resident on the other. The newcomer glanced at him, her eyes laden with guilt, but quickly looked away. He hadn't seen the woman take anything, but he had a feeling in his gut she'd taken that money. As soon as he could, he'd pull her aside and make her see the path she headed down was wrong.

Mildred came next, slower but no less spirited, if those narrowed eyes fixed on the sheriff meant anything. "Why's Jake in custody, Hal?"

"It's not exactly custody, Mildred. We're just talking."

"No need to spend the night behind bars to talk." She folded her arms. "What evidence do you have?"

"Two witnesses saw Smith leave the store in a hurry."

Callie huffed. "A guilty man wouldn't draw attention to himself. Did you ask Jacob why he left?"

"Claims he noticed something that made him suspicious, but can't or won't say what it was."

Mildred harrumphed. "Then we owe Jake our thanks."

The sheriff snorted. "Mildred, a toddler could come up with a better excuse."

"Hal Frederick, I diapered you more than once. Don't go getting uppity with me."

Elise giggled. "You're outnumbered, Sheriff."

Frederick's gaze swept the ladies, every one of them glaring at him. "You all need to settle down."

These women had come to Jake's defense. He hoped he wouldn't make a fool of himself and cry. But he didn't like them worrying. "Don't fret. God will take care of it."

Callie leaned toward him. "Did I hear you right?"

He shot her a smile. A smile she returned.

The sheriff motioned Jake to his feet. "Come with me. You're staying in that cell for as long as it takes to get to the truth."

"I'm the one you want," a soft voice said behind him.

Jake spun around to the speaker, the newcomer he'd seen in the store.

Callie put an arm around the girl. "Joanna, what are you saying?"

"I took the money."

The room turned silent.

Joanna reached inside the cloak she wore, odd for a warm spring day, and pulled out a wad of bills, shoving them into the sheriff's hands. "It's all there, except for the price of a bowl of soup and a glass of milk. I'm sorry." She laid an arm over the swell of her baby. "I was starving. The cash register drawer was open and I took it."

Jake took Joanna's hand. "I understand desperation, being alone in the world with no one to turn to." He glanced at the sheriff. "Ever known hunger, Sheriff? Ever seen it drive people to desperation?"

"Reckon I have."

"The waitress at the café told me about the home for unwed mothers, where it was. Callie took me in without one question. She fed me, gave me a bed to sleep in. If I'd known people like Callie Mitchell existed, I never would've done something so desperate. So wrong." Tears spilled down Joanna's face. "I was afraid to admit I took it. Afraid I'd have my baby in jail and they'd take it away." She sobbed. "But I couldn't let someone else take the blame."

Grace moved to her side. Soon all the women surrounded her.

Jake met the sheriff's eyes. "I'll pay the rest."

The sheriff nodded at Jake, his face clearing. "Case closed. You're both free to go. Smith, with my apology."

A surge of joy shot through Jake. *Thank You, God.*

Callie smiled. "God did take care of it."

Jake wanted to tell Callie he loved her. But he couldn't until he'd told her about his newfound faith. He'd taken a long time to see that when a man didn't walk with God, he wasn't much of a man. At least not the kind of man God intended.

And he understood why. Faith gave believers more than a clean slate. It also gave them strength, wisdom, purpose.

His new purpose would be a legacy to his mother. Even if the only part Callie allowed him to play in helping unwed mothers was signing over his mother's house.

Pastor Steele appeared at the door.

Callie gasped. "Oh, goodness, with everything that's happened, I forgot all about our meeting this morning."

"You folks feel free to come, too," Pastor Steele said. "We'll be talking about ways to help Refuge of Redeeming Love."

As Jake strode beside Callie on the way to the church, others questioned where they were headed, then joined the group until a crowd had formed. His imprisonment and the confession of the hungry newcomer swept through the throng. Some exchanged puzzled glances, more expressed doubts, a few grumbled about the riffraff invading the town. Obviously, everyone had an opinion and wanted their say. This was turning into a three-ring circus with Pastor Steele as the ringmaster.

Before they reached the church, Jake wanted Callie to know what had transpired in that cell last night. "I need to talk to you." He pulled her to the side, under the canopy of maples.

Off to their right, a family of ducks climbed out of the brook running alongside the town. Bringing up the rear, the last duckling struggled to keep up. So like Jake, the last one to find his way. "Callie, you may have already guessed from what I said at the jail, but I wanted to tell you straight out. I've found God."

A smile bloomed on her face. "Oh, Jacob. I thought you looked different. Happier than I'd ever seen you."

Dare he hope she cared? That the mixup over the house hadn't ruined his chance with her? Or was she just overjoyed that he'd found God, as she would for any nonbeliever?

"I've been reading the Bible, the prophecy, the promises fulfilled in the baby and sealed on the cross. But it all had seemed...illogical. Last night, in that cell, I had nowhere to turn. Callie... God showed up." He swallowed, fought for control. "I wasn't alone in that cell. I heard His voice. Not an audible voice but unmistakable, as clear as if He stood beside me."

Tears spilled down Callie's cheeks. She took his hands in hers, hanging on as if her life depended on it. Or knew his did.

"I put control of my life in God's hands." He grinned, wanted to shout from the rooftops. "And look, I'm free. Free from jail. Free from my past. Free from my sins."

God had answered Callie's prayers. She threw her arm around Jacob's waist and gave him a hug. "I'm so happy I could burst!"

"No more than I. I don't understand why the existence of God could seem irrational one minute and reasonable the next, but that's what happened."

"You opened your hardened heart, Jacob. That made all the difference."

"I credit you for the example of your life. For caring about where I spent eternity. I can never thank you enough."

Smiling, he took her hand and together they walked the short distance to the church and joined the others gathered out front. Pastor Steele stood on the steps, about to go in.

Across the way the family of ducks she and Jacob had seen earlier marched across the road, the hen in the lead, the babies in a straight line behind her, the drake bringing up the rear. But one duckling meandered alone, searching for something in the grass.

"Let's wait," Pastor Steele said, then stepped into the street and slowed traffic. "Make sure the ducks make it to the other side."

A buggy and wagon slowed for the parade of ducks, as the mother duckling led her babies across. The last duckling remained on the other side. The mother halted in the middle of the road and waited as the drake turned back and rounded up the duckling, shepherding it back in line. Once he waddled to the end, the mother moved ahead.

Pastor Steele's gaze swept the crowd. "I don't know about the rest of you, but those ducks are a lesson to me. They know by instinct what we need to learn—each one in God's family is important. We need to make sure none are lost. And when they wander, or lose their way, as that duckling did, we're to urge them to return and welcome them in to the family."

The parade of ducks ended at a patch of ground on the side of the church. They spread out, foraging for food as traffic resumed on the street. Though Pastor Steele didn't mention the unwed mothers, for Callie his meaning was clear. Folks remained motionless, staring at those ducklings milling around on the carpet of grass.

"Looks like they enjoy a fellowship dinner as much as I do," Pastor Steele said with a grin.

"Pastor, what if that duckling was rebelling? Left his family on purpose?" someone called from the back.

"We don't know why that duckling fell behind. Perhaps he was slower. Perhaps he was rebellious. Or maybe only distracted, but the mother duck's decision to wait wasn't based on the duckling's behavior. Her decision was based on love, wanting none of her family to be lost."

No one said anything for a moment, not even the naysayer. But within minutes, people started coming up to Callie, offering to help.

Hal removed his hat and put in the first dollars. "Reckon you could use some money to make a go of the place, Callie." Loretta joined her husband and they passed the hat through the crowd until it all but overflowed with money.

Off to the side, Commodore stared at those ducks. How long had he been standing there? He moved toward the church steps with slow, measured steps.

Hal stopped his progress. "Commodore, Jake didn't take the money. Here's what was missing." He pulled the bills from his pocket and handed them to Commodore.

Like it burned his fingers, Commodore dropped the money in the hat. "These young women need it way more than I do."

Her mouth gaping, Callie whirled toward Jacob. She couldn't remember the last time she'd been speechless.

Commodore stepped past the sheriff and stopped in front of his wife. "A man can live his life with regrets. Regrets that eat him up inside. It's rare when that man gets a chance to make things right."

What was this about? The wobble in Commodore's voice alarmed Callie.

"But I have that chance today. At least, I hope I do." He took his wife's hand. "Long before I knew you, Dorothy, I fell in love with a young woman. And she fell in love with me. I hope it doesn't hurt you to hear that."

Dorothy never took her eyes off her husband. "No, that was a long time ago."

"The girl's father refused to let us marry. He said I wasn't good enough for his daughter." His eyes turned soft. "She saw it differently." He gave a sad smile. "I'm not sure what she saw in me. But she'd be disappointed in the man I've become. I've not been a good husband to you. I apologize for that."

Tears welled in Dorothy's eyes but she didn't speak. Or couldn't.

"This young girl and I… We, ah, well. We got in a family way. Her name was Irene Squier."

Commodore's words, words Jake could barely comprehend, bombarded his brain, turning it to mush. He tightened his grip on Callie's hand. She leaned into him, holding him steady.

Around him, people gasped and whispered.

Commodore looked at his wife, then swept his gaze over the bystanders. "Jake's name isn't Smith. His real name's Jacob Mitchell."

Dorothy grabbed her husband's arm. "Jake's your son?"

Commodore nodded then turned to Jake. "You resented my attitude toward that house of Callie's. It's a constant reminder of heartache. Losing Martin. Failing Irene. Failing our boy all these years." Tears welled in his eyes. "I'm ashamed of my spinelessness."

Dorothy wept openly. "Why didn't you tell me? We could've talked about it. Worked it out."

"Guess that would be fear. Fear you'd hate me for what I'd done. I'm sorry. So sorry about all of it."

Jake fought the resentment flaring up inside him.

This man who had hounded him from the first moment he'd arrived in town, was his father? "You've known who I was all this time?"

"I had no idea who you were—until I found those postcards in the lean-to." Commodore shook his head. "They weren't from your mother, Jake."

Jake closed his eyes and prayed for strength as an image of a petite young woman with dark hair filled his mind.

"I'm sorry, so very sorry about…your mom, about everything. I—" Commodore looked away, as if unable to meet Jake's gaze. "I wrote and mailed those postcards, signed them 'Your mother.'" He scrubbed a hand over his brimming eyes. "I thought that's what she'd want me to do."

Jake snorted. Why not admit that he'd sent them to ease his guilt?

Sheriff Frederick handed Callie his money-filled hat. "If you sent those postcards, Commodore, why didn't you recognize Jake's name?"

Wasn't that just like a lawman, always investigating? "He sent those postcards to Jacob, in care of the orphanage. No last name," Jake ground out.

"But surely other boys named Jacob resided in that home."

Jake sighed. "Not with that same birthdate."

Her eyes laden with sympathy, Loretta put an arm around him and Callie. "I knew your mother, Jake, and I see her in you. She'd be proud of the man you are."

Those simple words brought Jake comfort. "I'd like to talk to you about her."

"I'd like that, too."

Loretta faced Callie. "I'm sorry. Sorry for fighting

the unwed mothers' home when underneath I knew what you wanted to do was right." She sighed. "I let fear control me. Well, no more. I've got some talking to do to Tillie Sunderland, too. It's time to heal wounds, to start anew." She lifted a hand. "I hope you will forgive me."

Tears flooding her eyes, Callie drew Loretta into a hug. "Of course I forgive you. Thank you."

Smiling, Loretta headed off, no doubt in search of Mrs. Sunderland.

On shaky legs, Commodore moved closer. He appeared to have aged overnight. "Irene loved you, Jake. The minute she knew…she wanted you. We planned to get married." Tears filled his eyes. "But her father moved her out of town the night we told them about the baby. I didn't know where they took her."

"That's terrible," someone said.

And it was. Jake looked at Elise, surrounded by her parents, holding little Katie Marie, then on to Grace and Joanna, all of them with tears running down their faces.

A couple of women came up and gathered Joanna and Grace in their arms. Jake's heart stuttered in his chest. One of those ladies was Mrs. Sunderland. Maybe something good had come from this after all.

Commodore grabbed a handkerchief from his pocket and handed it to Dorothy, then tucked her in his arms. "In early May, I got a letter from Irene, telling me she loved me. How much she loved our baby, who was soon to be born. She promised that once she turned eighteen, we'd be together.

"I held on to that. I'd make something of myself, show her father I wasn't some riffraff from the wrong side of the tracks." His voice broke. "A few weeks later,

I got another letter, this one from the senator. Irene died in childbirth, he said. He'd put the baby, a boy she'd planned to name Jacob, in an orphanage. He told me where I could find him if I wanted to claim the baby"

Like a knife wound to his gut, it stabbed at Jake that his mother's parents hadn't wanted him, most likely blamed him for their daughter's death. Now they were gone, too.

His face contorted with emotion, Commodore turned to Jake. "I went to that orphanage. Saw you lying in that bed, so tiny and helpless. You frightened me. I didn't have money, any means of caring for you. So I walked away." He sobbed. "By the time I opened the store and had the means to care for a child, I'd met Dorothy." He turned to face his wife. "I wasn't sure how the scandal would impact our marriage. I couldn't bear to lose another woman I loved…so I went on denying my son's existence." A sob. "I've wondered if Martin's fall from the roof of that house was my punishment for not claiming my firstborn."

Pastor Steele shook his head. "God wouldn't kill your son to punish you."

Dorothy put her arm around Commodore. "You've made some big mistakes. Mistakes that have shaped our lives. At least now I understand that wall between us, a wall I could never penetrate, but I never stopped loving you."

"I love you, dear wife." Commodore's face crumpled as he turned to Jake. "I know you despise me and I don't blame you." He turned to walk away. "I don't deserve your forgiveness."

All eyes turned on Jake. He glanced at Elise. Her father, a stubborn man, had hurt her time and again. Yet,

Elise had forgiven him. And because of that forgiveness, look what they had.

A family.

Jake knew he should be angry, but he couldn't find any other emotion except one. Forgiveness.

The crowd had grown silent. People stood with heads hanging, eyes downcast, several were crying.

Jake lifted a hand and stopped Commodore as he and Dorothy started to walk away, looking deep into his father's eyes. "I forgive you."

His expression blank, as if Jake's words hadn't sunk in, Commodore sputtered something garbled that Jake couldn't make out. Then, weeping, he swayed and fell into Jake's arms.

Something frozen, inside Jake since he was a boy of seven, softened, then melted then slipped away. He had a father. Not a perfect man, but then who was? In each other's arms, they wept for lost time and for Irene who somehow seemed to be part of the wonder of that moment.

Dorothy patted her husband's back. "We lost one son, but God granted you another chance with Jake."

Swiping at his tears, Commodore straightened. "Will you stay in town, Jake, and give me time to know you?"

"I'll stay if I can spend it with Callie." He took her hands in his. "The house is yours. I have no intention of taking it. I know I've hurt you. For that I'm sorry." Though the prospect of losing Callie slashed at his heart, he forced out the words he had to say, "I'll move on if that's what you want. All you have to do is say the word."

Looking into those green eyes filled with such hope but also with dread, Callie's eyes glistened. Why had she ever believed Jacob was capable of treachery?

The answer came, not an easy one. She'd let her marriage to Martin color her view of Jacob. Unable to bear another disappointment, unable to handle more hurt piled on the pain of her past, for surely another loss would destroy her, she'd refused to see Jacob with unbiased eyes.

She'd refused to trust the steps toward God she'd seen him take. She'd refused to trust his love, yet his actions made that love unmistakable. Her lack of trust made it easy to believe that he'd rip the home she loved from under her.

Her faith might've kept her strong, but she hadn't forgiven, not really. She'd held on to her anger at Martin, at Commodore, and let that determine who she was, the actions she took, and the things she believed. Fear of failing in another marriage had kept her heart closed.

Yet Jacob, a brand-new believer, just taught her what genuine forgiveness looked like when he'd taken the man who'd denied his fatherhood and badgered Jacob at every turn into his arms and wept with him.

"Oh, Jacob, I'm sorry. I'm the one who hurt you. I didn't trust who you were when you were exactly as you appeared—a man I can respect." She raised a palm to his jaw. "If you'll forgive me, I'm ready to take a chance on love again."

He wrapped Callie in those strong arms of his. "You're the woman I want to be my wife." Then he opened his arms wider to include Commodore and Dorothy—his parents—and Grace and Joanna as they stepped close and joined an ever-widening circle of love, of family. Clearly showing by his actions that he would not only love her, he'd share her mission to care for unwed mothers.

Mrs. Sunderland came forward. "If folks weren't so fast to judge, perhaps Commodore would've stepped up and raised his son." She glanced over at Pastor Steele. "I've learned a lesson today. A lesson I won't forget."

Glancing at Callie, eyes wet and apologetic, Loretta patted Mrs. Sunderland's back. "We'll show these young women God's love."

Mildred wiggled into the circle. "And to show Jake how much I respect his skills, what he's made of himself, I want him to remodel my home, shed its years and purpose, turn it into Peaceful's Historical Museum. I've got enough stuff to fill it," she said with a laugh, then offered her hand. "I'm your first client in that business you plan to start."

Jake took her hand. "It's a deal. If you'll keep us stocked in gingerbread boy cookies."

Mildred chuckled. "I'll save the smiles till last."

"I don't need any smile but Callie's." Jake squeezed Callie's hand and gazed into her eyes with such intensity that the crowd faded, and all she could see was the man. A man who cherished family and commitment, a man of faith and integrity, a man she could trust.

"I've repaired your home, but I want more than a business arrangement with you, more than three meals a day and a roof over my head. I love you, Callie Mitchell."

At his declaration, the lonely shell surrounding her spirit shattered, releasing her from the pain of her past. "Jacob Squier Mitchell, I love you. You've repaired more than my home." Tears stung her eyes. "You've repaired my heart."

"As you have mine. I've wanted a family all my life. I love that baby you're carrying. I want to be more than an uncle to him. I want to be a father. We'll start that family with three. Add Commodore and Dorothy, Mildred here and the ladies of Redeeming Love and their babies—" He laughed. "I'm losing count. But we've got plenty of love and that big old Victorian."

Jacob shared her dream, wanted it as much as she did. He would be a wonderful father, a considerate husband. What had she ever done to deserve this man?

He dropped to one knee. "Callie, will you be my wife?"

With her heart overflowing with peace and love, knowing God had brought exactly the right man into her life that day when a drifter had shown up on her porch, and now took residence in her heart, Callie smiled down at him. "My answer is yes. I want to marry you, Jacob, have a family with you." He rose and tugged her into his arms, arms that felt like home. "No other man will do."

* * * * *

Janet Lee Barton loves researching and writing heartwarming romances about faith, family, friends and love. She's written both historical and contemporary novels, and loves writing for Love Inspired Historical. She and her husband live in Oklahoma and have recently downsized to a condo, which they love. When Janet isn't writing or reading, she loves to cook for family, work in her small garden, travel and sew. You can visit Janet at janetleebarton.com.

Books by Janet Lee Barton

Love Inspired Historical

Boardinghouse Betrothals

Somewhere to Call Home
A Place of Refuge
A Home for Her Heart
A Daughter's Return
The Mistletoe Kiss
A Nanny for Keeps

Visit the Author Profile page
at Harlequin.com for more titles.

A PLACE OF REFUGE

Janet Lee Barton

Cause me to hear thy lovingkindness in the morning; for in thee do I trust: cause me to know the way wherein I should walk; for I lift up my soul unto thee.
—*Psalm* 143:8

To the family I was born into, and the one the Lord has given me, for always giving me their love and support. And most of all, to my Lord and Savior, for showing me the way.

Chapter One

New York City
February 1896

A knock on the door this time of evening was never a good sign. Luke Patterson paused at the staircase and frowned, looking around for Mrs. Heaton, the owner of his boardinghouse. Neither she nor Gretchen, the maid, were anywhere to be seen and everyone else had scattered after dinner. The knock sounded once more and he took it on himself to answer the door.

"Sir, I've a young woman in my hack and was told to bring her to this address." The man at the door handed Luke a familiar-looking card. It was one of Mrs. Heaton's, embellished simply with only Heaton House, then the address and telephone number underneath. She often gave the cards to young women she thought might be in need of a safe place to come.

"What is it, Luke?" Mrs. Heaton asked as she hurried out of her study.

"This man has a young woman in his hack. He says

he was told to bring her here." He handed Mrs. Heaton her card.

"Well, tell her to come right in," Mrs. Heaton said.

"She's in bad shape, ma'am. She passed out on the way over. In fact I think she's more in need of the hospital right now than anythin'. My wife's a friend of her sister's and they told me to bring her here, and that's what I've done. They told me you'd given her the card."

Mrs. Heaton's brow furrowed. "I'm sure I did. Luke, please help this young woman in."

"Of course." Luke didn't bother putting a coat on against the cold February night air. He hurried out to the hack alongside the driver. The man grabbed a small carpetbag, helped him get the young woman out of the hack, up to the front door and into the house.

"I've got to get back to the family, sir. I hope she's all right." He dropped the bag on the floor and let go of the woman, leaving her to slump against Luke.

Luke immediately lifted her into his arms as the man hurried out the door. She was light as a feather and when she moaned, he shifted her in his arms, hoping to make her more comfortable.

"Where do you want me to take her, Mrs. Heaton?"

"Let's get her upstairs, so I can see what she needs, Luke. I've had Gretchen call the doctor and let the other women know a man will be in the upper hall."

Male boarders were normally not allowed on the upper floors, but there really wasn't any other way to get this young woman upstairs. She wasn't in any shape to maneuver the steps. As they passed under the light in the foyer, Luke cringed at what he saw. The woman in his arms looked as if she'd had a fist shoved in her face. Several times. And she had a cut on the side of her temple that oozed blood through a makeshift bandage. What had happened to her?

He followed Mrs. Heaton up the stairs to the landing and waited while she turned to go up to the third floor. Then she paused. "No, let's put her in Violet's old room. There's no need to jostle her any more than necessary. I'm sure she's in a lot of pain or she wouldn't have passed out, poor dear."

Mrs. Heaton hurried into the room and lit a lamp before turning back the cover on the bed. "Lay her down easy, Luke. The doctor should be here any moment now."

He did as told and then tried to step back to let Mrs. Heaton see to her. But the young woman held on to his hand and wouldn't let go.

"Pull up a chair, at least until the doctor gets here. For right now it appears she doesn't want you to go anywhere," Mrs. Heaton said.

Luke grasped the chair by the side table with his free hand and pulled it a little closer, sat down and clasped the young woman's hand with both of his. If he could convey that she was safe, he'd sit there all night. "Do you have any idea who she is?"

From the other side of the bed, Mrs. Heaton lowered the hood of the woman's cape and looked down on her. Luke could hear her sharp intake of breath. "It's hard to tell with her face so bruised and swollen, but with that red hair of hers, I do believe she's the young woman we met in the park last summer—the one you'd helped defend."

Luke leaned closer. The young woman's hair cascaded over the pillow and his heart gave a sharp twist at her moan. Its deep red color told him she might well be the woman in the park. Aside from the fresh bruising and swelling, he could see a fading bruise under her left eye—apparently she got beaten up on a regular basis. His fist clenched at the very thought of anyone treating a woman that way. And if she was the same woman from last summer, he had a good idea who did it.

Footsteps sounded on the stairs and Gretchen and another woman, whom he recognized as one who came to some of the benevolent committee meetings Mrs. Heaton often hosted, entered the room. She was probably a member of the Ladies' Aide Society as was Mrs. Heaton, but he wasn't certain.

"Clara! What brings you—"

"Kathleen's sister contacted me and let me know she'd sent her to you. I've been afraid something like this might happen."

"Kathleen? Is that her name? How do you know her?" Mrs. Heaton asked.

In what Luke thought was an effort not to disturb the injured woman, his landlady led Clara over to the windows. But in the quiet of the night, he could still hear what was being said.

The woman Mrs. Heaton had introduced as Clara Driscoll lowered her voice. "She works in my department at Tiffany Glass Company and yes, her name is Kathleen O'Bryan. Evidently her brother-in-law lost his job *again* and came home drunk today. When Kathleen got there, she found them in the middle of a fight and she tried to stop him from hitting her sister. That's when he came at her, hit her and knocked her down and hit her again. He left saying she'd better be gone when he came back."

White-hot anger surged through Luke as the young woman moaned. How dare the man touch her! He—

The doctor arrived just then and Mrs. Heaton turned to Luke. "Why don't you wait downstairs, Luke? I'll let you know what the doctor says and how Miss O'Bryan is doing in a little while. Thank you for helping me get her upstairs."

"You're welcome." Luke tried to slip his hand out of the young woman's, but she held on tighter. Her eyes fluttered open and she hoarsely whispered, "Thank you."

He leaned close and whispered, "You're welcome. And you're safe here. Doc and Mrs. Heaton are going to take care of you now."

Only then did she let go of his hand. He watched her eyelashes drift downward and turned to leave as the doctor took his place.

Luke cringed as he heard a louder moan this time and he fought the urge to rush back to her side. But the doc was the one who could make her feel better now. He'd only be in the way.

"Please do let me know how she is, Mrs. Heaton."

She gave a short nod. "I will."

Luke's heart twisted in his chest as he hurried down the stairs to the main floor and then down the next flight to the first floor where he and the other male boarders' rooms were. He'd try to get some work done—at least a scene or two on the book he was writing. Otherwise he'd only pace the floor waiting for Mrs. Heaton to let him know how Miss O'Bryan was.

He flipped through a few typewritten pages to get back into his writing, but in only moments Luke realized he wouldn't get any work done this far away from what was going on upstairs.

He gathered a tablet and pencil and went back upstairs and settled at Mrs. Heaton's desk. He knew she wouldn't mind; she'd offered to let him work in here before. Maybe he could at least make a few notes about his next chapter. Luke tried to concentrate on what he was writing but the connection to it and the woman upstairs was so apparent he couldn't concentrate on anything but her.

If not for meeting Miss O'Bryan that day in the park, he might not even be writing this book. Her name fit her well, or at least the woman he remembered from that day in the park last summer, when her brother-in-law was threatening both her and her sister.

She'd shown such dignity that day, but the look in her eyes told him how vulnerable she really was. Ever since that encounter, he hadn't been able to get her out of his mind and every time he caught a glimpse of hair the color of hers, he took a second look—at the park, on a trolley, in the tenements, when he'd gone on an assignment from his boss, Michael Heaton. Michael was Mrs. Heaton's son and owned his own detective agency. Until his marriage this past December, he'd lived here, too.

Michael felt he had reason to believe that his sister who'd been missing for several years might have wound up living in the tenements. He didn't want his mother to know of his fears, but he'd confided in Luke that he'd almost given up hope of finding her at all.

It was the traveling in and out of the tenements that had precipitated the change in his writing career. He liked writing the lighter dime novels that made him a living, along with occasional investigative work for

Michael, but over the past few months, his goal had changed. He wanted to make a difference in people's lives with his writing. What he was working on now was a book that depicted life for those less fortunate in the city, and Luke hoped it would continue to call attention to their plight as Jacob Riis had done with his book, *How the Other Half Lives*.

Tonight he realized the woman upstairs had everything to do with the direction his writing had gone in—because of the way she and her sister had been treated that day in the park. The conditions he was afraid they lived in. And seeing her tonight—

"Luke?" Mrs. Heaton broke into his thoughts.

He jumped to his feet and came around the desk. "Yes, ma'am? How is she?"

"The doctor says Kathleen is going to be all right. But he said she's going to be in some pain for the next few days. He thinks she may have cracked a rib, too. Clara is giving her this week off and we're going to try to find out how best to help her. She'll be staying with us for now."

"That's good, I'm glad." Relief washed over him, knowing she'd be here. He couldn't explain the strange connection he felt for the young woman, but it was there and it was strong.

"Evidently her sister's husband has beaten Kathleen several times, probably because she comes to her sister's defense and keeps her from taking the beating," Mrs. Heaton continued. "Clara says Kathleen's sister, Colleen, is expecting a child. However, after tonight, she realized she had to get Kathleen out of there. Colleen was afraid that if she didn't, her husband might hurt Kathleen even worse."

Luke felt his lip curl in disdain for the man. "Kathleen will be safe here. I'll see that she is."

"I know you will. She's awake now and trying to remember what happened and why she's here. Things are slowly coming back to her. I'm going to take a food tray up to her and see if we can get her to eat something. I'll let her know you were asking about her and helped to get her upstairs."

"If you need me for anything at all—"

"Thank you, Luke. I know where to find you and I'm thankful you are here. We're going to take care of her."

Luke watched his landlady leave the room, thankful that she'd given Kathleen her card last summer. The pretty redhead might not know it, but she was in the best place she could be right now.

The vision of Kathleen's face, so lovely under all the swelling and bruising, came to him. He clenched his fist once more and went to look out of the window. He didn't know how long it would take, but he was going to find that no-good brother-in-law of hers. If the man were lucky, the cops would get to him before Luke did.

Kathleen opened one eye and then the other. A sliver of sunlight creeping through the slit in the draperies told her it was morning. The last thing she remembered from the night before was the nice lady… Kathleen closed her eyes and concentrated. Mrs. Heaton. Yes, the woman who'd given her a card last summer and who owned the home she'd been sent to…last night?

She took a deep breath. Why was she having such a hard time putting her thoughts together? Her face, her temple, her whole head ached, but nowhere near as bad as the night before—until she reached up to touch the bandage on her temple. The light contact was enough to make the throb feel like a pounding hammer.

She closed her eyes against the pain and held her breath until it eased off a bit. Then she lay as still as she could until she felt she could open her eyes once more.

Her mind flooded with unconnected memories. She remembered telling her coworkers good-night and leaving work. Money had been especially tight lately, so, though she was tired, Kathleen hadn't given in to the urge to take the trolley. Instead, she'd trudged over to Second Avenue and down to Eighth Street to the tenement building where she lived with her sister and her family. They seemed to have traded one pitiful existence for another since they'd left Ireland two years ago. Believing they'd have a better life in America, they'd pooled what little they had to make the trip, only to find life wasn't any easier here.

She didn't think the dreadful place could ever be home to her or her family. All the buildings in the area seemed the same to Kathleen. They were made of brick, with stoops in front. The six and seven stories housed scores of families, some even larger than hers, crowded in two-and three-room apartments. One had to know the number of the building and where it set on the street to be sure of where they were going.

But last night, as she'd neared their tenement and saw her nephews sitting on the stoop, her heart had dipped into her stomach and she'd felt a little sick. She'd known something wasn't right. Collin and Brody had looked at her with their big blue eyes and she could see they'd been crying. She'd bent and hugged them when they ran to her.

"What's wrong? What's happened?" she'd asked.

Collin had answered, "Papa came home early and started yelling and—"

"He was really loud." Brody wiped a hand across his eyes. "Mama started crying, and he yelled more."

"Mama sent us out."

Kathleen's heart constricted with dread. "Well, now, I'm sure things aren't as bad as you're thinkin'. Your papa does get worked up a bit at times. I'll go see what all the ruckus is about."

She hadn't wanted to take the boys, but—

A knock sounded on the door, bringing her out of her thoughts. The door opened just a crack and she heard a whisper. "Kathleen? It's Mrs. Heaton. Are you awake, dear?"

"Yes, ma'am."

"May I come in?"

"Of course." This was Mrs. Heaton's home after all and she'd opened it to her, a total stranger except for that chance meeting in Central Park last summer.

Mrs. Heaton entered the room and hurried over to her. "Are you still in pain?"

"Some." Kathleen tried to scoot up in bed and grimaced.

"I think a little more than that. Let me give you some of the medicine Doctor Reynolds left for you. Then we'll see if you feel like a cup of tea and maybe some toast."

"Yes, thank you." She opened her mouth as Mrs. Heaton brought a spoonful of medicine to her lips. Kathleen swallowed the liquid and prayed it would work quickly to ease the pounding in her head.

"You were out again when I brought a tray up last night and I didn't want to wake you. I did check on you several times throughout the night and you seemed to be sleeping."

Mrs. Heaton talked as she straightened Kathleen's covers and pulled back the draperies on one of the windows—just enough to let a bit of light in, but not so much that it bothered Kathleen's eyes.

"Let me look at you." The compassion in the woman's eyes touched Kathleen's heart. She'd been nothing but kind to her. She sighed now and shook her head. "Doc said your bruising might look worse before it gets better. I'm afraid he was right. But don't you worry, you'll be back to your lovely self before you know it."

"Thank you for taking me in and for being so kind."

"You're welcome. I'm glad you kept my card and were brought here. Try not to worry about your sister. Mrs. Driscoll said she would check on her and get word to you on how she and your nephews are."

Kathleen let herself relax a little at Mrs. Heaton's words. Tears sprung to her eyes just thinking about the only family she had left. She tried to remember…why was she here? "I have so many questions about what happened, and I just can't seem to remember. Everything is just so disconnected and yet I feel I've been here before."

"You were. But only for one night last spring."

"I was?" Kathleen tried to remember but couldn't.

"Don't struggle with it, dear."

Kathleen tried not to show how much pain she felt leaning forward while Mrs. Heaton plumped her pillow and added another to prop her up. She bit her bottom lip as the woman eased her back onto the pillows.

"Doctor Reynolds said you might not remember everything right away but he thinks your memories will all come back to you in time. He said it was a good sign that you knew your name and Mrs. Driscoll's, and where you work."

"Work. I..." Kathleen furrowed her brow and looked at Mrs. Heaton.

"Mrs. Driscoll said not to worry about coming in today. She gave you the rest of the week off and said she would be back today to see how you are."

Kathleen released a relieved sigh. *Thank you, Lord.*

Another knock came on the door and Mrs. Heaton went to answer it. "It's Gretchen, I'm sure. I asked her to bring a tray up."

A woman dressed in a maid's uniform came into the room. She appeared to be around Kathleen's age of twenty-four. Her hair was blond and curly and her eyes were light blue.

"Put the tray on the dresser, please, Gretchen."

"Yes, ma'am." She turned to Kathleen and said, "I hope you feel better today, miss."

"Thank you," Kathleen said.

"If you need anything more just let me know, Mrs. Heaton."

"Thank you, Gretchen." The maid left the room quietly and Mrs. Heaton turned to Kathleen.

"Perhaps, after you've had some tea and toast, Gretchen and I can help you to the bathroom so you can freshen up. That might make you feel better."

The thought sounded wonderful to Kathleen. "That would be nice."

"Well, then, lets get some tea in you. One or two teaspoons of sugar?"

"Two, please." The pain medication seemed to be working, for the pounding in her head had eased to a lesser throb. Mrs. Heaton placed the tray in front of her and Kathleen picked up the teacup and took a sip.

"By the time you finish, Gretchen and I will be back to help you—"

"Mrs. Heaton, I don't know how to thank you for everything."

"You've already thanked me, dear. Just let yourself heal and know that you are safe here."

Kathleen managed a small nod.

"Are you up to a little more light, dear?"

"I believe so."

Mrs. Heaton opened the draperies fully on both windows and sunlight flooded the room, but it didn't bother Kathleen's eyes. She liked the way the light filtered through the lace panels behind the drapes.

"I'll be back in a bit," Mrs. Heaton said. She hurried off and Kathleen took another sip of her tea.

Only then did she really see the room she was in. It was huge—and more than just a bedroom. Decorated with lavender-and-yellow wallpaper and bed coverings of the same colors, the room was beautiful.

There was a comfortable-looking chair in the corner between the bed and a window. And there was even a small sofa in front of a fireplace. An armoire that matched the headboard of the bed was on the other side of the room. She'd never seen anything this nice in her life and wished Colleen could see it.

Tears gathered in her eyes once more at the thought of her sister and nephews. *Dear Lord, please keep them safe. And please help me to remember all that happened to bring me here. In Jesus's name, I pray. Amen.*

Kathleen couldn't remember when she'd eaten last, and even though she didn't feel hungry, her rumbling stomach told her she was. She picked up a piece of toast and took a bite. By the time Mrs. Heaton returned, she'd managed one slice and had finished her tea.

"Oh, good. I'm glad you got something down. Gretchen is coming, and we're going to help you to the bathroom. You'll be sharing it with Elizabeth. She's at work now, but you'll meet her this evening."

Kathleen wasn't sure she was ready to meet anyone else, but she didn't have the inclination or the energy to argue with this woman who'd done so much for her.

Gretchen came in just then and the two women helped her into a bathroom that was just off her room. She couldn't believe the size of it. She and her sister's family had to share a bathroom with the other tenants on their floor. This was so clean and large compared to that one—and she was to share it with only one other person? A room almost as large as their apartment and a bathroom connected to it? Such luxury was too much to take in.

By the time Mrs. Heaton and Gretchen had helped her into a fresh gown and back to bed, she was quite drowsy.

"I can't believe I'm sleepy again," Kathleen said as Mrs. Heaton plumped her pillow once more.

"I'm afraid I tired you out with all my talking earlier, dear."

"Oh, no. I'm sure it's the medicine."

"Could be. But the doctor said rest was the best for you right now. You let yourself sleep whenever you can. I'll go let Luke know how you are doing today."

"Luke?"

"Luke Patterson. He helped me get you upstairs last

night. He's the young man who came to your defense that day in the park last summer."

Memories crept in. Of strong arms picking her up and holding her close, of not wanting to let go of his hand. They came to her now, as did that day in the park when the handsome man had tried to help her and Colleen. They were one and the same? "He lives here?"

"Yes, he does. And I know he was quite worried about you last night. You wouldn't let go of his hand for the longest time. I must let him know you are on the mend. I'll be back with some lunch a little later. You get some rest now." Mrs. Heaton slipped out the bedroom door.

Kathleen leaned back against the pillows and released a pent-up breath. The hammering she had felt no longer pounded in her head, but in her chest. Luke Patterson. The man who'd become her hero in one brief encounter and whom she'd dreamed about several times since then had a name. And he lived here.

Kathleen's memories were so jumbled in with her dreams and nightmares of the night before, she wasn't sure what was real and what wasn't. But evidently, hearing that deep, husky voice she'd become familiar with in her dreams and the comforting feeling of being lifted and carried gently in a pair of strong arms hadn't been a dream at all.

"Man in the hall," Mrs. Heaton called as she led Luke up the stairs. She'd finally given in to his wish to see how Kathleen was doing for himself, although it'd taken a lot of persuasion to get her to agree.

Luke heard several doors slam as they reached the landing and he was sure the women weren't thrilled with his invasion into their domain. He looked straight ahead as he followed Mrs. Heaton to the room she'd given Miss O'Bryan.

He waited as his landlady knocked on the door. "Kathleen, dear, it's Mrs. Heaton. May I come in? I've brought you supper."

"Yes, ma'am. Of course you may," Kathleen answered.

Luke opened the door for his landlady and stood to the side while she entered. She turned to him. "You stay right here until I see if she's up to seeing you."

"Yes, ma'am." Luke hoped that she was, for he wouldn't barge in on his own, but he felt the need to see her, to hear her voice, to make sure she was all right.

It was but a few minutes before Mrs. Heaton returned. "You may see Miss O'Bryan, but not for long. She's still recovering, you know."

Luke nodded and entered the room with Mrs. Heaton right behind him as decorum demanded. Kathleen was propped up against a pile of pillows, covers pulled up to her neck. As he got closer he could see the bruising was still evident, maybe even worse than the night before, but her coloring seemed much better.

"This is Luke Patterson, Kathleen. He's not let me rest until I finally said he could come see for himself that you are improving. He's the young man we talked about earlier."

"Yes, I remember."

She looked up at him and for a moment Luke felt he might drown in the deep ocean blue-green of her eyes.

"Thank you so much for coming to my aid that day in the park and again last night."

"You're more than welcome, Miss O'Bryan. You

look… I…" Luke was at a loss for words. He couldn't say she looked wonderful, for she still looked battered and bruised. "Ah, better."

"It's all right, Mr. Patterson. I know how I look. But rest assured, I'll recover and be the stronger for it all."

The lilting sound of her Irish accent made him smile. "I can see that by the glint in your eyes and I'm glad for your attitude. You were brought to the right place. Mrs. Heaton is going to take good care of you."

"She already has been," Miss O'Bryan said.

Luke nodded. "I can see that. I'm sure she'll have you joining us for dinner in no time."

"That's what Mrs. Heaton keeps telling me."

"You'll find that she is rarely wrong. I look forward to seeing you downstairs soon."

"Thank you."

"She'll be joining us soon," Mrs. Heaton said with a smile. "But it's time for you to go, Luke. The girls will be wanting to go down to dinner soon."

"Yes, ma'am." Luke smiled at Miss O'Bryan and gave a little nod. "Good night."

"Good night. Thank you for checking on me."

"You're welcome. Hopefully, you'll feel even better tomorrow." He turned to Mrs. Heaton. "Thank you for letting me see for myself that she is on the mend."

"You're welcome, Luke. Please tell the other men dinner will be served soon."

"Yes, ma'am." He resisted the urge to look at Kathleen once more and headed out the door, releasing a sigh as he headed down the stairs. She was going to be all right. And he was going to see she stayed that way.

Chapter Two

Kathleen leaned a little closer to the mirror. After almost a week her bruises were fading, but not fast enough. Mrs. Heaton had assured her that she only looked as if she'd been sick recently, but was on the mend. Kathleen hoped she was right because she'd agreed to have dinner downstairs with the other boarders tonight. If she was going to stay here, she figured she might as well get to know them.

She picked up the letter from her sister that'd been delivered the day before. While it did give her comfort to have word from Colleen, her heart twisted at the realization that she didn't know when she would be seeing her sister or her nephews again.

Kathleen sighed and reread the words once more.

Dear Kathleen,
Mrs. Driscoll has told me that you are healing and in the safest place you could be in this city. It relieves my heart to know that. I don't want you to worry about the boys and me. We are all right. Clancy knows how upset I am about what

he did to you and is trying to make it up to me.
He's found a job, but he is insistent that you not
come back and I feel you are better off away from
here. We can keep in touch through Mrs. Walsh.
Just use her address next door and she'll get your
letter to me. I'll send mine through her, too.
The boys and I miss you, but one day we'll find a
way to get together again, even if just for a short
while. Until then, take care of yourself and know
that I love you.
Your sister,
Colleen.

Kathleen willed herself not to cry. At least they could keep in touch with letters. That would have to suffice for now.

A light knock sounded on the door of the bathroom and she knew it was Elizabeth Anderson, the young woman with whom she shared the bathroom. Mrs. Heaton had introduced them the second night she was there and Kathleen really liked her.

"Come in."

Elizabeth peeked around the door. "Do you need any help getting ready? It's about time to go down."

"I only need your assurance that I look all right." Her fears diminished when Elizabeth came in wearing a brown skirt and tan shirtwaist, similar to what she had on, only her skirt was blue and her shirtwaist white.

"You look just fine. We don't dress for dinner here except on the weekends. Mrs. Heaton says we work hard and are tired at the end of the day, and she's not going to make us dress up just to eat dinner every night. And then, when we do dress on the weekends and holidays, dinner feels special."

"I'm afraid I don't have anything any dressier than what I have on now."

"Don't worry. I have a couple of outfits I think will fit you. We're about the same size. Writing for *The Delineator,* I see all the newest styles and sometimes I buy on a whim. But the colors don't always look good on me and I haven't known what to do with them. I think they'll look beautiful on you and I'll be glad to let you have them."

"Oh, Elizabeth—"

"Now, don't try to say no. You'll be doing me a favor. As long as they're taking up room in my closet, I don't feel I can go buy anything new."

Kathleen knew Elizabeth would have made the offer even if the clothing fit her and she loved it all. She'd been so kind from the very beginning; Kathleen felt she had found a real friend in her. "All right. I'll accept and I thank you for your offer."

"I'm glad. I'll get them to you later."

"I'm nervous, Elizabeth. I've never even been in a home as nice as this, let alone had dinner in one. I'm not sure I'll know which fork to use or—"

"Just watch me and do what I do. You'll be fine."

"I really don't belong here."

"You belong here as much as any of us do—perhaps more," Elizabeth said. "Although there are some male boarders living on the first floor, Mrs. Heaton started her boardinghouse primarily for young women, after her daughter, Rebecca, went missing several years ago. And one of her priorities is to open her home to those who have a real need for a safe haven, sometimes for a short while, sometimes as a regular boarder."

"She's been wonderful to me. I'm so sorry to hear about her daughter." Her heart hurt for Mrs. Heaton. She knew what it felt like to be separated from loved ones and not know how they were.

Oh, Mrs. Driscoll had been very good to let her know that she'd checked on Colleen and the boys and that they were all right. But that held true only for that moment and there was no way of knowing what might have happened since the last report.

"It's been very difficult for her, but she carries on and takes care of all she can. I'm glad you kept the card she gave you that day in the park."

"You were there? I don't remember—"

"There's no reason you should. You had your hands full that day. But yes, I was there and so were some of the others. So quit worrying about how they will react to you. They'll be as glad as I am that you kept Mrs. Heaton's card."

She gave Kathleen a quick hug. "Come on, now. I could smell the roast chicken as soon as I came home from work today. You're in for a treat."

They headed out the door to the landing and were met there by another woman.

"Kathleen, this is Julia Olson. She works at Ellis Island and is a good friend."

"I'm pleased to meet you, Kathleen," Julia said. "Mrs. Heaton told us there was a new boarder, and we've been hoping you'd be able to join us for dinner soon."

"Thank you, Julia. It's nice to meet you, too."

Kathleen followed the two girls downstairs, trying

to calm her jittery nerves. Julia had been very nice and
if her attitude was any indication of the kind of boarders Mrs. Heaton had, everyone else would be, too. She
hoped so, for part of her wanted to run right back to her
room and hide, while the other part desperately needed
a diversion from worry about her sister and nephews.

Elizabeth led them to what Kathleen thought was the
parlor, only it was much grander than any she'd ever
seen. She tried not to show how out of place she felt as
she took in the fine furnishings. The parlor suites were
covered in a burgundy silk, along with several chairs
upholstered in a gold-and-burgundy-striped fabric. The
draperies were made of the same striped material, making the room look inviting.

There were several very comfortable-looking chairs
clustered around a round table in another conversation
area in one corner of the room. A piano sat in the opposite corner.

"It's beautiful," Kathleen said.

"It's very comfortable," Elizabeth said. "It's a great
place to gather after dinner and we do so quite often."

Kathleen walked around the room looking at the
various photographs here and there. There was one of
a pretty young woman who reminded her of someone,
but try as she might, she couldn't place her.

Male voices were heard in the foyer and Kathleen
turned to see three gentlemen enter the parlor.

"Ben, John, come meet Kathleen O'Bryan. Luke,
you've met her already," Elizabeth said.

At the mention of Luke's name, Kathleen looked past
the two men headed her way and caught her breath as
the man who'd come to her rescue walked toward her.
He was as handsome as she remembered—if not more

so. He hadn't been smiling that day in the park. But now his lips turned up in a smile that had her heart hammering in her chest to each step he took toward her.

"Kathleen, this is Benjamin Roth, a teacher, whom we call just Ben," Elizabeth said, pulling Kathleen's attention to the men standing in front of her. "Ben, this is Kathleen O'Bryan."

"Pleased to meet you, Miss O'Bryan." He had blond hair and blue eyes.

"And this is John Talbot. He's a reporter for the *New-York Tribune*."

"I'm glad you could join us this evening, Miss O'Bryan," the man with hair the color of rust said. His eyes were a cool blue-green.

"I'm pleased to meet you both."

Suddenly Luke appeared behind them, taller and broader than either man, and they seemed to move to the side to make way for him.

"And I believe you've met Luke Patterson," Elizabeth said.

"I have. Good evening, Mr. Patterson," Kathleen said.

Luke held out his hand and Kathleen found herself slipping her own into it. "It's good to see you are finally able to join us for dinner."

His voice was husky and deep just as she remembered and her heart warmed at the sound of it. The others had moved away, giving them a chance to speak in private.

"Mrs. Heaton has refused to let me come up to see you again, but she's been good to let me know you were getting better each day. Still, it's not quite like seeing for myself," he said. "I'm glad you're healing."

But when he reached out and touched her chin, it took her by surprise and she flinched. Instead of this man, she saw Clancy coming at her for the second time that night he'd beaten her and her hand went up to protect herself.

"I'm sorry, Miss O'Bryan," he said. "I should have known—"

His words brought her back to the present and she shook her head. "No. I'm sorry, Mr. Patterson. I just… remembered Clancy coming at me with his fist raised and—"

"I shouldn't have—"

"No, it's all right. Thank you for your concern, Mr. Patterson. And thank you for helping me the other night and—"

"Oh, good, it looks as if you've all met Kathleen. I'm glad," Mrs. Heaton said, coming into the room. "I came to let you all know that dinner is ready. Luke, will you escort Kathleen into the dining room? And Ben, would you escort me?"

"I'd be delighted to," Ben said.

"Miss O'Bryan?" Luke crooked his elbow and looked down at Kathleen.

She wasn't used to gentlemanly actions and wasn't totally sure what she should do, until she saw Mrs. Heaton glide her arm through Ben's arm. Kathleen mimicked what the older woman did, slipping her hand through Luke's crooked arm and resting it on his forearm.

They followed Mrs. Heaton and Ben and left John Talbot to escort both Elizabeth and Julia to the table. Once Luke had seated her and taken the seat to her left, she breathed a sigh of relief that she'd managed not to embarrass herself.

She was glad Elizabeth was sitting across from her so that she could see what fork and spoon to use. Why anyone would need so many utensils to eat one meal was beyond her. At home they only used what was needed, a spoon for soup or porridge, a fork for everything else and a knife only when needed.

"John, will you say the blessing, please?" Mrs. Heaton asked as soon as everyone was seated.

"Certainly." He bowed his head and Kathleen bowed hers along with the others.

"Dear Lord, we thank You for this day, we thank You that Miss O'Bryan is well enough to join us and we thank You for the food we are about to eat. Please help us to do Your will. Amen."

Kathleen was touched that he'd included her in his prayer and her heart filled with thanksgiving that she'd wound up in this home.

Gretchen and Maida, her twin sister who'd greatly confused Kathleen the first few days when they would come into her room, began to serve the meal of roast chicken, creamed potatoes, peas with baby onions and piping-hot rolls.

Kathleen thought this kind of meal was served only in fancy restaurants, the kind she could never afford. For a moment she wondered what Colleen and the boys were eating and swallowed hard. It didn't seem right that she should be treated so well when her sister was stuck in such horrible circumstances.

"Miss O'Bryan? Are you feeling all right?" Luke asked.

"I— Oh, I'm sorry. I'm fine. I was just thinking

about my family and wondering…" She shook her head. "I'm fine, really."

She glanced over to see that Elizabeth had used the large fork, and picked up her own. She took a bite of potatoes and tried not to embarrass herself as she gave her attention to the meal.

Elizabeth smiled across the table at her. "We've been thinking about going to the Metropolitan Museum of Art tomorrow. Would you like to go with us?"

"Oh, I don't know, I—"

"It will do you good to get out in the fresh air for a bit, Kathleen. If you are feeling up to it, that is," Mrs. Heaton said.

Kathleen had never been to the museum. Some of the girls she worked with had talked about going, but she'd never had the opportunity to go. She was curious to see all the museum held, and it would give her something to do. Her room was lovely but she was beginning to feel a bit confined. Now that her face was looking more normal she wouldn't feel self-conscious about being out in public. "You're right. It would do me good. I'd be glad to join you, Elizabeth. Thank you for inviting me."

"So we're all going?" Elizabeth asked.

"I'd like to," Luke said.

"Count me in," Julia said.

"John and I were the ones who first brought it up, so we're going," Ben added.

"Well, I'm going to visit Michael and Violet," Mrs. Heaton said. She looked at Kathleen. "Michael is my son and he and Violet Burton got married last December. They don't live far from here and you'll be meeting them on Sunday. They usually come to Sunday dinner."

"I look forward to meeting them." Kathleen was relieved to know the woman had a son who lived nearby. When she and her sister's family had come here to America, she'd dreamed of falling in love and having a home near her sister's.

But that had never happened. Instead it was all Clancy and her sister could do to pay the rent and feed their children—and that only with Kathleen's help. She wasn't sure Colleen and Clancy would be able to get along without what she'd contributed to their income and she vowed to send her sister what she could. It seemed that was all she could do. Kathleen needed to accept it and quit feeling guilty that life for her had changed for the better.

Apple pie was served for dessert—something that only happened on special occasions with Kathleen's family. She watched as Elizabeth picked up the smaller fork and did the same, praying that no one noticed that she had no idea what utensil to use.

Luke would have kicked himself if he could. He should have realized that Kathleen might be skittish about any man who entered into her space, touched her without being asked. He'd seen the fear in her eyes and known he never should have reached out to touch her.

He didn't understand it, nor did he particularly welcome it, but something about Kathleen O'Bryan called out his protective instincts in a way no other woman had ever done.

He didn't think she realized how lovely she was or how badly he wanted to get hold of her brother-in-law and teach him a lesson for what he'd done to Kathleen. She'd looked so vulnerable as he walked toward her in the parlor. And yet, there was a dignity about her that made his chest feel tight with an emotion he couldn't name.

Sitting beside her, Luke could tell she was unsure of what utensil to use by the way she kept watching Elizabeth. But why should Kathleen know which fork or spoon to use? He doubted her meals were anything like the ones he and the others had become accustomed to.

When the meal came to a close, he heard Kathleen release a small sigh and was almost as relieved as she sounded.

He quickly drew her chair out for her.

"Thank you, Mr. Patterson."

"My pleasure, Miss O'Bryan. Will you be joining us in the parlor?"

"Oh, I don't know. I—"

"Some of the boarders usually gather there for a bit after dinner and continue with whatever conversations they were having, or speak to someone else they didn't have a chance to speak with. It's a way for you to get to know the others," he added, hoping to persuade her to join them. The week had been overly long waiting for a glimpse of her just to know for sure that she was recovering.

"I suppose I should get to know everyone. It appears I might be here for a while."

"I'm glad to hear that," Luke said, a little unsure whether to offer his arm to her again. Everyone else headed toward the parlor singly and he didn't want her to feel awkward.

She saved him from making a decision as she began to walk unaccompanied. He fell into step beside her, feeling a bit awkward himself, but needing to ask. "How are you feeling?"

She stopped and turned to him. "Much better, thank you. I'll be going to work on Monday."

"That's good news." He was glad to know that she was getting better physically, but…he had to know. "How are you adjusting? I'm sure it's hard to be away from your sister and nephews."

Kathleen looked at him questioningly.

"They were there that day in the park." Luke remembered them pleading with their aunt not to send their papa to jail that day. How hard that must have been for her. The man should have been locked up. But she'd chosen to honor her nephews' pleas instead of assuring her and her sister of a few days of peace.

"Yes, they were." Her gaze met his and her eyes were bright with what he thought might be unshed tears. "I—Mr. Patterson, I never really had a chance to thank you that day. You saved my sister and me from his fists and I'd like to thank you now."

"I just happened to be in the right place at the right time. I only wish I could have saved you from this last episode." He nodded toward her face.

Her hand came up to touch her cheekbone and she smiled. "But you did save me from crumpling at Mrs. Heaton's feet."

"I'm glad I was here. Have you heard from your sister?"

"I have. I received a letter from her just yesterday and that's made me feel better. At least she and my nephews were all right when she wrote it. And we'll be keeping in contact through a neighbor. I still can't remember all of what actually happened that night. I only know what

I've been told and the bits and pieces that come to me. I must admit, I'm relieved I won't be going back, but I don't know when I'll see my sister and the boys again."

They'd reached the parlor by then and Luke said quietly, "I'll be praying for them to stay safe and for you to be able to see them soon."

"Luke, Miss O'Bryan, come on in. We're going to play charades," Ben called.

"Charades?" Kathleen asked as they entered the room and took a seat on one of the sofas.

"Is it new to you?" Luke asked.

"I don't know. How do you play it?"

"It's a game where we guess a word or phrase from one's pantomime."

Kathleen shrugged and smiled. "I'm not sure. I'll watch tonight and perhaps play another time."

"All right. But once you catch on, feel free to join in," Elizabeth said.

For the next half hour, the others put on quite a show, trying to draw Kathleen into the game. But she held her ground and, while Luke was sure she'd caught on, she only watched and laughed at everyone's antics.

She had a light melodious laugh, one he would like to hear more often. Hopefully, he would. She'd be staying here, at least for the foreseeable future, and it relieved his mind to know that she wouldn't be living in the tenements. Never again would she live in those conditions, if he had anything to do with it.

Suddenly feeling exhausted, Kathleen said, "I think I'll go up now, if you'll all excuse me."

"Are you all right?" Luke asked in a quiet voice.

She nodded her head. "I'm just a bit tired."

"We're glad you joined us," Elizabeth said. "You are going with us tomorrow, aren't you?"

"I am. What time do I need to be ready?"

"I don't think we need to leave until after lunch, do you?" Elizabeth looked around the group for confirmation.

"That won't give us a lot of time," Ben said, "but perhaps for Kathleen's first outing, we shouldn't make it a long day."

"I don't want you changing your plans for me. I can go another time," Kathleen said.

"Oh, no. We want you to come along," Julia said. "We'll go back again."

"Then I'll be glad to go. Thank you all for making me feel so welcome tonight."

"It's nice to have a new boarder. With Michael and Violet married and gone, we've felt a bit…" Elizabeth's voice trailed off.

"Bored with each other, is what she's trying to say," Luke said. He grinned down at Kathleen.

"I did not mean that, Luke," Elizabeth said. "But now that you mention it, you might be right."

Everyone laughed, including Luke. Circumstances had always been serious when they were together and Kathleen had never heard him laugh. The sound was deep and husky like his voice, and it flooded her with warmth and seemed to brighten her mood. It was good to know there was laughter in this home.

"Good night," Kathleen said as she left the parlor. She went upstairs and readied herself for bed, thinking how nice all the boarders had been. Mrs. Heaton was right. They didn't ask questions she didn't want to answer, as she'd feared they might when she finally joined them for dinner tonight. Instead, everyone had gone out of their way to make her feel comfortable.

Kathleen thought it would be a while before she really felt at home here—at least until she learned to choose her eating utensils without checking to see what everyone else was using.

She pulled out her Bible and read *Psalms* 121:8 about the Lord preserving her going out and coming in from now on and for always. Peace stole over her. She was safe here. She prayed that Colleen and her boys would remain safe across town in a completely different world than the one she was in now. And she thanked the Lord for seeing her safely here. He had a plan. Kathleen knew He did. She only needed to trust that the Lord would reveal it in His time.

As she closed her eyes, her last waking thought was about Luke. There was something about his smile that put a hitch in her breath, and the concern in his eyes made her feel special in a way no one ever had. He made her feel a sense of safety she'd never known before. And yet, she warned herself that even Luke might not be the kind of man he seemed to be. From what she'd seen of men in the last few years…one never knew.

Chapter Three

Kathleen went down to breakfast for the first time the next morning to find Mrs. Heaton, Elizabeth and Ben already at the table.

"Good morning, Kathleen." Mrs. Heaton smiled from the head of the table. "I'm glad you felt like coming down this morning. As you can see, we all eat breakfast at different times. Just help yourself, dear." She motioned to the sideboard.

Kathleen was a bit disappointed that Luke wasn't there, but tried not to show it as she picked up a plate on the sideboard and chose some fluffy scrambled eggs, bacon and a biscuit. She was going to have to watch that she didn't gain weight living here, for the fare was much more than she was used to.

"Good morning. Have the others already had breakfast?" Kathleen took the seat she'd sat in the night before and was happy to see the utensil setting was one she could manage—one knife, one fork and a spoon.

"I'm not sure, but possibly," Elizabeth said. "I slept in today."

"Luke ate earlier. I ran into him on my way in," Ben

said. "He went down to get some writing done so he could go on the outing with us."

Kathleen was glad Luke was coming. She really didn't know him any better than the others, but she felt safe when he was around. "What does he write?"

"He writes dime novels," Mrs. Heaton said.

A writer? Somehow that surprised Kathleen.

"I'm glad you feel up to going to the museum, Kathleen," Mrs. Heaton continued. "Have you ever been before?"

Kathleen shook her head and swallowed the bite she'd just taken. "No, ma'am. But I've been told it's wonderful."

"It is. You'll love it," Elizabeth said. "Some of my friends have said that the Michelangelo collection is magnificent."

"Yes, I've heard that, too. Mrs. Driscoll has talked about it." She didn't mention that she really wasn't familiar with Michelangelo or his work as she'd never been to a museum of any kind. Hopefully she would be well acquainted with it by that evening.

"You can all tell me about it at dinner," Mrs. Heaton said, pushing back her chair. "You know, I don't believe you've seen all of this floor, Kathleen. Would you like a tour so that you know your way around?"

"Oh, yes, I would, please." She was finished eating and she pushed back her chair.

"Let's start with the kitchen," Mrs. Heaton said, leading her through the door on the other end of the dining room.

It was large and sunny and smelled wonderful. Gretchen turned from the sink to say, "Good morning, Miss Kathleen. It's good to see you this morning."

"It's good to see you as well, Gretchen."

Mrs. Heaton led her back to the hall and to a room across from the kitchen. "This is the back parlor where you may bring a guest. Gretchen and Maida are always happy to prepare refreshment for you and your company. It's a nice place to come to read or write letters or just a place to relax."

It was a very inviting room, smaller but just as beautiful as the larger parlor, and done in blues and greens with a homey feel to it. After that was a smaller room, very cozy with a wall of shelves filled with books.

"This is my study. You're welcome to borrow any book you'd like," Mrs. Heaton said.

"I do like to read, but haven't had much opportunity to in a while." Kathleen couldn't remember when she'd last had the time to read for pleasure.

"Feel free to help yourself anytime."

"Thank you, I will."

They walked out and Mrs. Heaton showed her where the telephone was in an area under the staircase. "Mrs. Driscoll has this number in case she needs to call you in. And I have hers if you should need to speak with her."

They were back to the foyer and Mrs. Heaton said, "That's about it for this floor—except there is a small garden out back. Downstairs is where the men's rooms are, and the next floor up from yours is where Maida's and Gretchen's rooms are, with a few other rooms that are used from time to time."

"It's beautiful, Mrs. Heaton."

The telephone in the cubby behind the staircase rang just then and Mrs. Heaton took it on herself to answer. She put her hand over the receiver and whispered, "This is a call I need to take. I'm sorry, I—"

"Oh, no, please take your call. I'll see you later."

Kathleen gave a little wave and hurried upstairs to her

room. A room she'd never thought to live in and wasn't sure she could afford to, until after she knew what Mrs. Heaton would be charging her. The woman had refused to discuss it until after Kathleen went back to work, telling her that she didn't owe a penny until then.

She'd hate to leave, but after seeing the rest of the house, she couldn't imagine that she could actually afford to stay. She might have to look into the YWCA. Kathleen made her bed—refusing to let Gretchen and Maida do it for her. They had enough work to do.

The bathroom was empty and she decided to wash her hair for the outing that afternoon. She toweled it dry as best she could and combed it out, knowing it would dry into near-uncontrollable curls.

When she entered her room, she noticed the door to her armoire was open slightly and went to close it. But color caught her eye and she opened it to find it full of clothing and a note attached to a gold dinner dress. At least that's what she thought it was from the magazines some of her coworkers had brought to work.

She unpinned the note and read, "Kathleen, these are the outfits I told you about. As you can see, the colors are much more suited to you than to me. This gold dress will work nicely for dinner tonight. I hope everything fits. If not, we can alter them. I took a sewing course from Violet Heaton last summer."

Kathleen hurried back into the bathroom and knocked on Elizabeth's door. When her new friend opened it with a smile, Kathleen threw her arms around her neck.

"I don't know what to say, except thank you, Elizabeth. I'm not sure I can accept your generosity though— it's too much."

"It is not too much, Kathleen. Aside from my buy-

ing on a whim, I have an aunt who buys clothes for me
without taking into consideration the colors or styles
I like. I wore them each once for her. I'll not be wearing them again. If you don't like them—" Elizabeth
shrugged "—we'll just gather them up and I'll—"

"Oh, no. I do love them. And I'm sure they'll fit.
Thank you."

"You are more than welcome. Come on, try them
on and let's see if they need to be taken up anywhere."

They spent the rest of the morning with Kathleen
trying on outfits, including a warm coat Elizabeth had
assured her she didn't need.

"I have another newer one, Kathleen, and I like it
better. This one is just going to hang in my closet or be
given to someone else."

The coat fit perfectly, as did everything else, and
all Kathleen could do was thank Elizabeth once more.
As she tried on one outfit after another, Elizabeth ran
back and forth between rooms to find the accessories
that went with them. It was almost too much to take in.

By the time she and Elizabeth joined the others in
the foyer to go to the museum, Kathleen felt as if she
were the most blessed person on earth. Hard as it'd been
for her to understand why things never seemed to get
better for her sister's family, now she couldn't understand why things had changed so drastically, in the best
possible way, for her. All she knew was that the Lord
had blessed her beyond anything she'd ever imagined.

When Luke saw how happy Kathleen looked as she
and Elizabeth came downstairs, he was very glad he'd
written enough that he could take the afternoon off.

"Are you ready? Are your shoes comfortable?" he asked Kathleen.

"I'm ready and yes, my shoes are comfortable. Elizabeth gave them to me and she broke them in well."

"That was nice of her." Luke smiled and nodded at Elizabeth. He'd been sure the women at Heaton House would take care of any shortage in Kathleen's wardrobe. They seemed to have plenty and were always bringing in more from a shopping trip on Ladies' Mile.

"They look comfortable and that's good, because you're going to be walking a lot."

They all left the house and he fell into step beside Kathleen as the group headed for the trolley stop.

"This is a very nice neighborhood," she said. "I thought it would be, since Heaton House is so beautiful, but I haven't been out since the night I was brought here."

"Gramercy Park is a good neighborhood. It's an old one, but very well kept as you can see. The park is nice, too. We'll have to show it to you one day."

"There's a park?"

"Yes," Elizabeth said from behind her. "It's a small private one, open only for those living in the neighborhood. It really is a kind of oasis of sorts and you can't get to it without a key."

"It sounds lovely."

The trolley to the museum arrived and Luke made sure to be right behind Kathleen as they stepped up into it. He had their fare paid before she could open her reticule.

"That's all right, miss. You're paid for," the driver said.

Luke wasn't sure how she would take him paying for

her but it didn't take long to find out. He found empty seats for them and motioned for her to take the one by the window.

As soon as they both had sat down, she turned to him, her eyes flashing. "Thank you for getting my fare for me, Mr. Patterson. But I have a job and I don't expect you or anyone else to pay my way."

"Please don't be upset with me, Miss O'Bryan." He smiled down at her. "I know you haven't worked this week and I don't want you to go short until you get your next pay. Forgive me if I've insulted you."

Kathleen closed her eyes and gave a little shake to her head before releasing a sigh. "I'm sorry if I've insulted you after all you've done for me, Mr. Patterson. You and Mrs. Heaton know I didn't arrive with much and I realize you are only trying to help me. Please forgive me for being so prideful."

His heart twisted in his chest. This woman… "There is nothing to forgive you for, Kathleen. Not a thing. And if you want to pay me back, you can—after you get paid again."

Then she smiled at him and said, "Thank you."

"You're welcome." The tightness in his chest eased somewhat but he felt awful for injuring her pride. He'd have to be more careful from now on.

"Mrs. Heaton told me you write dime novels."

He was relieved that she'd changed the subject. "I do. Do you like to read?"

"Yes, although I haven't done much of it in a while. Where do you usually set your stories?"

"Oh, all over. Out West at first, but lately, I've been setting them closer to home."

"Does Mrs. Heaton have any copies in her library?"

"I believe I gave her some."

"Then I'll have to borrow one."

He wanted to tell her he could give her copies of her own, but he didn't want to upset her again. "Let me know what you think. Not everyone likes dime novels."

"I look forward to reading your work."

"I hope you enjoy it." Luke felt nervous—would she like his writing? He hoped so.

They'd arrived at the stop right outside the museum and he stepped into the aisle to let Kathleen out. Once out of the trolley, the group gathered to go inside. He hoped Kathleen liked the museum as much as he did.

As they toured the museum, Luke saw again why the Metropolitan was one of his favorite places. Though it was full of all kinds of art, the paintings interested him the most. With the special Michelangelo collection on exhibit, they spent most of their time looking at these works.

From the look on Kathleen's face, he was sure she was as enthralled with the paintings as he was.

He knew she was when she whispered, "I've never seen anything like this. The Lord certainly gave him a talent, didn't He?"

"He did. I think I could spend several days straight, right here, looking at his work."

"I'm so sorry we aren't going to see everything in the museum today. Now I know why Ben wanted to get an earlier start."

"Oh, we'd never be able to see it all in a day, Kathleen," Elizabeth said from behind them.

"And I might not have been able to come if I hadn't had a chance to get some writing in. Besides, it gives us a reason to keep coming back."

"Oh, I would love to come back."

"You will." Luke smiled down at Kathleen. He'd certainly like to bring her again.

Hours later when they decided to call it a day, they went outside to find the weather had turned much cooler.

"Why don't we go to the nearest drugstore soda fountain and get some hot cocoa?" Ben asked. "It'll warm us up for the ride home."

Everyone agreed and before long they were all sitting at a round table sipping the sweet chocolaty drink. He watched as Kathleen interacted with the others. She seemed to be enjoying herself and so was Luke. He couldn't remember when he'd had such a good time on one of their outings.

Kathleen had never had an outing quite like the one that day, with men and women going together as a group. Everyone she knew was too tired to do much more on a weekend than get ready for the next workweek.

Which was what she proceeded to do when they got back to Heaton House. But she'd been surprised to find that her laundry had been done for her. She'd hurried downstairs in search of Mrs. Heaton. They hadn't discussed her rent yet, but Kathleen knew she couldn't afford to have someone do her laundry and she needed to let Mrs. Heaton know.

Kathleen found her in her study, sitting in front of the fireplace. "May I speak to you, Mrs. Heaton?"

"Of course you may. Come in, dear." She motioned for her to take the empty chair next to hers. "Did you have a nice time at the museum?"

Kathleen sat down. "Yes, ma'am, I did, thank you. But, Mrs. Heaton, I must speak to you about my laundry. I'm not sure I can afford to—"

"Kathleen, dear, don't worry. It's included in the rent."

"Yes, well, that's something we haven't talked about. I need to know what it is, please."

Mrs. Heaton quoted her a figure that seemed much too low. "Oh, Mrs. Heaton, that can't be right. I was paying my sister more than that for living with her and Clancy. I insist on paying you the regular amount."

"That is what I'm charging you, Kathleen, dear. I didn't start this boardinghouse to make money, but to help young women have a safe place to call home. And I set the rent accordingly." With that Mrs. Heaton put up a hand as if to end the conversation.

Kathleen didn't know what to say next.

Mrs. Heaton reached out and patted her on the hand. "If it makes you feel any better, there are those in need who spend a night or two here occasionally, just as you did that one time. I call them my temporaries and I don't charge them at all for the time they spend with me."

"But, Mrs. Heaton, I'm not a temporary now and I don't feel right paying so little, and then to have you feed me and do my laundry on top of it?" She shook her head.

"Kathleen, food and laundry are part of the board you pay."

"But you're barely charging enough for the room, Mrs. Heaton."

"Kathleen, this is my boardinghouse and I charge what I want. I want to help you, not make life harder for you. I know you worry about your sister and her boys. If you have enough left at the end of a week, send a bit to them."

"I don't know how to thank you."

"Oh, child, it gives me comfort to know that I'm providing a safe home for you and the others. That is all the thanks I want."

Remembering what Elizabeth had told her about Mrs. Heaton's daughter brought tears to her eyes and all Kathleen could do was hug the woman and hurry out of the room before she saw them.

She'd no more than made it to the hallway before she ran into Luke. Or she would have if he hadn't put out his hands to keep the near disaster from happening.

"Whoa there—are you all right, Miss O'Bryan?"

His hands were gentle on her arms but the moment she gasped, he immediately dropped them. "I'm sorry. I just didn't want you to—"

"I'm sorry. I wasn't watching where I was going." She brushed back the tears and looked up at him.

"Are you hurting? What's happened to make you cry?"

She'd never met anyone who seemed to notice so much about her. "I'm not hurting. It's just— Mrs. Heaton has been through so much heartache, and still she reaches out to others and—" She swallowed around the knot of tears and shook her head.

"She does do that. And I'm very glad she reached out to you." He pulled out a crisp white handkerchief and, knowing that the man intended no harm, Kathleen allowed him to dab at a lone tear that'd escaped and ran down her cheek.

"So am I." She was very thankful that she was here,

thankful for Mrs. Heaton's support and for this man who stood there trying to help now.

He tucked his handkerchief in her hand. "You may keep it. If there is anything I can help you with, please don't hesitate to ask."

"Thank you. I'll wash it and get it back to you soon."

"There's no hurry. I have a lot of them."

Kathleen wasn't sure what to say next and was relieved when Luke spoke again.

"Are you going to join the others in the parlor before dinner?"

"Yes, but first I'm going to go up and freshen up."

"All right. I'll see you later, then."

"Yes. I'd better hurry before Mrs. Heaton calls us down." She hurried upstairs, aware of Luke's gaze on her as she did. He seemed too good to be true. She'd never met a man like Luke Patterson. And she liked him a lot.

But could she trust her instincts where he was concerned? That she didn't know. She'd seen too many men, abusive men like her brother-in-law, who treated their women badly. She thought it almost impossible to trust any of them. Still, believing it impossible didn't keep her from wishing it could be different.

Chapter Four

"Do you think that brother-in-law will come after Miss O'Bryan, Luke?" Michael Heaton asked. He'd asked for a few minutes with him while Sunday dinner was being put on the table and they'd gone to Mrs. Heaton's study.

"I don't know. But you can be sure I'll be on the lookout for him. I don't think Kathleen's sister will let him know where she is—she sent her here for her safety, after all."

Michael nodded. "I'm just concerned about Mother. And yet I'd never want to stop the good she does. But since I've moved out, I do worry about her. You can't be here all the time, but knowing you are around most of the time—actually more than I was before I married—and trusting in the Lord to watch over Heaton House…well, it gives me peace."

"I'm glad to know that."

"But I do remember that man from the park last year. He's a bad one."

"Yes, he is. I'm glad Kathleen—Miss O'Bryan got

out of there. But I believe she worries a great deal about her sister and nephews."

"I'm sure she does. Has she heard anything from her sister?"

Luke nodded. "They're corresponding through a neighbor. Still, I think she worries about the time in between letters."

"That's understandable," Michael said. "You know, she's quite pretty."

"Yes, she is." In Luke's opinion, *pretty* was an understatement. But then, Michael hadn't seen her come downstairs dressed in a gold dinner dress the night before. She'd looked beautiful. Her hair had been done up in what looked like a cloud of fire and he'd had a hard time keeping his eyes off her all evening.

She'd looked just as lovely today when she attended church with Mrs. Heaton, Luke and some of the other boarders. Michael and Violet were there when they arrived and Mrs. Heaton had introduced them to Kathleen before sliding into the pew to sit beside her daughter-in-law. She'd motioned for Kathleen to sit beside her and Luke had taken the seat on the other side of Kathleen. Ben, John and Julia slid in the pew behind them. Luke found he had to really concentrate to keep his mind on the sermon. It was from *Romans* 8, about how all things work together for the good of those who love God, those called according to His purpose. He sent up a prayer that all things were working for the good of Kathleen and her sister.

"Luke?"

"What?" Luke dragged his thoughts back to the present. "Did you say something?"

Michael laughed. "You must have been lost in your thoughts."

"I'm sorry. Apparently I was. What were you saying?"

"I said, one wonders why Miss O'Bryan isn't married with a family of her own."

Luke had wondered the same thing. "Her brother-in-law isn't the best example of a husband. Could be she doesn't want one. And if she had any suitors, he probably kept them away. If she married, he couldn't get part of her income to help out."

"True. I wonder what he's going to do now."

"I don't know. But it does weigh on my mind."

"Do you want me to assign a man to watch over Kathleen on her way back and forth to work?"

"No. I'll take on that job for now." Luke wasn't going to give over Kathleen's protection to anyone else.

Michael nodded. "All right. But if you need some help, let me know."

"I will."

A light rap sounded on the door just before it opened, and Violet, Michael's wife, peeked her head around it. "Dinner is ready, Michael."

"We're coming now, love." Michael quickly joined his wife and kissed her cheek.

Luke couldn't help but notice the smile Michael gave his wife and the look that passed between them. He'd known from the beginning that they were attracted to each other and gave himself some credit for getting them to admit it to each other. He was happy for them, but at the same time, seeing Michael and Violet together sometimes made him feel sorrow, too. It brought up memories of what could have been had his fiancée,

Beth, not been killed in a bank robbery before he'd ever come to the city.

In fact he probably wouldn't be here if not for losing her. He couldn't stay in Texas after that. Instead he'd decided to go somewhere totally different and had ended up right here at Heaton House. He hadn't shared his sorrow with anyone—nor the guilt he felt that he hadn't shown up to see Beth home from work in time to do something—anything—to save her. It was only lately he'd begun to forgive himself.

Luke followed the couple to the dining room and watched as Michael put an arm around Violet's waist and leaned close to whisper something to her. She giggled and blushed.

Much as Luke liked being footloose to go where he needed to research his books and work for Michael, he had to admit that sometimes he longed for a relationship like theirs. Longed for someone to love again. But he'd vowed never to let himself fall in love with anyone else. He never wanted to chance going through that kind of heartache again—ever.

Everyone was already in the dining room when they got there, and he took his customary seat next to Kathleen. Michael took the seat at the opposite end of the table from his mother after seating his wife adjacent to him.

Everyone bowed as Michael asked a blessing over the food and then there was clatter and chatter around the table as everyone served themselves from the dishes Maida started around the table.

Luke held the dish of scalloped potatoes while Kathleen helped herself to a spoonful. Then he took a portion for himself and handed it off to Ben.

As conversation flowed around them, he leaned toward Kathleen and asked, "Are you sure you're ready to go back to work tomorrow? Did the doctor give his okay?"

"He did. I'm sure I'll be fine. And I must get back to work. Mrs. Driscoll was good to give me a week off, but I can't ask for more time."

"Are you worried that your brother-in-law might show up there?"

She gave a little shake to her head. "Not really, but the thought has crossed my mind from time to time."

It'd crossed Luke's and Michael's, too. "Well, just to be on the safe side, I'm going to accompany you to work and back, at least for a while."

"I can't be taking that much of your time, Mr. Patterson. You have your own work to do."

"You aren't taking it. I'm giving it. And don't you think it's time we call each other by our first names? Everyone else here does."

She looked around the table and nodded. "Yes, they do. I suppose we should… Luke."

Luke liked the way she said his name in her Irish accent. "And I agree, Kathleen." He also liked the way it felt to say her name out loud. He watched soft color flood her cheeks and wanted to say more, but before he could, Violet captured Kathleen's attention from across the table.

"What is it you actually do in Mrs. Driscoll's department at Tiffany Glass Company?" she asked. Her question got the attention of all the diners at the table.

"I help cut the glass at times and I work on foiling the pieces with sheets of copper."

"Oh, how interesting," Violet said. "And how do you go about that? Foiling the pieces of glass?"

"Bee's wax is applied to foil sheets, which are then cut into strips. Then the strips are wrapped around the pieces. Once we tamp down the edges and reassemble them, our work is done. Then the copper is soldered to the adjacent pieces of glass."

"It sounds as though it's very tedious work," Ben said.

Kathleen nodded. "Sometimes it is. And it's tiring. But seeing the finished product makes it worthwhile."

"Would you change workplaces if you found something else that might be easier on you?" Mrs. Heaton asked.

"If it were something I felt qualified for, possibly. Mrs. Driscoll hasn't said anything to any of us, but I've heard through some of the girls that she might be thinking of remarrying one day and they won't allow a married woman to work there."

"Not even the supervisor?" Julia asked.

"I don't think so," Kathleen said.

"So, if you got married, you wouldn't be able to work there?"

"Oh, no. That's why there's a lot of turnover in the department. Someone is always in training because it seems one of the girls is always getting married. But if Mrs. Driscoll does get married, I'm not sure I'd want to stay." She looked at Mrs. Heaton. "Has she said anything to you about leaving?"

"Not really. But Clara is very quiet about her private life. I know she cares a great deal about her 'Tiffany Girls,' though."

"She does, that. I'll be sad to see her go if she does."

"But you're bound to marry one day," Violet Heaton said. "You'd be leaving then, too."

For some reason the conversation had Luke wondering if there were some young man in Kathleen's life and he wanted to ask, but thought it'd be impertinent to do so…at least in front of so many people.

"And is there a young man in your life that we should have notified, Kathleen?" Julia asked as if she read his mind.

Her timing couldn't have been better and Luke was thankful for it as he listened for Kathleen's reply.

"No. I've had no time for young men," Kathleen said.

Luke told himself that it shouldn't matter to him whether Kathleen had a beau or not. He barely knew her. But somehow…it did matter. He let out a pent-up breath he didn't even realize he'd been holding.

After breakfast the next morning, Luke was ready and waiting to accompany Kathleen to work. He helped her on with the coat Elizabeth had given her.

"Luke, you really don't have to go with me. I ride part of the way with Elizabeth. I'll be fine."

"But you don't ride all the way with her. Besides, it does me good to get out first thing of a morning. I'll walk part of the way home and think about the next chapter I'm writing."

There was nothing to do but accept his offer as he walked to the trolley stop with her and Elizabeth. The two women sat together and he stood, holding on to the rope hanging from the ceiling. When Elizabeth got off at her stop, he took her seat.

He smiled down at Kathleen. "Did you get a chance to get to know Violet yesterday?"

Michael and his wife had stayed awhile until supper Sunday night and she and Mrs. Heaton had invited Kathleen to join them for tea in the back parlor that afternoon. Violet was easy to talk to and they'd discussed all manner of things. Kathleen liked her. "I did. She's very sweet and remembered Colleen and me from that day in the park. I think she was quite taken with my nephews Collin and Brody."

"Everyone who was there that day was concerned about you all."

"I'm thankful that Mrs. Heaton gave me her card for so many reasons. But one is that as much as it pains me to know everyone saw what kind of man my sister married, it is a relief not to have to explain it all to everyone. Besides, there is still so much I don't remember."

"Kathleen, his actions are no reflection on you. You could have been killed trying to protect your sister and—"

"But I wasn't, thanks to you, Luke."

"Anyone would have done the same thing."

"No. Not anyone. I—"

The driver called out her stop just then and Luke moved into the aisle to let her out, and then followed her out of the trolley. He walked the block to Tiffany Glass Company with her.

"What time do you get off work?"

"At five-thirty."

Luke nodded. "I'll be here."

Kathleen felt certain it would do no good to tell him not to come, so she thanked him instead.

Several of her coworkers came up just then and she joined them to go inside. She turned back to see Luke standing by the curb. Evidently he was waiting until she got inside. She gave him a little wave and hurried through the door.

"Who is that, Kathleen? Do you have a beau?" a girl named Cindy said.

Kathleen's heart did a funny little twist at the very thought. "No. He's…just a good friend."

"That's too bad," another girl named Ruth said. "He's very handsome."

Kathleen was inclined to agree and yet she had no intention of giving her heart away to any man. Over the years, she'd seen Clancy change from the cocky young man her sister fell in love with to a hard-drinking, woman-beating, mean man. And no matter what her heart was doing at the thought of Luke being a beau, she was determined not to fall for any man. Not even the one who made her feel safe and cared for in a way she'd never experienced.

"I wouldn't mind having a friend like him," Cindy said. "If he's in the market for a wife and you don't want him, you can send him my way."

That thought didn't sit well with Kathleen at all.

She'd never had a man friend before. And deep down she knew that Luke was more than just a friend. He'd been there for her when she'd needed a defender the very most and he'd been there when she'd been brought to Heaton House. He made her feel protected and special. And she was not going to send him Cindy's way— or anyone else's for that matter.

As Kathleen stepped into the workroom, she put the thought of Luke paired with Cindy out of her mind.

"Kathleen, it's good to have you back with us," Mrs. Driscoll said. "I've got a new project all ready for you."

The rest of her coworkers welcomed her back and

all of them seemed glad to see her. Thankfully, no one asked many questions about why she'd been gone— probably because some of them lived in the same kind of conditions that Kathleen and her family did. And besides, they'd seen her bruised before. She didn't feel the need to tell anyone she was no longer living in the tenement and she knew Mrs. Driscoll wouldn't have said anything about it.

It was still hard for Kathleen to believe that she'd begun a new life, and now that she was back at work she found it even more difficult not to feel guilty that her sister was stuck in her old life. It hurt to think of Colleen and the boys putting up with Clancy. She would so love to be able to get them out of the tenements. Much as she loved her work, she did wish she were able to help others.

"Here you go, Kathleen," Mrs. Driscoll said, bringing her the design and the cut-glass pieces she wanted Kathleen to start on. "It's ready for the copper foil."

"Oh, it's lovely, Mrs. Driscoll."

"Thank you. It's one I've been working on awhile now. I'm eager to see it finished." She patted Kathleen on the shoulder and lowered her voice. "Should you get tired, let me know. I can send you home early."

"I think I'll be fine. Mrs. Heaton has taken wonderful care of me."

"I'm very relieved that you kept her card and that your sister sent you to her."

"Thank you for coming to check on me."

"You're welcome."

Mrs. Driscoll went to check on another piece of work, and Kathleen concentrated on getting back to her job. She imagined she'd be tired by the end of the day, but it was good to be back at work. She carefully painted the outline of the brass design on what would become a Tiffany lamp, and smiled thinking about the weekend. It'd been the nicest one she'd had in a very long time—maybe ever. And never had she gone on an outing in mixed company, except with family.

She'd thoroughly enjoyed going to the museum and then singing around the piano after dinner that night. Then, yesterday, she'd enjoyed getting to know Mrs. Heaton's son and his wife.

After Sunday dinner, the men were talking about an upcoming sporting event at Madison Square Garden and the ladies had adjourned to the back parlor for afternoon tea. Well, she and Mrs. Heaton and her daughter-in-law had. Elizabeth was still at her aunt's and Julia had gone to visit a friend.

They'd just settled down with their tea when Violet turned to Kathleen. "You know, at Butterick, I didn't have to leave when Michael and I got married, but I know that it is that way with many businesses and it greatly disturbs me. I can't help but wonder…what about the married women who need to help support their families? Or the ones who are widowed with families?"

"It's very hard for them to find work, although many companies do hire married women," Kathleen had answered. "Colleen takes in ironing and such from time to time, but it's not anything she can really depend on. And if she worked outside, she'd have to count on a neighbor to watch the boys—at least until they are in school."

"What this city needs is someplace women could drop off their children while they worked. Somewhere they'd be safe and well cared for until she got off work," Violet said.

"Oh, that is a wonderful idea, Violet," Mrs. Heaton said. "It really is."

"Yes, but getting it implemented—"

"Might not be as hard as you think," Mrs. Heaton had said. "Let me give it some thought and contact a few people."

"If anyone could do it, you could, Mother Heaton," Violet had said affectionately.

Kathleen could see the two women cared a great deal about each other, and she greatly missed her mother who'd passed away when she was only fifteen—and she missed her sister.

Now she shook her head and tried to concentrate on foiling the glass pieces. Pushing an errant strand of hair out of her eyes, she sighed. Maybe she'd have a letter from Colleen today. She hoped so.

By the end of her shift she was more than a little exhausted. Her back was hurting and she was almost convinced that she did have a fractured rib. Maybe tonight she'd sleep in the corset Elizabeth had given her. It had seemed to help the night she'd tried it.

She headed out with the others and her heart did a little flip when she saw Luke waiting for her just outside the doors. She smiled at him and hurried over.

"You look exhausted," he said, lightly grasping her elbow. "Perhaps you should have waited a few days to return to work."

His concern touched her heart but she didn't want him worrying about her. "I'll be fine. Just need to get used to being on my feet again."

"Kathleen!" Cindy called as she and Ruth came running up to her and Luke. "It was good to have you back at work. We missed you!'

Then she turned to Luke. "I'm sorry. I don't believe we've met before. I'm Cindy White and this is Ruth—"

"Moore," Ruth said, batting her eyelashes at Luke.

My goodness, they were brazen. But it didn't seem to affect Luke. "I'm Luke Patterson, a friend of Kathleen's. It's nice to meet you ladies, but as you can see, Kathleen's first day at work was very tiring for her. If you'll excuse us, I want to get her on the trolley so she can get off her feet." He tipped his hat and propelled Kathleen away.

Kathleen looked over her shoulder to see the two girls standing there with their mouths wide open. She couldn't help but smile as she turned back around. This man…she was blessed to have him as a friend.

Chapter Five

Luke didn't like that Kathleen looked so tired. And the trolley, with all its stopping and starting, didn't help, he could tell from the look on Kathleen's face. He'd rent a hack tomorrow. It might not be any more comfortable, but it'd get them there faster. He wanted to put his arm around her and let her lean on him, but he didn't have that right and he didn't want to frighten her. Carrying her upstairs when she was beaten and bruised was one thing. Pulling her close in public was something all together different.

He saw her wince as the trolley came to a less than gentle stop. "Are you sure you're all right?"

"My side is hurting a bit," she admitted. "But I'll be fine. I guess I've gotten lazy this past week."

Luke had a feeling there was nothing lazy about this woman. "I don't believe that. You're still healing. Can't you sit down to work?"

"Actually, it's easier to stand most of the time. But I might try it tomorrow."

Elizabeth got on at the next trolley stop and even she could tell Kathleen was tired. "Long day?"

"A little." Kathleen smiled. "It will get easier."

Elizabeth gave Luke a questioning look. He shrugged. "That's what she says. But I think maybe her rib is giving her trouble."

"We'll wrap it when we get home. That should help a bit."

"I'm sure it will," Kathleen said.

But Luke could tell she wasn't feeling any better. He didn't know who was more relieved to get to their stop—Kathleen or him.

Once they got to Heaton House, she and Elizabeth quickly disappeared upstairs and he wondered if she'd be back down for dinner. He quickly called the nearest livery and made arrangements for a hack to be delivered the next morning. Kathleen wasn't going to ride the trolley again until she was much better.

Mrs. Heaton came out of her study just as he ended the call. "How did Kathleen do today?"

"I think it was hard on her. She seemed to be in some pain—her rib, I believe. Elizabeth was going to help her wrap it, I think."

"I'll go up and see if we need to telephone the doctor."

"Good." Luke felt better just knowing Mrs. Heaton would be checking on Kathleen.

"It's going to take a while for her to heal," she said as she pulled a letter out of her pocket. "But I have something that I'm sure will make her feel better. She got a letter from her sister today—well, I think it's from her sister. It has her neighbor's name on it but Kathleen said that's how they would correspond so her brother-in-law doesn't find out."

Luke watched her go upstairs and prayed she was

right. Hearing from her sister was bound to make Kathleen feel better. He went downstairs to wash up before dinner, and afterward he made a few notes on ideas that'd come to him for his next chapter. But his mind was on Kathleen and he couldn't concentrate. He dropped his pencil and sighed. It was time for dinner anyway. He'd work later. He joined the others in the parlor and was pleased that Kathleen and Elizabeth joined them only minutes later.

Mrs. Heaton announced that dinner was ready and he had only a moment to reach Kathleen's side and ask, "Are you feeling any better?"

"I am. Mrs. Heaton and Elizabeth wrapped my rib. I should have gone to work with it wrapped today. I'll be sure to tomorrow."

He escorted her to the dining room and pulled out her chair for her. John Talbot said the blessing and once Mrs. Heaton began passing dishes around and everyone began to talk, Luke turned to Kathleen again. She hadn't mentioned the letter so Luke took it upon himself to ask. "Mrs. Heaton said you received a letter. Is it from your sister? Is everything all right with her?"

Kathleen's smile told him it was good news—at least for now.

"She said Clancy is still working and the boys are doing well. They were happy to hear from me and said to tell me they love me."

Kathleen's eyes seemed to mist for a moment and she quickly blinked back whatever tears had begun to well there. "She said they aren't happy with their papa that I had to leave but they've accepted it."

"Perhaps you and your sister will be able to get together one day."

"I hope so. But it will be difficult. I don't dare show up at the apartment. And it's hard for Colleen to get away when Clancy is at home."

Luke wished he could find a safe way for Kathleen and her sister to get together. He'd have to give it some thought.

Once the meal was finished he pulled back Kathleen's chair. "Are you going to join the others in the parlor?"

She shook her head. "Not tonight. I really am tired and I think I'll go on up. Thank you for seeing me to work and home again, Luke. But please don't feel you have to keep doing it. I—"

"I don't feel I have to. But I will be seeing you in the morning. I hope you sleep well and feel better tomorrow."

"Thank you."

Luke watched as Kathleen made her way up the stairs to the landing. She was holding her side and he knew she wasn't feeling as well as she said she was.

He headed back down to get some work done, praying that Kathleen's rib would heal quickly and completely. He'd come to enjoy evenings in her company. Chatting with the others didn't hold the same appeal without her.

The week actually passed faster than Kathleen had thought it would. And she was getting used to being back at work. She'd taken to sleeping in a corset and her side was feeling much better by Friday.

She gave part of the credit to Luke's kindness in procuring a hack to take her to work and bring her home. She'd tried to tell him not to, but she was fast learning that the man had a mind of his own, and for the rest of the week she rode in relative comfort. The girls at work teased her constantly about Luke, insinuating that he was courting her, but she kept insisting he was a very good friend.

And he was. She'd never thought she'd have a man friend, but she felt more comfortable in Luke's company than any of the other boarders except for Elizabeth—and of course Mrs. Heaton.

But now, as she left work for the day and saw Luke waiting for her, her heart skipped a beat. She told herself it was only because she was glad the week was over.

Luke helped her in the hack and took a seat beside her as the driver moved out into the traffic. He grinned down at her. "You made it. A whole week. How are you feeling this afternoon?"

"Glad it's the weekend." She chuckled, knowing that wasn't what he meant, and quickly added, "My side feels much better."

"Good. But I'm glad it's the weekend, too. Do you think you might feel up to going to Michael and Violet's this evening?"

The couple had asked everyone over to their new home for dinner that night. "I do. I'm looking forward to seeing them again."

"Good. We're all looking forward to it. It's the first time they're entertaining and I think they're looking forward to having us as much as we're all looking forward to going."

Kathleen had found that traveling by hack was much quicker than by trolley and they were back at Heaton House in no time.

They parted ways inside, Kathleen to go upstairs

to get ready for the dinner party and Luke downstairs to do the same. She felt excited to be going out for an evening. It wasn't something she'd ever done before.

Thankfully, Elizabeth had helped her choose what to wear and offered to do her hair. Kathleen still had trouble believing the life she was now living. Oh, she worked as usual, but the life she lived outside of work was so drastically different from where she'd been just weeks ago. She prayed that she wouldn't get so used to it that she couldn't go back, if she had to. But it wasn't easy. She wanted to see her sister and nephews, but she didn't want to go back to the tenements. She wanted her loved ones out of there!

She'd received another letter from Colleen telling her how glad she was that Kathleen was with such good people. Colleen only wanted what was best for Kathleen, but Kathleen wanted the same for her sister. Only she didn't know how to go about helping her to get it. At least, not now. All Kathleen could do was send what money she could—made possible only by Mrs. Heaton's generosity to her.

She was blessed. There was no other word for it. And whether it lasted or not, for now, Kathleen was determined to try not to feel guilty for it and to enjoy this new life the Lord had seen fit to give her—for however long it lasted.

Now she twisted and turned in front of the mirror, as much as her still-tender ribs would let her, and was pleased with what she saw. The dinner gown Elizabeth had given her fit perfectly and the emerald-green color complemented her coloring. Elizabeth had swept up her hair into a fashionable knot on top of her head and added a green feather to it.

"You look beautiful," Elizabeth said, coming out of the bathroom. "I did a good job on your hair, if I do say so myself."

"You made me look beautiful."

"Oh, Kathleen, one only has to look into those eyes of yours to see beauty. It shines out of you. You could wear a flour sack and look lovely."

Kathleen laughed. "You aren't of your right mind, are you? *You* look gorgeous in that color." Elizabeth was dressed in a rose-colored gown that looked wonderful on her. "And your hair looks great, too."

"Well, let's go see how Julia looks. She said she was wearing blue."

The three women met up in the hall and Julia did indeed look lovely in a deep blue gown. They hurried downstairs to join the others. Mrs. Heaton looked wonderful as always, dressed in an ivory silk. She, too, sported a matching feather in her hair and her eyes sparkled. It was easy to tell she was excited about her son's first dinner party.

The men all looked quite nice, and not at all uncomfortable in their evening dress.

Kathleen found Luke by her side to help her with her evening cape—another gift, this one from Julia, who'd said she had too many. As he held the cape for her to slip into, he whispered, "You look lovely, Kathleen."

"Thank you. You look very nice, too. It's fun to dress up, isn't it?"

"I don't mind once in a while," Luke said. "But I'm certainly glad Mrs. Heaton doesn't make us dress for dinner every night."

"So am I," Kathleen said.

Mrs. Heaton had ordered an omnibus to pick them

all up and it was a high-spirited group that headed out into the still, cool night air. Kathleen was pleased that Luke took a seat next to her for the trip to Michael and Violet's home.

"I'm so glad you were all able to make it tonight," Mrs. Heaton said. "Michael and Violet are looking forward to seeing everyone. And a little nervous, too, I do believe."

"I can't wait to see their home now that Violet has it all decorated," Julia said.

"It's lovely. She has excellent taste," Mrs. Heaton said. "It's kept her very busy. But they did recently hire Gretchen and Maida's sister, Hilda, to work for them, although Violet does most of the cooking—with a little help from Michael."

Their home wasn't all that far from Mrs. Heaton's. One could actually walk there easily in warm weather, but Kathleen was glad for the warmth Luke provided sitting beside her.

"How fancy is this dinner?" she asked him in a whisper.

"Not much different than dinner at Mrs. Heaton's, I would imagine. Don't be nervous. You'll have a good time."

"It's those eating utensils I worry about," Kathleen surprised herself by admitting to him.

"Oh, that." Luke chuckled and leaned a little closer to whisper, "It can get quite confusing at times. I still watch what others are using."

"Yes, that's what Elizabeth has taught me."

"Well, even if we should pick up the wrong one, no one in this group would make fun of us."

Kathleen's heart warmed at the way Luke always made her feel better.

They were welcomed into a home smaller than Heaton House, but just as inviting. Michael opened the door to them and he and Violet ushered them in.

"Do we get a tour now that you have it decorated to your satisfaction?" Julia asked as they all shed their coats and hung them on a coatrack in the foyer. "Last time I was here, I was helping to move things over after your wedding. We saw the house, but not the home."

Violet laughed. "Of course you get a tour—right after dinner."

"And to that end, let's go to the dining room," Michael said. "I'm starving."

Violet had set place cards at each place setting and Kathleen's was adjacent to her host's end of the table and next to Luke. She appreciated the woman's effort to make her feel welcome and comfortable.

Once they were all seated, Michael said the blessing. "Dear Lord, we thank You for this day and for this gathering of family and friends to warm this home of ours. Please bless each one and keep us all Yours. Please bless the food we're about to partake together. In Jesus's name, Amen."

A woman—no doubt Hilda, who looked to be about Gretchen and Maida's age—began to serve bowls of soup. Kathleen wasn't sure what it was until Elizabeth said, "Oh, mock turtle soup. I haven't had this in a long time!"

Kathleen had never had it and watched to see which spoon to use. Once she took a taste, she was quite pleased. It hadn't sounded very good to her but it was surprisingly delicious. The rest of the meal was just as good—a salad of lettuce and tomatoes, fillets of beef with mushroom sauce, green peas and creamed potatoes.

As they ate, conversation flowed around the table. Kathleen had never been to a dinner party in her life. Having dinner at Heaton House had been the closest she'd ever come to it, and she found she quite liked sharing a meal with people who made dinner—or supper, as her family called it—an important part of the day. It was quite pleasant to have a meal with others who conversed with each other in a congenial way, instead of shoveling food in their mouths, complaining about their day and the meal. Or who left others at the table when one was through eating, as Clancy had always done. Much as she missed her sister and nephews, she did not miss anything else about living with her family. Only the three of them. And, oh, how she wished she could get them out of the tenements.

"Did you make all of this, Violet?" Elizabeth asked.

"Oh, no. Hilda is quite the cook and she did most of it. I did make the dessert, though," Violet said just as Hilda brought in a lemon pie piled high with a golden meringue.

"It's all wonderful," Kathleen said.

"Thank you," Violet said. "I'm glad you're recovered enough to be back at work and that you felt like coming this evening."

"So am I. Thank you so much for including me in your invitation."

"You're welcome here anytime, Kathleen. And you never need an invitation to stop by."

Violet's words touched Kathleen's heart, for she could tell the young bride meant them. She looked around the table and realized that she'd made friends of each person there. Michael had prayed God's blessing on each of them. But the Lord had already blessed her by bringing these people into her life.

True to her word, after dinner Violet showed them the rest of their home. The parlor was across the way as in Heaton House, and a bit smaller. Decorated in yellows and blues, it was quite inviting. There was no second parlor, but a small library connecting to the parlor.

"This is where Michael works and I read," Violet said. It was quite cozy with two chairs pulled near the fireplace.

They headed upstairs afterward and there were three nice-sized bedrooms, a bathroom and one smaller room attached to the master bedroom.

"This is perfect for a nursery," Elizabeth said.

"And will be used for just that one day," Michael said.

Kathleen couldn't miss Violet's blush as her husband looked at her. It was more than a little refreshing to see a couple so in love with each other. She remembered her parents' devotion to each other but she hadn't seen that kind of relationship in a very long time.

She'd often wondered if her sister's marriage had ever been a happy one. Was it the eventual struggle to get by that had made it an unhappy one?

Once in a while even in the tenements, she'd see couples happy and pulling together to make it. Still more often than not, she'd seen the total opposite—men mistreating their wives and children—so much so that she thought what her parents had shared was no longer possible. And yet, if what she saw between Violet and Michael was real, could it be possible for her?

"Your home is beautiful, Violet," Kathleen said as they all headed back downstairs.

"Thank you. We think so and of course, we love it. Up on the third floor are two other rooms and a bath. Hilda has one and, well, if Heaton House should ever be so full that Mother Heaton can't take in a temporary in need, as she calls them, we can offer a room."

It was obvious the Heatons put helping others at the top of their priority list and Kathleen was a grateful recipient of their generosity.

After playing charades for a while, they were served hot cocoa before going back out into the cool night.

"Spring is right around the corner," Michael said, "but it's been hard to tell the last few weeks."

"I'm looking forward to picnicking in Central Park," Julia said. "It won't be long before we can."

Kathleen glanced at Luke to find him gazing at her. She'd love to go to Central Park—and she'd love to run into her sister and the boys. But with them came Clancy and he was someone she never hoped to see again.

Once they were back in the omnibus, with Luke by her side once more, he turned to her and spoke quietly. "You know, when we can go to the park again, I don't want you to worry about running into your brother-in-law. He won't hurt you again, Kathleen. I won't leave your side—not for a moment. I promise you that."

"Thank you, Luke."

No wonder she felt safest around this man. Somehow he'd appointed himself her guardian and for that she could only be thankful.

Chapter Six

The next few weeks were some of the best Kathleen could ever remember as she settled in more at Heaton House. Her rib hurt less each day and she no longer came home from work totally exhausted.

Evenings were always enjoyable and she along with the other women had gone on several outings to Ladies' Mile, to browse and see what would be in fashion that spring. So far she'd never come home with anything, but she at least was learning how to accessorize the clothes Elizabeth, Julia and even Violet had given her. She particularly liked browsing at Macy's and Lord & Taylor.

She and the other girls from Heaton House enjoyed window-shopping as much as anything, watching the wealthy come out of stores with their servants trailing behind, carrying their purchases.

Kathleen had never really had good women friends except for her sister and she greatly enjoyed getting to know the women of Heaton House.

She'd learned that Violet and Michael had been neighbors back in Virginia where they both were from, but it wasn't until Violet came to the city to try to pay off the mortgage to her family home that they'd fallen in love.

"I'm so glad you've found true love, but I'm not sure I can ever give my heart to a man," Kathleen said one Saturday afternoon when they were having tea at a small café along Ladies' Mile.

"Oh, Kathleen, don't think that way. There are good men out there."

"But how does one know they'll remain good? My sister Colleen thought Clancy was a good man when she first met him. But it didn't take long after they married for her to find out otherwise. Only by then she loved him and thought she could change him." Kathleen shook her head. "She's been miserable ever since they married."

"I'm sorry about that, Kathleen. But you can't let yourself believe that all men are like your brother-in-law. They aren't. You already know that. Look at my Michael and then of course there's Luke."

Luke. He did seem to be the exception of—

"And there's John and Ben," Mrs. Heaton added. "They're all good Christian men, Kathleen."

"They seem to be." Kathleen sighed. "But how does one ever know if they'll change when they marry or if they are only on their best behavior during the courting stage? Living in the tenements, I've seen some good men who treat their wives right. But I've seen so much more of the opposite kind of men. I'm just not sure I'll ever be able to trust my heart to anyone."

"I'm going to pray you change your mind, dear," Mrs. Heaton said. "A loving man and a good marriage are a true blessing. Just let the Lord guide you—" her gaze took in Kathleen, Elizabeth and Julia "—all of you—in your choice of a husband. Listen to your heart and the Lord and you won't go wrong."

Her words gave Kathleen something to think about as they started back to Heaton House, but still she didn't see marriage in her future. It had to be easier not to depend on a man for either your livelihood or your happiness. It certainly hadn't been for her sister.

When they returned there was a letter waiting for her from Colleen and she hurried upstairs to read it in private. She settled down in the comfortable chair by the window and slit the letter open with the beautiful letter opener Mrs. Heaton had given her.

Dear Kathleen,

It is always so good to hear from you. I'm glad to know that you are recovering and beginning a new life out of this place. Thank you for the money you sent. It has come in very handy this week as Clancy lost yet another job. He's been in one of those moods and I'm glad you aren't here to see it.

The boys say to tell you they love you and thank you for the penny candy you provided through the money you sent. Of course you know that I love you, too. I'm so thankful that we can at least keep in touch by letter. I hope to report that Clancy has a new job next time. Pray for us, won't you? Love always, your sister Colleen

Clancy without a job was not a good thing. Kathleen bowed her head and whispered a prayer. "Dear Lord, please watch over Colleen and the boys, please keep them safe and keep Clancy from hurting any of them. Please let him find a job soon. In Jesus's name I pray, Amen."

She brushed at the tears just thinking of her nephews and her sister brought about. She wasn't there. She couldn't do anything other than leave it all in the Lord's hands—and trust that He'd watch over her loved ones.

Kathleen sighed and pushed herself out of the chair, her side giving a small twinge as she did. She freshened up and changed for dinner. She'd write Colleen tonight when she came back up and tell her she never stopped praying for them.

That evening, Michael and Violet joined them for dinner and everyone was in high spirits as they discussed going to the symphony the next week. Kathleen had never been before and was very excited about it.

Just as Kathleen and Violet were heading to the parlor with the others after dinner, a knock came on the door. Kathleen had learned that a visitor this time of evening was rare, and they stopped to see who was at the door Gretchen opened.

Kathleen felt a sliver of apprehension seeing one of the policemen who'd been at the park the day Luke had come to her defense.

"Evening, ma'am," he said to Gretchen. "I'm Officer O'Malley and I'd like to speak to Kathleen O'Bryan, if I may."

Dread flooded Kathleen's heart as she stepped forward. "I'm Kathleen O'Bryan, Officer. What do you need to talk to me about?"

She was barely aware that Luke stood by her, if for nothing else but support, as did Violet and Michael who moved to stand on the other side of her.

"Miss O'Bryan, there is no easy way to say this. I'm sorry to report that your sister has been shot and is in the hospital, ma'am."

"No!" If not for Luke's quick grasp of her arm, Kathleen was sure she would have crumpled at his feet. "Is she—"

"The doctors say she will be all right. But she is asking for you."

"I must go to her." Trying to gather her thoughts, Kathleen turned away then back again. "Yes. I must go now. The children. Where are they?"

"They're with a neighbor. I believe her name is Mrs. Walsh."

"Good." Kathleen nodded and released a deep breath before asking, "And Clancy? Colleen's husband?"

"He is dead, ma'am."

Kathleen felt herself begin to slump for a moment but again Luke was there to hold her up. She pulled herself together, let out a deep breath and stood straight once more. "What hospital is my sister in, Officer?"

"Bellevue. We can take you—"

"I'll take her, Officer. I have a hack on the way now," Luke said.

Kathleen assumed that he'd had someone call for one and was proved right when Michael came back to say the cab would be right there.

"We'll be going with you," Michael stated.

"All right, then." The officer nodded. "As long as she's not by herself. The neighbor said not to worry about the children, ma'am. She'll take care of them until you can get there."

"Thank you, Officer."

"I'm sorry to bring such news. I'll see you at the hospital."

The hack arrived and Luke helped her out to it. The ride to the hospital was one of silence, no one knowing what to say. Kathleen did the only thing she knew would help. She prayed silently and continually.

When they arrived at the hospital, they were taken to a room on the second floor and led through a row of beds on each side of the room. They passed other patients, some moaning and groaning in pain, others just lying there staring out into the room, and still others curled up and seeming to be asleep.

They stopped about midway down the aisle and Kathleen could no longer keep her composure as she saw her sister, her face black and blue from what must have been a beating, but with a huge bandage over her shoulder and part of her chest. She couldn't hold back a deep sob.

A nurse was with her and she turned to Kathleen. "Are you her sister?"

Kathleen nodded, wiping at her eyes. "Is she…is she going to be all right?"

"Yes. But—" The nurse shook her head and leaned closer to whisper, "I am sorry to tell you that she lost the baby."

Kathleen closed her eyes, but the only sound that came out of her mouth was a small moan as the nurse continued, "She just drifted off, but she's been waiting for you. I'll see if I can find a doctor…and here comes Officer O'Malley. He can tell you what happened before she came here. Perhaps you'd like to talk in the hallway?"

Kathleen hesitated while the officer stood by her side.

"I promise she's going to be all right, but it will take time to heal and get over the sorrow," the nurse said.

With a short nod, Kathleen and the officer headed toward the hallway with Luke, Michael and Violet following behind.

Officer O'Malley led Kathleen to a bench and sat down beside her. "You may get more information from your sister when she can talk more easily, or from her neighbors, but this is what I know. About five o'clock, one of the neighbors alerted us that there was a huge ruckus going on in your sister's apartment. They'd heard her screaming and the children crying."

Violet brushed at the tears that seemed to flow of their own accord.

"When we got there, we had to break down the door. Your brother-in-law had a gun in his hand and from the looks of her face, that's what he beat her with," Officer O'Malley continued. "Soon as we yelled for him to stop, a shot when off and, well, that's when he shot your sister. He turned, we told him to drop the gun and he shot again. I don't know whose shot killed him but both my partner and I pulled our triggers about the same time."

Kathleen closed her eyes and began to rock to and fro. Violet quickly sat down on the other side of her and put an arm around her.

"I'm sorry, ma'am. I hate this part of my job." The look in the officer's eyes said he was telling the truth.

"Oh, no. Please…" Kathleen paused, shaking her head. "Thank you for saving my sister's life. If you hadn't been there, she might not be here right now."

From the corner of her eye Kathleen saw a youngish man come up to them. "Miss O'Bryan?"

"Yes." She turned to him.

"I'm Doctor Addison. I just wanted to let you know that your sister will be all right."

Kathleen sighed with relief and swallowed around the knot in her throat.

"She's very lucky. If that bullet had hit her a little lower, she'd be gone. As it is, she'll be very sore for a while and won't be able to lift much, but she'll recover. It may take longer for her to get over the losses she's suffered tonight, but in time, she will. She'll be here a few more days before she can be released, but she seems to be worried about her children and kept calling for you."

"I'll try to set her mind at ease," Kathleen said. "Is she awake yet?"

"Let's go see."

Kathleen stood and followed the doctor back to her sister's bed. She sat down and reached out for Colleen's hand. *Thank you, Lord, for bringing her through. Please heal her completely and quickly. Please help me to know how to help her now.*

"I have to get back to write up the report," Officer O'Malley said. "Please tell Miss O'Bryan that I'll be checking on her and that if she has any questions before then to contact me."

"We will," Luke said. "Thank you, Officer O'Malley."

The policeman inclined his head and headed down the hall.

Restless, Luke got up and went to the door of the hospital room. He watched as Kathleen pulled up a chair to sit by her sister. His heart broke as he saw the expression on her face when she reached over to take her sister's hand.

He sighed and pinched the bridge of his nose as he

sent up a prayer asking for the Lord to heal Kathleen's sister and be with her and her family.

Michael came up behind him and nudged his arm as he looked at Kathleen once more. "Come on, Luke. It could be a while. Let's take a seat."

Luke nodded and the three of them sat on the bench Kathleen had vacated earlier. He turned to Michael and Violet. "I want to give her all the time she needs. You two can go on home. I'll get her to her nephews or wherever she wants to go when she's ready."

"We'll wait awhile. We probably should go with you. No telling what the apartment looks like. If there's blood—" Violet stopped and shuddered.

Michael put an arm around his wife and pulled her close. "At least she won't have to worry about that brother-in-law taking his rage out on her family or her anymore."

Or about me getting hold of him one day. Luke began to pace the floor. He wanted to be by her side, should she need him, but she hadn't asked him to go with her and he didn't have the right to impose himself on her at this time. He couldn't help but wonder what Kathleen would do now that her sister's husband was no longer a threat to her or her sister and nephews. Would she go back to live with them? He didn't want her to leave Heaton House.

Luke continued to pace for what seemed like hours. In reality it was probably less than one before Kathleen joined them again.

"She seems to be sleeping peacefully now. And I promised her I'd go home to the children. I'm sure they're quite frightened and I need to get to them and assure them their mama is all right."

Her eyes were bright with unshed tears and she shook

her head. "I don't know what to tell them about their papa." She looked around. "Is Officer O'Malley still here? I'll get him to take me home."

"He had to go, but he said he'd be checking on you," Luke said. "I'm going to take you wherever you need to go."

"We're all going with you," Violet said.

"Violet, I'm not sure that's a good idea, you—"

"Kathleen, your sister's children need you now. I want to help." Violet put an arm around her friend. "Let's get you to them."

Kathleen looked at Luke and then Michael.

"But—"

Michael shook his head. "No sense in arguing with her, Kathleen. Violet has her mind made up. And she's right. You don't know what you're facing when you get there and we want to help."

Finally, she nodded. "All right. Let's go."

It didn't take as long as Luke feared to procure a hack to take them to Kathleen's sister's building. As the driver pulled up to the tenement, there was no little amount of curiosity about the arrival of a hired vehicle from those still on their stoops and the street outside.

Luke and Michael helped the women out of the hack and Kathleen led the way inside. Several people recognized her and asked about her sister. No one expressed condolences about her brother-in-law, which told Luke the man wouldn't have many mourning his demise.

He followed Kathleen up the stairs. The hall was dark and dingy, stuffy and smelling of everything imaginable, and Luke didn't want her to move back here. Ever.

Chapter Seven

Luke could tell that Kathleen was distressed that they were seeing where she'd lived by the way her back stiffened as he followed her up the narrow staircase. With each flight he tried to ignore the heat that rose with them, the aromas that assailed them. When they reached the fifth-floor landing they started down the dark hallway. Somewhere a baby needed a diaper change and someone else must have cooked cabbage. He could hear a couple arguing as they passed one door.

Kathleen seemed to hold her back even straighter as they continued on. Midway down the hall she stopped and knocked on a door. The door creaked open only an inch or so and a man peeked out. Luke recognized him as the man who'd brought her to Heaton House. Once he saw Kathleen, he opened it a bit wider. "Sorry about your sister, Kathleen. I'll get Rose."

He'd barely turned away before he called, "Rose! Kathleen is here for the kids."

A woman came to the door, wiping her hands on a dish towel. "Oh, Kathleen, how is Colleen?"

"They say she'll be fine, but she doesn't look it. She's

badly bruised, and you know she was shot, don't you? And…" Kathleen paused and swallowed hard. "She lost the baby."

"Oh, I'm so sorry." Rose reached out and put a hand on Kathleen's shoulder.

"She insisted I come see about the children and I knew she wouldn't have any peace until I did. Nor would I."

"I tried to get them to eat, but they only pushed their food around on their plates. They are welcome to stay here until you can make arrangements—"

"No, thank you, but I need to see them, please." Kathleen's voice broke and Luke could only imagine how she felt. It'd been a while since she'd seen the nephews she loved so much.

Rose nodded. "Let me get them for you."

"Thank you, Rose."

It was only a moment before two little boys came running. "Aunt Kathleen!"

Luke heard Kathleen's stifled sob as she dropped to the floor and gathered the two little boys into her arms. They began talking over each other, telling her about their mama and papa arguing and papa hitting mama and all the blood, sobbing as she gathered them closer and rocked them back and forth.

"I'm here now. And Mama's going to be all right in time. It's going to be all right."

They clung to each other and Luke looked away as his emotions threatened to get away from him. He saw Violet put a hand to her mouth and tears gather in her eyes as Michael pulled her closer to him. Evidently they were touched just as much.

Kathleen stood and looked at her neighbor. "Thank you, Rose. I—"

"No need, Kathleen. I'll keep them tomorrow while you go see about Colleen. Just bring them over when you get ready. And I'll help out when she gets home. A woman shouldn't be treated the way Clancy treated her. She'll be better off without him."

Kathleen only nodded. "Thank you. I'll see you tomorrow."

From there, they formed a little caravan, with Kathleen and her nephews in front, Luke behind her and Violet and Michael in the rear. She stopped at a corner apartment and unlocked the door. The children clung to her as Kathleen turned to him and Michael and Violet.

"Thank you for bringing me home. I appreciate it more than I can say, but we'll be all right. I'll arrange to get my things in a few days—"

Luke's chest tightened. She intended to stay here.

"Nonsense," Violet said. "We'll get your things to you and we aren't leaving now. I'm going to see if you need help in cleaning up…" She swallowed hard and pushed her way inside.

"Violet, I can do it." Kathleen followed her and Luke could hear the relief as it whooshed from her chest.

He looked around but there was no evidence of a gunfight in the room they were in. Someone, probably Rose, had cleaned up what must have been a horrid sight and Luke was thankful for all their sakes. "You do have some good neighbors, Kathleen."

She nodded as she looked around. "Even better than I thought. Thank you for seeing us home. Please, everyone, your evening has been taken up—"

"Kathleen, stop talking like that. You are our friend

and we care about you," Violet said. "Let's light a lamp or two. It will be better for the children."

Luke and Michael did as she suggested, quite certain that Violet was going nowhere until she was convinced Kathleen and the children would be all right.

"Do you think the children would eat if I make something?"

"Thank you, Violet, but I doubt it. I'll make them something if they get hungry later."

"I'd be glad to make you all something." She looked around and Luke could see the disgust she was trying to hide from Kathleen that anyone had to live in these conditions. There were only three very small rooms in the apartment and no bathroom. It appeared they had to share one down the hall, or maybe even on another floor. The kitchen, if it could be called that, was in a corner. It consisted of a small sink, a tiny range and a small icebox.

The blood might have been cleaned up, and it appeared that Kathleen's sister tried to keep the apartment clean best she could, but the overall squalor of the building and the neighborhood couldn't be fixed so easily.

"Kathleen, why don't you go back to Heaton House with us? You know the children would be welcome."

"No, Michael, but I thank you. I can't impose on your mother any more than I already have."

"Please come back with us, Kathleen," Luke said. "The boys can share my room."

Kathleen shook her head. "Thank you for the offer, Luke. But I can't. I'm not being stubborn. I'm doing what is best. If we were to go back to the boarding-house, that would show the children a side of life they can't live in forever and it would make it harder for them to come back here. We'll get out of here one day, but until then we must accept that this is our life. It won't be forever, I assure you."

"But it doesn't have to be now, either."

"Yes, Violet, it does. My sister will come home, Rose will help her and watch the children while I work and we'll get on our feet. It will be easier without—"

She looked down at the two boys who still clung to her skirts. "We will be all right. And I will be in touch. Don't worry."

Luke could only watch as Violet looked at the children and swallowed hard. She turned back to Kathleen. "All right. We'll get your things to you."

"Thank you." Kathleen reached out an arm to hug Violet. "Your friendship means more to me than I can say."

She turned to Michael. "As does yours and your mother's. Please tell her I will be in contact and thank her for all she's done for me. Now, please go so that I can explain things to the children and comfort them."

Luke saw the resolve in Kathleen's eyes. She needed them to leave. But he wasn't going just yet.

"You two go on. I'll be along shortly," Luke said in a quiet voice, looking Michael in the eye, trying to convey his need to talk to Kathleen alone.

"All right."

Even Violet seemed to be more at ease knowing Luke wasn't leaving just yet.

"We'll be checking on you."

Kathleen nodded and Luke had a feeling that she was just trying to appease Violet so that she would leave.

"Come, Violet. I'll bring you back," Michael said.

Violet nodded and followed him out the door.

Kathleen turned to him. "Thank you again for being with me once more in my time of need, Luke."

"Kathleen, let me help you get the boys to bed. And then I'll go. Please."

He thought she was going to turn him down, but she nodded instead. "This is Mr. Patterson, Collin and Brody. He's a friend of mine."

Collin nodded. "I 'member him. He helped you and Mama at the park that day."

Luke remembered the way they'd clung to their mother's skirts that day, hiding behind her in fear and yet begging Kathleen not to send their papa to jail.

He bent down to their level and looked the one called Collin in the eyes. "It's good to meet you again, Collin. I remember you, too."

Luke held out a hand and the young boy looked at him for a moment before slipping his smaller hand into Luke's. Luke gave it a shake and then turned to the younger boy. "And you're Brody?"

He nodded and sidled closer to Kathleen.

"I'm pleased to meet you, too. Your aunt has missed you very much."

Tears welled up in both boys' eyes.

"We missed her, too," Collin said.

"Well, you'll be seeing a lot more of her again now. Will you let me help Aunt Kathleen get you ready for bed?"

Brody stuck a finger in his mouth and nodded. Luke picked him up and looked at Kathleen. "Tell me what to do."

Brody put a hand on Luke's cheek and turned his face to look at him. "Didn't your mama teach you how to wash for bed? Ya put water in a bowl, get a clean rag and scrub your face and hands and then yer feet."

Luke chuckled and even Kathleen joined in as they set about getting her nephews ready for bed.

Much as she'd wanted everyone to leave, Kathleen had to admit Luke was a great help and his presence comforted her.

But once the boys were ready to be tucked in, she turned to him. "Thank you for helping me, Luke. But it's getting late and I need to make sure they go to sleep assured their mama is coming home."

"I understand, but I still wish you'd take them back to Heaton House, Kathleen. It's not too late and we'll all help out with them."

"But, Luke, they can't stay there and it would be so much more difficult for them to have to come back here again." She knew firsthand how hard it would be.

Luke only nodded. "Go on and tuck them in, then. I'll be here when you get through. I know how to make myself a cup of tea."

"But you can't—"

"I'll only stay until you have them asleep and I know *you* are all right."

There was a glint in his eye that told her she might have won the battle over her staying here with the boys, but he wasn't going anywhere until he spoke to her again.

She gave a brief nod and headed to the room she'd shared with her nephews. They were both sitting on their pallets waiting for her.

She gathered them close and rocked back and forth, thankful they were all right and she was with them again. But talking to them about their mama and papa was the hardest thing she'd ever done—after seeing Colleen in that hospital bed, her face black-and-blue, all bandaged up and knowing she'd lost the baby. She had to keep reminding herself that the doctor and nurse said she would be fine…eventually. But her sweet sister certainly didn't look like she'd be all back to normal anytime soon.

"Mama's going to be all right, Aunt Kathleen?" Collin asked as she'd cuddled them and tried to assure them. "She's not going to die, is she?"

"Oh, no, Collin, your mama isn't going to die. She'll have to stay in the hospital for a little while, but she's going to be all right. And you'll have to be good boys and help her some. But I know you'll do that."

"Oh, we will," Collin said, his eyes big and overly bright. She wasn't sure if he was going to cry or not. He looked at his little brother. "Won't we, Brody?"

Brody solemnly moved his head up and down and cuddled closer to Kathleen.

"But your papa won't be coming home." Kathleen held her breath waiting for them to ask why.

Instead, Collin only asked, "Never again?"

"Never again." Kathleen felt guilty for the surge of relief that washed over her at the realization that her brother-in-law would never be able to hurt her sister again. That he was gone for good and that he got what he deserved. *Lord, please forgive me. I know I should feel sad for him, but right now all I can feel is relief that he won't hurt anyone again. That I can be part of my family's life again.*

Whether the boys realized their papa was dead or not, she didn't know. They didn't ask. Nor did they cry.

Collin had only said, "He won't be able to hurt Mama or you again."

"He won't be able to hurt anyone." Kathleen didn't tell them about the baby, she'd let Colleen do that or at least ask her if she should when she saw her again. For now, the boys had heard enough bad news. She looked down on the innocent faces and thanked the Lord for answering her prayers and for letting Colleen be alive, for letting the boys be unharmed.

After saying their prayers with them and kissing them good-night, she slipped out of the room, leaving the door cracked so she could hear them if they needed her.

Then she went out to find Luke standing at the window, waiting for her. She joined him there.

"Are they asleep?" he asked.

"Not yet, but it's been a tiring day for them. I'm sure they will be soon."

"I can see why you've missed them so much."

Kathleen drew a ragged breath and nodded. She tried to blink back the tears that fought to be let loose.

Luke reached out to brush a tear and she flinched. His hand stilled. This was Luke, she reminded herself. Not Clancy. He only wanted to comfort her. At that knowledge she leaned her cheek into his hand and sighed.

Luke pulled her into his arms and for the first time in a very long time, Kathleen gave herself over to the emotion. Her breath released on a sob and she let the tears come. He rocked her back and forth and rubbed her back with one hand until her tears were spent. Then he raised her chin so that he could look into her eyes.

"I'm sorry. I've got your shirt all wet and—"

Luke stopped her words with his fingertips on her lips. "It will dry. You needed to cry it out."

She nodded but didn't know what to say next. She didn't want him to go and yet, she knew she must send him away.

"Thank you for being here. I—"

"And you need some rest. I don't want to leave you, but I'll check on you tomorrow. There is a telephone in this building somewhere, isn't there?"

She nodded. "The landlady on the first floor has one."

"If you need me for anything, you telephone me."

"I will."

"Promise?"

"I promise."

His arms were still wrapped loosely around her and he placed his forehead against hers. "I'm sorry about your sister, Kathleen. But I'm so glad you weren't here when it happened. You might have ended up in the hospital, too. Or worse. And I..." He pulled back slightly and raised her chin. He shook his head and sighed. "You lock up good. I won't leave until I hear all these locks click."

"All right."

"The kettle is hot. Make some tea and I'll see you tomorrow."

She nodded.

He went through the doorway and pulled the door shut behind him. "Lock up now."

Kathleen did as he said, turning the three locks.

"Good night," Luke said from the other side of the door.

"Good night." Kathleen heard his footsteps fade before she turned and then hurried to the window. She pulled the thin curtain back and glanced down just as Luke left the building and looked up. She didn't know if he saw her or not but she waved, just in case. He waved back and she touched the windowpane, as if she could touch this man who'd begun to mean so much to her.

Once he was out of sight, she went to check on the boys and found them fast asleep. She pulled the covers up over them and kissed their cheeks.

She pulled the kettle from the back of the stove and poured it over tea she'd placed in a small pot, then went to look out the windows while she waited for it to steep.

The view was the same as it was when she left. Buildings, just like the one they lived in, lined up across and down the street. So many people living in squalor. Such an extreme difference in the way she'd been able to live these past weeks.

She'd been relieved when Violet and Michael left. They were wonderful friends, but she hated for them to see the conditions she'd lived in before she'd come to Mrs. Heaton's home. Hated that they had to know the ugliness that happened in the tenements at times. Hated that they knew it had happened in her family. And yet she knew they cared. They would treat her and her family the same as they had from the day they took her in and she would always be grateful to them.

Still, it had hurt to see Luke go, knowing that she wasn't going back to Heaton House anytime soon, if ever. At that thought her heart tightened as if it were being squeezed by a vise and she swallowed around the knot in her throat. She'd known it was too good to be true.

Would she see her friends again? Or would they go

on about their lives? She certainly couldn't expect them to come here. And with Colleen in the shape she was, it'd be up to her to take care of her sister and the boys. They were all the family she had and she loved them. At least Clancy couldn't hurt any of them again.

But, oh, how she longed to be back at Heaton House, longed to have gone with Luke and taken the boys with her. Still, she had to do what was best for the boys.

She looked around the apartment and saw a mouse come out of hiding and skitter across the floor. It was a sight she'd seen often but it still sent a shiver down her back.

Living here was horrible, especially after living at Heaton House. But now she was more determined than ever to get her family out of the tenements and into something they could call home. And one day she would.

Chapter Eight

Luke let himself in Heaton House with a heavy heart. One of the hardest things he'd ever done was to leave Kathleen and her nephews in that apartment. And when he'd looked up to see her looking out her window, he'd almost rushed back in to insist she come with him.

But she had a stubborn streak and he couldn't really argue with her reasoning. It would be hard on those boys to live at Heaton House and then have to go back. They'd be dealing with enough in the weeks to come. And Kathleen—how hard must it be for her to have lived here and then have to return to that apartment?

"Luke? We're in the parlor," Mrs. Heaton called. "Please come join us."

Luke was a bit surprised to find Violet and Michael had come back there and were waiting for him to return. They were in the parlor with the others and had filled them in on what they knew of the evening.

"How are Kathleen and her nephews?" Mrs. Heaton asked. "I remember those little boys from that day in the park."

Luke smiled. "I'm sure they're better now that they

have their aunt Kathleen. I believe they were almost asleep when I left."

"And Kathleen? How is she?" Violet asked.

Luke swallowed hard, remembering her sobs. "It's been hard on her, but Kathleen will do whatever she needs to."

"We told Mother that we tried to get her to bring her nephews here, but that she said no," Michael said.

"Well, they aren't going to stay there for much longer, rest assured of that. Not if Violet, Elizabeth and I have anything to do with it," Mrs. Heaton declared. "We've been working on a project for a while now—even before Kathleen came to stay. And even harder once she did."

"What is it?" Luke asked. "What do you have planned?"

"It will take Kathleen and her sister both working, unless one of them marries and possibly even then, to afford a decent place to live," Mrs. Heaton said. "But they have no child care apart from depending on a neighbor and that isn't something they can depend on permanently. And it's not getting them out of the tenements.

"So, we are going to try to get some kind of child care started," his mother added. "Surely there are those who love children and would be thrilled to be paid to keep them while their mothers work. Or maybe it will be a chance for some mothers to work and have their children with them while they watch over other children, since not all employers want to hire married women—especially mothers—although some of them are the most in need of work."

"Are you hoping that some businesses or benefactors

will see the need and provide the space?" If so, the idea made good sense to Luke.

"Yes. That's it, exactly." Violet seemed pleased that he was interested.

"It's a good idea," Michael said. "I'll run it by some people I know. If you can get a few started in different parts of the city, then it will be easier to get more people on board. What about our churches? If we could get them to sponsor or help to sponsor one or two children or the homes, that would help."

"That is a wonderful idea, son. Would you bring it up to the church elders?"

"Certainly I will. I must say, I'm quite proud of you all for coming up with this idea," Michael said.

"You know, I'd like to write an article about the need," John said. "I can't guarantee that it will get in the paper or, even if it does, that it won't be buried on the back pages, but it might generate some interest."

"Oh, John, that is a good idea," Elizabeth said. "I'll run it by my editors at *The Delineator*. Maybe they will ask to reprint your article or ask for another."

"Thank you, Elizabeth."

Luke hoped the plan worked. He wanted Kathleen and her family out of the tenements as soon as possible.

Everyone seemed very enthusiastic about the project and Luke could see that Mrs. Heaton, Elizabeth and Violet were quite determined to carry it through.

"For now," Mrs. Heaton said, "Clara has excused Kathleen from work, but she won't be able to do it indefinitely. And of course that doesn't fill their immediate need for food and all—"

"Why don't we take up a collection? I'm sure everyone here will chip in and maybe Mrs. Driscoll could collect from work," Elizabeth said.

"That's another great idea," Luke said. He'd been planning on sending something to Kathleen anonymously but he'd add his contribution to the rest. "How long do you think this plan will take to firm up?" Luke asked.

"We're hoping to be able to tell Kathleen and her sister about it in a few weeks," Mrs. Heaton said.

Luke nodded. That wasn't all that long. Not really. So why did it feel like forever?

Luke knew the tenements would look much worse in the daylight, but when he accompanied Mrs. Heaton and Elizabeth to take Kathleen's things to her the next afternoon after Sunday dinner, he was still taken aback by the utter hopelessness in the faces of some of the tenants.

He'd been in and out of areas like this one before, but never had someone he cared about lived in those conditions. Much as it bothered him before, having Kathleen move back there lit a fire inside him to complete his book.

Many of these people had come to this country to have a better life than where they'd come from, just as Kathleen's family had. But if this was better—and he didn't possibly know how it could be with people so crowded together—he hated to think of what it must have been like in their homelands.

From the look on Mrs. Heaton's and Elizabeth's faces, they were dealing with the same kinds of feelings. Luke lifted Kathleen's satchel out of the hack and

Mrs. Heaton and Elizabeth grabbed the bags of extras they'd brought.

If possible, the stairwells and halls were dingier in the daylight where what sunlight did find its way in caught up all the dust moats and illuminated the filth. The odors clung to the air and the yelling seemed even louder, although not quite as menacing as in the dark of the night before.

They didn't know if Kathleen would be home or not, but were hoping that she was as they made their way down the hall to her sister's apartment. Luke knocked on the door and waited. He thought he heard the murmur of voices, but couldn't be sure where it was coming from.

Just as he'd decided to check with the neighbor and see if Kathleen had left the boys with her and gone to the hospital, the door opened slightly. Kathleen peeked out and then opened the door a bit wider. She stood there with her two young nephews peeking out from behind her skirt.

"You didn't have to do this today," Kathleen said. "I would have come to collect my things."

"We wanted to check on you and your family," Mrs. Heaton said, smiling at the children. She brushed past Kathleen and into the apartment. "And your sister? How is she, do you know?"

"I haven't had a chance to go see her yet, but I'm praying that she is better."

"Well, let's take care of that," Mrs. Heaton said. "Luke can take you to the hospital and Elizabeth and I will stay with the children until you get back."

"Oh, no, Mrs. Heaton. I couldn't ask you to do that. Thank you so much, but this is no place for you. I'll leave them with the neighbor later on and go see about Colleen."

"No place for me? It's no place for you and your family, either. It is no place for anyone, Kathleen, dear. But if you insist on staying here for now, then you must expect to see us from time to time. You've become dear to me and to all of us, and we'll not let that connection be lost."

"I—"

"Please, Kathleen, let us help you," Elizabeth implored. "The children will be fine with us and we brought them a treat."

"Might as well say yes, Kathleen," Luke said. "We aren't leaving and you may as well let me take you to the hospital to find out how your sister is doing."

"I…" She looked around the room and then gave a shrug as if she didn't want them to see it, but as they were already inside, there was nothing she could do about it. "All right. Thank you."

She turned to the boys. "This is Mr. Patterson from last night. Do you remember him?"

Both boys nodded and Luke smiled at them.

"And this is Mrs. Heaton, the lady whose home I lived in while I was gone, and this is Elizabeth. She's a good friend, too. They are very nice people and they're going to watch you while I go see how your mama is doing. You behave yourselves, you hear?"

The boys nodded again, Brody with a thumb stuck in his mouth.

"I'll tell Mama that you miss her and want her home quickly." She kissed the tops of their heads and nodded to Luke. "Let's go."

The boys continued to hold on to her skirt, looking

first at Elizabeth and then Mrs. Heaton. Then the older boy—maybe five or six years old—whispered to his little brother. The little one nodded and smiled at the women. Still keeping one hand on Kathleen's skirt, he gave a half wave as if a little afraid to fully acknowledge seeing them before.

"It'll be fun. We brought you a treat," Mrs. Heaton said, looking at Kathleen and giving her a wink.

"Gretchen sent some of her molasses cookies and some other things she thought you could use," Elizabeth explained, digging into one of the bags and bringing out a smaller bag of cookies.

The boys looked to their aunt and at her nod, they immediately let go of her skirt and hurried over to Mrs. Heaton, who handed each of them a cookie.

"Thank you," Kathleen said as she and Luke walked out the door.

She walked ahead of him and Luke could tell by now that when she held herself so rigid, she was trying to hide her emotions.

But last night, just for a few minutes, she'd let her guard down and let him see a side of her he was sure not many did. And somehow that made him feel that she might be coming to trust him. Maybe, just a little. Only time would tell.

Kathleen let Luke help her into the hack he'd kept waiting outside. As they had last night, children and others had surrounded it—they didn't see many hired vehicles in this part of town.

But many of them asked about her sister and told her they'd say a prayer for her. Kathleen kept assuring herself that the hospital would have gotten word to her if

Colleen had taken a turn for the worse, but she wouldn't rest until she saw her.

"Thank you for coming," she said, turning to Luke. "I was about to take the boys to Rose, but they were afraid to leave in case their mama came home today. I tried to tell them that she'd have to stay in the hospital a few days, but they don't really understand and I couldn't bring myself to tell them about the baby."

"That's understandable, Kathleen. It'd be difficult for any of us." He reached out for her hand and she slipped it into his, somehow needing his touch. Luke covered her hand with his larger one and gave it a light squeeze. "Maybe you'll have good news to share with them when we get back."

"I hope so. Right now my prayer is just for Colleen to get better."

"I'm praying the same, as I'm sure all the others at Heaton House are."

"Thank you, Luke. It does comfort me to know that."

They arrived at the hospital just then and Luke helped her out of the hack and then kept a hand on her elbow as they went inside and up to Colleen's room.

Kathleen turned to him at the door. "I'm not sure if you— She doesn't know you, other than what I've written in my letters and…"

"It's all right, Kathleen. You go on in. I'll wait over on that bench for you." He pointed to a bench right across from the doorway where he could see into the room. "If you need me, just wave."

Kathleen nodded. She really wished he could come with her. Colleen had looked so terrible last night, that even though the doctor said she'd recover, Kathleen wasn't so sure. She'd like some support when she saw her for the first time today. But she didn't know how Colleen would react to seeing Luke or anyone besides her and she didn't want to stress her any more than she already must be.

She made her way down the aisle to the last bed. Colleen's eyes were closed and Kathleen pulled a chair up to her side as quietly as she could. Her sister's color looked a little better than last night—at least where it wasn't bruised.

Kathleen bowed her head to pray and placed a hand over Colleen's. Her touch made her sister jerk awake.

"Ahh… Kathleen, 'tis you. How are my boys? Where are they?"

"Shh, don't get yourself all wound up. Collin and Brody are fine. I wouldn't have left them if they weren't. But they are anxious for news of you and I had to see how you are."

"I lost the baby…. Did they tell you?"

"They did. I'm so sorry, Colleen. But I'm thankful that you are still here with us. The boys and I need you."

"And I need to get out of here so I can take care of them."

"Colleen, you need to recover more before you even think of coming home. I'm taking care of the boys until you can."

"Where are they? Are they with Rose?"

Kathleen shook her head. "No, Luke—Mr. Patterson—came by to bring me to see you, and Mrs. Heaton and one of my friends are with the boys at your apartment."

Colleen looked around. "Luke—he's the man who helped us that day in the park? The one you've written me about?"

"Yes."

"Where is he now?"

"He's in the hall. I wasn't sure how you'd be or how you'd feel about seeing a stranger with me."

Her sister surprised her by saying, "Please ask him to come in. I'd like to meet him."

Kathleen stood and looked down the aisle to see Luke looking into the room from his bench. He hadn't grabbed a paper to read. Instead he seemed to be doing just as he said he'd do. Waiting to see if she needed him. She smiled and waved him in.

Luke smiled and nodded as he stood and made his way into the room.

"Here he comes now."

As Luke made it to her side, she turned to Colleen. "This is Mr. Luke Patterson, Colleen. Luke, this is my sister, Colleen Sullivan. She wanted to meet you."

"I'm pleased to meet you, Mrs. Sullivan. And I'm very sorry about your loss."

Kathleen saw the tears well up in her sister's eyes as she nodded. "Thank you, Mr. Patterson. And thank you for helping us that day in the park and for being there for my sister the night I sent her to Heaton House."

Luke smiled down at her sister, who looked so battered and bruised, much as she herself must have looked when she arrived at Heaton House. "You're welcome, but there is no need to thank me. I would hope any other man—"

"Oh, no. Not just any man would have come to our aid that day. But you did. And for that, Kathleen and I will be forever grateful."

Kathleen could tell Luke didn't know what to say and he seemed a bit uncomfortable, so she quickly changed the subject. "Do you know when your doctor will be in to see you?"

"You just missed him. He came in earlier and said that I might be able to go home tomorrow."

"That seems awfully early after all you've been through."

"I'll heal better at home than here. I want to be with my boys. And besides, look around, Kathleen. They don't have any empty beds in this ward."

Kathleen glanced around the ward and found her sister was right. Last night there'd been a couple of empty beds, but today it looked as if those were filled and a couple more brought in.

"Well, I'll be there to help you. I do have to let Mrs. Driscoll know why I didn't come in today."

"I would imagine that Mrs. Heaton has already done that. She mentioned that she'd telephoned her this morning," Luke informed her.

Kathleen saw her sister smile. "I'm so glad Mrs. Heaton gave you her card, Kathleen, and that you kept it. It appears I sent you to the right place."

"Oh, there is no doubt about that, Mrs. Sullivan," Luke said. "None at all. I'll be glad to help Kathleen get you back home tomorrow, if the doctor does release you."

"That would be nice of you, Mr. Patterson. Thank you."

Luke's offer didn't surprise Kathleen but it warmed her heart and gave her some peace. Her new friends—or family, as she'd come to think of most of them—weren't going to forget her just because she wouldn't be living at Heaton House. They'd already shown they'd be there for her and her family. She had much to be thankful for.

Chapter Nine

Colleen had been allowed to come home the next day. Luke had helped get her home, but she still seemed to be very fragile and he could tell Kathleen was afraid to leave her alone.

Once she was settled in her room, Kathleen came out and said, "Would you mind staying for a few minutes while I run and ask Rose if she can come over while I go to the grocers and the pharmacy?"

"I will, but there's no need to ask Mrs. Walsh. I can run any errands you need," Luke said. "I can take the boys with me and you can stay with Colleen."

"I don't want to impose on you." She shook her head.

"Kathleen, you aren't imposing on me." Luke rubbed the back of his neck and sighed. "I'm your friend—at least I hope you consider me one. Please let me help you."

"You have work to do, Luke. You can't keep taking off for me."

"I can write at night—one of the blessings of being a writer." He pushed an errant strand of her beautiful hair behind her ear. He'd love to pull her in his arms and tell her not to worry, that as she took care of her sister, others were trying to find a way to help them both. But he didn't want to say anything in case Mrs. Heaton and the others' plans fell through.

And just because she'd let him hold her once didn't mean it would ever happen again. He could see the wariness in her eyes and quickly lowered his hand. "Now, please give me a list. Your sister needs to nap and it will do the boys good to get out in the fresh air and quit worrying about their mama for a bit."

Collin and Brody had been overjoyed to see their mother and now they each sat on the bed beside her. But Colleen looked exhausted and they looked worried.

Kathleen nodded and began to write a short list. Then she handed him some bills and called to the boys. Luke stuffed the money in his pocket, knowing she'd never take it back.

"Want to go to the store with Mr. Patterson?" she asked the boys. "He's going to pick up a few things for us and you two know what items your mama uses and can help him, if he has any questions."

Both boys grinned and nodded, and Luke had a feeling they didn't get to go to the grocery very often. He'd be sure to pick them up some candy while they were out.

"You stay right with Mr. Patterson, do you hear?" Kathleen said as they headed out the door.

"Yes, Aunt Kate," Collin said.

Kate. Luke quite liked that name. He turned and said, "I'll make sure they do… Kate."

Her cheeks turned pink when he winked at her and shut the door behind him. Yes, he liked that name just as much as he liked Kathleen. Perhaps it was because he'd come to care for the woman—no matter what her name.

The air inside the halls hadn't freshened any at all and as he and the boys stepped outside, they all seemed to inhale deeply, even though the air outdoors wasn't all that fresh, either.

Both boys slipped a hand in each of his and looked up at him. His heart went out to them. Losing a father—even though the man hadn't deserved the family he had—then finding out they weren't going to have a baby brother or sister after all, and seeing their mother in such bad shape had to affect them. And yet they looked up at him trustingly, and a familiar protective feeling washed over Luke. He could easily come to care for Kathleen's family, almost as much as he cared for her. He wanted them all out of the tenements as soon as possible.

They picked up the boys' mother's medicine first and then headed for the grocer she used. Collin and Brody were very good in the store, helping him pick the things they were familiar with, pointing out which brands of canned goods his mother used, along with staples.

"Aunt Kate can fry the best potatoes," Collin said with a sigh.

They weren't on Kathleen's list, but he put a bag on the counter along with several other things he could tell the boys might like and that he thought Kathleen might need but not have the money to buy.

He made arrangements for the groceries to be delivered and then let the boys each pick out a stick candy. They grinned as the grocer handed them their choices.

"Thank you, Mr. Patterson!" they both said at the same time.

"You're welcome." Luke wondered how long it'd been since they'd had a piece of candy.

They took their time getting home and when they did, it was to find that the groceries had already been delivered. He thought Kathleen might be angry with him for adding to her list, and figured she'd tell him all about it when she sent the boys in to see their mother.

"She's awake and asking for you," she told the children.

They hurried into her room and Luke turned to Kathleen, ready for whatever it was she had to say.

But she surprised him. Hands on her hips, she looked at him and shook her head before advancing toward him. "Luke Patterson, you are a good, kind man. It appears the boys let you know of their fondness for fried potatoes."

"They say you make the best. I wouldn't mind trying them out." He grinned at her, relieved that she didn't appear mad.

He looked down at her as she stood in front of him, and he had the strongest urge yet to pull her into his arms and hold her. But his instincts told him that holding her in his arms the night everything happened had been an exception and she'd permitted it only because of the stress she was feeling at that moment. Kathleen still seemed skittish around him most of the time and he didn't want to damage the fragile friendship they appeared to be developing.

"Thank you." Kathleen made an abrupt turn and went back to putting the groceries up. "I'm sure you have things to do, but you may come back for supper, if you'd like."

"Oh, I'd like. Thank you. What time should I be here?"

"About six, if you can make it by then."

"I can."

"Did they thank you for the candy?"

"They did. They are very good boys, Kathleen. You have every reason to be proud of them."

"They're pretty special."

"They are that—just like their aunt Kate. Thank you for the invitation. I'll see you at six."

Rose had asked Kathleen to let the boys come play with her son later that afternoon while Colleen slept and Kathleen took that time to straighten up and wash a few of the boys' clothes. She was hanging them up on a makeshift line strung out the window when a knock came on the door.

She opened it to find Mrs. Heaton and Violet. It was so good to see them that she fought down the humiliation of having them in this neighborhood and this building, and opened the door wide.

"It's so good to see you, Kathleen, dear," Mrs. Heaton said. "We miss you a great deal."

"I miss you all, too." And she did. More each day.

"How is your sister, dear?" Mrs. Heaton asked.

"She's very weak, but I think being home will help her. The boys cheer her up."

"Where are they?"

"With a neighbor. She has a son Collin's age and she thought Colleen could rest better if they played with him for a while. They seem to keep wanting to check on her just to make sure she's here, I think."

"That's understandable."

"Let me make us some tea."

"We don't want to make more work for you."

Kathleen was already putting the kettle on. "It's not

work and I'm ready for a cup. Please take a seat at the table."

"We'll join you, then," Mrs. Heaton said, sitting down at the table. Violet did the same. "We have something we'd like to tell you."

"Tell me?" Kathleen sat down. "What is it? Not bad news, is it?"

"Oh, no, dear. And we certainly wouldn't burden you with any more of that right now, even if it were."

"Then what?" Kathleen couldn't imagine what it was they wanted to tell her.

"Well, you know we love you at Heaton House." Mrs. Heaton smiled. "And if you didn't know, let me assure you we do. We and your coworkers have been very worried about you and your family, too. And, well, none of us want you to worry about money while you are helping out your sister." She pulled an envelope out of her parasol and placed it on the table. "We all want you to have this."

"Oh, Mrs. Heaton, I can't—"

"Kathleen, you *can*. It's for your family and we aren't going to take no for an answer."

Kathleen looked from one woman to the other.

"Mrs. Heaton is right. We aren't taking it back, so you might as well accept it and use it to help Colleen and the boys," Violet reiterated.

Kathleen swallowed around the clump of tears in her throat. "I don't know what to say. I can't begin to thank you all for everything you've done for us."

"We just want you to feel free to help your sister, but know that we are already thinking about ways to help her, too."

"What do you mean?"

"Well, we can't tell you just yet. But, Kathleen, we aren't going to just let you and your sister fend for yourselves. I wish you'd bring them all to Heaton House."

Kathleen shook her head.

"I am trying to understand why you think it's best not to. We want you back at Heaton House."

"Oh, Mrs. Heaton, I'm not sure I'll be coming back. I—"

"You'll be back, dear." Mrs. Heaton reached over and patted her hand. "You'll be back, if for no other reason than to visit. Don't think for one moment we're not going to expect that."

Kathleen wasn't sure what to say. Wasn't sure of anything at that moment except that she loved these two women. They'd become family to her in the short while she'd known them and she couldn't wait for Colleen to meet them.

Mrs. Heaton pushed the envelope over to her. "Now take this for your family's sake, Kathleen. Please."

"Everyone wanted to contribute, Kathleen," Violet said. "This will make it easier for you until you can work again."

Kathleen had no idea when that would be. Colleen had to get much stronger before she could. "Thank you. Please thank everyone for me."

Overwhelmed with gratitude, Kathleen got up to pour boiling water over the tea leaves in the teapot that'd belonged to her mother and left it to steep before wiping her eyes and turning back to her guests.

"I hope there comes a day when I can repay you by helping others as you've all helped me and my family." Oh, yes, she'd been truly blessed the day she'd been taken to Heaton House.

She turned back to pull down cups and saucers for their tea and tried to get her composure. *Thank you, Lord. For all of those who've reached out to help, and especially for Mrs. Heaton and Elizabeth...and for Luke.*

Over the next few days, Luke spent his time going back and forth between Heaton House and Kathleen's sister's apartment. He'd enjoyed the fried potato supper she'd prepared on Monday and fought the urge to overstay his welcome when he left that night.

Colleen seemed to be improving each day, but still appeared quite fragile. But by the middle of the week she was up and around and had even told Kathleen that she thought she'd be all right if Kathleen needed to go back to work. Mrs. Walsh had offered to help her with the boys.

Now, Luke listened as Kathleen used him as a sounding board.

"I'm not sure what to do. I can't stay off work indefinitely, but I don't feel Colleen is well enough to be left alone yet." Kathleen added some seasonings and stirred the soup she'd put on earlier. "At least with the collection that Mrs. Heaton took up for us, I don't have to worry about rent for the next month and we can eat. But Mrs. Driscoll can hold my position for me for only so long."

"Don't be worrying about it right now. She gave you all of this week off. Take the time, Kathleen." Luke was afraid that after all she'd been through even before her sister's near murder, she could easily have a setback herself if she tried to do much more. "Your sister and the boys need you and by Monday you'll feel better about leaving your sister for the day."

"That's true, I will."

There'd been several meetings in the small parlor at Heaton House about Kathleen and her sister's situation and the plan for child care homes. Luke knew what was going on because Mrs. Heaton, Violet and Elizabeth had kept him and Michael apprised of the situation, but until they had everything firmed up, he'd promised not to say anything to Kathleen and her sister. And he didn't want to get their hopes up in case it all fell through. But he prayed daily that the plan would come together and Kathleen and her sister could move out of this neighborhood.

Colleen appeared in the doorway of her small room and Kathleen hurried over to help her to the kitchen table. "Mr. Patterson, it's good to see you. I believe I've been sleeping my life away these past few days. Kathleen tells me you've been keeping my boys in treats. Thank you."

"It's been my pleasure. You have good boys, Mrs. Sullivan."

"Please, call me Colleen. Mrs. Sullivan makes me feel old."

And probably reminded her of the husband who nearly killed her, he thought. "Colleen it is. And I'm Luke."

He didn't want anyone feeling he should be invited to eat each night and thought that Kathleen's sister would feel more comfortable if he left. She did have better color now, but he could tell from the sorrow in her eyes and the way she wrapped her arms around her middle that she mourned the baby she'd lost, possibly the husband, too, and she still had pain from the gunshot wound. But these two sisters were made of tough stock and he prayed the Lord would ease their burdens.

"I'd best be on my way." Luke got up and headed toward the door. "I told Mrs. Heaton I'd be there for dinner tonight. I've imposed on you enough this week."

"You've done nothing of the sort. You've been a great help and the boys love having you around," Kathleen said, walking him to the door. "But we take up enough of your time."

"No, I believe it's the other way around. I know it goes against your grain to let me help, but you've been very gracious in letting me." He grinned and winked at her when he was sure Colleen wasn't looking. "I'll see you tomorrow."

"Luke, you don't have to—"

"I know. But I'll see you tomorrow anyway."

He finally won a smile.

"See you then. Good night."

"Good night, Kathleen."

He spoke to several people as he passed their apartments on his way to the stairs. And he'd gotten used to the stuffiness and the smells—well, maybe not totally. What he'd learned was not to breathe deeply until he reached the street, and found it helped a lot.

He walked outside amid people trying to escape both the heat and the odors, he supposed, and walked as fast as he could over to Third Avenue and toward Gramercy Park, taking deep breaths of the fresh air. He hated leaving Kathleen and her family in the tenements more each time he had to.

Seeing them up close on a daily basis, even getting to know some of the tenants, had given him new insight and understanding of the struggles most of them faced. While he'd never use the names of Kathleen and her family, or those he was getting to know, their plight lent new energy to the writing of his book and he'd been staying up late into the night working on it.

But the days and early evenings, he saved for Kathleen and her family. He'd come to look forward to visiting with Collin and Brody, and Colleen, too, when she felt up to it. The hardest thing was leaving them and coming back to Heaton House.

Much as he loved living there, it felt lonely to him without Kathleen's presence and the few hours he spent with her and her family weren't the same as seeing her first thing in the morning at the breakfast table and again in the evening for dinner and then spending time in the parlor after dinner. He missed the outings they'd had and—

Luke sighed. Kathleen had to do what she could to help her family. He knew that and his esteem for her grew daily. She never complained, never whined about how her life had changed. And yet he was sure she wondered what the future held for her and her family.

He wondered the same. And he wanted to fix it all, only he didn't know how. And even once Mrs. Heaton's plan was put into place, he didn't know if Kathleen would be moving back to Heaton House or not.

He arrived home just in time for dinner and took his seat, trying not to think of Kathleen's empty one beside him. Nor did he want to compare the meal Mrs. Heaton served to the simple one Kathleen's family would be eating.

When Elizabeth asked about Kathleen and her family he was more than glad to talk about them.

"The boys seem to be doing all right and Kathleen's

sister was up when I left there. But I hope your plan comes together soon, Mrs. Heaton. I'd surely like to see them get out of there."

"That may be sooner than you think, Luke," Mrs. Heaton said. "We had a meeting today. Thanks to word getting out and Elizabeth's and John's articles, several business leaders have heard of our idea and, well, we're getting some good backing. Our initial plan to help Kathleen and her family is going to end up helping many others in the same predicament."

"What's happened?"

"We've begun looking for a house for the first child care arrangement. I'm going to talk to Kathleen and her sister tomorrow about it, but if Colleen thinks she'll be able to run it, she'll get the first one. And we'll have to find another woman who needs to provide for herself or her family to help. It will provide a home for two different families and at the same time provide care for others who must work outside the home. We still have to decide how many children each home will be able to care for."

"What about Kathleen?"

"We have an offer for her, if she'll take it. We need someone who can find out which families have a real need for what we're doing, as well as who can run a child care home."

"But what about her job?"

"Clara says this would be a much better position. The salary will be more than Kathleen is making now or anytime in the future, according to Clara. And we've been asked to come up with someone who can relate to what those living in the tenements are going through in their day-to-day lives. Who better to fill that position than Kathleen?"

"I certainly can't think of anyone," Luke said. Still, he didn't like the idea of her having to be in the tenements on a regular basis. But if she didn't have to live there... "Will Kathleen be living at the home with Colleen?"

Mrs. Heaton shook her head. "No. She'd come back here. We all know how devoted she is to her family and that is all well and good. But it's doubtful there will be enough room. And even if there is, Clara and I believe Kathleen needs to have a life of her own. She'll be able to see her sister and nephews anytime she wants. She just won't have to feel responsible for all their needs."

"When will you be presenting the plan to her?"

"First thing tomorrow."

"Good." For the first time in days Luke felt the heaviness in his chest lift. If his prayers were answered, Kathleen would soon be moving back to Heaton House.

Chapter Ten

After Mrs. Heaton and Violet's visit, Kathleen knew something was in the works to help her family, but she wasn't sure what. When Mrs. Heaton sent word by Luke that she and the ladies would like to bring lunch to her and Colleen on Saturday, Kathleen had a feeling they were about to find out more.

Luke had asked if he could take the boys to Central Park and fly kites with them, since the weather was unseasonably warm, and of course Colleen had agreed. They were all becoming fond of Luke, and the boys loved going on outings with him.

Kathleen kept looking out the window, watching for the ladies' arrival. Finally, a rented hack pulled up and Mrs. Heaton stepped out carrying a huge picnic basket. The other ladies followed her into the building.

Earlier, when she'd told Colleen about the ladies' visit, her sister had hesitated. Kathleen had insisted.

"We can't be rude, Colleen. These women care about us."

"You're right, to be sure. I'm just a little nervous about havin' company here."

Kathleen had understood. She'd felt the same way until she'd come to realize these people genuinely wanted to help her and her family. And just as she knew they would, Mrs. Heaton, Mrs. Driscoll, Elizabeth and Violet all put her sister at ease immediately by showing their concern for her health, for her welfare and the boys', as well as for Kathleen's. They talked to her as if they were lifelong friends and with as much respect as they would give one another.

Kathleen was pleased to see that her sister began to relax as soon as they started to eat the meal Mrs. Heaton had brought over.

"My dears, we've come to tell you some good news. At least we think it is and we're hoping you both do, too."

"What is it, Mrs. Heaton?" Kathleen asked.

"Well, we've found a place for your family to live outside the tenements. It's not overly far from Heaton House and it's—"

Kathleen could see the tension in her sister's face as she sat a little straighter and shook her head and interrupted Mrs. Heaton.

"Aw, now, we can't be taking charity, even though I know your hearts are good and you mean well," Colleen said with a sigh. "We'd never be able to pay for a place the likes of what you're describin' with Kathleen's wages and what I can bring in doing laundry for others."

"Oh, but my dear, please wait until you hear us out. We have a plan for that also."

By the time the ladies finished explaining that Colleen could run one of the child care homes they were establishing around the city, Kathleen could see the hope she felt deep inside reflected in her sister's eyes.

Not only did the plan offer a better life for Colleen and the boys, but also the hope of a future for Colleen's children—and her own if she ever had any.

"I assure you, Colleen, you'll be earning every penny you receive," Mrs. Heaton said. "Please don't consider anything we are doing as charity. We've just figured out a way that we can all help you and your family and others to have hope again."

"You say there'll be another woman living there, too. What about Kathleen?" Colleen asked.

"Well, we have an offer to make to Kathleen, too."

"Oh?" Kathleen looked from Mrs. Heaton to Mrs. Driscoll. "And what is that? Do you want me to run another of the homes?"

Mrs. Heaton shook her head. "No, dear. We want you to find others we can hire to run the new homes as we can start them up. And most of all we need you to identify those who are in real need of child care while they work."

"But what about my job at Tiffany Glass? Will I be able to work around it?"

"Kathleen," Mrs. Driscoll said, "I love having you work in my department. You are one of the best workers I have. But this is a much better position. It will pay you more than you are making now—or, for that matter, more than I'm making."

"How can that be?"

"The backers of this project have the money to do it right," Mrs. Heaton said. "And they want someone who has lived in the tenements, who can relate to the women in need. Because it involves talking to women, a man isn't going to be able to do the job as well as you. Many of the women would never even talk to a man."

"And you've expressed a desire to help others," Violet added. "We thought this would be ideal for you to be able to do that in a way we can't."

"But where will she live?" Colleen asked.

"She has a room at Heaton House as long as she wants it," Mrs. Heaton said.

Kathleen felt the sting of tears behind her eyes. She wanted to move back to Heaton House, but— "I'm not sure Colleen is up to this so soon."

"I'll be fine, Kathleen. And now that I know you can go back to Heaton House where you have so many friends, my heart is at ease. You've given up so much over the years to help us and—"

"But, I—"

"Kathleen, it will be a few weeks yet before we get things in place. By then Colleen will feel even better. We don't want you leaving her until you both feel comfortable about it," Mrs. Heaton explained, looking from one to the other. "In the meantime, you could try to find someone with the need of a job who could help run the house and who would be a blessing to your sister. I'm sure you know several people that are friends already who might want this opportunity."

"You know there are, Kathleen," Colleen said. "I can think of several right now."

Mrs. Heaton smiled. "I thought that might be the case. It would be good if it were someone you know and like, Colleen. So, ladies, will you help us?"

Help them? Kathleen looked at her sister and nodded. She saw Colleen's smile before it even reached her mouth and knew she'd agree to the plan. How could she not?

"Oh, yes, ma'am," Colleen answered. "I can't thank

you enough for the opportunity you are offering us. I promise you'll never be sorry."

"We're pretty certain of that, dear. Otherwise, we wouldn't be here." Mrs. Heaton smiled and looked at the women who'd come with her. "Well, ladies, I think we can put our plan in motion."

"Thank you." Kathleen hugged the older woman who'd taken her into her home for no other reason than just to help her for a few days or weeks. Now she'd helped her for all time.

Luke enjoyed flying kites with the boys. They loved being at the park, running and playing, letting the kites he'd bought them fly higher and higher in the sky.

They were tuckered out by the time they headed home that afternoon—so much so that Brody had fallen asleep on the trolley ride, and Luke carried him from the trolley stop to their building and up the stairs to their apartment.

Luke had prayed all afternoon that Kathleen and her sister would accept Mrs. Heaton's offer for what it was and not refuse it as charity. He realized they were both proud, but surely they'd see that they would be helping others as well as themselves.

And hopefully Kathleen wanted to move back to Heaton House as badly as he wanted her to. Oh, he knew she loved her family, but she needed a life of her own, too. Clancy was no longer a problem and Luke couldn't bring himself to be anything but glad about that. Kathleen could see her family anytime she wanted without fear of her sister's husband, and she no longer had to fear that her sister or the boys would be hurt.

Collin ran ahead and knocked on the apartment door.

When Kathleen opened the door to them and saw her nephew in Luke's arms, she smiled and he tried to read what her decision had been as she reached out and took Brody from him.

"Come on in. Colleen is napping, but I've got some coffee on and Mrs. Heaton left cookies."

"Cookies? May I have one, Aunt Kate?" Collin asked.

"You may. You can keep Luke company while I put Brody down."

Collin led him to the cookie jar in the center of the table. "Mrs. Heaton brings the best cookies." He looked into the jar, reached in and pulled out a huge sugar cookie.

Luke put his hand in and pulled out one for himself. He'd fed the boys lunch on the way to the park, but all the activity had made them hungry.

Kathleen came out of the tiny bedroom the boys shared and poured him a cup of coffee just as a knock came on the door. Collin ran to answer it and found Roger, the neighbor's son, asking if he could come play.

"May I go play with Roger, Aunt Kate?"

"You may." She pulled another cookie out of the jar and handed it to Roger. Then she stood and watched them enter the Walsh apartment before coming back to the kitchen.

"How were they? Did they tire you out?" Kathleen asked as she poured herself a cup of coffee and joined Luke at the table.

"Pretty near. But we had a good time. It didn't take them long to catch on to the art of kite-flying." He took a sip of coffee and met Kathleen's gaze. "How did the meeting go?"

If the sparkle in her eye was any indication, it went well.

"Did you know of the offer Mrs. Heaton and her group were going to make us?"

"I did. But it wasn't my news to tell and I—"

"I understand. I just didn't know how much to tell you and I'm still not sure I believe it." She smiled and shook her head. "That we're all getting out of the tenements is such a blessing. Colleen couldn't contain her tears once they left. It's a lot to take in."

"You accepted the position they offered you, too?"

"I did. At first I didn't think I'd be qualified for it, but then Mrs. Heaton explained that they want someone who has lived here, who can relate to those who do. I think it's my chance to help others as she's helped us and I'm so grateful for the opportunity."

"I'm a little concerned about you coming and going all the time."

"Luke, I've lived here for a long time. I'll be fine. And Mrs. Heaton has made me promise not to be out and about after dark. I don't do that now, so it was an easy promise to make."

Luke leaned back in his chair, relief washing over him. His prayers had been answered. Kathleen and her family would be out of here before long. And she would be back at Heaton House. It couldn't come soon enough for him.

By the end of the month, things had come together so well that Mrs. Heaton was asking for volunteers to get Kathleen's sister moved into the first home that would serve as both home to her and her boys, along with a friend of Colleen's who'd be helping to run the home and do a lot of the cooking. It would serve as a child care home for one of Kathleen's former coworkers from Tiffany, one from Butterick, and two others who lived in the same tenements as Kathleen and her sister.

Colleen and the other woman they'd hired, Ida, would be watching ten children altogether, and everyone agreed that would be enough at least until they saw how things went. But Colleen would be in charge and with her salary and a furnished home, she'd be able to make a decent living.

"What did Kathleen say when you told her everything was in place?" Elizabeth asked.

Mrs. Heaton had visited her just that afternoon. "She cried. And then she hugged us. Clara and I told her together." Mrs. Heaton clasped her hands together and smiled. "I can't wait to get her family moved in the new home and Kathleen moved back in here."

Luke felt the exact same way. Oh, he'd seen a lot of Kathleen at her and her sister's apartment. But that was nothing like having her in the same house.

"What about furnishings? Will they have enough for the house?" Elizabeth asked.

"We've had wonderful donations of items to furnish it and all of that is already in place. It won't take very long to move the rest of their belongings. There isn't much," Mrs. Heaton said.

"Luke and I are leaving here at nine in the morning. Michael and Violet will meet us at Colleen's. Any of you who wish to help are welcome to come with us."

Julia and Elizabeth immediately offered to help at least part of the day, as did John and Ben.

"I am so eager to get them out of there. The memories they have to live with would be enough reason to find something else, even if it wasn't such an awful place to live," Luke said.

But it was awful, and thinking about all the children living in similar conditions had kept him up late into the night working on his book.

"Once they are out, maybe they can begin to put those awful memories behind them. I pray Collin and Brody can forget that night." Luke had become quite fond of those boys. It was a pity their father hadn't cared enough to throw the bottle out and treat his family the way they deserved.

"I hope so, too," Mrs. Heaton said. "But I'm not sure they can—at least not now. Perhaps, in time, they will."

"Perhaps their mother will remarry one day and hopefully, another man, a good man, will help wipe out those memories," Julia said.

"I have been relieved to know that Officer O'Malley has been checking on them from time to time," Elizabeth said.

What mattered to Luke most right now was getting those children out of that apartment, out of the shadows and into a home where there was sunlight—and hope for their future.

The next morning most of Mrs. Heaton's boarders, all except for Julia, who'd been called in to work at the last minute, showed up to help Kathleen and Colleen get moved.

Kathleen watched her sister. While she would have been embarrassed at one time, today she was happy to see them and thankful for their help.

There was Mrs. Heaton, Elizabeth and Violet, of course, and Luke. But also Michael, John Talbot and

Ben rolled up their sleeves and got to work. Kathleen's heart warmed that they cared enough to give up their Saturday to help her and her family.

"It is so good to see you again and know that you'll be living at Heaton House once more." Elizabeth hugged her. "And your sister will be close enough to visit."

"I know. I'm so thankful for that. Thank you for your help and your friendship," Kathleen said, hugging her back.

Everyone began gathering up boxes or crates to carry down the stairs and it seemed a madhouse for a while. But Luke and Michael had rented a couple of wagons, and soon they were loaded and on their way to the new house by noon.

In short order they pulled up in front of a well-kept, modest two-story home on a nice quiet block not all that far from where Mrs. Heaton lived. It was the first time Kathleen and her family had seen the house Colleen and the boys would be calling home. Kathleen only had to see the expression on Colleen's face to know what her sister was feeling.

"Are we at the right place?" she asked Mrs. Heaton.

The older woman patted her hand. "This is it, dear. Colleen's new home."

Kathleen was speechless. It was…so much more than either she or her sister had imagined when Mrs. Heaton and Elizabeth had told them about it. She felt as if she must still be sleeping and would wake up soon, still in the tenement and finding this was all a dream. It was only when Luke offered his hand to help her and Colleen out of the wagon that she began to believe it was real.

Violet and Mrs. Heaton went in with them while the

others began to unload the wagon. Kathleen looked around at the parlor…and put a hand to her mouth as she took in the furnishings. There was a real parlor suite of blue and gold that actually matched. There were paintings on the walls and drapes at the windows. The furnishings were in good condition, if slightly worn. But they made the parlor look homey, comfortable and beautiful in her eyes.

Then she spotted the dining room across the way and saw that it, too, was furnished. The pieces didn't match but they fit each other and all she could do was shake her head as they made their way upstairs and picked out the rooms Colleen and her boys would have. The boys would share a connecting room. There was a room like Colleen's across the hall and she chose it for Ida. "If Ida doesn't like it or wants a different room, she can choose when she arrives."

All the rooms were big, bright and clean, and Kathleen was thrilled. She wouldn't feel so guilty living in Heaton House again, now that Colleen and the boys had such a nice place to live.

The bedrooms were furnished with beds and armoires—the boys would each have their own bed for the first time in their lives. Kathleen turned to Mrs. Heaton. "Oh, we've never had such nice furnishings. Do these come with the house?"

"They do," Mrs. Heaton said. "Many of my friends and I have things in our attics that were in good condition and just sitting there, not being used, Kathleen. It gave everyone who donated something much pleasure to know how it would be used, I can assure you of that."

Colleen looked dazed. "I've never seen such fine things. I don't know how we can ever repay you."

"Just help someone else, dear. And you'll be doing that by keeping the children of others in need."

"But I'll be paid for that. This is all…just too much to take in." Colleen sank into a settee and looked around the parlor. "I've never seen anything so grand and that it will be ours…"

"Yours it is. It will feel like home before long," Violet said. "At least we hope it will."

The group started bringing things in and asking where to put the different boxes, and Colleen stood to take one.

But Mrs. Heaton turned to Colleen as she stood and shook her head. "You just sit here and get used to everything, Colleen. You still don't need to be lifting and all. You'll have your work cut out for you when you start keeping the other children in a few weeks. For now, just tell us where you want certain things put and try to get used to this being your home."

Tears came to Kathleen's eyes as she turned to Elizabeth and Mrs. Heaton. "I truly don't know how to thank you both for all you've done for us. If it weren't for you, we'd have no hope."

"You both have grit, Kathleen. You would have made it. We just wanted to hurry things along."

"You've certainly done that. Thank—"

Mrs. Heaton held her hand up. "You're welcome. And we're glad to have some part in your future. But it is your future and we know that you will both make the best of this new chapter of your lives. You've had a tragedy, to be sure, but you know the Lord can work all manner of things to the good of His people. And He will use you to help others. By understanding what others like you and Colleen have been through, you will be more able to help them."

"I promise you that we will do all we can to be worthy of all of this." Kathleen knew she'd be on her knees for a very long time that night. That the Lord had seen fit to have them helped in such a way was most humbling to her.

"Kathleen, you've always been worthy of help, dear. I'm just glad you came to us. But you know, the Lord has had a plan all along. We've just been a part of it."

"To my way of thinking you've been the best part of it."

"Kathleen, do you know where Colleen might want these things?" Elizabeth asked, a big box of clothing in her arms. Julia had shown up after her half day of work and was right behind her with two smaller boxes.

"I think those go upstairs." Kathleen took the top box from Elizabeth. "Come on and I'll show you where to put them. Or at least where I think Colleen might want them."

"I'll go get some more boxes," Violet said.

"No." Elizabeth turned to her. "Michael said for us just to help put it all up. He and the men will bring the rest of it in."

"All right. It will probably go faster that way."

"Well, I'm going to go get Colleen some tea and help Gretchen get lunch together," Mrs. Heaton said. She'd sent Gretchen over earlier to stock up the kitchen and prepare a lunch for everyone.

Luke came in just then with Kathleen's two nephews right behind him. They each held a couple of items he'd handed them. "The boys think these go in their room. Do you know which one it is?"

"I do. Follow me, boys. I'll show you your new room." Kathleen was glad to get to work on getting her nephews settled in their new room.

"Is this really our new home, Aunt Kathleen?" Collin asked, looking up at the stairs. "Do we have an apartment here?"

"This house is your new home, Collin. The whole house. Do you think you'll like it?"

He looked as dazed as his mother as he followed Kathleen up the stairs. "Oh, yes, I do."

Brody scampered up beside him. "Me, too. I like it lots."

"Well, let's go find your room." Kathleen glanced back to see Luke looking at them. Her chest felt a little funny when he smiled at her and Kathleen turned to hurry up the stairs. As she topped the landing she didn't know if it was the climb or Luke's smile that had her feeling all breathless and fluttery inside.

Chapter Eleven

Luke and Michael had helped Ida get her things up-stairs when she arrived later that afternoon. By then nearly everything had at least been put into the rooms they belonged in, and everyone began to go their separate ways.

It'd been a tiring day and once most of the work was done, Michael and Luke took off to return the wagons back to the livery, and brought back a hack to get them home. Michael took his mother and wife home and Luke stayed behind to bring Kathleen back to Heaton House when she was ready.

He didn't rush her, as he knew it wouldn't be easy for her to leave her sister after all they'd been through. Just as he'd figured she wasn't ready to go until she helped Colleen get the boys in bed.

But she came back downstairs with a smile on her face. "Brody fell asleep in the middle of saying his prayers and Collin is barely holding on until he says 'Amen.'"

"I'm sure they're tuckered out. They worked hard today carrying boxes up the stairs and putting things away," Luke said. He'd come to care for her nephews a great deal. "They're good boys."

"They are."

Her tone sounded a little wistful to him. "Are they upset that you're leaving?"

Kathleen shook her head. "Not too much. We've been preparing them for it and they know we can see each other whenever we want now, so they're happy about that. And I promised them I'd see them tomorrow."

But Luke saw a hint of sadness in her eyes. "How about you? Are you wishing you were staying here, too?"

"I have mixed feelings about it all. But I know it's for the best for us all."

"It is," Colleen said as she came up behind them. "The boys are fast asleep."

"I didn't think it would take long. I hope you all sleep well in your new home, Colleen," Kathleen said.

"I believe we will. But what you were saying about things being for the best—they are, you know. You'd only begun to have a life of your own and start to enjoy it when Clancy—" Colleen stopped and took a deep breath. "When I ended up in the hospital. I don't want you feeling you're responsible for me any longer, Kathleen. We've been truly blessed by Mrs. Heaton and the others' efforts. And we're going to make them proud."

"Yes, we are," Kathleen said.

"You go on now. I'm going to lock up, make Ida and me some tea and help her finish getting settled in."

"I know you must be quite exhausted," Kathleen said. "Are you sure—"

"I am. And the tired I feel is the best tired I've ever

been. I know I'll sleep well tonight and I hope you do the same back in Heaton House."

"I think everyone will sleep well tonight," Luke added.

"I believe you're right, Luke. Go on, now, take my sister back to her other home."

"Kathleen?" He nudged her elbow. "Are you ready?"

She turned to him, her eyes filled with an emotion he couldn't name. "I am. Or at least my sister is ready for me to go. She thinks I spoil the boys too much, you know. She's ready to get me out of her hair."

"Now you know that's not so," Colleen said, shaking her head.

Kathleen kissed her sister on the cheek and gave her a hug. "I do. I love you, Colleen. You do have a telephone, you know."

"I didn't. Where is it?"

Kathleen led her to a small table tucked under the staircase. "Right here. And the Heaton House number is right there beside it. If you need anything—"

Colleen turned her around and gave her a little push. "I'll be sure to telephone you if I need you. I promise."

Luke wondered if Kathleen realized her sister was walking her to the door as she spoke.

"Lock up tight," Kathleen said.

"I will. See you tomorrow."

There was nothing more to do but walk outside. The door shut right behind them and they heard the lock turn.

Kathleen turned to Luke. "I think she was ready to get rid of me."

He chuckled. "It did seem that way, but perhaps she's

just wanting to relax and she couldn't do it with me there."

Kathleen laughed and shook her head. "Oh, no, that's not it. I know my sister. I think she's ready to start this new life she's been given without me having to protect her from Clancy."

"And it sounds as if she wants you to be able to start your new life without having to worry about him."

"I'm sure she wants the best for me, just as I do her."

They reached the walk and Luke helped her into the hack he'd called to pick them up, then he got in himself.

"Where to? Are you hungry?"

"A little bit. But you must be starved after all you've done today. I'm sorry, I should have left earlier."

"It's all right. I understood you wanted to see the boys settled down for the night. But I am a little hungry. How about we stop for supper on the way home?" He pulled out his pocket watch and looked at it. "It's getting late and I'm sure they've already eaten at Heaton House."

At Kathleen's hesitation, he added, "Mrs. Heaton will fuss over us if we haven't eaten."

"You're right. She's fussed over others long enough for one day. I'll be glad to have supper with you, Luke."

He leaned toward the driver and gave him directions to a restaurant he liked and then settled back in his seat and looked at Kathleen. "It will do you good to have a time to relax, too, and I know just the place. You've been busy taking care of Colleen and the boys for weeks now, not to mention packing and getting ready for this day, and then getting Colleen and her family settled in. You've got to be exhausted."

"Well, it wasn't only me. You did your part, too. And so many others helped to make it possible."

They arrived at a restaurant that was still quite busy, as Luke knew it would be, but they didn't have to wait and were quickly whisked into the dining room and shown to a table facing a courtyard.

Kathleen ordered only a bowl of clam chowder, but Michael ordered a full meal and shrugged when the waiter left the table. "I suppose it was lugging all those boxes downstairs from the apartment building and then upstairs at the house, but I'm ravenous."

Kathleen's smile made him glad he'd brought her here. "As well you should be after all that work. Thank you for getting the actual moving organized for us, Luke."

"You're welcome. I was glad to do it. Those boys of Colleen's made the day for me. I doubt they'll have trouble sleeping in the new place after all the traipsing up and down stairs they did today."

Kathleen let out a deep breath. "I'm just glad you were there to catch Brody when he slid down the banister."

"So am I. That was too close for comfort. But I think I frightened him enough with what could have happened that he won't be trying it again too soon."

"I certainly hope so." Kathleen put a hand to her heart and shook her head. "I thought for sure he was going to go flying across the room. My, but weren't they happy with their room, though?"

"And that they each had a real bed to sleep in. I think that touched me about as much as anything."

Luke couldn't get the look of wonder in their eyes out of his head.

"I know. It touched me the same way. For so long they've slept together on a mat on the floor. They both looked really happy today. I can't tell you how wonderful it is to see that look rather than the one of worry they usually have," Kathleen said.

"Now I can understand why you didn't want to bring them to the boardinghouse the night Colleen was shot," Luke said.

Kathleen bit her bottom lip and for a moment, Luke wondered if she might cry. But she only said, "You don't know how badly I wanted to. I am just so thankful that they'll never have to live in those conditions again. To see them smile so readily now…" Her expression suddenly darkened. "Still, I'll never forget that night."

"Neither will I." For more reasons than one. Luke's thoughts strayed from the horror of the shooting to a bittersweetness he'd never experienced before when he'd held Kathleen in his arms and she'd sobbed on his shoulder. He'd wanted to kiss her so much that night. And yet he'd been afraid she'd fly right out of his arms had he done so.

Luke's gaze traveled from Kathleen's eyes to her lips and lingered there. When he managed to pull his glance away, it was to see color flooding her cheeks. She ducked her head. Was she remembering, too? He hoped so. He reached across the table and—

The waiter brought their supper just then and Kathleen quickly pulled her gaze from his. Luke sighed. His timing seemed to be atrocious where Kathleen was concerned. Once the man departed, Luke said a blessing, thanking the Lord for letting them be a small part of helping Colleen and her family be able to have a fresh start.

Fearing Kathleen had been embarrassed when the waiter came to the table, Luke tried to keep the conversation on impersonal matters while they ate. This woman had worked her way into his heart and he didn't have the faintest idea what to do about it.

The look in Luke's eyes sent Kathleen's thoughts back to the night he'd held her in his arms and sent her heart pounding like crazy. Something had changed between them since the night her sister had been shot by Clancy. Before then he'd been her hero, her rescuer—the person who'd protected her from Clancy. Then he'd become her friend.

But she wasn't ready for him to become what her heart seemed to want him to be. He was a wonderful man. But she'd seen the dreams of her sister and those of her coworkers disappear when the love they'd felt for the men they'd married turned to fear and insecurity. She couldn't—didn't dare let herself—begin to think of him as anything more than a very good friend. And be thankful to call him that.

She tried to concentrate on her dinner and prayed that the heat she felt in her face was due to the hot soup she'd been served and not the attraction she was fighting toward Luke.

"Are you excited about starting your new position as liaison for the day care homes?" Luke asked.

Kathleen breathed an inward sigh of relief at his change of subject. Did he know how uncomfortable she'd been remembering that night he'd held her in his arms and let her cry? Could he possibly know that she hadn't wanted him to let go? That she'd wanted— Kathleen squashed the thought and quickly pulled her attention back to his question.

"Excited? I am. I'm also a little nervous about it. I have a meeting on Monday where my duties will be explained more clearly and hopefully, after that, I'll feel better about it all."

"I'm sure you will. And remember I'd like to accompany you to the tenements."

"Luke, there is no need to—"

"We've already had this discussion, Kate. I know you know your way around, but you haven't been in every tenement in your neighborhood. Let me go with you until we know you are safe traveling in and out of the buildings. Please."

"I don't need—" She'd started to insist that she didn't need his protection, but she couldn't bring herself to say the words. She *had* needed his protection several times already. And he knew it as well as she did. "Maybe for the first few times."

Luke grinned across the table at her. "Thank you. That will put Mrs. Heaton's mind at rest, as well as mine. Besides, it's a good place for me to do research."

"What kind of research?"

"For my writing."

Kathleen wasn't sure how she felt about that. "Isn't that taking advantage of those less fortunate?"

"I don't see how it could be, if it's meant to help them, similar to Jacob Riis's book."

The name was vaguely familiar to Kathleen, but she'd never read anything by him…or Luke either, for that matter. Exhausted as she was by the end of the day the only book she managed to read was her Bible.

And she didn't know how writing dime novels could

possibly help the people she knew, but she knew first-hand that Luke's heart was good and he was probably just using his writing as an excuse to get her to think she wasn't wasting his time while he was accompanying her.

This time it was she who changed the subject. "I still can't believe how my and Colleen's lives have changed so suddenly. I'm so happy to be going back to Heaton House. I've missed everyone."

"And we've all missed you. I think we're going to have another boarder or two soon to add to the mix," Luke said.

"Really? Have you met them?"

He shook his head. "No. But I heard from John that Mrs. Heaton said a new man might be moving in next week. Michael's old room is free now that he married Violet. And while you have her room there is still one more on your floor. I did hear that she'd interviewed a young woman yesterday. So we may have a full house again soon."

Kathleen smiled. "Anyone who moves into Heaton House is very fortunate to be there. I don't think all boardinghouses are run the way Mrs. Heaton runs hers."

"I doubt it." Luke leaned back in his chair and smiled. "Mrs. Heaton's house is not just a boardinghouse to me. It's home. Has been for several years now. I can't think of anywhere I'd rather live at the moment."

"She has a way of making everyone feel they're part of her family," Kathleen said. "I know I do."

"There've been a couple of boarders who didn't seem to fit in since I've been there, but they're few and far between."

The waiter returned to the table just then and asked if

they wanted dessert. Luke looked at Kathleen. "Would you like something?"

She shook her head. "No, I'm fine, thank you."

Luke settled up with the waiter and they started back to Heaton House. "Want to walk or ride?"

They weren't far and Kathleen didn't want him spending more money on her than he already had. It wasn't too cool out and it was a bright starlit night.

"Let's walk."

Luke crooked his arm and she slipped her hand through, resting it on his forearm. His pace was just right. Not too fast or too slow.

"I love the city lights at night," Kathleen said. "Especially in this part of town. But in the tenements, I wish there were more. It's never light enough there at night. Still, it always gave me comfort to look out the windows and see a light on here or there in the apartments across the way."

"I can see how it would. We'll have to go to Gramercy Park one evening. I love it there where you can see lights on in all the homes surrounding it." Luke looked up at the sky. "But it's a nice night out tonight with that full moon and so many stars."

"Yes, it is." Kathleen had heard mention of Gramercy Park and hoped she would get to see it one day, but she was enjoying her time alone with Luke too much to say it to him. She should have told him not to come with her to the tenements. It probably wasn't wise to spend much time with him—it only made her want to see him more.

It didn't take long to get to Heaton House and seeing lights in its windows made her feel happy and warm.

"I can't tell you how glad I am you're back here,

Kathleen," Luke said. "It hasn't felt quite the same with you gone."

"Why, thank you, Luke."

"I mean it. You've made a place for yourself here. You do fit in and it's not just me who thinks so."

As they walked up the steps and he opened the door, Kathleen felt as if she had come home. Not to the tenements, not to the house Colleen would be calling home. But here to the place where she'd finally felt safe and cared for.

"Kathleen! You're home at last." Elizabeth came out of the parlor and hugged her. "We've all been waiting up to welcome you back."

Mrs. Heaton and the rest of the boarders all welcomed Kathleen back home as Elizabeth led her and Luke back into the parlor.

They all said how glad they were to have her back and Kathleen had to blink several times to keep her tears at bay. These people had come to mean so much to her in such a short time. She couldn't explain it, but she felt that the Lord had orchestrated it all—from Luke keeping Clancy from hitting her that day in the park, to Mrs. Heaton handing her card to Kathleen before she left. Then to be brought here the night of her beating—she could only believe that the Lord had known all along where she needed to be.

"I can't tell you all how glad I am to be back. And I want to thank each of you for all you've done to help Colleen move into her new home. You've become family to us and we'll be forever grateful to you all."

"That's what family is for, Kathleen, dear," Mrs. Heaton said. "My goal has always been for my boarders to feel they have family here in the city. And I hope that your sister and her boys will soon come to feel as welcome in this house as you are."

Kathleen looked around at all the faces she'd come to care about. They all did feel like family to her. Well, all except for Luke. And he—

She looked over to see Luke smiling at her and the wink he gave her sent her pulse racing. She wasn't sure what Luke was to her—but she knew he owned at least a corner of her heart and always would. And she was determined not to let him claim any more of it.

Thoughts of what Clancy had done to her sister, and to her, clouded the joy of the moment. She wasn't sure she'd ever be able to let any man lay claim to her heart. Not now, and maybe not ever.

Luke watched Kathleen as the others gathered around her. She seemed almost as happy as he was that she was back at Heaton House. And yet, she seemed to be avoiding eye contact with him.

Maybe that wasn't a bad thing. Every time his eyes met hers and she smiled at him, his chest tightened in a way that told him he could care deeply for her if he allowed himself to. But he wasn't going to. He couldn't let himself care that way about anyone again. Couldn't bear the thought of anything happening to her. He still had nightmares about what happened to Beth, holding her in his arms while she took her last breath. Oh, no. He never wanted to experience that kind of pain again. And yet he couldn't deny that he was strongly drawn to Kathleen and very protective of her. But he couldn't fall in love with her.

Gretchen brought in freshly baked cookies and as everyone gathered around her to grab one, Luke forced his thoughts away from the woman who'd been dominating them lately and onto his writing. Seeing how people who truly cared had been so much a part of helping Kathleen and her sister out of the tenements gave him more confidence that his book could give hope to others facing the same struggles.

Instead of trying to write a book much like Jacob Riis's *How the Other Half Lives,* in which he tried to inspire others to reach out and help, Luke wanted to provide hope to those still living in the tenements. To assure them that their lives could change for the better. And that if offered a helping hand, they needed to be willing to accept it.

He knew that had been difficult for Colleen, but it was easy once she felt she would be helping others as much as she would be helped. Maybe that was the key to it all.

Suddenly he felt a need to get back to work. He waited until the welcome-home party broke up, and was glad it didn't take long. Everyone, Kathleen especially, seemed ready to call it a day.

After good-nights were said and they began to head to their rooms, Kathleen began to follow Elizabeth and Julie and then turned back to him. Luke smiled at her as she approached him.

"Thank you again for all your help today and for dinner," she said.

"You're welcome. I'm glad you've moved back."

"So am I. It feels as if I've come home from a very long trip."

He nodded. It felt that way to him, too. "I'll see you in the morning. Sleep well."

"You, too." She started up the stairs and then turned

back. Her lips parted as if she wanted to say something else. But then she gave a little shake of her head and only said, "Good night."

"Good night, Kathleen." Luke watched her up to the landing and then turned to head down to the lower floor. He took the stairs two at a time, wanting to get his thoughts about changes in his manuscript down on paper before he forgot them.

He had a direction for his book, now more so than ever. And once again it was Kathleen and her family who were the inspiration behind it.

Chapter Twelve

The next week passed swiftly for Kathleen. She was in meeting after meeting at the United Charities Building on Fourth Avenue and Twenty-second Street. The building had been set up to assist all the benevolent societies in the city as they tried to help those less fortunate.

The Ladies' Aide Society with their newly formed Child Day Care Program was one such society and it was no surprise to Kathleen that Mrs. Heaton sat on its board. The society had a small office in the building but Kathleen was told she could work from Heaton House where Mrs. Heaton had set up a desk for her in the small back parlor.

She was feeling overwhelmed by the job she'd been hired to do, and as the week progressed she became more and more nervous.

Luke must have sensed her worry, for after dinner on Thursday night he sought her out and asked if she'd like to take a walk.

"Yes, I believe I would, thank you."

They met Mrs. Heaton in the hall and told her they were going for a walk.

"Why don't you take Kathleen to Gramercy Park? I don't believe she's been there yet, has she?"

"No, I haven't," Kathleen answered for herself. "I'd love to see it, though."

"That is a great idea, Mrs. Heaton. I've been meaning to show it to her."

Mrs. Heaton nodded and went to the table in the foyer. She opened the drawer and pulled out a key. "Here you go, Luke. You two enjoy the nice evening."

"Thank you, we will," Luke said.

He swept Kathleen out the door and down the steps and onto the sidewalk. "You'll love the park. It's a great place to go when you need time alone or when you need to talk without worrying about someone walking in on your conversation."

"That might be nice." She loved Heaton House, but it wasn't always easy to have a private conversation with anyone.

Luke tucked her hand in the crook of his arm and they sauntered down the walk until they came to the gated park. Kathleen was a bit surprised when Luke pulled out the key Mrs. Heaton gave him and unlocked the gate.

"I still can't believe this park is private." Kathleen didn't know of another that was.

"It is. And each home only has two keys. It's been that way since the beginning and no one is inclined to change it. It's fairly small and was put in specifically for the residents of the neighborhood."

He led her into the park and Kathleen could see why the residents wanted to keep it to themselves. It was lovely, with trees that'd grown tall through the years and bushes that were sure to be filled with roses or other kinds of flowers as soon as it warmed enough for them to bloom. Luke led her into the middle of the garden and stopped at one of the benches. "Want to sit a little while?"

"Yes, I think I would, thank you." The park seemed an oasis in the middle of the city, much quieter than Central Park and very private. Yet, the lights in the homes surrounding it did make it feel like a safe haven of sorts.

She took a seat and Luke sat down beside her. "Now, tell me what's bothering you. You've become quieter each evening since you started your new position. Are you regretting your decision to work for the Ladies' Aide Society?"

He'd come to read her entirely too well. Kathleen shook her head. "Oh, no, I don't regret it, but I'm afraid they might regret hiring me."

"Now, why would they do that?"

"I don't want to disappoint Mrs. Heaton in any way, Luke, but I fear I'm not educated enough for this position. I—"

"Kathleen, did anyone ask for your credentials?"

"Well, no, but—"

He raised an eyebrow at her. "Did they ask how far you went in school?"

"No, but—"

"Do you know the tenements and relate to those living there?"

"Yes, of course I do. But, Luke, I don't want to fail or disappoint anyone counting on me to hire the right people to run the houses or recommend those that need the day care help. I don't have much experience in that kind of thing."

"I can assure you that none of the women you are working for have the kind of experience you do. They don't understand what it is you and Colleen and your neighbors have gone through. They have good hearts and they want to help, but it's going to take your experiences and your understanding of the people they want to help to be successful. *You* are the person they need, Kathleen."

For the first time that week, the kinks in Kathleen's neck seemed to relax. From the first meeting on Monday until right this minute, she'd begun to doubt her abilities. But Luke made sense.

She did know what it was like to live in the tenements. She knew what it was like to wonder where her next meal was coming from, to worry about physical abuse, to worry about her family. And she could honestly tell the people she talked to that she understood. She could do this job. Everything would be all right.

"My fear was getting the best of me, I'm afraid. I haven't been leaving things in the Lord's hands like I should."

"Oh, maybe not in this instance. But I've watched you, Kathleen. I've seen you pray with your nephews, and I know you put your faith in the Lord to get you through hard times. I believe you trust the Lord more than most people I know."

Kathleen smiled. "I know He's watched over Colleen and the boys, and me." He'd also used Luke to help them, but she wasn't sure Luke realized it.

"That He has. And the Lord is going to use all you've been through for good. You'll see. You are the right person for this job, Kathleen."

"Thank you, Luke. Your encouragement means a lot

to me." It meant more than she could say. No one had ever been there for her in the way Luke had been. But she was going to have to fight the attraction she felt for him. It was simply too easy to be around him.

"That's what friends are for, isn't it?" he asked.

Friends. They could be that, at least. "Yes, but I think you've been a better friend to me than I have been to you."

Luke shook his head. "Not so."

He looked as if he were about to say something more and decided against it. "I'm glad we're friends."

"I am, too." For that's all they could be—at least for now—and maybe for always.

Luke looked up into the star-filled sky and stifled the sigh his chest fought to release. *Friends.* There was no doubt he wanted to be her friend, wanted her to be his. And that was a good thing. And yet, his heart longed for more—in spite of the heartbreak of his past.

First his mother had left him and his father for another man when he was young. From then on, he'd had to live with a bitter man warning him never to trust his heart to a woman. And for years he'd believed him.

But as he'd gotten older he'd realized it was his father's bitterness and not his own, and he'd fallen in love with Beth. He'd been happier than at any time in his life, looking forward to their life together. And then she'd been killed. And he'd vowed never to fall in love again.

Much as he'd begun to care about Kathleen, he couldn't let his feelings turn to love. He could not go through that kind of heartache again. He was better off living at Heaton House amidst those he considered family.

So why did he suddenly feel…so lonely? He'd been doing just fine, living at Heaton House, enjoying everyone's company. He hadn't wanted more until—

"I suppose we should be getting back," Kathleen said, interrupting his thoughts. "Thank you for bringing me here and helping me feel better about everything."

"You're welcome."

They both stood and sauntered back to the gate. The night was deepening and the stars shone brightly as Luke locked the gate behind them and they started back to Heaton House. "When is it you're going to start visiting buildings in the tenements?"

"I hope to begin Monday morning. I've been mapping out which ones to go to first. I thought I might start with our old neighborhood, with the people I know. They might also be able to suggest someone to run the other houses."

"I think that's a good idea. Might as well start with a familiar area. You'll do fine."

"I think I'll feel better once I get started."

"I'm sure you will. It's the unknown that has you unsettled. After a few weeks you'll have more confidence."

"I hope so. Right now I just want to get to Monday."

"Why don't we see if Colleen and the boys would like to go with our group to the park on Sunday? They love flying kites and I like helping them. I'm sure John and Ben would, too."

"The boys would love it. I'll talk to Colleen about it."

"Good. How are they doing?"

"I stopped by on my way home today and they're doing fine. They're settling in and really looking forward to making new friends, and Colleen and Ida are just ready to get the day care started."

"Much like you wanting to get started in your new position?"

"Exactly." She chuckled. "Now that you mention it, I think we're all a little nervous and excited all at the same time. Kind of silly, I suppose."

The tinkling sound of her laughter lightened Luke's heart. His admiration for her grew even more that she could laugh at herself after all she'd been through.

"Not at all. I think everyone is a bit nervous when they're faced a major change in their lives."

"You're not just trying to make me feel better?"

"No. I know what it's like to start over. It is difficult, but it gets easier with time."

Or it did—until memories surfaced and brought back all the pain of losing a loved one and reminded him why he'd decided never to fall in love again.

They arrived back at Heaton House to find that the new boarder had arrived.

"Kathleen, Luke, come meet Matthew Sterling, our new boarder," Mrs. Heaton said.

They entered the parlor to see a man who appeared to be about Luke's age. But he was a little taller, had almost black hair and blue eyes and was quite tan, as if he worked outside most of the time.

"Matt is the son of one of my childhood friends from Virginia. He's an iron worker come to help finish up the American Surety Company Building and then he'll be helping build the Park Row Building starting in October."

Luke strode across the room and held out his hand. "A pleasure to meet you, Mr.—"

"Oh, please call me Matt. Mrs. Heaton has assured me everyone goes by their first name here."

"All right, Matt. I'm Luke Patterson—just Luke is fine. Welcome to Heaton House. It's always good to have another man in the mix here."

"And this is Kathleen O'Bryan," Mrs. Heaton said as she pulled Kathleen forward. "She's been our newest boarder until you came."

"How do you do… Kathleen?"

"It's nice to meet you, Mr.—ah, Matt. You'll find Heaton House is truly a home, just as the rest of us have."

"I'm already feeling at home here, thank you."

"I've heard the Park Row is going to be one of the tallest buildings in the city," Luke said. "How is it working so high up?"

"Well, I've worked on some tall ones and I love it. But this one is going to be 391 feet. I think it will be the tallest once it's finished. I can't wait to get to work on it."

"Oh, it sounds very dangerous," Kathleen said.

Matt shrugged and grinned at her. "It can be. But we're careful up there."

"Luke, I've given him Michael's old room, of course, but he hasn't had time to get his things downstairs. Everyone had gone to their room when Matt arrived. Would you mind?"

"I'll be glad to help him get settled. Whenever you're ready, Matt." And the sooner the better. Luke could see the interest in the other man's eyes as he looked at Kathleen and he didn't like it at all.

Matt turned his attention to Luke. "I'm ready now. I've got to report in early tomorrow. I didn't bring a lot." He motioned to the two cases on the floor at his feet.

Luke grabbed one of the cases. "Follow me." He

barely looked back as he said, "Night, Kathleen, Mrs. Heaton. See you in the morning."

"Good night, Luke. Thank you for showing me Gramercy Park. I enjoyed it very much."

"So did I. We'll have to do it again."

"See you both in the morning," Mrs. Heaton said.

Matt followed Luke out the door, down the hall and then down the stairs.

Even though he had no claim on Kathleen—and was determined not to—Luke didn't mind if this new boarder thought he might. Mrs. Heaton might have known the man's mother a long time ago, but none of them knew the man.

"You've got a nice room. It's next door to mine, and Ben's and John's are across the hall. They're good men. You'll meet them tomorrow."

"How many boarders are there?" Matt asked as he unlocked the room with the key Mrs. Heaton had given him.

"Right now there are four men, including you, and three women. You met Kathleen, and there is Julia and Elizabeth. I believe Mrs. Heaton will be adding one more woman before too long. And then there are the two maids, Gretchen and Maida. They live here, too." He didn't feel the need to explain that Mrs. Heaton sometimes took in temporary boarders. He'd find that out soon enough.

"Mrs. Heaton's son—where is he now?"

Luke grinned. "Not all that far from here. He married one of the lady boarders—an old friend of the family— at Christmas last year and they set up housekeeping a few blocks away. You'll get to know them, too."

"Sounds kind of like one big family."

"It is. And it's quite nice to have it here in this huge city. That's what Mrs. Heaton strives for. It'll be home to you before you know it."

"I hope so."

"If you need anything or have any questions, just knock."

"Thank you."

"See you in the morning. You just go up when you're ready for breakfast and help yourself to whatever is on the sideboard. I'm sure Mrs. Heaton explained it all to you, and she'll be there to introduce you to the others."

"Thanks for your help, Luke."

"You're welcome."

Luke wondered if Kathleen and Mrs. Heaton were still upstairs. He'd wanted to get Matt out of the room so fast he hadn't really had a chance to reassure Kathleen again.

He hurried back upstairs to see if they were around, only to find Gretchen in the kitchen.

"Mr. Patterson, is there anything I can get you? I have some apple pie left from tonight."

"No, I'm fine, Gretchen, thank you. Do you know if Mrs. Heaton and Kathleen are still in the parlor?"

"No, sir. I believe they just went upstairs. Is it important? I can tell them you'd like to talk to them."

"No. That's all right. I'll see them in the morning. I will take a cup of that coffee with me though, if you don't mind."

"You know I make a fresh pot for you this time of night. Help yourself."

"Thank you, Gretchen."

"You're welcome."

Disappointed he hadn't caught Kathleen before she

went upstairs, Luke poured himself a cup of coffee and headed back to his room. He'd see her in the morning and talk to her then. For now, he might as well see if he could get any writing done.

For Kathleen, having a new boarder in the house proved a good distraction from worry over her new position. It was quite entertaining to watch everyone at dinner. Kathleen mostly listened and watched as Elizabeth and Julia engaged Matt in conversation, with all kinds of questions about what it was like to work so high up in the air.

But if the scowl on John Talbot's face was any indication, he wasn't too happy about the attention Elizabeth was giving to the other man. Ben was quieter than usual, but Luke was hard to read. She couldn't tell what he thought of the other man. Still, having someone new at the table made for interesting conversation.

"You're from Boston?" Julia asked. "I'd think there was plenty of building going on there."

Matt chuckled and shrugged. "There is. But it's not New York and I wanted a change. And the buildings are getting taller here."

"You really like working that high up?" Elizabeth asked.

"I love it."

Kathleen couldn't imagine working so high in the sky. The fifth floor she'd lived on in the tenements was plenty high up for her.

"Enough about me. What is it the rest of you do?" His interest picked up when he heard Luke was a writer of dime novels.

"Luke Patterson," Matt said. "I do believe I've read

some of your novels. You capture the West quite effectively. I'll have to write my father and let him know that I've met you. He'll be bragging to everyone. He loves your stories."

"Why, thank you, Matt. I appreciate knowing that. I'd be glad to send him a signed copy of my newest one. It comes out next month." Luke smiled at the new boarder.

"I thought you were working on something besides dime novels, Luke," John said.

"I am. But it's not finished yet. I'll have several dime novels out before then."

"Are all your novels set out West?"

"No. I set them here, too. And I've set a few down south."

"And you've been to all the places you've written about?"

"Not all, but most of them. I like traveling."

Somehow that surprised Kathleen. Luke seemed so settled here. Of course, he didn't say he wanted to move—just that he liked to travel. Kathleen had thought she would, too, until she'd come here by ship. That had been a most unpleasant trip and it'd been hard to leave her homeland.

But the thought of traveling now and again, coming back home to the city, might be something she'd enjoy someday. Right now she just needed to concentrate on her new position and getting through the first few weeks until she knew whether or not she was capable of handling the job.

"Are you all right?" Luke whispered to her as the conversation turned to something else.

"I'm fine. Just thinking about my job."

"Please quit worrying about it, Kathleen. You are going to do a great job. If Mrs. Heaton and the others didn't think so, they would never have offered it to you."

"Thank you, Luke."

"I'm not saying it just to make you feel better, although I hope it does have that effect on you. I truly believe it. And I've heard Mrs. Heaton talking about how blessed they were to be able to talk you into taking the position. They don't know the tenements like you do."

"But I'm afraid I don't know them as well as they think I do."

"You know all you need to know. It will all fall into place, you'll see."

Luke's encouragement went a long way in helping Kathleen through the rest of the week. By the weekend she was more excited than nervous to begin her work on Monday.

She spent most of Saturday with her family and was a bit surprised to find that Officer O'Malley had stopped by several times to visit Colleen and the boys in the last week. Before they'd moved, he'd stopped by the apartment a time or two, but Kathleen had put it down to him doing his job, following up on a crime he'd been called in on. But now she wasn't so sure his visits weren't for some other reason. Although if he were attracted to Colleen, he'd better be prepared to wait a good long while for her to be able to even think about remarriage.

As far as Kathleen could tell, except for Collin and Brody, the only thing marriage had brought her sister was heartache. And if witnessing it had made Kathleen leery of giving her heart away, she could only imagine how Colleen felt.

But her sister seemed quite willing to accept the policeman's friendship and it did give Kathleen a measure of comfort to know that he'd be watching out for Colleen and the boys.

Just as she was about to leave, she remembered to ask about going to the park after church the next day. "Luke thought the boys would enjoy flying the kites he bought them. And Mrs. Heaton always has plenty of food for the picnic. She'd love for you to join us."

"Well, now, that is very nice. But I've already asked Officer O'Malley to come for Sunday dinner."

"Oh?"

Colleen shrugged. "The boys seem to like him and—of course they like Luke, too."

"Well, maybe he could come with us. Think about it, okay?"

"I'll think on it. But you have a good time, either way, all right?"

"I will. But Mrs. Heaton meant it when she said she wanted you to feel welcome with all of us."

"I know she did. But, Kathleen, you need a life of your own without worrying about me every minute."

"I'm not worrying all the time anymore. I just want you to begin to enjoy life again."

"I know. And I will. I just have to give it time."

Kathleen nodded. It wasn't easy to put all the sorrows and fears of the past behind. She knew that as well as Colleen did. She could only pray that one day they would.

Chapter Thirteen

Kathleen's first day out in the tenements wasn't as bad as she'd feared. Having Luke along made her feel safer, although it also resulted in having a few doors shut in their faces.

As they left the third building in the neighborhood Kathleen had lived in, she tried to find words that wouldn't offend Luke. But it'd become very obvious as they'd knocked on first one door and then another that he couldn't accompany her on her interviews.

As they walked outside toward the next building, she gnawed her bottom lip before finally saying, "Luke, I'm sorry, but I think you're going to have to let me do this alone or wait downstairs or out of sight in the hallway while I try to talk to these women. They just aren't comfortable talking to both of us."

He rubbed his forehead. "Much as I hate to admit it, I know you're right. I'll wait in the hall and if that doesn't work, I'll wait in the foyer downstairs."

"Thank you." Kathleen was relieved that he'd agreed so readily. Maybe he felt a bit uncomfortable in talking to the harried women holding babes in their arms and other children clinging to their skirts. No. That wasn't fair. It hadn't seemed to bother him that Collin and Brody had clung to her skirts. In fact he'd been very empathetic.

She wondered what kind of childhood he'd had and realized that there was much about Luke she didn't know. How selfish of her—she'd never even asked, letting him see to her and her sister's needs instead of trying to get to know him better.

Where had he come from and what had his life been like before he came to live at Heaton House? It was time she showed some interest in him and his life, after all he'd done for her and her family.

But now wasn't the time. She did have a job to do and she'd like to be able to report that she'd found several people who either could use day care or were interested in helping run one of the homes. Of course, she really couldn't make a decision about anyone from one interview—or without checking them out and getting references. But she'd like to have a few leads at least.

They entered the next building and Kathleen was relieved when Luke said he'd stay out on the stoop and see if he could find anyone to talk to. She supposed it was in connection with his writing and though she still wasn't sure how she felt about his interviewing the less fortunate for a novel, she decided to trust that his intentions were honorable.

"All right," she told him.

"Take your time, but yell if you need me."

"I will." Although Kathleen doubted that he'd be able to hear her, still, she felt better knowing he was near. And she had no doubt that he'd come looking for her if she didn't come back soon enough to satisfy him.

As she began knocking on doors and went from one apartment to another, Kathleen was pleased to find that she actually recognized several of the tenants.

"Well, if it isn't Kathleen O'Bryan! 'Tis good to see you, dear," an older woman named Mrs. Connor said. "Come in and have a cup of tea with me."

Kathleen knew Mrs. Connor wouldn't need day care, as she lived with her daughter and son-in-law who both worked and had no children, but she might know someone who did. "I'd love a cup of tea."

"Good. Take a seat and I'll make us a cup." She motioned to a small table that'd been placed in front of a window looking down upon the street. Mrs. Connor was a widow and Kathleen supposed she spent a lot of her day looking out that window and watching the comings and goings of the other tenants.

Kathleen watched her hostess prepare a pot of tea and bring it and two cups to the table. This apartment was even smaller than the one she and her sister's family had lived in, but Mrs. Connor seemed quite happy in it.

"It's good to have company. I'd heard you all moved out after... How is your sister doing?"

Kathleen quickly assured her, "Colleen is doing well, thank you. We did move. We were both offered wonderful opportunities that we hope will help others as well."

"Oh?" Mrs. Connor poured their tea and settled back in her chair. "Tell me about it."

"Well, Colleen is actually running a day care home the Ladies' Aide Society has started. It's the first of many they hope to start. That's why I'm here. I'm the liaison for them, hoping to find those women who can benefit the most from having somewhere safe for their children to stay while they are at work."

"Really? Why, how much would that cost them?"

"Nothing."

"How can that be?"

"There are people in this city who really want to help. And they try to find ways to do so. Colleen and I have been the recipients of their help and through that, they've enabled us to be able to help others. Do you know anyone who might benefit from the day care?"

Mrs. Connor took a sip of tea and leaned her head to one side. "I might. There's a young mother living upstairs who might be interested. She takes in washing and ironing to support her and her daughter, but I think if she could get a regular job, she might be able to get them both out of here one day."

"Do you know her name?"

"It's Reba..." Mrs. Connor shook her head. "I can't remember her last name. But she lives in 4C. She might be there now, but I don't know."

"Do you think she'd talk to me?"

"I don't know. She's very private. I could tell her you might be coming around in the next few days and find out."

"That would be wonderful, Mrs. Connor. May I check back with you tomorrow?"

"Yes, of course you may. You stop by anytime. I'll try to think of others who might need your help the most. And I'll ask around."

"Thank you. I truly do appreciate that."

"It will give me something to do and if I can help one or two women get out of here, I'll feel I did something good, too."

Kathleen nodded. That was what she was happiest about with her new position—the chance to make a real difference in someone's life. She knew how it felt to look forward to a future in this country she'd come to love. But that had only truly happened because of the help of Mrs. Heaton and Luke and the others.

Oh, her job would bring her back here, but she'd be able to go back to Heaton House at the end of the day. Still it would keep her humble, remembering where she'd come from and counting her blessings.

She took the last sip of tea and stood to leave. Luke was probably thinking she was making her way from one apartment to another by now.

"I'll check back with you tomorrow. Is there any time that is best for you?"

"I'm here most of the day unless I need to run an errand—and I don't have any of those to take care of tomorrow. But should I leave for any reason, I'll leave a note on the door."

"That will be fine. But should you need to talk to me, here is the number of the Ladies' Aide Society's office. They'll let me know to get in touch with you." Kathleen handed Mrs. Connor one of the calling cards the society had made up for her.

"I'll keep it where I can find it. Thanks for sharing a cup of tea with me today."

"Thank you for having me," Kathleen said.

She knocked on a few more doors in the building, but no one answered and she hurried back down the stairs and outside where Luke waited for her on the stoop.

His smile welcomed her back. "You look happy. It must have gone well. Did you find anyone to help?"

"I'm not sure. Possibly." She explained about Mrs. Connor and the young woman she'd told her about. "I should find out more tomorrow."

"Are you ready for some lunch?"

"I'd like to visit one more building. And I really don't want to keep you from your work, Luke. Why don't you go on and—"

"I'm not leaving until you do. Go on to the next building and do whatever you need to do. We can grab something to eat after that."

Kathleen could see from the look on his face that he wasn't going anywhere today until she was through. Hopefully after a few weeks he'd realize she was safe here and that she knew her way around.

In the meantime, she'd count him and his concern as blessings and get on with her work.

Luke watched Kathleen disappear into the next building and then took a seat on one of the steps outside. The air was somewhat fresher out here than inside the buildings—but not much with trash building up outside. Kathleen must have a stronger stomach than he did, for the smells in some of the buildings they'd been in that morning had been nauseating.

He pulled the notepad from his pocket and looked around, watching people come and go on the streets, seeing unsupervised children playing in the middle of them. He wrote down his thoughts and descriptions of different people he saw. There was the older woman who was returning from the grocers or a street vendor. Her bag looked heavy but she shook her head when he offered to carry it home for her.

She kept looking back as she passed him, as if she expected him to follow her. He couldn't blame her for being suspicious of a man she'd never seen before, but it saddened him he couldn't help her.

He was busy writing down his impressions and questions he'd like to ask, should he get a chance to interview anyone, when Kathleen came outside.

"That didn't take long," he said, stuffing his pencil and pad back into his pocket.

She chuckled. "I was in there nearly an hour. You must have been writing longer than you thought."

"Possibly. But at least that proves you aren't keeping me from working." He pulled her hand through his arm and looked down at her. "Let's go get some lunch. Want to go to a street vendor or…there's a little café a few blocks away that's pretty good."

"Wherever you want to go is fine with me," Kathleen said. "After waiting on me all morning, I think the least I can do is give the choice to you."

"Well, let's go to the café. You could use a break, I'm sure."

As they were a bit later than the normal lunch hour, they were seated right away in the small café over on Third Avenue. While Kathleen looked over the menu, he wondered if she was disappointed in him for not helping out one of the street vendors who possibly lived in the tenements.

"I suppose we could have gotten some clams at one of the vendors. I—"

"No, it's all right, Luke. I don't know many of the vendors and I'd only feel safe buying from one I did know. Not all of the carts are as clean as I'd like and I just talked to a woman who said she got sick from eating oysters at one only last week. I'd have gone had you picked one, but I'm glad you chose someplace you know is good. What do you recommend?"

"Their daily special is usually the freshest and today

it's creamed chicken with rolls. I've had it before and it's very good."

"I'll have it, then."

Once they'd given their order Luke smiled across the table at Kathleen. She'd dressed in a plain skirt and shirtwaist, much as she'd worn to work at Tiffany Glass. He'd overheard her and Mrs. Heaton talking about what to wear and Kathleen had wanted to be sure she looked just like she had when she lived there. She didn't want anyone she knew to think she was putting on airs just because she'd moved out of the tenements.

"How did things go this time? Did you find anyone you could recommend?"

"I found several, but either their husbands don't want them to work outside the home even though they might need for her to, or they are too prideful to accept free and reliable child care. I think that could be one of the biggest problems and I'll have to be careful on how I present the offer. I can understand the pride. I've had my share of it, too, and wrongfully so. *Proverbs* talks about pride coming before destruction and having a haughty spirit comes before a fall. I don't want either of those things happening to me, so I must be watchful always to be neither haughty or prideful."

"I suppose we all have trouble with those two feelings."

"Yes, but we can't quit fighting against them."

"True." He admired this woman more all the time. She had such high morals and love for the Lord—more so than any other woman he knew.

"I'm sorry. I don't mean to sound preachy. I—" She leaned back in her chair and sighed. "I've been so blessed that coming back here makes me feel kind of bad, almost guilty that I've moved out and so many are still there. Will always be there."

Luke nodded. "I understand. I felt somewhat that way as I waited for you. Knowing I didn't have to live there and so glad that you don't either. But don't feel guilty, Kathleen. You are going to be able to help many people over the years."

"I suppose I might feel better when I know that I've been able to do so. Hopefully Mrs. Connor will talk to the young woman she thinks needs child care. Of course we don't have another home up and running just yet—I have to find someone for that soon. But perhaps, if the need is great enough, Colleen and Ida could take one more child. But it's made me realize that my first priority is to find people to get the new homes started."

Their meal came just then and they spent the next half hour talking about where to look for someone who could run one of the homes. "I'm trying to think. Maybe… Mrs. Walsh is wonderful with children. Her husband does work, but I'm sure they could use the extra money and—"

"You know, if he's handy, it's possible that Mrs. Heaton and the others would want someone who could take care of the homes and—"

"Oh, Luke, that is a wonderful idea! I need to run it by Mrs. Heaton before I even think about talking to Rose about it. I'm not even sure how handy her husband is, but maybe—" She broke off and looked at Luke, her expression one of hope. "Maybe he can learn what he needs to—if he needs to?"

"There are all kinds of trade schools around. I'm sure he could learn anything he needs to."

"The homes will be in good shape when they are

moved into and by the time something goes wrong perhaps he will know what to do." She gave a little laugh. "I'm getting way too excited about this, but it could help them get out of the tenements and, well, I know Rose would be wonderful at running one of the homes."

"I think Mrs. Heaton will like the idea."

Kathleen nodded. "Yes. So do I. And although this was started to help working women, I don't think anyone would object if it helped a man out of the tenements, either. He could keep the job he has now, I would think."

"I'm sure he could. And you knowing the couple would probably make the ladies feel better about hiring them."

By the time they left the restaurant, Luke wasn't sure who was more excited about his idea—him or Kathleen.

When Kathleen and Luke returned to Heaton House and presented Mrs. Heaton with the proposal to hire Rose and her husband to run the next child care home, she was almost as excited as they were.

"Oh, my dears, I love the idea. I will have to run it by the others, of course, but I don't think there will be one objection to it."

Kathleen leaned back in the chair in Mrs. Heaton's study and released a pleased sigh and smiled at Luke. "I told Luke it was a wonderful idea."

Mrs. Heaton looked from one to the other. "Well, you're right. I'll get on the telephone and try to have an answer for you by dinnertime."

"Thank you, Mrs. Heaton. I suppose I should go write up notes on what I did today and about the young woman Mrs. Connor told me about. I'll fill you in on that at dinner. But right now, I'll leave you to make your call."

"Oh, and we have a new boarder. She'll be joining us for dinner tonight. Her name is Millicent Faircloud and she's a photographer. I think you'll both like her."

"I'm sure we will. I'll be sure to welcome her, if I see her before dinner," Kathleen said.

"Thank you, dear. I appreciate that. And please tell the others."

"Yes, ma'am," Luke said. He followed Kathleen out of Mrs. Heaton's study and into the hall.

Kathleen turned to him. "I think Mrs. Heaton likes your idea as much as we do, Luke."

He smiled at her. "I told you it was going to be all right, Kathleen."

"Thanks to you—you're the one who came up with the idea that might get us our next home up and running."

"You probably would have thought of it on your own, but I'm glad to help in any way." They reached the staircase and Kathleen turned to Luke. "I do appreciate you going with me today and for lunch. But—"

"If you are going to tell me I don't need to come tomorrow, don't. Please. I actually got some good ideas from people-watching while waiting for you. You are not hindering my writing in any way. I've always worked better late at night."

"But you aren't going to get enough sleep."

"I don't require a lot."

"I'm not going to convince you, am I?"

"No, ma'am. You aren't. I'll either be going along with you or following you—at least for a while." He smiled. "But I'll go get some work done now so you don't have to worry about keeping me from it. See you at dinnertime."

Kathleen watched him hurry downstairs before she headed upstairs to get her notes in order. She couldn't honestly say she was disappointed in Luke's response. She had felt safer with him along, but he couldn't shadow her everywhere all the time. She was going to have to become more comfortable coming and going in the area she'd lived in for so long.

She'd never really thought about her safety as much as her sister's before now, but going in and out some of the buildings today, she'd realized she'd have to be very aware of her surroundings. And there would be some buildings she might not enter. Once she got the word out to those she trusted, eventually people would end up contacting her for the day care opportunity. Then maybe Luke wouldn't feel quite so responsible for her. And she wouldn't feel quite so—

"Kathleen, wait up!" Elizabeth hurried up the steps to join her at the landing. "How did your day go?"

"It went very well. I have a lead on someone who might really need to put her child in the day care home and Luke gave me an idea on who I might talk to about running the next one."

"That is wonderful! I heard we have a new boarder. Have you met her yet?"

"No, not yet. But I'm looking forward to it."

"So am I. I do hope she's easy to get along with," Elizabeth said.

"I'm sure she will be. I can't imagine anyone Mrs. Heaton has accepted as a boarder wouldn't be."

"Oh, you'd be surprised. There have been one or two. But thankfully, they're no longer with us."

"Well, I look forward to meeting Miss Faircloud."

"It's always interesting to find out more about our boarders. Matt has been a nice addition."

"Yes, he has. I don't think John likes the attention you give him, though."

The smile on Elizabeth's face told Kathleen that was not bad news for her.

"Really? I didn't think he noticed."

"Oh, he's noticed."

"Hmm," Elizabeth said.

She'd never mentioned being interested in John, but anyone who sat at the dinner table with the two of them would have to be blind not to know they cared about each other.

The two women parted at the top of the stairs to get ready for dinner and Kathleen found she was looking forward to it a great deal. She was excited to hear what Mrs. Heaton had found out about taking an offer to the Walshes—and to see how everyone took to the newest boarder. Living at Heaton House was never boring.

Chapter Fourteen

Dinner was every bit as entertaining as Kathleen thought it might be. Millicent Faircloud was petite with light blond hair and blue eyes, and she captured the attention of most everyone at the table the moment she took her seat.

"A photographer, you say?" John asked. "And you're going to start up your own business?"

That fact seemed to take everyone a little by surprise. It certainly wasn't normal to see a woman going into business on her own, but to the women at the table it was quite an admirable thing to try.

"It's what I want." Millicent gave a little shrug. "But it might be a while before I get a name big enough to actually make it work. I truly would like to photograph weddings and families, capturing just the right shot to show people at their best for years to come. But in the meantime, I've set up appointments with several magazines and newspapers this week, to show them my work and try to get on their list of photographers."

"Did you put *The Delineator* on your list? I'm sure

they'd be interested," Elizabeth said. "If you didn't, I'd be glad to talk to my supervisor and—"

"You work there?" Millicent leaned across the table toward her.

"I do."

"I love that magazine and I definitely have them on my list. I'm supposed to meet with them on Friday."

"Good." Elizabeth nodded. "I hope you're successful in starting your own business and I will mention that I know you."

"Thank you, Elizabeth."

"It's refreshing to see women taking advantage of all the opportunities available to them today," Mrs. Heaton said. "I hope you all know how blessed you are."

"We truly are," Kathleen added. She still couldn't quite believe the changes in her life.

"Well, I wouldn't have this opportunity had my grandmother not left me enough to live on until I can get started," Millicent said. "But I need work so I don't have to dip into my little nest egg too much. And of course, had Mother not known you, Mrs. Heaton, I know I wouldn't have been able to come to New York City."

"I'm glad she sent you to Heaton House, Millicent."

"I am, too."

Kathleen knew firsthand how blessed the young woman was to be here and she'd soon know it, too.

As dinner progressed and conversation flowed around the table, Kathleen noticed that Elizabeth didn't look any happier about the attention John was giving Millicent than he'd been about the attention she'd given Matt a few evenings earlier.

"Do you think those two will ever admit their feelings for one another?" Luke whispered to her.

"Maybe they're trying to deny how they feel." She could understand if they were. She'd been trying to ignore a few feelings lately herself.

Luke shrugged. "I suppose they might be. But they seem made for each other. She works for a magazine and he works for a newspaper. They even cover some of the same stories."

Kathleen had been at Heaton House long enough now to know that John covered much of the social goings-on in the city. He entertained them with stories often. And Elizabeth occasionally covered some of the same things for *The Delineator.* Yet they sometimes seemed in competition with each other—maybe that was the way they fought their attraction to each other. But hard as they might try to ignore their feelings for each other, Kathleen didn't think there was anyone at the table who didn't believe they cared for each other.

Her heart suddenly skipped a beat, and then another. Could everyone at the table tell how she struggled with her growing feelings for Luke? Oh, she hoped not. She—

"Kathleen, dear, I have news for you." Mrs. Heaton broke into her thoughts. "You've been given permission—no, actually you've been greatly encouraged to see if the Walshes might be interested in running the next home. Everyone thinks it a wonderful idea just as I did."

"Oh, that is fantastic news, Mrs. Heaton! I'll be sure to go see Mrs. Walsh first thing tomorrow."

"We don't have a home ready yet, but all should be in place within the next few months. So that would give them time to prepare."

"I will let them know."

"Might I ask what these homes are?" Millicent asked.

Mrs. Heaton explained about the day care homes and how Kathleen was working to identify the families in need.

"Aren't you a little frightened going to the tenements?" Millicent asked Kathleen.

She shook her head. Even if she were at times, she wasn't going to admit it—not with Luke listening to her every word. Still, she didn't want to lie. "So far I've mostly been visiting the area I lived in and—"

"You lived there? Oh, I would love for someone to show me around."

"I've heard it's not a place for anyone to go alone, unless they are very familiar with the area," Matt said from across the table. "So don't be taking off by yourself, Millie."

"I do not like being called Millie, Mr. Sterling. And furthermore I don't like being told what to do by someone I've just met. I said I'd like someone to show me around. I have no intention of going by myself."

"Oh, I'm sorry if I overstepped, Miss—"

"You may call me Millicent and I'll call you Matt. I've been told everyone is on first-name basis here."

"Yes, that's what I've been told, Millicent."

Mrs. Heaton cleared her throat as she passed a basket of rolls down the table. "It's so nice to have a full table again."

Luke nudged Kathleen's elbow and leaned a little nearer to whisper, "Seems like those two might have lit a spark of some kind between them."

It certainly seemed like it. She could almost feel the electricity in the air. Or was it her reaction to Luke's nearness she was feeling?

Tired from her first day out in the tenements, Kathleen didn't want to linger in the parlor for too long after dinner. But she wanted to stay long enough to make Millicent and Matt feel welcome. She knew how much it'd meant to her to have everyone try to make her feel at home in Heaton House.

Julia played the piano and they gathered round to sing along with her. Kathleen liked all the songs— "After the Ball," and "Daisy Bell," but her favorite and that of most of the boarders was "The Sidewalks of New York." When Julia played it, everyone knew it would be the last song of the evening.

The group put their all into it and Kathleen loved hearing Luke's rich baritone from right behind her. It gave her goose bumps and made her shiver, while her heart turned kind of mushy at the same time.

If he ever quit writing, he could probably make a good living singing.

The last note died away and everyone began to go their separate ways. Luke touched her elbow before she headed out the parlor door, sending tingles up her arm. "I'll see you in the morning. I'm eager to find out what the Walshes say about your offer."

"Yes, so am I." She almost told him once more that he didn't have to accompany her, but she knew it would fall on deaf ears and besides, it was his idea to include Mr. Walsh. He deserved to know what their reaction was. "See you tomorrow."

The next day Kathleen and Luke set out for Mrs. Connor's first. They took the trolley as far as Third Avenue and then walked by foot amid the hustle and bustle of the city streets.

The days were getting warmer and the street venders began hawking their goods earlier.

"We'll go to visit Rose a little later. But right now, I really want to find out if Mrs. Connor had a chance to speak to the young woman she told me about. And I believe it will be fine for you to come with me to both places. I think Mrs. Connor gets lonely while her family is at work and of course you've met Rose. I don't think either of them will mind talking to me with you there."

"Are you sure? I don't want to get in the way of you doing your job."

Kathleen grinned at him. "Don't worry. I won't let you hinder my work. If I have a chance to speak to this woman, I'll ask you to wait for me. Or better yet, if she comes to Mrs. Connor's you can just tell me you'll wait outside for me."

Luke seemed to appreciate that she didn't want to appear to be telling him what to do in front of other women. He gave a little nod. "That will work well."

Luke followed her up the stairs in a building much like the one she'd lived in. There wasn't much difference in the apartment buildings in this neighborhood—only whether or not the buildings were kept up by the owners and how well the tenants took care of their own apartments.

She'd felt quite comfortable in Mrs. Connor's and was sure that Luke would, too. The apartment was as clean as one could make it and the older woman was happy to welcome them into it.

Kathleen lightly touched Luke's arm. "This is a friend of mine, Mrs. Connor. His name is Luke Patterson."

"How do you do, ma'am. I'm pleased to meet you."

Luke gave her a smile that Kathleen was sure would melt the older woman's heart—it always did funny things to hers.

"Thank you. If you are a friend of Kathleen's, you're as welcome here as she is. Please, take a seat and I'll make some tea—or would you prefer coffee, Mr. Patterson?"

"I'll have whatever you ladies are having, thank you."

She'd obviously been expecting Kathleen, for she had a small plate of cookies ready and the kettle was steaming on a back burner. "Won't take but a minute to steep the tea."

"Were you able to speak to the young woman you told me about, Mrs. Connor?" Kathleen got right to the point.

"Reba? Yes, I did. And she's very interested, but said she'd have to meet you and anyone she'd be leaving her little girl with before she'll commit to anything."

"Oh, I understand completely. I'd want to do the very same thing," Kathleen assured her.

Mrs. Connor brought a tray of cups and the teapot to the table and poured them each a cup before taking her own seat. "She lives on the fourth floor and I believe she's home. She's in 4C, if you want to go up. Mr. Patterson can stay and keep me company."

"I'd like to talk to her. I—" She looked at Luke.

"It's fine with me, Kathleen. If Mrs. Connor doesn't mind I'd really like another one of her cookies."

The older woman smiled at the compliment and Kathleen had no doubt that both of them would get along just fine while she was away. "Will Reba be expecting me?"

"I told her I'd send you up if you came by today. Oh, and her last name is Dickerson."

Kathleen took a last sip of tea and stood. "I'll be back in a bit then."

Mrs. Connor showed her to the door and Kathleen took the stairs to the fourth floor. The stuffiness in the hallway seemed to make the breakfast smells, along with every other aroma in the building, linger longer. She was careful not to breathe deeply as she knocked on apartment 4C.

"Yes? Who is it?"

"Mrs. Dickerson? It's Kathleen O'Bryan. Mrs. Connor told me she talked to you about me and—"

The door cracked open ever so slightly and all she could see was one blue eye and some reddish-blond hair. Kathleen smiled and the woman opened the door wider. "Come in."

A little girl of about three or four peeked around her mother's skirts. She had her mother's blue eyes but her hair was blonder and had no red in it. She had a finger stuck in her mouth and as Kathleen smiled down at her, she ducked behind her mother.

There was something familiar about the young woman, but Kathleen couldn't place her. She stood straight and proud as Kathleen entered and looked around, and she recognized the stance well. There was a time when she would have reacted the same way. And not long at all since her sister had. She hurried to put Mrs. Dickerson at ease.

"This apartment is much like the one I used to live in down the street."

"You're from the tenements?"

"I am, yes. I've only recently moved out."

Kathleen could see the young woman's stiff stance begin to relax. She picked her child up and motioned to the worn sofa. "Please, have a seat while I get Jenny occupied with her toys."

Kathleen looked around the two rooms she could see—the small parlor and tiny kitchen. They were both clean with only a bowl at the table where the child had most probably been eating.

The young mother was back in only a few minutes. "Would you like some coffee or tea?"

"I'm fine, thank you. Unless you'd like something and in that case I'll join you."

"Come, take a seat at the kitchen table and tell me more about this child care home Mrs. Connor mentioned."

Kathleen wasted no time in doing just that as Mrs. Dickerson poured them both a cup of coffee. She pulled a few flyers from her bag that explained the day care homes and other things the Ladies' Aide Society wanted to do.

"And it doesn't cost anything?"

"Not a cent. There are people in the city who have money and truly do want to help others."

"I sure would love to have some regular income. I take in laundry, but it doesn't go near far enough."

"With child care, you'd be able to take a job that pays better. I think you're a perfect candidate for the service, Mrs. Dickerson."

"Please, just call me Reba. It does sound wonderful. I've thought of applying at Macy's for a position, but—"

"You could do that now. Please, think about it. Pray about it. If you let me know soon I can get you on the top of the list for the next home."

"There isn't an opening now?"

"Well, I could see if there is room for one more, if you should find employment before the other home is up and running."

"I think I'd like that. I'll see if Mrs. Connor can watch Jenny so that I can go apply at a few places."

"I'm sure she'll be happy to. She's a very nice woman. I'll check back with you in a few days or you can leave a message for me at the Ladies' Aide Society." She handed Reba one of her cards.

Reba took it. "Thank you."

"You're welcome. I'll be praying you find the right job. You do that, and we'll find a place for your little girl."

Kathleen left the apartment with a light heart. It felt wonderful to see the expression in the woman's eyes change from resignation to hope. Kathleen sent up a silent prayer that she would be able to help her.

As soon as Kathleen returned to Mrs. Connor's apartment, Luke could tell from the expression on her face that things went well. So, apparently, could Mrs. Connor.

"She said yes, didn't she?" the older woman said.

"Well, she seemed very interested," Kathleen replied. "She said she's going to see if you will watch her daughter while she puts in applications."

"Of course I will. I want that young woman to have a better life."

Kathleen nodded and Luke knew she wanted the same thing.

"Thank you for telling me about her, Mrs. Connor. Seeing her with her little girl, knowing that making their living is up to her…well, I'll pray she finds something quickly."

"We'll leave it in the Lord's hands. It's for sure He will work it all out in the best way."

Luke had a feeling the woman prayed often. Something he needed to do more.

"We all need to be praying about it," Kathleen said. "I told Reba to pray about it also. I'm sure the Lord will guide her. You know, there is something about her—I feel I've seen her before."

"That's possible. She lives in the same neighborhood that you did. More than likely you've passed her on the street."

"That's true. We probably passed each other numerous times." She seemed to be in deep thought and then gave her head a shake. "I suppose we should go now. I have a few more people to see today."

"Thank you for putting up with me, Mrs. Connor," Luke said. He'd had quite an enjoyable time talking to the woman. She'd given him all kinds of insight into the kind of people he wanted to help.

"Thank you for keeping me company, Mr. Patterson. It was a pleasure to meet a real author. You come back anytime and I'll see if I can come up with any more memories for you. Or just come by for coffee when you're in the neighborhood."

"Thank you, ma'am. I may very well take you up on your offer."

"I hope you do." She turned to Kathleen. "Thank you for bringing him with you, Kathleen. Something about this young man reminds me of my son."

"You're quite welcome. I'm sure we'll be seeing you again."

"I'm counting on it."

She let Kathleen and Luke out and then locked the door behind them. Kathleen sighed as they began to walk away. "I wish I could get her and her family out of here, too."

"I know. But you know she's much better off than some. She's not dreaming of getting out as much as she's trying to help others."

"We can learn a lot from Mrs. Connor. She reminds me of Mrs. Heaton in many ways."

"Yes, she does me, too."

They made their way up the street to Kathleen's old building. It looked the same to Luke, and he was surprised when she said, "It doesn't feel the same now that we don't live here. And we haven't been out very long. How can that be?"

"I don't know. It seems the same to me."

They climbed the stairs and Kathleen wrinkled her nose and began to chuckle. "It smells about the same."

"It does."

They passed an apartment where loud arguing was heard. "And it sounds much the same."

"Like I said. Only difference is that you don't live here any longer."

They reached the Walshes' apartment and Kathleen knocked on the door. For a moment Luke thought everyone must be gone, but then the door opened a crack and Mrs. Walsh peeked out.

"Kathleen! Mr. Patterson! My, but it's good to see you. Come in, come in." She opened the door wide and Luke followed Kathleen inside.

"Please take a seat and tell me what brings you here. Colleen and the boys are all right, aren't they?"

"They are wonderful. She'd very much like you to come see her, and the boys would love to see Roger."

"I've been meaning to visit but I thought perhaps she's been so busy getting everything set up. I think it is such a fine thing the Ladies' Aide Society is doing, Kathleen. And I'm so glad it's provided you and Colleen a better life."

"So are we. And, well, Rose…would you like to… what would you say if you were offered the same kind of chance?"

"What do you mean?"

"The city is in need of more day care homes and the Ladies' Aide Society is wanting to get the next one going as soon as possible."

"But I have no need of it, Kathleen. My husband doesn't want me to leave Roger to go to work."

"What if you didn't have to leave him? And what if your husband could continue to work at his job but earn a little more?"

"What are you talking about, Kathleen? Do tell me."

Kathleen explained the offer to her and Luke could tell Rose was trying to contain her excitement about it. "You mean we'd be running another house? We'd be able to move out of here?"

"If your husband agrees to it, yes."

Rose put a hand over her heart and tears gathered in the corners of her eyes. "I don't know what to say. I—"

"You don't have to say anything just yet. Talk to your husband and let me know as soon as possible. And if you have any other questions, you are welcome to come talk to me and Mrs. Heaton."

"Oh, I'm sure there'll be questions. But it sounds too good to be true."

"Have no worries, Rose. You'll be working, probably harder than you ever have, taking care of a passel of children—but it's a chance to have a life out of here. You'll have a nice home, make good money and have a future—not to mention that you'll be helping others at the same time."

Luke watched Kathleen's former neighbor as she put a hand over her mouth and nodded. "I don't know what to say. Thank you for thinking of this."

"It wasn't just me. Luke actually came up with the idea that your husband could be hired to help keep up the houses—if it's something he'd like to do."

"I think he'd love it. I can't wait for him to get home so that I can talk to him about it. But I can't see how he'd even think of turning it down."

Luke was glad to hear it. He had a soft spot for this family. After all, it was Rose's husband who'd brought Kathleen to Heaton House. He deserved some kind of reward in Luke's eyes for that very reason.

The two women chatted for a few minutes and then Kathleen looked at Luke. "I suppose we should be going now."

Rose saw them out. "Thank you. I'll be getting in touch with you as soon as I can."

"I look forward to hearing from you, Rose. And you know, you and your husband can always ask Colleen about the position and how she's liking it."

"I might just pay her a visit today."

"I'm sure she'll be very glad to see you."

The two women hugged and he and Kathleen left the apartment.

"Another good day for you," he said to her as they made their way down the flights of stairs.

"Oh, yes, I think so. Now all I have to do is wait for answers."

"You'll get them soon, I'm sure. I can't imagine anyone turning down the offers you've made today."

"Neither can I." They reached the bottom floor and Luke wondered if Kathleen realized they both took a cleansing, deep breath at the same time.

The grin on her face and the gleam in her eye told him she did. "You were so right. It hasn't changed a bit. I don't think I really knew how bad it was until I moved away. Oh, I knew, but it didn't matter as much because most of the people I worked with and knew lived in the same conditions. But there is so much more out there—so many opportunities if only…"

"I know. But we can't help everyone at once, Kathleen. Just a few at a time. And we can get the word out about how much more help is needed and what opportunities there are. And then we have to leave things in the Lord's hands."

"I know. I'm not always very good at that, though."

"None of us are. But I believe you are better at it than you think you are. I think it comes naturally to you." She was a wonderful example of being there for her sister, of doing what she could to protect her and the boys, to help support them when her brother-in-law either couldn't or wouldn't. And she'd even gone back to help once she'd gotten out of this place. She'd given up living at Heaton House to come back and help her sister. And she'd have kept doing it as long as she had to.

"No, Luke, I—"

"Kathleen." Luke stopped in the middle of the walk and turned to her. "Anyone can see you look to the Lord to guide you. And you do what you believe He wants you to do—even if it might be the last thing you want."

"Luke, I only wish I was like that. I know deep down that I'm not. I'm not brave and I'm not willing to go out on a limb in many ways. I have a hard time trusting others and—"

"Do you trust the Lord?"

"Of course I do. But—"

"Then just trust that the Lord will bring people into your life whom you can trust. Like Mrs. Heaton." *And me.*

He wished she knew that she could trust him to be her friend, to be there to protect her, but, because of all she'd been through, he understood why she found it extremely difficult to trust men—including him. He'd like to change that, but it might mean making a commitment that he couldn't make now—and wasn't sure he ever could.

And yet who did he think he was telling Kathleen that she should trust the Lord when he needed to do the very same thing?

Chapter Fifteen

Kathleen had visited both Reba and Mrs. Connor later in the week and the younger woman was busy putting in applications for work but hadn't found anything yet. Rose and her husband had visited with Colleen to find out more about what to expect and promised to have an answer by the coming Monday. Kathleen had no choice but to wait for their decisions and as frustrating as that was for her, Mrs. Heaton and the other ladies were hopeful and encouraged by her first real week out in the tenements.

At dinner on Friday evening everyone began talking about the weekend.

"We should have a group outing. We haven't done that in a while," Elizabeth suggested.

"You know what? It's getting warmer out. Maybe we should go to Coney Island this weekend? It's still much too cool for a swim, but we could enjoy the amusement parks and perhaps have lunch there."

"I've never been to Coney Island," Kathleen said. "But I heard a lot about it when I worked at Tiffany. The group went once in a while, but I..." Her voice trailed off, thinking about the outings she'd been asked to go on but always refused because of money or just not feeling right about enjoying her weekend when Colleen and the boys were stuck with Clancy. But she didn't have that worry now. "I'd love to go."

"So would I," Millicent and Elizabeth said at the same time.

"We'd need to get an early start. We can take the El partway and then use the trolley," Luke said. "Does everyone want to go?"

"Yes, let's." Julia grinned. "I'm off this Saturday and I haven't been in ages."

It appeared everyone would be able to go—even Mrs. Heaton.

"I'd like to join you all, and I'm sure Michael and Violet might like to go, too."

"The more the merrier," Luke said.

"May I ask Colleen if she'd like to take the boys?" Kathleen asked. For now her sister and Ida had decided to take turns watching the children on Saturdays as only a few were left there on that day. And they were both off on Sundays. She thought Ida would be in charge this Saturday. "They've never been, either."

"Of course!" Elizabeth said. "They'll love it."

"I'll walk over with you after dinner so you can ask, if you'd like," Luke offered. "Or you can telephone her."

"Thank you, Luke. I'd love to go visit them for a bit." Mrs. Heaton didn't have many rules but she was firm about not letting the women go out alone after dark. One of the male boarders would escort them where they wanted to go and back to Heaton House.

Once dinner was over, Luke said, "Are you ready?"

"Let me run up and get my wrap and I'll be right back," Kathleen said.

He nodded. "I'll be in the parlor. Just call me when you're ready."

Kathleen met up with Elizabeth, Julia and Millicent at the landing. They were talking about what to wear the next day.

"Oh, I need some advice for that, too. But I don't want to keep Luke waiting and I'd like to see the boys before Colleen puts them to bed."

"Just come to my room when you get back," Elizabeth said. "I'll tell you what we're wearing and we can choose something for you."

"Thank you, Elizabeth. I'll do that. See you all later."

Kathleen hurried to her room and grabbed a lightweight shawl before heading back down to the parlor.

Evidently Luke had been waiting for the sound of her footsteps, for he joined her just outside the parlor door.

"I'm ready if you are," Kathleen said.

"At your service, ma'am." Luke opened the front door and they headed to her sister's.

Luke offered her his arm and she took it, knowing by now that he was only being gentlemanly. Still it brought her into closer contact with him and her heart fluttered. But she didn't want to appear rude by not taking his arm. Thankfully, he never overstepped the bounds of being a gentleman and she was sure he never would.

"Are you looking forward to tomorrow?"

"I am. What's it like?"

"Oh, it's very interesting and there are a lot of rides I'm sure the boys will love. Have you ever been on a roller coaster?"

"No, I never have and of course neither have they. But we've seen pictures of them."

"What about a carousel? Have they ever ridden one of those?"

"No."

"Well, then, I'm getting more excited by the minute about showing it to you and them. It's going to be a fun day."

"But what if Colleen doesn't go?"

"I'll look forward to showing it to you and then again to them at another time."

The evening was quite nice and Kathleen enjoyed the walk to her sister's. They were welcomed in as if they hadn't seen them in a very long time. The boys hugged Kathleen and then gave their attention to Luke.

"I'm not sure whether to be insulted or not."

Her sister looked at her. "Oh, Kathleen, you know they love you. But they haven't seen Luke in a while and he found a place in their hearts when I was so sick and he took them to fly kites."

"I know. I was only teasing."

"Well, come out to the kitchen with me and I'll get some refreshment while they are playing with Luke. What brings you over tonight? Have you heard from Rose?"

She shook her head. "She said they'd have a decision by Monday."

"I'm sure they are going to say yes. They'd be plumb crazy not to and I told them so when they came over this afternoon."

Kathleen took a seat at the kitchen table and watched her sister pour glasses of lemonade—a treat they'd rarely been able to afford.

"I made some cookies today. The boys will be happy to have another before bedtime."

"Well, before we go in, I'll let you know one of the reasons we came this evening."

"You have a reason other than you miss us?" Colleen grinned at her and Kathleen smiled back. It was so good to see her sister the way she used to be—long ago before Clancy.

"I do. We're all going to Coney Island tomorrow and wondered if you and the boys might want to join us."

"Oh, my, they would love to go. And Ida is in charge tomorrow. So, yes! We will go." The smile left her face but joy was in her eyes. "Oh, Kathleen, do you know how good that felt? To say 'yes, we will go'?"

"I have an idea." Kathleen crossed the room and hugged her sister. They rocked back and forth for a few moments and then Colleen brushed at her eyes.

"The good Lord has seen us through, hasn't He?" she asked.

"Oh, yes, He has."

Colleen let out a big sigh and smiled. "Let's get these things on a tray and go tell the boys they are going to Coney Island tomorrow. I don't think they'll believe me."

Kathleen laughed as she took in the tray of cookies while her sister took in the lemonade she'd made earlier. "If they don't now, they will tomorrow."

"You know, I don't think I will tell them tonight. They'll never get to sleep if I do. I'll wait until the morning."

"Good idea."

And it was. The boys were already wound up, playing with Luke. Kathleen smiled as she watched them arm wrestle. He won once and then let the boys each win once. He was so good with them. He should have children of his own to play with. Her heart skittered at the very thought. He'd have to be married first and— She didn't want to think about that. If he found someone and got married, she knew their friendship would never be the same. At that thought her heart twisted. No. She couldn't think about it. Wouldn't let herself.

She lifted the plate of cookies high. "Cookie, anyone?"

The boys hurried over and Luke followed. She gave the boys theirs and then handed him a cookie, leaning forward to whisper, "Colleen said they'll go but she doesn't want the boys to know. Said they'd never sleep if she did."

Luke chuckled. "She's probably right. They're pretty wound up. She might not let me come see them at night anymore."

"I shouldn't." Colleen came up behind them. "But I wouldn't deprive any of you from having such a good time."

"Thanks, Colleen." Luke took the glass she handed him. "I'll try not to get them quite so wound up next time."

They didn't stay much longer so that Colleen could get the boys settled down and into bed. Luke promised Collin and Brody he'd see them soon and that made both boys happy. Kathleen couldn't wait to see their faces the next day when they realized they'd spend the day with him.

They headed back home under a moonlit, star-filled sky. Kathleen loved the quiet of the evening.

"Those nephews of yours have changed so much since they moved. They seem full of life and happy. Has your sister said anything about the boys missing their father?"

Kathleen shook her head. "No, not really. We don't talk about Clancy much. She'll talk when she's ready."

"And you? How are you feeling?"

"I still don't remember what happened the night I came to Heaton House. Only vague images and, well, I don't try to remember any more. And I don't want to ask Colleen—she has enough awful memories to live with. I survived that night and he's gone. And my sister and the boys are safe. I've got a lot of blessings to count."

"Perhaps I should do some of the same."

"What's that?" Kathleen turned her head to look at him.

"Try not to remember the past and count my blessings."

"You have memories you'd like to forget?"

"I do."

Of course he did. Didn't everyone? But he always seemed so strong and sure of himself, Kathleen had never asked much about him. She recalled her vow to start. "Would you like to talk about it?"

"I don't want to burden you with—"

Kathleen stopped in the middle of the walk and turned to him, hands on her hips. "Luke Patterson, I can't believe you said that. You have watched over me and protected me from the first day we met. You've even let me cry on your shoulder." She let out a sigh. "How could you possibly think that listening to you could ever be a burden to me?"

Luke raised his hands in surrender. "I'm sorry. It's not that I've tried to keep any of my life secret—not really. I just haven't wanted to talk about it. It hurt too much for a long time and then, well, you've had a lot to deal with on your own, Kate."

"I'm sorry, Luke. I shouldn't pressure you to talk. It's none of my business anyway. I just want you to know that I am here for you, too."

Luke's heart slammed against his chest and he wasn't sure how to reply. Her words made him want to pull her into his arms and hold her, pour out his heart to her. But she wasn't ready for that—nor was he. What was he thinking? She hadn't declared love for him. She'd only made the offer of a good friend and here he was letting his thoughts run away from him.

"Thank you, Kathleen." Luke took a step forward and began to speak, Kathleen keeping pace beside him. "I haven't told anyone at Heaton House—haven't really seen the need to, but your words about not trying to remember made me realize that I haven't let go of the memories I can't do anything about. Perhaps I need to sort through them and keep the good ones and say goodbye to the bad ones once and for all."

"Perhaps it would help to tell someone—it doesn't have to be me if you aren't comfortable talking to me about it. But maybe Mrs. Heaton?"

"I have no problem telling you." He took a deep breath and forged ahead. "Before I came to Heaton House, back home in Texas, I was engaged to be married. My fiancée was a bank teller." Memories came flooding back and Luke swallowed around the lump in his throat.

"There was a robbery and my Beth was shot. I arrived only moments after, and—" His voice broke and he cleared his throat. "She died in my arms. If only I could have gotten there earlier. I—"

Kathleen stopped and both hands grasped his arm. Luke could never remember her touching him at all other than when they were walking. But now she was grasping his arm and looking at him with tears in her eyes.

"Luke, I'm so sorry. I didn't mean to bring you pain. I'm sorry about your Beth, but you must know by now that what happened wasn't your fault."

Her words soothed his aching heart and he let out a cleansing breath. "I do now. But it's been a long time coming. And then there's been guilt when the memory of her face began to fade. I did love her…with all my heart. But she's no longer here and—"

"Luke, I believe that is normal. I think anyone would feel the same way. If not for the pictures I have of my parents, I wouldn't remember what they looked like, either. But you have the memories, even if her face isn't clear to you."

"Those are fading now, too, Kate."

"Maybe it's the Lord's way of easing the pain?"

Luke had never thought of it that way.

"Maybe He's paving the way for you to find someone else?"

He shook his head. The Lord above knew better than anyone that Luke didn't plan on ever falling in love again. "I don't think so. But thank you for your thoughts and for listening. It has helped to talk about it."

"I'm glad. Anytime you want to talk about it, remember I'm here."

"I'll remember." He did feel better. "Now maybe I can put the bad memories to rest and concentrate on my blessings."

"I hope so."

Her smile lightened his heart even more. He was blessed to have this woman as a friend. "So do I."

They walked back to Heaton House then and they

entered the foyer. A peek into the parlor told them everyone had gone their separate ways.

"They probably want a good night's sleep before tomorrow. I am so looking forward to it!" Kathleen said. "I suppose I should see if Elizabeth is still up. She promised to help me pick out something to wear. Thank you for escorting me to Colleen's—and for sharing with me."

"Thank you for listening, Kathleen." He wanted to pull her into his arms but he settled for looking deep into her eyes, seeing the compassion there. "You are one of the blessings I'll be counting tonight."

He could hear the quick intake of her breath and his own breath caught in his throat. He watched her chew her bottom lip as if she didn't know what to say next. Had he overstepped?

"Thank you, Luke. You're high on my list, too. I suppose the Lord knew we both needed a good friend. Good night. See you in the morning." With that she turned to hurry up the stairs, leaving Luke to watch.

She disappeared around the landing and suddenly Luke realized Kathleen was much more than just a friend to him—and that his feelings for her seemed to grow with each passing day. And he didn't have the faintest idea what to do about it. So, he did the only thing he knew to do. He prayed.

There was a holiday feel to the day the next morning at breakfast when Kathleen came downstairs dressed in the lightweight beige skirt and shirtwaist that Elizabeth had loaned her.

"It will reflect the heat off you. Being outside most of the day, you'll need it," she'd said.

Kathleen was pleased to find she was dressed similarly to the other women in the house. And even Colleen had seemed to know what to wear as she showed up in a light-colored dress. The boys both had on light brown knickers and white shirts.

Instead of taking the trolley, Michael had hired an omnibus to take them out to Coney Island. As they all piled in, it was Brody and Collin who had everyone's attention. There was nothing quite like seeing things through a child's eyes.

"Where we goin', Luke?" Brody asked.

"We're going to Coney Island."

"Is there pirates there?" Collin asked.

"No. Well, maybe, but not real ones. There are lots of amusements."

"What's amusements?"

"Amusements are places that are for entertainment—to have fun at."

"Oh!" Brody said. "I like to have fun. Is it like arm wrestlin' with you?"

"Oh, I think you'll like it better," Luke said.

"Okay." Brody grinned and looked out the window. "Is it a long ways?"

"It's farther than you've been before, Brody," Colleen said. "And we're going to go over a bridge to get there."

"The Brooklyn Bridge?" Collin's eyes flashed with excitement.

"Yes, that's the one," Kathleen said as she brushed his hair out of his eyes.

"Oh, boy! I can't wait to go over it." He turned around and got on his knees to join Brody in looking at the passing scenery.

"I can't wait to see the look on their faces when

they actually see the Elephant Colossus!" Luke grinned. "They are going to love everything."

"I think I am, too. What's the Elephant Colossus?"

"You'll see."

The boys' excitement was contagious and Kathleen couldn't wait to see the sights any more than they could. Going over the Brooklyn Bridge was quite breathtaking as they left Manhattan behind and headed toward Brooklyn and then Coney Island. It was quite the ride and Kathleen understood why they wanted to get off early.

It was midmorning before they arrived at Coney Island and Luke didn't have to point out the Elephant Colossus. The boys were overwhelmed at the sight.

"Look, Aunt Kate! Look at the Elephant!" Brody yelled.

"How big is it?" Collin asked.

"It's 150 feet tall and has all kinds of amusements inside. There are even telescopes inside where you can look out his eyes."

"I don't know if I want to get that close to him," Brody said.

"He won't hurt you, Brody. It's not a real elephant after all," Collin assured him.

Everyone piled out of the omnibus and Kathleen found herself looking to Luke for direction. "Where do we go first?"

"Doesn't matter. We can just take off in any direction, stop when something interests you or the boys. We've got all day and can backtrack if we need to. Just stick with me and we'll see it all—well, most of it. What we miss now, we'll see another time. I'm sure the boys would love to go swimming when it warms up."

"Yes, they would love it," Colleen said.

"I thought you might ask Officer O'Malley to come with us," Kathleen said to her sister as they walked along.

"Actually, I did telephone him after you left last night. He's on duty today and couldn't come. He was excited for the boys, though. He's pretty taken with them."

"Who isn't?" Luke nodded his head toward Michael, Violet and Mrs. Heaton, who were carrying on a conversation with the boys in front of them. "They're pretty hard to resist."

Kathleen's heart warmed as it always did when Luke talked about Brody and Collin. He was very taken with them himself.

"They don't get sick easily, do they?" Luke asked Colleen.

"Not that I know of, but they've never been on rides like this."

"Well, we'll try some of the tamer ones and see how they do. If they make it through those, maybe we'll go on the Switchback Railway and then the Serpentine Railway roller coasters. I haven't been on any of these in a while."

After the first few tamer rides, Colleen said they'd be fine and for the next few hours they rode roller coasters, carousels and anything else that struck the boys' fancy. By noontime everyone was starved and they all picnicked on hot dogs and lemonade.

Afterward everyone separated into groups to go their own way with an agreement to meet back up by four o'clock. The Heatons wanted to see the Sea Lion Park that had opened the year before.

Some of the others hadn't had their fill of rides and took off in search of more.

"I think we'll just walk around for a bit," Colleen said once they'd finished eating. "I'm not sure it'd be a good idea to go on a ride so soon after eating. But you two go on. We'll catch up with you later or see you at four."

Luke looked at Kathleen and grinned. "Want to ride something else, or do you want to stroll for a bit, too?"

"I think I'll opt for strolling. That last ride had my stomach taking a dive." She pointed across the way. "What's that long building out there?"

"That's the Brighton Beach Hotel. There's a boardwalk right on the water and benches to sit on. Would you like to see it?"

"I'd love to." She turned to her sister. "Colleen? Do you and the boys want to go?"

"We'll walk with you as far as the first bench, then I think the boys and I will just enjoy watching the people and the water while you two take your stroll."

They made their way to the boardwalk and true to her word, Colleen settled herself and her boys on the first empty bench they came to. "Now you two go along and enjoy your walk."

"Are you sure?"

"I'm sure, Kathleen." Brody leaned against his mother and yawned. "I think the boys might enjoy a bit of a nap with the sound of the water and the light breeze. I might nod off myself."

"All right, then. We'll be back this way soon."

Luke offered his arm and Kathleen slipped her hand through, resting it on his sleeve as they sauntered down the walk.

It'd been late into the night before she'd fallen asleep the night before—she couldn't get her mind off what Luke had told her about his fiancée. How heartbreaking that must have been for him. That he shared it with her, when he hadn't told anyone else, meant a great deal to

Kathleen. In the past it was only her worries and problems they'd shared. Now that she'd seen a glimpse of his, she felt they were on more even footing than ever before.

"Kathleen," Luke said, breaking into her thoughts as he led her over to the railing overlooking the water, "I wanted to thank you again for listening to me last night. I didn't realize how much better I would feel just telling someone about Beth."

"You don't need to thank me, Luke. You've been there for me on numerous occasions. And I was glad to listen. I'm so very sorry you had to go through that kind of heartbreak."

He broke his gaze from hers and looked out to sea. "It's gotten easier over the years, but I still needed to talk about it. I slept better than I have in years last night."

"I'm glad. You know you can talk to me anytime."

She didn't tell him that she'd had a hard time going to sleep. Or that along with hurting for him, she had another ache inside of her—one she couldn't name, but it felt a little like jealousy.

She had no right to be jealous, especially of someone who'd passed away. So why should she feel so disturbed that Luke had been in love before? Could it be that her growing feelings for him were more than friendship? Was it possible Luke was the one man she could ever trust with her heart? And what was she going to do about it?

Chapter Sixteen

Luke had enjoyed the weekend immensely—spending time with Kathleen and her family, having time with her alone and sitting by her in church on Sunday. They'd shared a hymnal and he'd loved the sound of her alto mixed with his baritone.

He could spend hours singing with her. After church, she spent most of the day with her sister and as daylight waned, he debated going to escort her home. However, she arrived just before dark and in time for dinner. But she seemed quieter than she had the past few days and he wondered if something had happened to upset her.

As soon as dinner was over and she made to leave, he quickly pulled back her chair and spoke quietly, "Are you all right? Would you like to talk?"

She bit her bottom lip and nodded to him.

"Let's go to Mrs. Heaton's garden. No one else will be out there now."

"All right."

They waited until everyone had either entered the parlor or gone to their rooms and then headed out to the small garden Mrs. Heaton tended to so lovingly. There were a couple of small benches set in the garden and Luke led her to one that couldn't be seen from the house. He waited for her to sit down and then sat down beside her, taking care to put some distance between them.

"What's happened to upset you, Kathleen?"

"Nothing, really. It's just that Colleen told me she'd asked Officer O'Malley to dinner and, well, I'm afraid he's sweet on her and I'm not sure how she feels about him."

"Did you ask?"

"Yes. And she got upset. Said she was a grown woman and I didn't have to be looking out for her anymore. That it was time I—"

"Time you what?"

Kathleen let out a deep breath and shook her head. "I just don't understand how she can trust another man after all Clancy put her through. And it seems much too soon for her to…"

"Do you think she's fallen in love with Officer O'Malley?"

"I don't know. She says she cares a lot for him and that she trusts him and…" Kathleen closed her eyes. "He seems a very good man, I'll give him that. But she has only known him a short while and I don't want her doing something rash like marrying him just because she's lonely or wants someone to take care of her. She should only marry for love."

"I agree."

Kathleen let out a shaky breath. "But then she did that the first time and look where it got her."

She seemed so confused and upset, Luke wanted to ease her mind. "Kathleen, maybe Colleen's love for Clancy died a long time ago—after he changed and put her through so much. Maybe she knows what it is she's looking for this time—before she gives her heart away. And maybe, because of that love dying, she's ready to love again."

"I hadn't thought of it that way. I guess I was just thinking about how hard it is for me to trust after the way I saw her treated."

It was plain to Luke that Kathleen was finding it more difficult to trust men than her sister was. His heart constricted at the very thought that she might never get past it.

"I'm sorry, Luke. I want her to be happy, to find true love if that's what she wants. I just don't want her to rush into another marriage."

"I understand. The best thing you can do is pray for the Lord to guide her. For Him to keep her from doing anything rash but also for her to know if the time and the person are right."

"That's true. And I will."

"Did she say anything about marriage? Or if Officer O'Malley has asked her to marry him?"

"No. Not really. I suppose I could be jumping to conclusions."

"You might be. And Kathleen, remember that Officer O'Malley was there that night. He was at the hospital and knows what shape she was in. He's the one who might have shot Clancy. I don't think he's going to rush her into anything."

"I hope not. And I hope he's not…just trying to get past the guilt he might feel over Clancy's death."

"You and your sister are beautiful women, Kathleen. It's highly unlikely that Officer O'Malley is keeping Colleen company because of guilt. Besides, whichever officer shot Clancy, he saved Colleen's life. There's no need for him to feel guilty over it."

Luke had leaned closer as he talked and he could almost feel Kathleen's shoulders relax as she sighed. "That's true. Thank you for reminding me, Luke."

"You're welcome. It was my turn after the other night."

"Oh, Luke, after all the encouragement you've given me, all the times you've been there for me, you have a lot of catching up to do."

He chuckled. "As long as I don't have to do it all at once."

"No, you don't. Thanks for listening again and for your thoughts. You gave me a lot to think about and I think I owe it to my sister to let her make the decisions that are important to her. I have been overprotective of her and sometimes I forget that Clancy is no longer here to hurt her."

"Or you." Luke regretted his words the moment they left his lips.

Just as he opened his mouth to say he was sorry, he heard Kathleen whisper, "Or me."

Her fingers covered her mouth and she looked up at him. He could see her eyes shimmer with unshed tears in the moonlight. But she swallowed hard and blinked them back. Luke wished he could cry for her.

He reached out his hand to touch her cheek and she stilled but didn't flinch. He could see the wariness in her eyes, and something else that pulled him nearer. His fingers grazed her cheek. "You are the strongest woman I've ever met, Kate. Clancy is gone. He'll never hurt you again."

"Never again." She closed her eyes and nodded. She

reached up and covered his hand with hers. "Thank you, Luke."

"You're welcome." He turned his hand over and captured hers. His glance lowered to her lips and back to her eyes. He'd never wanted to kiss anyone more, and it was all he could do to keep from pulling her into his arms. But the wariness lingered in her eyes and he leaned his forehead against hers. If-onlys whirled through his mind. If only she could trust again. If only he could, too.

He glanced at her lips once more and cleared his throat. "We'd better go in before—"

"Someone wonders where we are?"

No. Before he threw caution to the wind, pulled her into his arms and kissed her.

Kathleen punched her pillow one more time. She'd tossed and turned for hours, it seemed, thinking about Luke and their time in the garden.

She didn't know what to do. The more time she spent with Luke the more time she wanted to be with him. He'd become her confidant and if she wasn't mistaken, she'd become his. One minute she thought she should distance herself from Luke in order to keep her feelings for him from deepening. The next she told herself that she couldn't desert him just as he'd begun to confide in her.

If she made him feel she didn't want to listen to him, what might that do to him? After all Luke had done for her, all the times he'd been there for her, there was no way she could not be there for him.

Still, she had to find a way to guard her heart, to keep from letting her growing feelings show. If there were one man in the world she could trust, it would be Luke. But he'd lost the love of his life and she didn't want to come in second to the memories of another woman. If she ever gave her heart to a man, she wanted to be first in his life, after the Lord. Always.

Besides, he'd given no indication that they were any more than friends. Except, there was a look in his eyes tonight that made her wonder what it would be like to be kissed by him.

"Arrgh!" She turned her pillow over and punched it once again. She needed to get to sleep. Tomorrow promised to be a busy day and she wanted to be fresh. She had to quit thinking of Luke. Still, she wondered, had he wanted to kiss her as much as she'd wanted him to? For one short moment she'd thought he would. And then he'd said they should go in.

It was for the best. She knew it was. She closed her eyes and prayed. *Dear Lord, please help me to quit thinking of Luke in a romantic way, please help me to quit longing for the impossible. Or please show me if it is possible for me to trust my heart to—*

The only man she could imagine trusting her heart to was Luke. And she didn't even know if he wanted it. Tears sprung to her eyes.

I don't know what to do, Lord. Please help me to know Your will for my life and guide me to do it. In Jesus's name, Amen.

Only then was she able to drift off to sleep.

"No!" Luke yanked himself out of the nightmare, breathing deep and hard. His brow damp with sweat, he flung off his covers and sat up on the side of the bed, trying to get his bearings. He was awake; it wasn't real.

None of it was real. He took one deep, cleansing breath after another until he quit shaking.

He got up, crossed over to the small window that looked out at street level and rubbed the back of his neck. Dawn was breaking and he was more than ready for the night to end and day to begin. He'd tossed and turned all night, moving from one nightmare to another.

First he'd relived Beth's death as he still did from time to time. But somehow as he'd held her lifeless body and bent down to kiss her brow, the woman he'd been holding in his arms had turned into Kathleen.

He'd barely roused himself out of that nightmare when he'd begun to dream of the day in the park when he'd first seen Kathleen being badgered by her brother-in-law and come to her aid.

The ache in his heart as she left the park, wondering if she would be all right, was as real as it had been that day. Just as it was when the dream moved to him carrying her up the stairs when she'd arrived at Heaton House. He kept waking himself, thinking it wasn't real. Kathleen was here now and she was safe. Only then did he fall into a deeper sleep.

But the dreams of the past turned into his fear of the present. He watched Kathleen go in one tenement building after another, only he wasn't with her. No one was with her.

Luke went to the bathroom and splashed cold water in his face, fighting the memory of what happened next. But his breathing became shallow as the last nightmare came back to him full force.

He was in the tenements looking for Kathleen when he heard a moan in an alleyway. He rushed in and his heart stopped as he saw a woman, with hair the color of Kathleen's, lying there, motionless.

He'd gathered her up in his arms. Somehow, the nightmare switched to the day Beth died, and then back to him holding Kathleen in the alleyway, trying to assess her injuries. But he felt something wet and warm at her side. She'd been shot and he'd prayed, *Dear Lord, please don't let me lose Kathleen, too.* Her head lolled to the side and that was when he'd yanked himself out of the nightmare and jumped out of bed.

He'd failed Beth. He couldn't fail Kathleen.

When Kathleen joined the others at the breakfast table she noticed Luke looked as if he hadn't slept any better than she had. Much as she'd like to think it was because he was thinking about her as much as she'd thought about him, she figured he'd probably stayed up too late writing. She'd been taking up way too much of his time. And she had to put a stop to it. It wasn't fair to him.

"You ready?" he asked as they finished breakfast and she laid her napkin on the table.

"I am, but really, Luke, I don't need you to go with me today. I'm just going to the Walshes' and to see Reba. I know the way and I will be fine."

He slid her chair out from the table. "I'm going to see you there safely, Kathleen."

"Luke, I can't keep taking up your time. You have your own work to do and I'm feeling bad that you're staying up late to catch up."

"I told you, that's when I write best. Come on, at least let me see you there safely and—" He sighed deeply.

"I really wish they'd find a safer way for you to do your job."

"I'm safe, Luke. I went in and out of those tenements for years. I know my way around and I'll be fine."

Mrs. Heaton walked into the dining room. "Excuse me, but you have a phone call, Luke. I think it's your publisher."

Luke turned to Kathleen. "Wait for me. I'm sure this won't take long."

When he had left the room, Mrs. Heaton sat down next to her. "I couldn't help but overhear part of your conversation with Luke, Kathleen. You know he has a point and I'm going to take it up with the ladies. Perhaps we need to hire someone to go along with you, or find a way to get the word out and have the interested parties come to you."

"But you wanted someone who knows their way around the tenements and who can relate to those living there."

"Yes, and you fill that qualification perfectly. But we don't want you in any kind of danger. Let me see what we can come up with. And in the meantime, please let Luke go with you when he can. If anything happened to you, I'd blame myself."

"Oh, Mrs. Heaton, you mustn't take that burden on yourself."

"Please let Luke accompany you until we can come up with a plan, Kathleen."

After all the woman had done for her and all she'd been through, Kathleen couldn't bring herself to refuse. "Yes, ma'am, I will."

"Will what?" Luke asked, coming back into the room.

"Let you accompany me to the tenements."

Mrs. Heaton turned to him. "I'm going to talk to the board. We're going to come up with a way to make sure Kathleen is safe going in and out of the tenements."

"I'll see that she is."

"Yes, but you have your own work to do at times and you won't always be able to accompany her. But I appreciate you taking care of it now, Luke."

"It's not a problem at all." Luke turned to Kathleen. "I'm ready whenever you are."

There was nothing to do but go with him and try not to let Mrs. Heaton see how frustrated she was at Luke for starting all this. It hurt that they didn't feel she could do the job by herself. "Let's go. See you this afternoon, Mrs. Heaton."

"You two have a good day," the older woman said as they headed toward the front door.

Once they were on the trolley, Luke turned to her. "What was that all about?"

"Mrs. Heaton overheard you talking about my safety and decided you were right. But, Luke, it's the job they hired me to do. I can't always have someone with me."

"Maybe it is a job for two people."

Kathleen sighed. "I don't want them thinking I can't handle it."

"They aren't going to think that for a moment. But they aren't going to want you in danger any more than I do."

Her pulse skittered at his words. How was she going to distance herself from him when he turned her heart to mush?

Chapter Seventeen

Luke went with Kathleen to the Walshes' and was welcomed into their apartment right along with her. Mrs. Walsh had the kettle on, along with a pot of coffee.

"Which do you prefer, Mr. Patterson?"

"Coffee, please."

She set a cup in front of him and brought a teapot and two cups to the table for her and Kathleen.

"Well, what is your decision?" Kathleen asked once the woman joined them at the table.

She let out a huge sigh and grinned. "We would very much like to run the home if the Ladies' Aide Society wants us to."

"Oh, Rose, I'm so glad. With Colleen running the first one, I don't know anyone I'd trust more to run another than you and your husband."

"And Harold is as happy about it as I am. To think we'll be able to get out of here for good. I can't thank you enough for thinking of us, Kathleen."

"Well, I have to give Luke credit for suggesting that Harold might be able to have work, too."

"Thank you, Mr. Patterson."

The sheen of tears in her eyes was hard to ignore. "You're welcome, Mrs. Walsh."

"I'll let you know when your interview will be with the board," Kathleen told the woman, "but I know they are going to be very pleased to have you and Harold in charge of the next home."

"I certainly hope they are. I'll be waiting anxiously to hear from you."

The two women hugged and then he and Kathleen were on their way to see Reba and find out if she'd landed a job yet.

Kathleen seemed to be in better spirits after the news Rose gave her and he was glad. He knew she was upset with him over bringing up her safety in Mrs. Heaton's hearing.

Luke hadn't meant to make her feel incompetent in any way. He just didn't want anything happening to her. Maybe he'd talk to Michael and get some ideas from him on how to protect her without her knowing it. There had to be a way for her to do her job, be protected and not feel smothered.

When they arrived at Reba's building she turned to him. "I think I need to go by myself to visit Reba, Luke. I'm barely getting to know her and I want her to trust me. I'm afraid she might feel uncomfortable with you along."

"I understand. Do you want me to wait outside or visit with Mrs. Connor?"

"It's your choice."

Her tone was a little cool and Luke really didn't know what to do about it other than to let her do her job. "Well, Mrs. Connor isn't expecting us, so I'll wait for you out here on the stoop. I brought my notepad, and I'll stay busy. Take all the time you need."

"I will, thank you." She started up the steps and then turned back. "I'm sorry I've been grouchy today. I do appreciate that you want to protect me, and—"

"It's all right, Kate. The last thing I want is for you to feel suffocated while you work. And you won't always be coming here so often. For now—"

"For now, we'll do it your and Mrs. Heaton's way. But only for a while."

Kathleen hurried up the stairs. She didn't know whether to be relieved or disappointed Luke wasn't with her. Much as she protested and felt bad that he was giving up writing time to go with her, she did appreciate it and she liked his company.

But that was the problem. She liked his company too much for her own good and she was dangerously close to falling in love with him.

Reba opened the door slightly and after recognizing Kathleen, she smiled and let her in. "Good morning. I was hoping you would come today. Would you like some tea?"

Though Kathleen had already drunk two cups at breakfast, she didn't want to offend Reba. "Yes, please."

Reba's daughter was at the kitchen table and gave Kathleen a shy smile when she sat down opposite her.

"Good morning, Jenny. You look very pretty today."

The child didn't speak but her smile grew.

"Tell Miss O'Bryan thank-you, Jenny."

The little girl ducked her head. "Thank you."

"You're welcome."

Reba brought the tea to the table along with some

gingersnaps that reminded Kathleen of the ones Mrs. Heaton made. "Well, have you any news for me? Did you hear back from any of the places you applied for?"

"I did. In fact I'm to go back for an interview at Macy's this afternoon. Mrs. Connor is going to watch Jenny for me and I'll let you know as soon as I know. I do hope I get to work there. But if so, I'll need someone to keep Jenny on a regular basis soon. Mrs. Connor has said she'd help, but I don't want to impose on her for long."

"I think I can get Jenny in the child care home my sister is running. I'll check and see. Otherwise, my old neighbor is going to be running the next home but I'm not sure how long it will take to get it going. I'll check on it as well."

"This is such an answer to prayer, Kathleen. I can't tell you how blessed I feel that you came by to see me."

"Well, Mrs. Connor gets the credit for that. But she didn't tell me a lot about you other than you are raising your daughter alone. My sister is raising her sons alone since her husband..." Kathleen didn't want to go into all the details just yet. "Since he died. Are you a widow, too?"

She felt horrible at the look on Reba's face. "I'm sorry. That is certainly none of my business."

Reba took a sip of her tea and looked at her daughter. "All done with breakfast?"

Jenny nodded. "Can I go play now?"

"Yes, you may play in our bedroom."

The little girl scooted out of her chair and ran to the bedroom. The door was open and they could see her pull out a small cloth doll.

"Mrs. Connor made that for her. She doesn't have a lot of toys like I—"

Kathleen felt sure that Reba hadn't always lived this way. She seemed to be educated and there was a manner about her that bespoke of better times in the past. Of course, a lot of the immigrants in the tenements had had better lives before coming to America—at least at one time. However, Kathleen didn't think Reba was an immigrant. But she'd already pried when she shouldn't have. She wasn't going to ask.

"Do you mind if I iron while we talk?" She put her iron on the stove to heat up and pulled out her ironing board.

"No, of course not." There was no way Kathleen would object—this was how the woman made her living after all. But the fact that she hadn't just asked her to leave made Kathleen think she might want to talk.

Reba took a shirtwaist, sprinkled water on it and began to iron. "I—I actually ran away from home with the man I loved—or thought I loved. He promised a great life if we came to the city and it all sounded so wonderful. My mama didn't approve of him and, well, we ran off."

She looked over to where Jenny was playing in her room and smiled, then she looked at Kathleen. "Jenny is the blessing that came out of it all, but I never thought I'd be raising her alone."

"She's very pretty and quite sweet." She'd never answered whether or not she was a widow, but it didn't matter. What did matter was that Reba appeared to have been duped by the man she loved—the man she thought she could trust. More than ever Kathleen wanted to help her be able to raise her child and get out of the tenements one day.

"Thank you. I just want a better life for her. I'm not an immigrant—I'm actually from Virginia."

"Did you ever think about going back? Do you have

family there?" There she went again, asking questions she had no right to ask. "I'm sorry, Reba. I'm being quite nosy today."

"It's all right. I expected some questions. I won't go back to Virginia."

Kathleen nodded. There were things she'd decided she wouldn't do, too.

They talked a bit more and she saw Reba's hope and optimism for the future.

"I was beginning to think it'd never be possible to leave here," she said, "but thanks to Mrs. Connor and you, I believe it is."

"So do I." Kathleen took the last sip of tea. She knew a little more about Reba than before and she liked the young woman. Still, she couldn't shake the niggling feeling that she'd seen her somewhere before. But if she was from Virginia, then it must have been just passing in the street or the grocer, as Luke and Mrs. Connor had suggested.

She got up to leave. "No need to see me out. You keep working. I'll be back in the office this afternoon, so just let me know how your interview turns out. I'll be praying all goes well and you have a job when I hear from you."

"Thank you, Kathleen. I need all the prayers I can get."

Kathleen let herself out, and headed back downstairs, praying all the way that Reba got the job today, and that Colleen would make room for Jenny.

Kathleen opened the door to the outside to see that Luke was observing the people around him and making notes. She supposed that all writers enjoyed watching people. He'd explained to her that he might hear a snippet of conversation that might make it into one of his stories, or see a particularly interesting person whose looks might fit a character he was writing about.

Now her heart did a little twist and dive as he looked up at her and smiled. "Well, how'd it go?"

"Good. She's going for an interview this afternoon, so say a prayer she gets the job. She really wants it."

"I'll certainly do that. Where to next?"

"I've got to stop by Colleen's and see if she has room for one more child before I go to the office. I want to be there in case Reba calls me later."

Luke pulled his watch out of his pocket. "Want to grab something for lunch from one of the street vendors?"

"Why don't we see if Colleen has something? No need spending money when we can get something better for free."

"Now, that's a better idea. Let's go." He stuffed his notepad and pencil stub in the inside pocket of his jacket and held out his arm.

Kathleen took it and they were on their way. They caught a trolley on Second Avenue and got off on Twenty-fourth. From there it was a short walk to Colleen's.

"Why and what brings you two here just in time to eat today?" Colleen asked, motioning them into the dining room where the children were seated around the table. "The children are almost finished, but we've plenty of stew for the two of you. Come into the kitchen."

"I was hoping you'd say that. Can you keep us company for a few minutes? I've something to ask of you," Kathleen said.

Colleen ladled up the stew and set it down before them. "Take a seat and I'll let Ida know."

Luke said a blessing and they'd just begun to eat

when Colleen came back into the room. She ladled a bowl for herself and sat down with them.

"Now, what is it you want to ask?"

"Well, first I've got a bit of good news for you. The Walshes are going to run the next home."

"Oh, but that is good news, isn't it?"

"It is, for sure. And the other news is that Reba Dickerson, the young woman I told you about, is close to getting a job at Macy's. But she'll need care for her little girl quickly if she gets it."

"Ah, and I know what the questions is, then. Of course we'll make room for one more child."

"It might only be until the other home is up and running, but I'd like to be able to tell her that Jenny can be taken care of as soon as she gets the job."

"Tell her, then. Actually, Ida and I have been thinking we could take a few more on."

"Thank you, Colleen. I knew you'd agree. And if you can take on several more children, I know that will be good news for Mrs. Heaton and the others."

"Now that you've got someone to run the next home I'm sure it won't take long to fill it up—at least according to what the parents of our children tell me."

"An idea just came to me," Luke said. "Colleen could ask for referrals from the women who are bringing their children here. Perhaps that would make it easier on you, Kathleen."

"That is a good idea, Luke," Colleen said.

Kathleen smiled and gave Luke a little shake of her head. She had a feeling his motive came from trying to keep her out of the tenements as much as possible but how could she be upset at him for caring enough to try to keep her safe? "It is a very good idea. You seem to be full of them lately."

"Let me know when you're ready for me to start gettin' a list of names together."

"I will. I'll try to find out how long it will take to get the other home up and running first. I don't want to get anyone's hopes up too fast."

"I understand that, I do. I am so glad Rose and Harold want to do this. It is such an opportunity for them. For so many people. When I think of all the people the Ladies' Aide Society will end up helping because of the child care homes, it makes me want to cry. Every day I see the mothers of these children relieved that they can help their families and it's only because they have someone to look after their children. I am so happy to be part of it."

"I know that feeling," Kathleen said. She'd never thought to see her sister as happy as she was now. She took her and Luke's bowls to the sink and washed them out, laying them on the drain board. "Thank you for lunch. I need to get back to the office now, but I'll telephone you and let you know what I find out from Reba."

"Good. In the meantime, I'll let Ida know we'll be getting at least one more child soon."

Kathleen and Luke said goodbye to Ida and the children as they went back through the dining room on their way out. With the exception of her grouchiness to Luke that morning, it'd been a good day. Now if only Reba got her job, it'd be a great start to the week.

Chapter Eighteen

Kathleen was the last one in the office when Reba telephoned to let her know she got the position at Macy's and that she was to start the next Monday. Kathleen promised to return the next day to have her fill out the paperwork needed for Jenny to be accepted for the day care and to take her to meet Colleen and Ida and see the home herself.

She had convinced Luke that she could get to her office without him accompanying her there and back, only now she missed him as she took the trolley back to the stop nearest Heaton House. She couldn't wait to share the news of the day with everyone.

But Mrs. Heaton wasn't in her study and Luke was nowhere to be seen. Maybe he was working. Kathleen hoped so. She headed upstairs to get ready for dinner. Her news would just have to wait until then.

She freshened up and redid her hair, pulling it up in the newest style she and Elizabeth had been trying out. As it was a Monday, she kept on the brown skirt and beige shirtwaist she'd started the day out in.

She was the first to get to the parlor, which was unusual, but she used the time to look at some of the pictures around the room. She'd been told that Mrs. Heaton changed them every so often, adding newer ones and putting older pictures in a box. She walked around the room, picking up first one and then another. There was one of Michael and Violet at their wedding and another of the group of boarders on an outing at Central Park, before she became part of the group. She grinned as she spotted one Elizabeth had taken the day they went to Coney Island. It was nice to feel she truly was one of the family of boarders now.

She moved to another table and caught her breath. Her heart began to pound as she picked up the frame and looked closer at the photo.

The woman in the photograph looked very much like Reba. Only younger by several years at least, and her hair was done much differently. She was dressed much nicer but she so resembled Reba that Kathleen had to wonder if they could be the same woman. But that was impossible. Or was it? Perhaps she'd been a boarder at one time? No, if she was important enough for Mrs. Heaton to have a photo of her in the parlor, Kathleen was sure she'd never have ended up in the tenements. Still, she looked so much like Reba—

"Kathleen, you're down early," Luke said as he crossed the room and came to stand beside her. "How did things go? Did you hear from Reba?"

"I did. She got the job!"

"That's wonderful news."

"It is. But, Luke, who is this young woman? Do you know?"

"I do. It's Mrs. Heaton's daughter, the one who is missing. Do you know about her?"

"Yes. Elizabeth mentioned her to me."

"Well, for a long time, she couldn't bring herself to put Rebecca's photo up, but then there was a letter or something that gave her and Michael hope that she is still alive and I believe she finally felt able to have her photo up where she could see it."

Tears burned the back of Kathleen's eyelids. Could Reba be Mrs. Heaton's daughter?

"Luke, I—"

"Good evening, you two," Elizabeth said as she entered the parlor.

"Good evening, Elizabeth."

The room quickly began to fill up as Julia and Millicent, John, Ben and Matt entered.

"You were going to tell me something?" Luke asked as the others greeted each other.

"Yes but not now. Maybe after dinner if you have time?"

"Yes, of course. Is it something— Would you like to go to the park?"

The man read her entirely too well. She didn't want to talk about her suspicions where she could be overheard. "That would work well, thank you."

"Thank you."

"Whatever for?"

He smiled and leaned closer, sending her heart galloping. "For—"

"Dinner is served," Mrs. Heaton said from the doorway.

"Later." Luke held out his arm and Kathleen took it with no hesitation at all, knowing she trusted him more with each passing day. Trusted him to keep her safe, to be ready to listen to anything she had to say, to be there for her. Her heart longed for her to trust him with it as well, but could she? After hearing how Jenny's father had treated Reba she wasn't sure she ever would.

Luke thought Kathleen had never looked lovelier as she told Mrs. Heaton and the boarders about her day. She was so animated there was no doubt that she was as happy to be helping others get out of the tenements as she'd been herself.

He wanted to know what it was she'd been about to tell him when the others came into the parlor, but as Mrs. Heaton asked them both to her study after dinner, he knew it was going to have to wait.

They settled in the chairs across from her desk and she clasped her hands together and grinned. "I am so happy about your news, Kathleen. We've got things going on the purchase of the next house and it won't be long before you'll be needing to fill it up."

And that meant more visits to the tenements for Kathleen. Only she would be protected whether she liked it or not.

"I can't tell you how happy I am."

Kathleen's smile warmed his heart.

"You don't have to, dear. It shows," Mrs. Heaton said. "I know we have the right person as our liaison in you. But we are going to come up with some ways to assure your safety as you go in and out of the tenements."

"What are you thinking?" Kathleen asked.

Luke knew, for he'd talked to Michael Heaton about it after leaving Kathleen that afternoon. But he thought Kathleen would take it better if it came from Mrs. Heaton instead of him.

"I'm getting Michael's advice on it and of course we

want to hear what you think, Luke. But the Society is thinking of hiring someone to accompany—"

"Oh, Mrs. Heaton, please don't—"

Mrs. Heaton held up her hand and waved it once in a way that everyone came to know meant "say no more."

"Kathleen, dear, I know you are a strong woman and not afraid to come and go in the tenements. But we are afraid for you to. I'm not sure you've been told about my daughter?"

"Yes, ma'am. Elizabeth told me when I first came here. I'm so sorry. I…"

Mrs. Heaton nodded. "Well, we have recently learned that she is still alive, but we have no idea where she is. I can only pray that she is safe."

Luke saw Kathleen swallow hard. It was heartbreaking to think of all Mrs. Heaton had been through.

"I must ask that you allow us to make sure you are safe in your work for the Ladies' Aide Society. The fact that you lived in the tenements once might keep you safe—or the fact that you've made it out might cause someone to—" She took a deep breath and shook her head as if she couldn't bear to continue.

"You must let us do what we feel is in your and our best interests. It wouldn't do us any good to have something happen to our liaison, now, would it?"

"No, ma'am, I suppose not."

Luke breathed a silent sigh of relief at Kathleen's response. She might not like having an escort while she worked, but she would no longer fight it.

"Thank you. Now, you did say that Colleen has room for more children and that she had an idea on how to go about finding others who need our services?"

"Actually, it was Luke's idea. I'll let him explain it to you."

Luke did, and when he was finished, Mrs. Heaton smiled. "I love it! Who better to get names from than neighbors and friends of those in need? Eventually, it will cut down on having to knock on so many doors and actually make it safer for you, too, Kathleen." She nodded. "We'll meet again soon and see what Michael and Luke come up with."

"Yes, ma'am."

"And in the meantime, you'll be seeing this young mother, Reba, and getting her daughter enrolled?"

"First thing tomorrow."

"Good. I'm glad we can help her. Thank you for the report. I've got to telephone the others now. I know they'll be as happy as I am with your news."

"I hope so."

Kathleen stood and Luke did the same. He wondered if she still wanted to go to the park or if she was too upset about having to be escorted from now on. He didn't have to wait long as she turned to him almost as soon as they walked out the door.

"May we go to the park now, or is it too late? We can go to Mrs. Heaton's garden if need be, but I must talk to you."

The urgency in her voice had him going to the table where the park keys were kept and he grabbed one and held it up. "Let's go."

They managed to get out the door without anyone noticing and once they were out of sight of the house he turned to her. "What is it? What's so important?"

"I think I may know where Mrs. Heaton's daughter is."

* * *

Luke seemed to be at a loss for words as he hurried Kathleen to the park, unlocked the gate and led her to a bench.

"What are you talking about? How could you know where Rebecca Heaton is? No one has heard anything from her except for a letter she'd sent to Violet's mother months ago letting them know that she was alive at that time."

"I think Reba Dickerson may be Rebecca Heaton."

"What?" Luke jumped up from the seat. "Why would you think that?"

"She looks almost exactly like the photo in Mrs. Heaton's parlor, only a little older and more mature. It's uncanny, Luke."

"This is what you were about to tell me before dinner?"

"Yes. I wanted to tell Mrs. Heaton, but I can't get her hopes up if Reba is not Rebecca."

"No, you can't do that. She's been through way too much already. But surely, Kathleen, if it were Mrs. Heaton's daughter, why would she be living in the tenements?"

"I don't know. I think it's possible she might feel she's shamed her family, but I'm not sure. When I go back tomorrow I need you to come with me at least long enough to get a good look at her."

Luke nodded and sat back down beside her. "All right, I will. It would be wonderful if she is Mrs. Heaton's daughter and they could be reunited."

"I know. But I'm not sure it will be easy. If it is her, there's got to be a reason she didn't feel she could go home and it might bring more heartbreak for everyone."

"It could, yes. We must pray it doesn't."

"But first, I need to know if you think it could be her. And then, could you help me to find out for sure?"

"I'll do all I can, surely you know that by now, Kate."

And she did. Luke was indeed the trustworthy person she knew and— She stopped, amazed at her own thoughts. Yes, in spite of Reba's story, and Colleen's, she knew Luke could be trusted. She felt it in her heart.

"Kate? Are you all right? You look a little bemused."

Bemused, bewildered, that she was. "I'm all right. I just…" Her heart began to pound as she looked at him, and she jumped up from the seat. "I suppose we should be getting back to the house. We left late and—" She turned and looked at Luke.

He had a slight smile on his face as if he were trying to figure her out. They needed to go—now—before he read her thoughts as he'd become quite good at. "Are you coming?"

"Yes, I'm coming." He lightly grasped her elbow and turned her toward him. "Kathleen, we'll find out if Reba is Mrs. Heaton's daughter. And as soon as possible. Trust me."

"I do." There, she'd said it out loud and to him.

He smiled and his eyes crinkled. "Thank you."

"You're welcome."

Luke leaned a little nearer and for a moment she thought he might kiss her. Was sure he would. Wanted him to. She stood still and held her breath. And then he closed his eyes and gave a little tug to her elbow, propelling her out of the park and up the street.

They walked back to Heaton House in quiet. Kathleen wasn't sure what to think. She was almost certain he'd been about to kiss her, but he hadn't. Why? She knew she was falling in love with Luke. And that she trusted him…to keep her safe, to help her find out who Reba really was. But could she truly trust her heart to him? And did he even want her to?

She trusted him. She'd said so. Luke's heart slammed against his ribs. But did she really? Just because she trusted him to help her find out who Reba really was didn't mean she trusted him in everything.

And yet, something was different. He hadn't seen the wariness in her eyes when he'd leaned nearer. But he'd heard her quick intake of breath. What had it meant— that she was afraid he would kiss her or wishing that he might?

Oh, how he'd wanted to pull her into his arms and kiss her. And yet, once he did, he'd be committing to… loving her. And he did. There. He admitted it to himself. Kathleen had come into his life that day in Central Park and he hadn't quit thinking about her since. She had his insides twisted up in all kinds of ways.

She'd replaced Beth—first in his thoughts, then his dreams, and finally in his heart. He loved her. Plain and simple. But to admit it to her, to woo her, to commit to her? To put himself in the position of possibly losing the person he loved most in life as he had Beth?

Luke wasn't sure he could do it. And even if he declared his love for Kathleen, could she trust her heart to him completely?

Maybe all they both needed was time. And helping her find out about Reba would give them some. Instead of just escorting her in and out of the tenements, they'd need to spend some time together, alone, to talk it over. Maybe then he could get a sense of how she felt about him.

It was when they arrived at Heaton House that he realized they hadn't spoken on the way back. He paused at the steps. "I'm sorry, Kathleen. I was lost in my thoughts."

"It's all right, so was I."

Had they been thinking along the same lines? "Kathleen, I—"

"I hope Mrs. Heaton won't be able to sense I'm keeping something from her. She reads me well."

Evidently not. "I don't think she sensed anything earlier."

Kathleen nodded. "No, I don't either. I'll just have to be careful, but oh, I hope we can find out for sure, and soon."

Much as Luke wanted Reba Dickerson to be Rebecca Heaton, he wouldn't mind it taking a few weeks to give him more time to spend with Kathleen. More time to figure out what he was going to do now that he could no longer deny how he felt about her.

Chapter Nineteen

Kathleen and Luke didn't tarry long at the breakfast table the next morning. In fact they were the first ones to leave the house.

"Oh," Kathleen breathed as they headed for the trolley stop. "I thought for sure Mrs. Heaton was going to ask me what I was hiding. I hope we find out something soon. I don't like not being open with her."

"You don't have to worry," he told her. "She really doesn't think you're hiding anything from her. Of course if we keep leaving earlier than everyone else, she might begin to wonder."

"Oh, no! Do you think?"

The trolley came to a stop just then and Luke chuckled as he followed Kathleen on and sat down beside her. This was a side of her he'd never seen. "Do you just find things to worry about?"

"Normally, no. Life gives us enough of that on its own. But I do hate to feel like I'm lying—although I'm not. I don't know who Reba really is, but still…"

"We can't say anything about it until we know for sure. It will be much better for Mrs. Heaton to know nothing than to think she's found her daughter and it turn out not to be her."

Kathleen leaned back in her seat and expelled a huge sigh. "Of course."

"So please quit worrying."

"I'll try. I don't want to hurt Reba, either, so I'll have to be careful on how I question her."

"That's true. But the forms you help her with should ask for some of the information we need."

"I'm glad I saw the photograph yesterday. Otherwise, I would just turn in the paperwork and not be able to get it back without explaining why or telling a lie."

It came as no surprise to Luke that she didn't want to lie—he'd known from the first she was a woman of integrity. It was one of the reasons he was so attracted to her. He'd tossed and turned most of the night again, flitting from one dream—one nightmare—to another. There was no doubt in his mind that this woman had replaced Beth in his heart.

When he'd awakened this morning realizing that it was only Kathleen who was on his mind all night, he'd felt almost guilty that it wasn't Beth who occupied his thoughts day and night. And then, he'd felt hopeful. He was moving on.

Maybe this was the Lord's way of telling him to put his heart on the line again. To give it to Kathleen, holding nothing back, and trusting in the Lord to help him keep her safe. In truth, he hoped so. Because denying he cared that deeply about her would be lying.

"Now, how do I introduce you to Reba? I don't quite know what she's going to think of my bringing you with me."

"Hmm. And we don't want to lie to her." He thought

for a moment. "How about you just say that I'm your friend. We are friends, right?"

Kathleen nodded. "Yes, we are."

"And that I'm accompanying you today because you want to go to lunch with me when you're through and I needed to know where to pick you up."

"Oh! Yes, that will probably work."

"How long will it take to fill out the papers and have your talk?"

"A few hours," she replied.

The trolley stopped and they got out on Second Avenue and walked the rest of the way to the building. Luke was eager to meet Reba Dickerson and see for himself if she looked like Rebecca Heaton.

When they reached her floor, Kathleen turned to him. "Are you sure this will work?"

"No. But I don't have any other ideas, and we're here."

"That we are." She reached out and knocked on the door, making sure that she was the one Reba would see when she cracked it open.

The young woman gave Kathleen a smile, but it quickly disappeared when she saw him.

"Reba, this is my friend Luke Patterson. Luke, this is Reba Dickerson. Luke came with me because we're having lunch together later and I wanted him to know where to meet me. Will it be all right if he calls for me around noon?"

Reba looked from one to the other and then smiled. Suddenly she did resemble the woman in Mrs. Heaton's photograph—a little older and more mature as Kathleen had said. Still, he wasn't certain she was Rebecca.

"Of course Mr. Patterson may pick you up."

"Thank you, Mrs. Dickerson." Luke turned to Kathleen. "I'll see you later. You two have a nice visit."

"Thank you, we will." Kathleen turned back to Reba, and Luke turned to leave. He'd have to look at the photograph of Rebecca again. He tried to commit Mrs. Dickerson's face to memory so that he could compare the two. And he'd see her again when he came to get Kathleen. He wondered how they could get a photograph of Mrs. Dickerson. Suddenly an idea came to him and he hurried back to the woman's apartment and knocked on the door.

Once again, Mrs. Dickerson cracked it open only far enough to see who was there. She smiled this time. "Mr. Patterson, you're a bit early, aren't you?"

Luke chuckled. "I'm sorry but I need to speak to Kathleen for a moment, if possible."

She must have heard her name, for she came to the door just then. "Luke? Is something wrong?"

"No, I just—" He hoped he wasn't overstepping, but it was the only way he knew to get his idea across to her. "I wondered—you didn't have your camera with you to take the pictures for your records—would you like me to bring it when I come back?"

He could see that she caught on quickly as she nodded and smiled. "Oh, yes, please. Thank you for thinking of it."

"You're welcome. I'll bring it back with me." He hurried down the stairs this time, feeling quite proud of himself for coming up with the idea. It could never hurt to have pictures of the people applying to the day care homes, or to run one. He'd tell Mrs. Heaton about the idea—if she saw him with the camera and asked about it. Then, once the film was developed, he and Kathleen could compare the photographs side by side. Then they'd know if Reba was who they thought she was.

Kathleen followed Reba back to the kitchen table where they'd just begun to chat while the tea steeped.

Luke came up with some of the best ideas. She'd never even thought of bringing a camera—not that she had one anyway—but it was a wonderful idea to include photographs with the application records. Not to mention it'd help in trying to find out who Reba really was.

"I didn't know you'd be needing a photograph. I'm not much on having mine taken."

Kathleen wondered if she were going to refuse to have her picture taken. "Neither am I, so I understand. But—"

Reba's hand came up and sliced the air—in almost the exact same way Kathleen had seen Mrs. Heaton do on numerous occasions. The breath caught in her throat as she waited to hear what Reba had to say.

"But since it's necessary... I'll have time to freshen up a bit before you take it."

Kathleen released a silent sigh of relief as Reba poured them both a cup of tea. "I'll need one of you and Jenny, if it's all right."

"I guess so, if you must have them for the record, I suppose I don't really have a choice. I'll go get her from Mrs. Connor's when you're ready."

"You know it never hurts to have a picture or two of yourself and your loved ones. We never know what might happen that we might need it."

The color drained from Reba's face and Kathleen quickly tried to explain. "My parents passed away before my sister and I came here. If not for their photographs, I think I would have forgotten what they looked like."

Kathleen was almost sure that there were tears in Reba's eyes as she quickly turned to get a plate of cookies and bring them to the table.

"I'm sorry for your loss, Kathleen. And you are right. Photographs would be good to have."

Glad that was settled, Kathleen pulled out the forms she needed filled out and they began to go over them. She let Reba fill them out, hoping that it would give her and Luke the information they needed to find out if she was Mrs. Heaton's daughter. She wasn't familiar with feeling deceitful to anyone and didn't like it, but they had to find out the truth.

Reba was from Virginia and she was twenty-one— younger than Kathleen—and on her own with a child to raise alone. "Does your family still live in Virginia?"

"As far as I know." Reba's head was bent over the paper as she filled it out.

Evidently she hadn't kept contact with them after she left. Kathleen opened her mouth to ask why, but that question was not on the form and she really didn't know Reba well enough to ask something that personal. At least not now. But her heart went out to the younger woman and she prayed that she might be Mrs. Heaton's daughter—and that if she were, it would bring joy and not heartache to both women.

Reba had finished filling out the paperwork and they were enjoying another cup of tea and getting to know each other a little better when Luke came back.

"Oh, my, time went by fast," Reba said. "I'd best run down to Mrs. Connor's and get Jenny so we can get ready for that picture-taking. Please, Mr. Patterson, have a seat and some tea. I'm sure Kathleen will be glad to fix you a cup. I'll be right back." With that she hurried out the door, leaving Luke and Kathleen waiting for her.

"We get to take a picture of her daughter, too?"

"Yes. I came up with that one on my own, thank you." Kathleen grinned at him.

"It's a good idea." He crossed the room in a hurry and pulled out his camera from its bag. "Have you used one of these before?"

"No."

"Well, this is a Number 2 Bulls-Eye Kodak and it's easy to use." He pointed out the features to her. "This is where you look through the lens and this is the key you use to advance the film. And this is the shutter to take the picture."

"And I just slide this to take the picture?" She touched the small slide.

"That's all you have to do." He handed it to her. "Here, get the feel of it before she gets back." He handed it to her and she looked through the lens at him, and he smiled. She quickly slid the slide and heard a click. "I think I got you."

"I think you did, too." He smiled and the look in his eyes had her pulse racing as he approached her. "Now just turn the key to advance the film. And now it's my turn."

He took the camera from her and stood back a ways. "You can't exactly refuse to let me take your picture when you took mine without even asking."

"I'm sorry, Luke." She laughed as he took aim through the lens. "But please don't take—" Kathleen heard the click.

He grinned. "Looks like I got you, too."

"Yes. And probably with my eyes closed and my mouth wide open."

"Nope. I don't take those kinds of pictures."

"Humph." She sighed. "But I suppose I really don't have the right to complain."

"You're right about—"

The door opened and Reba and Jenny entered. "It won't take but a minute for us to freshen up. We'll be right back." She smiled as she hurried her daughter into their bedroom.

"So, what do you think?" Kathleen whispered. "Do you think she could be Rebecca?"

"I think it's a good possibility, but I'm just not sure." He leaned close to her ear. "The photos will help. I'll have them developed as soon as I can. But what do you think?"

"Oh, I think it is a real possibility. She has this hand movement that is just like Mrs. Heaton's. You know the one. Like this." Kathleen mimicked the movement and Luke nodded. "I know it could just be coincidence, but I think it might be her. I really do."

The bedroom door opened and out came Reba and Jenny. "Well, I suppose we'd best get to this. I hope you take good pictures."

"You know, Luke is really better at taking them than I am. Let's let him do it. He says he doesn't take bad ones."

"If that's the case, then all right. I'd like it to be a good one."

Luke took several photos, near the windows where there was light, and Reba and Jenny posed for each shot.

"We'll make sure you get the extra photos for your own album."

"Thank you, that's very nice, Kathleen."

"It's the least we can do." And maybe she wouldn't feel so bad for taking them when as yet, they really weren't part of the application. She grabbed her bag and the papers Reba had filled out. "Tomorrow I'll take you to meet Colleen and the other children she's watching, if you'd like."

"Oh, yes, I would. That way Jenny will feel better when I drop her off. Thank you for thinking of it."

"Would around ten in the morning be all right?"

"It will be fine."

"I'll see you then."

Jenny smiled shyly at Luke and he tweaked her nose on the way out. She giggled and rubbed her nose. She was a delightful child. After Reba shut the door behind them and they were down the hall, Kathleen turned to Luke. "If Reba turns out to be Mrs. Heaton's daughter, can you imagine how she's going to feel finding out she not only has her daughter back but a granddaughter, too?"

After dropping the film off to a developer, Luke took Kathleen to lunch at a small café not too far from her office. After the waiter took their order they began to discuss the magnitude of what they might be on the brink of discovering.

"I really feel we should tell Michael about our suspicions, but I don't want to see him or Mrs. Heaton heartbroken if it's not her," he said.

"I know. Neither do I. But aren't they from Virginia?"

"Yes. Is Reba from there, too?"

Kathleen nodded and pulled out some papers from her bag. "She's from Ashland."

Luke blew out a huge sigh. "Mrs. Heaton is from Ashland."

"It's got to be her, Luke."

"Not necessarily, Kathleen. There are a lot of people who live in Ashland. We can't jump to conclusions. I'll get the photos late this afternoon and we'll look at them. If we are sure, then we'll have to at least tell Michael."

Kathleen nodded. "I agree."

"You know he's thought for a while that there might be a possibility that Reba might be living in the tenements."

"Why would he think that?"

"He thinks she might have—" How did he say it delicately? "—gotten into trouble…and was too ashamed to come home."

Kathleen blushed and Luke felt sure she knew what he was talking about. He shrugged.

"It's possible, I suppose. And it would explain why she wouldn't go home. When I asked if her family still lived in Virginia, she said 'as far as I know.' I thought that an odd answer at the time, but…" Kathleen's voice faded away and neither of them seemed to know what to say next.

Luke was relieved when the waiter brought their lunch. "Don't worry about it now. We don't know much more than we did this morning. Let's just pray for the Lord to guide us the rest of the way."

At Kathleen's nod, they bowed their heads and Luke did just that.

Chapter Twenty

Kathleen could barely look at Mrs. Heaton at dinnertime for fear of giving away what she and Luke now
believed to be true.

When she'd arrived back at Heaton House after work,
it was to find Luke waiting for her in the parlor. He'd
motioned to her to come in and after making sure no
one else was around, she hurried to his side. He had
several photographs he'd taken of Reba and Jenny and
quickly held them up to the photo of Rebecca.

To Kathleen's eye, they had to be one and the same
person. She was almost positive that they were. "What
do you think?"

He'd taken another look at the photos before slipping
them back into his jacket pocket. "I think Reba is indeed Rebecca. But now we have to prove it. Maybe we
should go to Michael's after dinner and let him know?"

Kathleen had nodded. "I don't think we should put
it off."

"No, neither do I. We'll go for a walk and end up at
Michael and Violet's."

"All right."

And now she made herself take a bite of the roast chicken on her plate when she really wasn't hungry—too afraid Mrs. Heaton would ask what was wrong with her if she didn't eat.

"Kathleen, dear," Mrs. Heaton called from the head of the table.

Her heart jumped. "Yes, ma'am?"

"I just wanted to tell you that I think it's a wonderful idea to take photographs of the mothers and children who will be using the day care homes. If anything should happen to one of the children while in our care or even out of it, there would be a photo to help identify them."

Kathleen breathed a sigh of relief that she hadn't asked what she was hiding. "I'm glad you think it is a good idea."

But she could see the pain in her sweet landlady's eyes and was sure she was thinking of her own daughter. *Oh, dear Lord, please let Reba be her, if for no other reason than that Mrs. Heaton will know she is alive and well. But if it is her, please let it bring joy and not heartache.*

"Oh, and Luke, did you get the letter from your publisher that came today?"

"I did." Luke's eyes lit with excitement. "He wants to see the complete manuscript as soon as I have it done and I'm not that far from it. But he liked what I'd sent him."

"I knew he would."

"That is wonderful, Luke." Kathleen was glad that he at least seemed to be getting his writing done even with all the time he'd been spending with her. He must require much less sleep than she did.

Once the meal was over and everyone began leaving the dining room, Luke turned to her. "Want to go for that walk?"

"I'd like that, yes."

"It's nice out tonight," Mrs. Heaton said. "You two enjoy yourselves."

"Thank you." Again Kathleen felt bad for keeping so much from Mrs. Heaton, but they simply couldn't tell her until they were certain about her daughter.

She didn't know whose sigh of relief was the loudest when they got outside—hers or Luke's.

Luke took hold of her elbow as they started down the walk. "I hope we get this settled soon. It is one thing to investigate for people you barely know, but this involves so many people I care about. I pray it turns out well for all of them."

"I know. That is my biggest fear—that if Reba is Rebecca, she might not want her mother and brother to know where she is."

"Let's don't even think that way."

"No. Let's don't." But she knew it was there in the back of both their minds as they made their way over to Michael and Violet's.

Hilda answered the door and showed them into the parlor where Violet sat reading a book. She jumped up when she saw them and hurried to greet them.

"Luke, Kathleen, how wonderful to see you. What brings you out tonight?"

"Well, we came to see you and Michael," Kathleen said, "but I suppose I should have telephoned first."

"Oh, nonsense, you know we don't hold to social protocol with you all. But Michael is out of town, so I hope it isn't a wasted trip for you." She motioned to the couch. "Please have a seat and I'll have Hilda bring us some refreshment."

"Oh, please, don't trouble yourself. We just got up from the dinner table."

Violet laughed. "Say no more. I know Mother Heaton takes care of her boarders very well." She took her seat on the couch and Luke and Kathleen sat down across from her. "Now, is there anything I can help you with?"

Kathleen and Luke exchanged glances and Luke nodded. "Actually, it might be best that we talk to you, first."

"Now you have my curiosity up. Whatever is it?"

Luke nodded to Kathleen. "It's your story."

She took a deep breath. There was no easy way to say it. "I think I may have found Mrs. Heaton's daughter."

Violet gasped, stood up and sat back down. "Rebecca? You know where she is?"

"I believe so." Kathleen explained about Reba and how she'd come to think she might be Mrs. Heaton's daughter.

"And her last name?"

"Is Dickerson."

Violet's face paled. "Mother Heaton's maiden name is Dickerson. What does she look like?"

Kathleen turned to Luke, and he pulled the photographs out of his pocket and handed them to her. Kathleen looked down at them, more certain than ever that this was Mrs. Heaton's daughter and granddaughter. She handed the photos to Violet. "She has a little girl."

Violet reached out and took the photos with trembling fingers. She looked at each one, placed a hand over her mouth and looked at Kathleen with tears in her eyes. "I think it might be. But I'd need to see her, hear her voice to know for sure. And I'm glad Michael isn't here. He'll be home tomorrow, but I don't want him to know anything until we are positive. Is there any way I can see her for myself?"

"I'm taking her and Jenny—"

"That's the little girl's name?" Violet released a little sob. "Rebecca always said if she had a little girl, she wanted to name her Jennifer."

Kathleen wiped at her own tears as she went to sit beside Violet and gave her a hug. "I know this must be so much to take in and I don't in any way want to bring pain to Mrs. Heaton or Michael and you, but I do believe this is Rebecca. I am taking them to meet Colleen and the other children tomorrow around ten. If you could be there visiting Colleen—"

"I'll arrange to take some time off. I'll be there. Oh, I pray this is her. But what if she still doesn't want Michael or his mother to know where she is?"

"I don't know what we'll do then. But if it is Rebecca, I will do all I can to bring them together unless you tell me different."

"All right. Thank you so much for coming to me with this. And I know it's hard, but I think it's wise not to let Michael and his mother know just yet. They've been through so much heartache with Rebecca—and I'm sure she's gone through her own. I know she was close to both of them and loves them. Oh, please pray that it turns out good for all of them."

By the time they left Violet's they had a plan in place. Violet was sure she would know if Reba was Rebecca once she saw her, and if she was, she'd let Michael know.

If that was the case, Kathleen would talk to Reba

and tell her she had a mother and brother right here in the city. And they all prayed they'd be able to get them together again where their love for each other would be obvious.

But Kathleen was awfully quiet as they left Violet, and Luke was pretty sure he knew why. He remembered the small park in Michael's neighborhood right around the corner from their house.

He took hold of Kathleen's arm and led her there. It wasn't gated and just as he thought, no one was there this time of night. It would be the perfect place to talk.

"We need to talk where no one will overhear anything about this. Want to sit for a few minutes?"

"Yes, that would be nice. I feel anyone who sees me will know something is going on. I need to get my thoughts together."

They found a bench that was just far enough inside that no one walking by would hear what they were saying. Once they were both seated he turned to Kathleen.

"You know, if this doesn't turn out well, it's not going to be your fault. No one is going to blame you."

"Oh, Luke, I don't want to bring heartache to any of them, especially after all they've done for me and my family."

"I know and I understand. I feel the same way. And remember you aren't in this alone."

"Oh, no. I probably shouldn't have dragged you into all this. I don't want them upset with you, either. I'll take all the blame—"

Luke stopped her words by lightly touching her lips with his fingertips. "Kathleen, shush. This is not your doing. The Lord brought Reba into your life through Mrs. Connor, who wanted to help her. You want to help her and Mrs. Heaton. Perhaps this is all the Lord's will and His timing." He moved his hand to her cheek.

"I've never thought of it that way. I just don't want any of you who have helped me so much to be hurt by my actions."

"Has it never dawned on you that you've helped all of us in your own way, too?"

"Oh, Luke, no, I—" She shook her head.

"Kate." He looked into her eyes. Oh, how he wanted to kiss her, to let her know of his growing feelings for her. Of how much she meant to him. But this wasn't the time or the place. "Don't you know the Lord is as capable of using you to help others as anyone else?"

Finally he saw her lips turn up in a smile. "Thank you. Again. For reminding me of what I already know."

"You're welcome." He cupped her cheek in his hand and tipped her face up—thankful that she no longer flinched if he touched her. "It's going to all work out, Kate. You'll see."

"I hope so."

Then he was no longer able to resist the temptation. He lowered his head and heard Kathleen's quick intake of breath. But she didn't move. He lowered his lips to hers. And she responded. Her lips were soft and sweet and— She broke it off and stood.

"I— We'd better be going, Luke."

"Yes, of course." She hadn't slapped him. Surely that meant something?

The rest of the walk home was in silence, but Luke didn't know if it was a good or a bad one. Was she upset about the kiss? And if so, was it because he'd kissed her, or that she'd kissed him back?

Once they arrived at the house, she started up the steps. "Kate?'

She stopped and turned to him.

"I'm sorry—" they both said at the exact same time.

"I should have—" again together. Finally they both chuckled and broke the tension between them.

"Let's leave this for another time—after all this with Reba is taken care of. But then we need to talk about us. Agreed?" He held out his hand and his heart hammered as he waited.

Kathleen slipped her hand in his. "Agreed."

Luke escorted Kathleen to Reba's apartment building as usual the next morning, but they didn't discuss anything other than their plans in regard to Reba.

They'd made a deal and taken it seriously. But Kathleen knew they would have a talk about what had happened between them the night before. Luke was a man of his word, and she was a woman of hers.

"I'll not be far away at any time, but you might not see me. If you need me, just call my name and I'll be there," Luke said just before she entered the building.

"All right. See you later." Kathleen hurried up the stairs, buoyed by just knowing that he would be near. And that she trusted that he would be.

She'd slept better than she'd expected the night before. The Lord must have known she needed to sleep instead of reliving Luke's kiss. But it'd been on her mind as soon as she'd awakened. She still couldn't believe she'd responded the way she had and deep in her heart she knew she could no longer deny that she was falling in love with him.

But for now she put it all out of her mind. Today

was about Reba and the Heatons and she needed a clear mind to handle whatever came of it once Violet saw the young woman.

Reba and Jenny were ready as soon as she knocked on the door and they both seemed to be in high spirits. Kathleen paid for the trolley for all of them and they were soon on their way. She could tell they rarely road the trolley from Jenny's excitement. She was such a pretty little girl and there was no way around the fact that she resembled Mrs. Heaton enough to be her grand-daughter.

She'd telephoned Colleen that morning and she knew to expect Violet first and then her and Reba and Jenny. Her sister opened the door wide and welcomed them inside as Kathleen made the introductions.

"Many of the children come before breakfast," Colleen explained, "so that is available to Jenny if you need to leave for work early. And of course we serve them lunch, too. You're welcome to stay for that today, if you'd like."

After they dropped Jenny off in the playroom and introduced her to the other children, Colleen took them on a tour. Kathleen wondered where Violet was. Would she make herself known or surreptitiously get a look at Reba?

Reba seemed quite pleased with the home as Colleen led her through one room and then the other, including the kitchen and the small garden out back where the children sometimes played.

"Oh, this is even nicer than I imagined," Reba said as they headed back into the house. "I know Jenny is going to love being here."

Colleen opened the door and the hallway seemed

dim after the bright sunshine outside. Kathleen heard Violet's voice say, "Oh, I'm sorry."

"It's all righ—" Reba took a quick breath and seemed to hold it.

"Ida said you were outside, Colleen. I was just coming to find you." Violet turned back to Reba. "I— You look so familiar, do I know y—"

"No, I don't think we've met before."

"Oh, I'm sorry. I truly thought—"

"No. I need to get Jenny now." Her voice seemed shaky.

"Oh, you don't want to stay for lunch?" Colleen asked.

"We can't—I—" She seemed to be getting more agitated by the minute.

"Come with me. I'll get her," Colleen said.

"I'll meet you by the front door, Reba," Kathleen said. But once they were out of sight she turned to Violet and whispered, "Well, could you tell?"

Violet's eyes were filled with tears. "It's Rebecca. I know it is."

Kathleen nodded. "I'll see what I can do."

"Thank you."

Kathleen hurried to the front door and waited for Reba to come with Jenny. Jenny hated to leave, but Colleen assured her she'd be back soon and calmed her down.

But the look on Reba's face as they walked to the trolley stop unsettled Kathleen and she prayed that she wouldn't change her mind about using the day care.

On the way to the apartment Jenny chattered about the day care and the children she'd met and how much she wanted to go back. Finally Reba assured her she'd get to go back and Kathleen was sure she was as relieved as Jenny was at that news.

"But now be a good girl and go change into your everyday clothes and play for a bit while I talk to Kathleen and make your lunch."

"Yes, ma'am." Jenny skipped off to the bedroom with a smile on her face.

She'd no more than left the room when Reba turned to Kathleen. "Who was that woman who thought she knew me?"

"She's a friend of Colleen's. She's not usually there—she works at Butterick."

"You're sure she's not always there?"

"I'm certain of it. She must have had the day off and stopped by for a visit."

Reba went to the kitchen and Kathleen followed her. She could tell the young woman was still upset by the way her hands shook as she filled her teakettle and put it on the stove.

"Are you all right, Reba? You seem upset."

Reba turned from the stove, tears flowing down her cheeks and Kathleen hurried over to her. "What is it? Is it Violet?"

Reba nodded and began to sob. Kathleen wrapped an arm around her. "It's all right, come sit down and tell me about it."

Reba let her lead her to the table and sat down. She pulled a handkerchief out of her pocket and blew her nose as Kathleen sat down opposite her. "Violet Burton was our neighbor in Virginia. I'm not sure why she's here."

Kathleen had to tell her what she knew. "She's Violet Heaton now."

Reba began to cry all over again. "She's my sister-in-law, then. I didn't know Michael had moved here."

"I'm sorry, I—"

"My name isn't Dickerson. It's Heaton and I've never been married. Dickerson is my mother's maiden name." Reba stood up and began to pace as the floodgates opened and she talked. "I left home and came here with a man I thought loved me, wanted to marry me. But it was all a lie and when he left me here, I was pregnant with Jenny and too ashamed to go home and face my family. I didn't want to bring shame on them and I—" She sat back down and began to sob in earnest. Kathleen grasped her hands until she was spent and sniffing.

"You are Rebecca Heaton?"

Reba nodded.

"I must be truthful with you. Your mother came here shortly after you went missing and she and Michael both have spent years trying to find you. They aren't worried about you bringing shame on them, Reba. They just want you back, to know you are alive and well and to be part of their lives again."

"Did they send you here?"

"No! They know nothing about you yet. But, oh, Reba, you have a family who loves you with all their hearts right here in the city. Please consider letting them know you're here."

"My mother is here? In New York City? She didn't go back after they couldn't find me?"

"No. She's always believed that they would find you—or you would find them when you were ready. And she's made it her life's work to help other young women who might need a place to stay. She runs Heaton House where I live."

"Please tell me more about her and Michael."

The kettle began to blow steam and Kathleen took it on herself to make them both a cup of tea as she told Reba all Mrs. Heaton had done for her and her family, how wonderful a couple Michael and Violet were and how she came to think Reba was Mrs. Heaton's daughter.

That Reba wanted to see them was as apparent as her fear of doing so. She was clearly at war with herself.

"I love your mother, Reba, and I don't want to see her go through any more heartbreak."

"But I'm afraid they won't want—"

"Reba, surely you remember the story of the prodigal son? And how his father welcomed him home? You must know deep down that your mother and brother will do the same with you."

"I know the Lord has forgiven me, but I don't want Jenny to suffer for my sins."

"There is no way that will happen and you know it. Your mother and brother and Violet, too, are going to dote upon her. Jenny deserves to know her grandmother and uncle, Reba. Please let me tell them about you."

Finally, Reba nodded. "Yes. You can tell them. But if they don't want to see me—"

"That's not going to be the case. I can promise you that."

Chapter Twenty-One

Kathleen no more than got out the door of Reba's apartment before Luke was there. She didn't even know where he'd come from but suddenly he was walking toward her.

"I didn't have to call you."

"No, you didn't. I was here all along. What happened?"

They walked and talked at the same time. "Reba is Rebecca and she's agreed to meet with Michael and Violet. But I don't want her to change her mind so the quicker we can make it happen the better."

"Let's go see Michael. He should be home by now."

Kathleen filled in Luke on what had happened with Reba on the way to Michael and Violet's. Once they got there, her heart went out to Michael.

His voice was filled with emotion as he asked, "Is this woman really my sister, Kathleen?"

"She is. She recognized Violet this morning even though she denied knowing her and when we got back to her apartment, she broke down and told me everything."

Michael turned away for a few moments and gathered his wife in his arms. Kathleen's eyes were full of tears as she looked at Luke and saw his were filled also.

Finally Michael was able to compose himself. "After all these years of looking for her it's hard to believe she's been found. Can you tell me more?"

Kathleen filled him in on everything, including the fact that Reba—Rebecca—was afraid they'd want nothing to do with her once they found she had a child out of wedlock. "I assured her that wasn't the case and finally talked her into letting me tell you about her. She's agreed to see you and Mrs. Heaton."

"When?"

"As soon as you can. I don't think she'll run away—I told her Jenny deserved to know her grandmother and uncle—but I'd say the sooner the better."

"I'll go get Mother and bring her over. Violet and I will prepare her. Can you and Luke bring Rebecca and Jenny back here?"

Kathleen looked at Luke and he nodded. "We can. We'll go now."

They headed back to the tenements immediately, and Kathleen prayed all the while that Reba would be home and that she hadn't changed her mind about seeing her mother and brother.

Luke went with her this time and Reba let them both in. She told the woman who Luke really was, that he lived at Heaton House, too. Then she relayed Michael's request to meet. "You haven't changed your mind, have you?"

"No. I haven't changed my mind. It wouldn't be fair to anyone after I told you I would. And you're right. My daughter deserves to know her grandmother and uncle. I've even told Jenny she was going to get to meet them. I can't go back now."

Only then did Kathleen begin to relax. It was going to be all right. She and Luke waited while Reba and her daughter got ready.

"I can't even imagine what Mrs. Heaton must be feeling right now. I'm so glad Michael went to get her and will explain it all to her. I'm not sure I could do it again."

Luke agreed. "We'll get to see the reunion. I can't wait for that."

"Me, either. But then I think we should leave them alone, don't you?"

"Yes, I do. How about you let me take you to dinner? So we don't have to answer the boarders' questions just yet?"

His smile had Kathleen's heart doing a funny little twist. "I'd like that, thank you."

Reba and Jenny came out of their room, excitement on the face of the child, and a bit of apprehension on her mother's. They walked out to Second Avenue where Luke procured a hack to get them there as quickly as possible.

When they arrived at Michael's, Violet let them in and immediately hugged Reba. "I knew it was you. I'm so glad…" She stopped and took a deep breath, then looked down at Jenny. "Hello, Jenny. I'm your aunt Violet and I'm very glad to meet you."

"I'm glad, too," Jenny said.

Just then the doors to the parlor opened and Mrs. Heaton and Michael came out. In spite of the fact that the older woman had been crying, her eyes were filled with joy for anyone to see.

"Mama." Reba ran to her mother who wrapped her in her arms and sobbed. "I'm so sorry, Mama. I never wanted to hurt you so."

"Shh, child. You're here. My prayers have been answered. These are tears of joy, not sadness." Mrs. Heaton wiped her eyes on the handkerchief she held in her hand. Then she looked at Jenny, who had a grip on her mother's skirt. "And you must be Jenny, my granddaughter?"

Reba picked her up and held her in her arms. Jenny nodded. "I think so."

"Oh, I know so. You look just like your mama did at your age. I'm very happy to meet you." She leaned over and kissed Jenny's cheek.

"Me too, Granma."

One could hear Reba swallow her sob as she turned toward Michael. "And this is your uncle Michael, Jenny."

Jenny gave him a smile and a little wave as Michael crossed the foyer and hugged them both. "I've always wanted to be an uncle, Jenny."

He held out his arms and the child fairly jumped into them.

Kathleen took the handkerchief Luke handed her to wipe the flow of tears before she turned and found herself in his arms.

"I told you it would be all right, didn't I?"

Kathleen nodded but before she could step out of Luke's arms, Mrs. Heaton was there, crying, hugging and kissing them both. "Kathleen, Luke, thank you, thank you."

"Oh, Mrs. Heaton, you are so welcome. We're just thankful it's turned out this way."

"You'll stay for supper?" Violet asked.

"No," Luke said. "Thank you, but Kathleen and I want this time to be yours. I'm going to take her to dinner and we'll celebrate with you all—"

"This weekend. At Heaton House," Mrs. Heaton said. "We'll all celebrate then."

* * *

Luke took Kathleen to a small Italian café where one didn't have to dress up and the lighting wasn't good enough to tell if one had been crying all afternoon.

Now as they each enjoyed the rich lasagna they'd ordered, Luke was relieved to see Kathleen smiling.

"I don't think I've ever seen anything quite so touching." Her eyes shone with unshed tears.

"Oh, it was that. I had a hard time there for a while. But I have also been witness to something just as touching. The night you went to your sister's side and then to get your nephews." He'd never forget that night, or this one either for that matter.

"Oh, Luke, did I ever thank you for being there for me?"

"Many times." He took a bite of the rich pasta dish and leaned back in his seat.

"This is wonderful. I don't think I've ever eaten any Italian food. I love it."

"It's a favorite of mine. And we can come here again anytime you'd like to." He hoped she'd want to come back with him.

"That would be nice."

She looked exhausted by the time they'd finished their meal and he got a cab to take them back to Heaton House. "Want to take the long way home so that maybe we don't have to run into anyone at home?"

"Yes, I think I would. I just…"

"No need to explain to me. I know it's been a long, grueling, wonderful day for you." He leaned forward and spoke to the driver and then sat back. "We're going to drive through Central Park. Have you ever done that at night?"

"No, I never have."

As they drove down the streets of the city, Luke knew there was no one he'd rather be with—now or forever. He loved this woman with all his heart and he wanted to tell her. But tonight wasn't the night to declare his love. She was worn out. He needed to wait until she'd had a good night's sleep and was rested. But he could tell her how proud he was of her.

"You know, you worried all for nothing. The Lord did have it under control and He used you in a huge way to get the Heaton family back together again. I can't tell you how much I admire what you've done and what you want to do to help those still in the tenements, Kate."

"Oh, Luke. Thank you. But you had just as big a part in helping the Heatons as I did. And I know you are as happy as I am at the outcome."

"I am. I do hope that my book will help people in the tenements as much as your work with the Ladies' Aide Society is going to."

"I'm sorry. I'm not sure how a dime novel could help, unless you give all the proceeds from it to—"

Luke laughed. "No, Kathleen. I thought you knew— that you realized I've been writing a different kind of book, one that I hope will give the people in the tenements hope that they can get out of there and make new lives for themselves like you and your sister have."

"Like us?" Kathleen sat up straight and he could see she was angry. "You used my family as examples? Luke, how could you?"

"How could I what? I'm trying to help, to—"

"You wrote about me and Colleen and our family? You used us to write your book?"

"No! Kathleen, I'd never—"

"Have the driver take us home. Now, please."

"Kathleen, listen to me."

"I've heard enough. That you could use our situation to your gain!"

Luke felt the blood rush to his face. How dare she accuse him of something like that?

"Driver," she called out, "there's been a change in plans. Take us to Heaton House now, please."

"Kathleen—"

"I have nothing more to say to you." She turned away and shut him out. There was nothing to do but pray that he'd find a way to make her see how wrong she was.

The driver had barely stopped the hack at Heaton House and she was out of it like a flash and in the house before Luke could pay the man.

"She's not very happy with you, mate."

"No. Nor am I with her." Luke handed the man his money and rushed up the steps to the house. He opened the door and resisted the urge to slam it. Kathleen was nowhere to be seen, but thankfully, neither were any of the other boarders. He took the stairs down to his floor and to his room.

What was she thinking? She had to know him better than to think he would do her or her family any harm! He slammed his fist down on top of the manuscript pages he had ready to send his publisher. That she could believe something like that left him with a knot in his gut and feeling as if a sharp knife had just pierced his heart.

Kathleen paced the floor of her room. How could Luke have used her and her family for research for his book? Just as she'd begun to trust him, he'd betrayed that trust. But what was worse, she could no longer deny she loved him. And it hurt unbearably that he'd done something like this.

There was a knock on her door and she went to answer, thinking it might be Mrs. Heaton back from Michael's. Maybe Reba was with her. She opened the door to find Gretchen there.

"Miss Kathleen. Mr. Luke wanted me to ask you to come to Mrs. Heaton's study. Said he needs to speak with you—"

"I don't want to talk to Luke right now, Gretchen."

"Oh, please, Miss Kathleen. He said if you don't come down he's coming up to get you and you know how that will upset Mrs. Heaton." She began wringing her hands.

Kathleen heaved a huge sigh. "All right. He's in Mrs. Heaton's study?"

"Yes, ma'am."

Kathleen marched down the stairs, indignant that he would use Gretchen in that way. He could get her into all kinds of trouble. She didn't bother to knock on the study door.

"Luke Patterson, what are you thinking? We have nothing more to discuss! And I don't feel like talking."

"You don't have to talk!" His eyes flashed. "But there are a few things I have to say, and you're going to listen. I understand how hard it might be for you to trust a man after all you've been through, but there's one thing you need to know."

Kathleen held her breath, waiting for his next words. "I love you with all my heart, even though I know you'll never trust me with yours. And I don't know what to do about it except give you this." He handed her a box.

"Take it." He thrust it at her and she had no choice

but to take it. "It's my manuscript, but it's yours to do with as you will. Burn it, tear it up—I don't care."

With that, he turned and left her speechless as he walked out the door.

Kathleen hurried up the stairs with it, ready to do just as he suggested. Before she'd let her family become a laughingstock she'd— Kathleen stopped in her steps. Would he really have given it to her if he'd done what she accused him of? Luke?

Kathleen sat down on the settee in front of the fireplace and held the box in her lap. She'd have to light a fire to burn it and it was really too warm for that now. She lifted the top off the box and took the pages out with trembling fingers. She could tear them up. She took the first page, held it in her hands and began to read.

Six hours later at the crack of dawn she was crying. Again. How could she ever have accused Luke the way she did? She'd come to trust him, so why did she light into him the way she had?

Maybe it had been hearing how Reba had been treated by Jenny's father—one more example of a woman trusting a man and being betrayed—that had brought up all of her trust issues again. But that wasn't Luke and she knew it. When the woman he'd loved died, he was by her side; he hadn't betrayed her.

And he'd been there for Kathleen, every time she'd needed him. To the point that she finally knew she had no reason not to give her heart to him. And that scared her with every fiber of her being. What if it didn't work out?

She blew her nose and wiped her eyes. Yes, she was afraid of giving her heart to Luke, but not doing so frightened her even more. She had to decide if she was going to be brave enough to do what her heart begged her to do, or if she was going to live the rest of her life in regret.

She slid to her knees and prayed. "Dear Lord, please forgive me for treating Luke so badly, for not having faith in You to help me trust my heart to him. For not letting go of my fear when I know I have nothing to fear with You by my side. I don't know if Luke can forgive me, but please give me the courage to ask him to. And show me Your will for us. In Jesus's name, Amen."

Kathleen dried her eyes, put the manuscript pages back in the box and ran back downstairs to the kitchen where she knew she'd find Gretchen even though no one else would be up by now.

"Gretchen, can you ask Luke to come to the little parlor? I need to speak to him."

She must think the two of them were crazy, but if so, she didn't say. "Of course. Actually he came up for coffee just a few minutes ago and asked if I'd seen you. I'll let him know."

"Thank you."

Kathleen hurried to the back parlor and paced back and forth, waiting to see if Luke would give her another chance, if he could forgive—

"Kathleen? Gretchen said you wanted to speak to me?"

He looked as if he'd lost his best friend and she was afraid she'd lost hers. *Oh, dear Lord, please help me here.*

"I did. I…" She swallowed around the knot of tears in her throat and picked up his boxed manuscript. "I wanted to give this back to you so that you can send it off to your publisher as quickly as possible."

He took it from her but his gaze never left hers. "You read it?"

"Yes. I'm so sorry for hurting you, Luke. I don't know

what got into me. Yes, I do. It was fear, plain and simple. Fear of giving my complete trust to you, even though you and the Lord have been showing me how very trustworthy you are for weeks now. I've asked for His forgiveness—now I ask for yours although I know I don't deserve it." She took a deep breath and continued. "I've known that I love you for a while now, but I've been afraid to admit it and trust that you might love me, too."

Luke dropped the box on the nearest table and pulled her into his arms. "You love me?"

"I love you. And I know I can trust your love for me. Will you forgive me for accusing you so wrongly? Can you still love me after hurting you the way I have?"

"Kate, I've had my own fears about loving you. I can't bear the thought of losing you the way I lost Beth. But the thought of living without you is too painful to contemplate and I'm going to trust that the Lord will see us through everything together. My love for you isn't fleeting, it's for a lifetime, if you want it."

Kathleen's heart filled with so much love for this man she thought it might burst with happiness. "Oh, yes, that's exactly what I want—today, tomorrow and always."

"Will you trust me to love you for the rest of our lives and become my wife, Kate?"

"I will trust my heart to you, Luke, and I'll be honored to become your wife."

Luke bent his head and she stood on tiptoe as his lips claimed hers in a kiss that assured her heart a lifetime of happiness and love. Kate kissed him back and sent up a prayer of thanksgiving to the Lord for bringing this trustworthy man into her life.

* * * * *

**WE HOPE YOU ENJOYED
THIS BOOK FROM**

LOVE INSPIRED

INSPIRATIONAL ROMANCE

Uplifting stories of faith, forgiveness and hope.

Fall in love with stories where faith helps
guide you through life's challenges, and discover
the promise of a new beginning.

6 NEW BOOKS AVAILABLE EVERY MONTH!

LIHALO2020

SPECIAL EXCERPT FROM

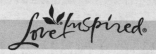

Could this bad-boy newcomer spell trouble for an Amish spinster…or be the answer to her prayers?

Read on for a sneak preview of
An Unlikely Amish Match,
the next book in Vannetta Chapman's miniseries
Indiana Amish Brides.

The sun was low in the western sky by the time Micah Fisher hitched a ride to the edge of town. The driver let him out at a dirt road that led to several Amish farms. He'd never been to visit his grandparents in Indiana before. They always came to Maine. But he had no trouble finding their place.

As he drew close to the lane that led to the farmhouse, he noticed a young woman standing by the mailbox. A little girl was holding her hand and another was hopping up and down. They were all staring at him.

"Howdy," he said.

The woman only nodded, but the two girls whispered, "Hello."

"Can we help you?" the woman asked. "Are you…lost?"

"*Nein*. At least I don't think I am."

"You must be if you're here. This is the end of the road."

Micah pointed to the farm next door. "Abigail and John Fisher live there?"

"They do."

"Then I'm not lost." He snatched off his baseball cap, rubbed the top of his head and then yanked the cap back on.

Micah stepped forward and held out his hand. "I'm Micah— Micah Fisher. Pleased to meet you."

"You're not *Englisch*?"

"Of course I'm not."

"So you're Amish?" She stared pointedly at his clothing—tennis shoes, blue jeans, T-shirt and baseball cap. Pretty much what he wore every day.

"I'm as Plain and simple as they come."

"I somehow doubt that."

"Since we're going to be neighbors, I suppose I should know your name."

"Neighbors?"

"*Ja.* I've come to live with my *daddi* and *mammi*—at least for a few months. My parents think it will straighten me out." He peered down the lane. "I thought the bishop lived next door."

"He does."

"Oh. You're the bishop's *doschder*?"

"We all are," the little girl with freckles cried. "I'm Sharon and that's Shiloh and that is Susannah."

"Nice to meet you, Sharon and Shiloh and Susannah."

Sharon lost interest and squatted to pick up some of the rocks. Shiloh hid behind her *schweschder*'s skirt, and Susannah scowled at him.

"I knew the bishop lived next door, but no one told me he had such pretty *doschdern*."

Susannah's eyes widened even more, but it was Shiloh who said, "He just called you pretty."

"Actually I called you all pretty."

Shiloh ducked back behind Susannah.

Susannah narrowed her eyes as if she was squinting into the sun, only she wasn't. "Do you talk to every girl you meet that way?"

"Not all of them—no."

Don't miss
An Unlikely Amish Match *by Vannetta Chapman,*
available February 2020 wherever
Love Inspired® books and ebooks are sold.

LoveInspired.com

SPECIAL EXCERPT FROM

LOVE INSPIRED
INSPIRATIONAL ROMANCE

Can the new teacher in this Amish community help the family next door without losing her heart?

Read on for a sneak preview of
The Amish Teacher's Dilemma *by Patricia Davids,*
available in March 2020 from Love Inspired.

Clang, clang, clang.

The hammering outside her new schoolhouse grew louder. Eva Coblentz moved to the window to locate the source of the clatter. Across the road she saw a man pounding on an ancient-looking piece of machinery with steel wheels and a scoop-like nose on the front end.

When he had the sheet of metal shaped to fit the front of the machine, he stood back to assess his work. He knelt and hammered on the shovel-like nose three more times. Satisfied, he gathered up his tools and started in her direction.

She stepped back from the window. Was he coming to the school? Why? Had he noticed her gawking? Perhaps he only wanted to welcome the new teacher, although his lack of a beard said he wasn't married.

She glanced around the room. Should she meet him by the door? That seemed too eager. Her eyes settled on the large desk at the front of the classroom. She should look as if she was ready for the school year to start. A professional attitude would put off any suggestion that she was interested in meeting single men.

Eva hurried to the desk, pulled out the chair and sat down as the outside door opened. The chair tipped over backward, sending her flailing. Her head hit the wall with a painful thud as she slid to the floor. Stunned, she slowly opened her eyes to see the man leaning over the desk.

He had the most beautiful gray eyes she'd ever beheld. They were rimmed with thick, dark lashes in stark contrast to the mop of curly, dark red hair springing out from beneath his straw hat. Tiny sparks of light whirled around him.

"I'm Willis Gingrich. Local blacksmith." He squatted beside her. "Can you tell me your name?"

The warmth and strength of his hand on her skin sent a sizzle of awareness along her nerve endings. "I'm Eva Coblentz. I am the new teacher and I'm fine now."

Don't miss
The Amish Teacher's Dilemma
by USA TODAY *bestselling author Patricia Davids,*
available March 2020 wherever
Love Inspired books and ebooks are sold.

LoveInspired.com

LIEXP0220

LOVE INSPIRED

INSPIRATIONAL ROMANCE

UPLIFTING STORIES OF FAITH, FORGIVENESS AND HOPE.

Join our social communities to connect with other readers who share your love!

Sign up for the Love Inspired newsletter at **LoveInspired.com** to be the first to find out about upcoming titles, special promotions and exclusive content.

CONNECT WITH US AT:

Facebook.com/LoveInspiredBooks

Twitter.com/LoveInspiredBks

Facebook.com/groups/HarlequinConnection

HARLEQUIN

*Heartfelt or suspenseful,
inspiring or passionate, Harlequin
has your happily-ever-after.*

With new books published
every month, you are sure to find the
satisfying escape you know you deserve.

HNEWS2020